The employees of the Lassiter Detective
Agency are facing their toughest cases
yet—to find their secret desires in the
most unexpected places

MOST WANTED

by
International bestselling author

DIANA
PALMER

Dane Lassiter and his secretary Tess Meriweather have
a troubled past that makes him the last person she
would turn to in a crisis.

Nick Reed returns to his childhood home for a break—
until Tabitha Harvey asks him for help.

When Kit Morris starts work at the Lassiter Detective Agency,
her old boss Logan Deverell is lost without her and is
determined to get her back into his life and heart forever.

'Nobody tops Diana Palmer. . . I love her stories.'
—Jayne Ann Krentz

DIANA
PALMER

MOST WANTED

SILHOUETTE®

*First published as a collection in Great Britain 2004
Silhouette Books, Eton House, 18-24 Paradise Road,
Richmond, Surrey TW9 1SR*

MOST WANTED © MIRA Books 2000

The publisher acknowledges the copyright holder of the
individual works as follows:

The Case of the Mesmerizing Boss © Diana Palmer 1992
The Case of the Confirmed Bachelor © Diana Palmer 1992
The Case of the Missing Secretary © Diana Palmer 1992

ISBN 0 373 60157 3

47-0604

*Printed and bound in Spain
by Litografia Rosés S.A., Barcelona*

CONTENTS

THE CASE OF THE MESMERIZING BOSS

Prologue

Richard Dane Lassiter stared down at the city of Houston from his office in the exclusive high-rise building, with eyes that didn't really see the misting rain in the streetlight-dotted darkness. He was wrestling with a problem that wouldn't go away.

Any minute now he was going to have to go into the outer office of his detective agency and chew out his secretary. Actually, she was almost a relative. Tess Meriwether was the daughter of the man his mother had been engaged to. Their respective parents had been killed just days shy of their wedding. So Tess wasn't really related to him, but he'd felt responsible for her for years, anyway. It was why he'd given her this job, why he was so protective of her. There were wounds between them that might never heal, but that didn't in any way diminish his feelings for her.

It could have been love, if he hadn't been so determined to send her running from him. He'd had a failed marriage and he'd been shot to pieces in a gun battle while he was still a Texas Ranger. The shooting had

changed him as well as his life. He'd had to give up
police work, so he'd founded this detective agency and
robbed the local police departments to staff it. He had
a reputation for being one of the most thorough and
discreet private investigators in the business, and he
was very successful. But his personal life was a mess.
He had no one, really. No one except Tess, and she
backed away whenever he came close. He felt guilty
about that sometimes. She didn't know, could never be
told, that it hadn't really been anger that had triggered
his physical demands on her. She thought he'd been
trying to frighten her away. That was funny. The truth
was that on that afternoon so long ago, he'd been out
of control for the first time in his life.

He turned away from the window, a tall, lithe man
with a graceful way of moving and an arrogant tilt to
his head. He looked like he'd had a Spanish ancestor
from whom he'd inherited his dark eyes, his black hair
and the olive tan of his skin. He was a handsome man,
but he was unaware of it. These days, he had little use
for women.

His own mother had despised him because he reminded her too much of his father, who'd deserted her
when Dane was only a child. He'd wanted to love his
mother, but she never had time for him. Her attitude
had scarred him deeply. He'd married while he was still
one of Houston's policemen, before he became a Texas
Ranger, but his wife had only been attracted to his uniform. His life with Jane had been a rocky one. She'd
wanted something he could not give her. It had taken
very little time for her to decide that she'd made a
terrible mistake. She didn't want him in bed at all, and
very quickly decided that she didn't want him out of
it, either. She just didn't want him. When he got

wounded, she walked out on him while he was still in the hospital. If it hadn't been for Tess, he wouldn't have had anyone at all throughout that nightmarish time.

Ironic, he thought, that Tess had been in love with him. She'd been only a teenager, just barely out of school, when they first met. Her father, Wyatt Meriwether, had neglected her, just as Nita Lassiter had ignored Dane. Wyatt had left Tess to be raised by her grandmother while he pursued his promiscuous lifestyle. Tess was innocent and gentle, and she attracted Dane as no other woman ever had. Even now, thinking about how it had been between them during his recuperation could make him ashamed of what he'd inadvertently done to her.

They'd experienced a tenderness toward each other that was overwhelming in its intensity. He'd fought it at first. He didn't trust or like women, and Tess was altogether too young. But she got under his skin. He'd never been loved like that, before or since. He'd thrown it all away in a moment's passion, and had frightened Tess so badly that she still backed away from him.

He ran an angry hand through his hair. He really had to stop looking back. It did no good.

Now Tess wanted to be an operative. He wouldn't let her. It was dangerous work sometimes. Dane didn't even like sending Nick and Nick's sister, Helen, out on assignments, like the stakeout that Tess had inadvertantly interrupted. He was going to have to give her hell for it. She hadn't blown their cover, but she'd come close. That couldn't be allowed. Besides, he didn't want Tess out in the field. He didn't want her at risk, ever. She kept pestering Helen to teach her things, to show her some martial arts throws, to show her how to use a gun. He usually managed to break up any tutorials, but Tess's persistence disturbed him. He couldn't bear the thought of having her in danger. She was relatively safe in the office, being his secretary. Out of it... Well, thank God, he didn't have to worry about that, now.

As for her interference with the stakeout, that was something he *did* have to worry about. He remembered the first time he'd met her, at a restaurant where their parents had invited them to get acquainted. Dane had tried to make her think he'd disliked her on sight. Actually, she'd appealed to him instantly. He almost seemed to know her, which was really disturbing, because he was married and had had his reluctant wife with him that night. Jane had been alternately sarcastic and obnoxious until he'd sent her home in a cab. Tess, on the other hand, had been quiet and shy and very curious about him.

His body began to tauten at the memory. He'd wanted Tess then, and the wanting hadn't stopped during all the years in between. He was resigned to living alone these days. He had a reason for not seeking commitment, for not ever wanting marriage. He couldn't tell Tess what it was. But it was devastating to his masculinity.

With a grimace he started toward the door that separated his office from the waiting room. Putting off the confrontation was cowardly, something he'd never been. It was just that Tess could look so wounded when he scolded her. He hated giving her more pain. Over the years, God knew, he'd given her more than enough.

But she had to learn that rules were meant to be obeyed. If he overlooked this infraction, he might put her at risk in the future. He couldn't have that.

Resignedly, he reached out and opened the door.

Chapter One

Tess Meriwether sighed hugely, feeling stiff all over from the tension of waiting for the axe to fall. She glanced ruefully toward Dane's closed office door. Today had really been one of those days. She'd blown a stakeout and gotten the cold shoulder from Dane all day for it. She hoped she could sneak out at quitting time without being seen. Otherwise, she was going to catch it for sure.

Dane Lassiter was her boss—the owner of the Lassiter Detective Agency—but he was also more. She'd known him for years; their parents had almost gotten married. But a tragic accident had killed them both, and the only one Tess had left in the world was Dane.

She carefully put away her equipment with a quick glance at the clock and reached for her trench coat. The coat was her pride and joy, one of those Sam Spade-looking things that she adored. Working for a detective agency was exciting, even if Dane wouldn't let her near a case. Someday, she promised herself, she was going to become an operative, in spite of her overprotective boss.

"Going somewhere?" he asked, suddenly appearing in the doorway, a cigarette smoldering between his lean fingers. He looked like the ultimate private investigator in his three-piece suit.

She had to drag her eyes away. Even after what he'd done to her three years ago, she still found him a delight to her eyes.

"Home," she said. "Do you mind?"

"Immensely." He motioned her into his office. Once she was inside, he half closed the door and came closer to her, noticing involuntarily how she tensed when he was only a few feet away. Her reaction was predictable, and probably he deserved it, but it stung. He spoke much more angrily than he meant to. "I told you not to go near the stakeout."

"I didn't, intentionally," she said, nervously twisting a long strand of pale blond hair around one finger. "I saw Helen and I waved. I thought the stakeout you mentioned was going to be one of those wee-hours-of-the-morning things. I hardly expected two professional detectives to be skulking around a toy store in the middle of the afternoon! I thought Helen was buying her boyfriend's nephew a present." Her gray eyes flashed at him. "After all, you didn't say *what* you were staking out. You just told me to keep out of the way. Houston," she added haughtily, "is a big city. We didn't all used to be Texas Rangers who carry city street plans around in our heads!"

He didn't blink. His dark eyes stared her down through a cloud of smoke firing up from the cigarette in his fingers.

She coughed as the smoke approached her face. Loudly.

He smiled at her. Defiantly.

Neither moved.

A timid knock on the door startled the tall, rangy, dark-haired man and the slender blond woman. Helen Reed peeked around the half-opened door.

"Is it all right if I go home?" she asked Dane. "It's five," she added with a hopeful smile.

"Take your ear with you," he said, referring to a piece of essential listening equipment, "and go with your brother. Nick needs some backup while he stakes out our philandering husband."

"No!" Helen groaned. "No, Dane, not four hours of lewd noises and embarrassing conversation with *Nick!* I *hate* Nick! Anyway, I've got a date with Harold!"

"You were supposed to tell sweetums here—" he nodded toward a glaring Tess "—where and when the stakeout was coming down, so that she wouldn't trip over it."

"I apologized," she wailed.

"Not good enough. You go with Nick, and I'll reconsider your pink slip."

"If you fire me," Helen told him, "I'll go back to work for the department of motor vehicles and you'll never get another automobile tag registration off the record for the rest of your life."

He pursed his lips. "Did I ever mention that I spent two years with the Texas Department of Public Safety before I joined the Texas Rangers?"

Helen sighed. She opened the door the rest of the way and made a huge production of going down on her hose-clad knees, her long black hair dragging the floor as she salaamed, her thin body looking somehow elegant even in the pose. She studied ballet and had all the grace of a dancer.

"Oh, for God's sake, go home," Dane said shortly. "And I hope Harold buys you a pizza loaded with anchovies!"

"Thanks, boss! Actually, I love anchovies!" Helen smiled, waved, and then vanished before he had time to change his mind.

He ran a restless hand through his thick black hair, disrupting a straight lock onto his forehead. "Next the skip tracers will be after paid vacations to the Bahamas."

Tess shook her head. "Jamaica. I asked."

He turned and tossed an ash into the smokeless ashtray on his desk. The entire staff had pitched in to buy it. They'd also pitched in to send him to a stop-smoking seminar. He'd sent them all on stakeouts to porno theaters. Nobody ever suggested another seminar. Dane did install big air filters, though, in every office.

Dane was a renegade. He went his own way regardless of controversy. Tess might disagree with him, but she had to respect him for standing up for what he believed in.

She watched him move, her eyes lingering on his elegant carriage. He was built like a rodeo cowboy, square shoulders and lean hips and long, powerful legs. When he was tired, he limped a little from the wounds he'd sustained three years ago. He looked tired now.

She watched him, remembering how it had all begun. When he'd opened the detective agency, he'd remorselessly pilfered the local police department of its best people, offering them percentages and shares in the business instead of salaries until the agency started paying off. And it had thrived—in record time. Dane had been a Houston police officer years before he made it to the Texas Rangers. He'd been a good policeman. He had plenty of clout in intelligence circles, and that assured his success.

Being a Texas Ranger hadn't hurt his credentials, either, because in order to be considered for the rangers, a man had to have eight years of law enforcement experience with the last two as an officer for the Texas Department of Public Safety. Then the top thirty scorers on the written test had to undergo a grueling oral interview. The five leading candidates to pass this test were placed on a one-year waiting list for an opening on the ninety-four-member force. Dane had been one of the lucky ones. He'd worked out of Houston, ranging over several counties to assist local law enforcement. A ranger might not have to fight Indians or Mexican guerrillas, but since Texas had plenty of ranchland left, a ranger had to be a skilled horseman in case he was called upon to track down modern-day rustlers. Dane was one of the best horsemen Tess had ever seen. Despite his injuries, he still was as at home on the back of a horse as he was on the ground or behind the wheel of a car.

She was awed by him after all the years they'd known each other. But she was very careful these days not to let him know how awed. One taste of his violent ardor had been enough to stifle her desire for him as soon as it had begun.

"You never send me out on assignments." She sighed.

He glanced at her, his expression guarded. He seemed to make a point of never looking too closely, or for too long, as if he found her very existence hard to accept. "You're a secretary, not an operative."

"I could be, if you'd let me," she said quietly. "I can do anything Helen can."

"Including dressing up like a hooker and parading down the main drag?" he mused.

She shifted restlessly, averting her face. "Well, maybe not that."

His dark eyes narrowed. "Or listening to intimate conversations in back-alley motel rooms? Taking photographs of explicit situations? Tracing an accused murderer across two states and apprehending him on a bail-bond forfeiture?"

She let out a long breath. "Okay. I get the point. I guess I couldn't handle that. But I could be a skip tracer, if you'd let me. That's almost as good as going out on cases."

He put out his cigarette angrily, a terse but controlled stab of his long fingers that made Tess uneasy. He was a passionate man, despite his cold control. She very rarely allowed herself to remember how he was with a woman. Just thinking about those strong, deft hands on her body made her go hot and shaky, but not with desire. She remembered the touch of Dane Lassiter's hands with stark fear.

He glanced at her suddenly, his eyes piercing, steady, as if he felt the thought in her mind and reacted to it. She went scarlet.

"Something embarrasses you?" he asked in that slow, lazy drawl that intimidated even ex-policemen.

"I was thinking about having to follow philandering husbands," she hedged. She clutched her purse. "I'd better go."

"Heavy date?" he asked with apparent carelessness.

She'd given up on men some time ago. He wouldn't know that, or know why, so she just shrugged and smiled and left.

The streets were dark and cold. The subdued glow of the streetlights didn't make much difference, either. It was a foggy winter night, stark and unwelcoming. Tess pulled her trench coat closer around her and walked toward her small foreign car without much enthusiasm. Tonight was like any other night. She'd go home to an empty apartment—an efficiency apartment with a tiny kitchen, a bathroom, a combination living room and bedroom, and a sofa that made into a bed. She'd watch old movies on television until she grew sleepy, and then she'd go to bed. The next day would be a repeat of this one. The only difference would be the movie.

Ordinarily, she might go out to a movie with her friend Kit Morris, who worked nearby. But Kit's boss was overseas for two months and Kit had had to go with him—even though she'd groaned about the trip. The older girl was a confidential secretary who got a huge salary for doing whatever the job demanded. Tess missed her. The agency did a lot of work for Kit's boss, hunting down his madcap mother, who spent her life getting into trouble.

With Kit gone, Tess's free time was really lonely. She had no one to talk to. She liked Helen, and they were friends, but she couldn't really talk to Helen about the one big heartache of her life—Dane Lassiter.

She looped her shoulder bag over her arm and stuffed her hands into her pockets. Her life, she thought, was like this miserable night. Cold, empty and solitary.

Two expensively dressed men were standing under

a streetlight as she appeared in the doorway of the office building. She stared at them curiously as one passed to the other an open briefcase full of packets of some white substance, and received a big wad of bills in return. She nodded to them and smiled absently, unaware of the shock on their faces as she walked toward the deserted parking lot.

"Did she see?" one asked the other.

"My God, of course she saw! Get her!"

Tess hadn't heard the conversation, but the sound of running feet caught her attention. She turned, conscious of movement, to stand staring blankly at two approaching men. They looked as if they were chasing her. There were angry shouts, freezing her where she stood. She frowned as the gleam of metal in the streetlights caught her attention. Before she realized that it was the reflection of light on a gun barrel, something hot stung her arm and spun her around. Seconds later, a pop rang in her ears and she cried out as she fell to the ground, stunned.

"You killed her!" one man exclaimed. "You fool, now they'll have us for murder instead of dealing coke!"

"Shut up! Let me think! Maybe she's not dead—"

"Let's get out of here! Somebody's bound to have heard the shots!"

"She came out of that building, where the lights are on in that detective agency," the other voice groaned.

"Great place you picked for the drop.... Run! That's a siren!"

Sure enough, it was. A patrol car, alerted by one of the street people, came barreling down the side street where the office was located, its spotlight catching two men bending over a prostrate form in a dark parking lot.

"Oh, God!" one of the men exclaimed. "Run!"

The sound of running feet barely impinged on Tess's fading consciousness. Funny, she couldn't lift her face. The pavement was damp and cold under her cheek. Except for that, she felt numb all over.

"They shot somebody!" a different voice called. "Don't let them get away!"

She heard more pops. Black shoes went past her face, as two policemen went tearing after the well-dressed men.

"Tess!"

She didn't recognize the voice at first. Dane was always so calm and in command of himself that the harsh urgency of his tone didn't sound familiar.

He rolled her gently onto her back. She stared up at him blankly, in shock. Her arm was beginning to feel wet and heavy and hot. She tried to speak and was surprised to find that she couldn't make her tongue work.

He spotted the dark, wet stain on her arm immediately, because the bullet had penetrated the cloth of her coat and blood was pulsing under it. "My God!" he ground out. His expression was as hard as a statue's, betraying nothing. Only his eyes, glittery with anger, were alive in that dark slate.

One of the policemen was running back toward them. He paused, his pistol in hand, kneeling beside Tess. "Was she hit?" the policeman asked curtly. "I saw one of them fire—"

"She's hit. Get an ambulance," Dane said, his black eyes meeting the other man's for an instant. "Hurry. She's bleeding badly."

The policeman ran back down the alley.

Dane didn't waste time. He eased Tess's arm out of her coat and grimaced at the gaping tear in her blouse and the vivid flow of blood. He cursed under his breath, whipping out a handkerchief and holding it firmly over the wound, even when she cried out at the pain.

"Be still," he said quietly. "Be still, little one. I'll take care of you. You're going to be all right."

She shivered. Tears ran down her cheeks. It hadn't hurt until he started pressing on it. Now the pain was terrible. She cried helplessly while he wound the handkerchief tightly around the wound and tied it. He shucked his topcoat and covered Tess with it. He took her purse and used it to elevate her feet. Then he turned his attention back to the wound. It was still bleeding copiously, and what Tess could see of it wasn't reassuring. He seemed so capable and controlled that she wasn't inclined to panic. He'd always had that effect on her, at least, when he wasn't making her nervous.

"Am I going to bleed to death?" she asked very calmly.

"No." He glanced over his shoulder as a car approached. He used words she'd never heard him use and abruptly stood as the squad car pulled up. "Help me get her in the car!" he called to the policeman. "She won't make it until an ambulance gets here at the rate she's losing blood."

"I just raised my partner on the walkie-talkie. He's on his way back with one of the perps," the officer said as he helped Dane get Tess into the back seat. "If he isn't here by the time I get the engine going, he's walking back to the station."

"I hear you." Dane cradled Tess's head in his lap. "Let's go."

Just as the officer got in behind the wheel, his partner came into view with a handcuffed man. Dane stiffened.

"M-20's on his way," the officer called to his partner. "I've got a wounded lady in here. Can you manage?"

"You bet! Get her to the hospital!" the other man called back.

The older man wheeled the squad car around with an expertise that Tess might have admired if she'd been less nauseated and hurt.

Minutes later, they pulled up at the municipal hospital emergency room, but Tess didn't know it. She was unconscious....

Daylight was streaming through the window when her eyes opened again. She blinked. She was pleasantly dazed. Her upper arm felt swollen and hot. She looked at it, curious about the thick white bandage it was wrapped in. She stirred, only then aware that she was strapped to a tube.

"Don't pull the IV out," Dane drawled from the chair beside the bed. "Believe me, you won't like having to have it put back in again."

She turned her head toward him. She felt dizzy and disoriented. "It was dark," she mumbled drowsily. "These men came after me and I think one of them shot me."

"You were shot, all right," he said grimly. "They were drug dealers. What happened? Did you get between them and the police, get caught in the crossfire?"

"No," Tess groaned. "I saw them pass the stuff. They must have panicked, but I didn't realize what I'd seen until they were after me."

He stiffened. "You saw it? You witnessed a drug buy?"

She nodded wearily. "I'm afraid so."

He whistled softly. "If they got a good look at you, and recognized the office building…"

"One got away."

"The one who shot you," Dane said flatly. "And they don't have enough on the one they caught to hold him for long. They'll charge him, but he'll probably make bail as soon as he's arraigned, and you're the gal who can send him up for dealing."

"His cohort shot me," she pointed out. "But the one they arrested was there. Can't he be arrested as an accessory?"

"Maybe, maybe not. You don't know how these people think," he said enigmatically, and he looked worried. Really worried.

"I'll bet you do," she murmured sleepily. "All those years, locking people up…"

"I know the criminal mind inside out," he agreed. "But it's different when things hit home." His dark eyes narrowed on her wan face. "It's very different."

She must be half-asleep, she decided, because he actually sounded as if he minded that she'd been shot. That was ridiculous. He resented her, disliked her even if he had felt sorry enough for her to give her a job when her father had died. He was her worst enemy, so why would it matter to him if something happened to her?

Dane stretched wearily, his white shirt pulled taut over a broad chest. "How do you feel this morning?"

She touched the bandage. "Not as bad as I did last night. What did the doctors do to me?"

"Took the bullet out." He pulled it from his shirt

pocket and displayed it for her. "A thirty-eight cali-
ber," he explained. "A souvenir. I thought you might
like it mounted and framed."

She grimaced. "Suppose we frame and mount the
man who shot me instead?"

His black eyebrow jerked up. "I'll pass that thought
along to the police," he said dryly.

"Can I go home?"

"When you're a little stronger. You lost a lot of
blood and they had to put you under to get the bullet
out."

"Helen will be furious when she finds out," she
murmured with a smile. "She's the private eye, and I
got shot."

"Oh, I'm sure she'll be livid with jealousy," he
agreed. He paused beside the bed, his dark eyes narrow
and intent on her face in its frame of soft, wavy blond
hair. He looked at her for a long time.

"I'm all right, if it matters," she said sleepily. She
closed her eyes. "I don't know why it should. You hate
me."

Her voice trailed off as she gave in to the need for
rest. He didn't answer her. But his eyes were stormy
and his mind had already registered how much it would
have mattered if her life had seeped out on that cold
concrete.

He got up and went to the window, stretching again.
He was tired. He hadn't slept since they'd brought her
in. All through the operation, he'd paced and waited
for news. It had been the longest night he'd ever spent.

A soft sound from the bed caught his attention. He
shoved his hands into his pockets and stood beside her,
watching the slow rise and fall of her chest. The un-
becoming hospital gown did nothing for her. She was

too thin. He scowled as he looked at her, his mind on the coldness he'd shown her over the years, the unrelenting hostility that had, eventually, turned a shy, loving girl into a quiet, insecure woman. Tess had wanted to love him, and he'd slapped her down, hard. It hadn't been cruelty so much as a raging desire that he'd started to satisfy in the only way he knew to satisfy it—roughly, savagely. But Tess had been a virgin, and he hadn't known. She'd run from him, in tears, barely in time to save her honor. Afterwards, she'd never come near him again. His pride hadn't allowed him to go after her, to explain that tenderness wasn't something he was used to showing women. Her frantic departure in tears had shattered him. She didn't know that.

He'd been antagonistic to hide the hurt the experience had dealt him, so it wasn't surprising that she thought he hated her. He'd even tried to convince himself he didn't mind the fact that Tess avoided him like the plague. To save his pride, he'd even made it appear as if his actions had been premeditated, to make her leave him alone.

He thought back to those dark days after he'd been shot. Everyone had deserted him. His mother had always hated him, despite her pretense for the sake of appearances. Even Jane, his wife, had walked out on him and filed for divorce, after being blatantly unfaithful to him. But Tess had been with him every step of the way, making him live, making him fight. Tess had been the light that brought him out of the darkness. And he'd repaid her loving kindness with cruelty. It hurt him to remember that. It hurt him more to realize that she could have died last night.

A faint tap on the door announced the nurse's entrance. She smiled at Dane and proceeded to check Tess's vital signs.

"Lucky, wasn't she?" the woman asked absently, as she waited for the thermometer to register. "Just a few inches to the side and she'd be dead."

The impact of the idle remark was as sharp as a tack. He blinked, his dark gaze steady on Tess's closed eyes. If she died, he'd be alone. He'd have no one.

The enormity of the thought drove him out of the room with a murmured excuse. He walked down the long corridor without seeing it, his mind humming all the way to the black Mercedes he'd had Helen drive to the parking lot for him while Tess was in surgery. He still had to call the office and tell them how she was. He checked his watch; it was time they were at work. He'd stop by on the way to his apartment to shower and change his clothes.

He unlocked the car, but he didn't get in, his hand on the door handle as he stared up at the hospital. Tess wasn't a relative in any sense at all. Their parents had never married. But they were both only children and their parents were dead.

With a rough sigh, he opened the car door and got in. He didn't start it immediately. He stared at the blood on his sleeve. Tess's blood. He'd watched it pulse out of her in the darkness as if it were his own. She could have died in his arms.

Once she'd been such a bright, happy girl, so eager to please him, so obviously in love with him. He closed his eyes. He'd killed that sweet feeling in her. He'd frightened it right out of her with his clumsy headlong rush at her that afternoon, when he'd given in finally to the need that had been tearing him apart. He'd never wanted anyone so much. But he knew nothing of tenderness, and he'd terrified her. It hadn't been deliberate, but maybe, subconsciously, he'd wanted her to back away, before she became his world. A failed marriage made a man gun-shy, Dane thought bitterly, looking back to the time three years ago when Tess and he had first met....

From the evening that Tess and Dane had first met— so long ago, at a restaurant where their parents had invited them to get acquainted—they saw very little of each other except on holidays. Dane and his wife, Jane, were not getting along. And even his mother, Nita, had mentioned cattily that Jane had been seen with another man. It was almost as if it pleased Nita to know that Dane's wife was being openly unfaithful to him....

Those days had not been good ones for Dane. Then, on the morning that Wyatt Meriwether and Nita Lassiter announced their engagement, Dane had walked into a shootout with some bank robbers and had wound up in the county emergency room fighting for his life.

Tess had rushed to the hospital as soon as she knew. Her father drove her, but when they discovered that Nita was still at home and that Jane couldn't be found, he'd left.

But Tess stayed, that night and the next day. Once she convinced a floor nurse that he was going to be her stepbrother, and that he had no one else, they allowed her to see him in intensive care. She held his hand, smoothed his brow and cringed at the damage the bullets had done, because she'd had a look at the torn flesh of his shoulder, spine and leg where the bullets had penetrated.

"Will I walk?" he managed in a pain-laced voice when he regained consciousness.

"Of course," Tess said with a gentle smile. She touched his lean face and pushed the hair away from his forehead with a possessive feeling.

His eyes closed and he groaned. "Where's my mother?" he asked harshly. "Where's Jane?"

She hesitated.

His black eyes opened again, fury in them. "She was sleeping with my partner," he said harshly. "He told me...."

She grimaced.

He laughed coldly and went back to sleep.

In the weeks that followed, Dane's life changed. Jane came to see him once, stiffly apologetic, only to inform him that she'd filed for divorce and was remarrying the minute the divorce was final. His mother peered in the door, remarked that he seemed prepared to live after all, and went sailing with Wyatt.

Tess, infuriated with the rest of the family, devoted herself to Dane's recovery.

God knew, he needed someone, she thought. What he'd found out about Jane had very likely distracted him enough to get him shot. Then Jane walked out on him. His own mother had deserted him. Not only that, but he even lost his job, because the surgeons agreed that he might never be fit enough for full-time work again because of the damage to his spine.

When they told him the bad news, he almost gave up, he was so depressed.

"This won't do," Tess said gently, recognizing instinctively the lack of life in his lean face. She knelt beside the chair where he was sitting up for a few minutes and took his hand in hers, holding tightly. "You can't give up, Dane," she told him. "They only said that you *might* not be able to work—not that you *will*. You can't let them do this to you."

"Can't? They already have," he said tersely, averting his eyes. "Why don't you get out, too?"

"You're my almost-big-brother," she said. "I want you to get well."

He glared at her. "I don't need a teenage sister."

"You'll get one, all the same, when our parents marry," she said pleasantly. "Come on, cheer up. You're tough. You were a ranger, after all."

His face closed up. "*Was* is right."

"So you won't be in prime condition for a while. So what? Listen, Dane, there are plenty of things you can do with your law-enforcement background. God doesn't close doors without opening windows. This can be an opportunity, if you'll just look at it in that light."

He didn't speak. But he listened. His dark eyes narrowed as they searched hers. "I don't like women," he began.

"I guess not. With all due respect, your life hasn't been blessed wtih nice ones."

"I married Jane to spite my mother. Not that I didn't want her at the time. She was all set to settle down and have children. That was all she wanted." He averted his face, as if the memory of her desertion was killing him. "Get out, Tess. Go play nurse somewhere else."

"Can't." She shrugged. "Who'll keep you from wallowing in self-pity?"

"Damn you!" he snapped, his eyes flashing warning signals as they met hers.

She grinned, refusing to be intimidated. That was the first spark of interest she'd seen since they'd told him he couldn't work. "That's better," she said. "How about a cup of coffee?"

He hesitated. But after a minute, he gave in to the irritating need to be fussed over. He nodded and she almost ran in her haste to get to the coffee machine down the hall. He stared after her with helpless need. He'd never been treated like this by a woman, by any woman. It was new and unsettling to have someone care about him, want to do things for him. With his mother, and especially Jane, it had been, "What can you do for *me?*" Tess was different. Too different. She was getting under his skin, and not just with her warm affection. He looked at her body and felt a kind of desire he hadn't experienced in years. She aroused him as Jane never had. That, he thought worriedly, could present some problems later on. She was only nineteen, even if she was probably experienced. Most girls were these days. He closed his eyes. Well, he'd cross that bridge later. Not now.

He began to think about what she'd said, about a new profession. His lips pursed thoughtfully and all at once he began to smile as wheels turned in his mind.

As the weeks passed, Tess came with time-clock regularity, sitting with him, talking to him. He accepted her presence and finally began to let his guard down with her. They grew closer, even as he fought his headlong attraction to her.

The attraction slowly began to undermine his efforts to be kind to her. He was overly irritable one Monday morning when she came to his apartment and found him lying listlessly in bed.

"You again? What the hell do you want?" he'd asked coldly.

Used to his flashes of temper by now, she only smiled. "I want you to get well," she said simply.

He lay back and closed his eyes. "Go away. Aren't you late for school?"

"I graduated. It's summer."

"Then get a job."

"I'm going to secretarial school at night."

"And working during the day?"

"Sort of."

His head turned on the pillow. "Sort of?"

She smiled. "Dad thinks I'm doing enough of a job helping you get back on your feet." She didn't add that her father had only agreed absently with her own comment on that score. Nita had been to see her son just that once, and had stayed less than five minutes. But Tess adored him. She'd worked to lose weight, to improve her appearance, so that he might notice her during his long recovery. It hadn't worked, but she was hopeful that it might one day.

"Are you qualified to practice psychiatry and physical therapy?" he asked with biting sarcasm.

It bounced right off. She knew he was hurting, so she didn't mind being a target. She put her purse aside and stood up, her ponytail swinging as she leaned over him.

"My father is going to marry your mother. When that happens, you'll be my big brother. I need to practice looking out for you," she said.

He glared at her. "I don't need looking after."

"Yes, you do," she replied pleasantly. Her eyes went to the visible scars on his upper arm in its white T-shirt. There were worse ones on his back. She'd seen them, though he didn't know she had. "It must hurt terribly," she said, her voice as gentle as the look she gave him. "I'm sorry you got hurt, Richard."

"Dane," he corrected. "Nobody calls me Richard."

"Okay."

"And I don't need a schoolgirl for a nursemaid."

"Why doesn't your mother come to see you more often?" she asked curiously.

He averted his eyes. "Because she hated my father. I look like him."

"Oh." She moved a little closer, hesitant but determined. "Wouldn't you like to be part of a family?" she asked, sounding more plaintive than she realized. "I've only ever had my grandmother, really, and she only kept me because she had to. My mother died when I was just little. Dad…" She shrugged. "Dad was never much of a family person. So I've really got nobody. And…I'm sorry…but it seems as if now you haven't got anybody, either." She clasped her hands tightly at her waist. "We could be each other's family."

His face had gone hard, and his eyes glittered at her. "I don't want a family," he said deliberately. "Least of all, you!"

"I might grow on you," she said, and smiled to hide the hurt caused by his words. Of course he didn't want her. Nobody ever really had.

He hadn't said anything else. He'd tried ignoring her, but she wouldn't go away. She came every single day, bringing books for him to read, tapes for him to listen to. She cooked for him and sat with him and talked to him, argued with him and encouraged him, and despite his hostility and lack of encouragement, she very quietly fell in love with him.

She didn't realize that her love for him was so obvious. It was impossible not to notice how she felt, when her face was radiant with it. Neither had she known that Dane noticed her without wanting to, his dark eyes growing more covetous by the day as his recovery brought her close and kept her there. He became used to her, enjoyed her, wanted her. She was so different from all the women he'd had in his life. Tess was loving and gentle, and there was an odd kind of vulnerability about her. He thrived on her attentions. He began to look forward to her company.

But even so, he eventually grew uneasy when he began to realize how attached he was becoming to her. He was afraid of involvement, terrified of it, after the disaster of his marriage. Even if he'd married Jane to spite his hard-hearted mother, who didn't approve of her, he'd been attracted to Jane at first, and she'd pretended to be in love with him. Then had come marriage and her distaste of intimacy with him. The crowning touch had been her reckless affair with his old partner on the Houston police force. That had been revenge, he knew, and she'd left him more crippled than the shooting had. Tess was a woman. She could very easily be deceiving him, too, overcome with compassion and what was probably physical infatuation.

His doubts led to a return of his former moodiness, and then to open hostility. He pushed Tess away at every opportunity, but she was stubborn and refused to believe that he really didn't want her around.

He got back on his feet and grew strong much more quickly than anyone thought he would. With good health came a revived male vitality that responded suddenly, and with devastating results, to Tess's femininity....

With her blond hair around her shoulders and wearing a white peasant dress with a colorful belt, she danced into his apartment at lunchtime one day carrying a homemade cake. Dane was in jeans and barefoot, his white T-shirt over his muscular chest damp with sweat from the workout he'd been having in his improvised gym. He limped a little because of his wounds, but he could walk. Now he was intent on walking without the limp, getting fit. But Tess was making him vulnerable all over again, draining him of strength.

He wanted her desperately, even if it was totally against his will. He'd been without a woman for a long time, and he needed someone. Tess was tempting him beyond bearing. She looked at him with eyes that wanted him, and the need had smoldered so long that it got away from him.

She hadn't seen the calculating look he'd given her as she deposited the cake on the counter in the kitchen, or the warning glitter of his black eyes.

"What's this?" he asked in a sensual tone he'd never used with her before, moving close.

"Just a pound cake," she said breathlessly, her eyes shyly glancing off his as she registered the devastating impact of his nearness on her pulse rate. Her eyes adored him. "I thought you might have a sweet tooth. How do you feel? You look...much better." Her eyes had dropped, as if the sight of him delighted her, embarrassed her.

He hadn't thought about her love life, or lack of it, or it might have prevented what happened next. His only intent at the time had been to ease the ache devouring him, in the quickest possible way.

"I've got a sweet tooth, all right," he'd said softly as he backed her up against the counter and leaned his body into hers. "You must have one, too. You spend half your life devouring me with those sultry eyes. I'd have to be blind not to know what you feel for me. Is this what you want, Tess?'' he asked huskily, and moved his hips blatantly against hers, letting her feel the stark evidence of his desire for her. She blushed, but he wasn't looking. His eyes were on her parted lips. ''God knows, I want you beyond bearing!''

Her mind had stopped working, shock mingling with fear. Before she could find the words to protest, his hard, hungry mouth covered hers, his hips pushing her against the counter behind her. His hands lifted her into the stark aroused curve of his body, and his tongue went into her mouth with enough lust to make even a virgin aware of his intent.

Tess had only been kissed once or twice, always by men who knew how sheltered her life was. Now she was being subjected to an embrace that only an experienced woman could have responded to, and it scared her to death.

She stiffened and pushed at his chest frantically, but her actions didn't penetrate the haze in his mind. One lean hand possessed her breast roughly while his leg suddenly stabbed between hers in an explicit movement that made her panic.

''Dane...no!'' she panted, wild-eyed.

He barely heard her. ''Yes,'' he groaned unsteadily. ''Oh, God, yes, yes...!'' His powerful arm contracted. ''You want me, don't you, baby?'' he'd asked blindly, his body shuddering as his mouth burned over her bare shoulders and throat, only to return, hot and heavy and rough on hers. ''Don't you? Right here.'' He groaned harshly, his hands moving under her skirt, holding her bare thighs as he shifted her so that she could feel the blatant need of his body pressing hungrily at the threshold of her innocence.

She gasped, her heart shaking at the sensations the

contact aroused. She moaned under his mouth, frightened.

"Here," he growled. "Right here, baby, standing up," he said shakily. His hands were on bare skin, touching her as no man ever had, as if his own need was paramount, as if she were simply a vessel for that need, to be used.

Then all at once, still breathing harshly, he let her slide to the floor and his head lifted briefly. His eyes were glazed, his body trembling faintly, like the strong, lean hands that smoothed roughly over her breasts as he crushed her mouth under his and groaned harshly. "This is too much for my back," he'd whispered. "We'll have to do it in bed, so that I can lie down...."

She knew it was the only chance she'd have to get away. She ducked and tore out of his arms. Her fear of him was so evident that it managed to penetrate the glaze in his eyes, the raging, headlong helplessness of his need. The threat of intimacy without emotion made her panic. She wept, her sobs loud in the room as she backed away from him, her gray eyes tragic and wide.

"Get away...from me!" she cried as he came toward her, his intentions written in his dark eyes. "Leave me alone!"

It registered, finally, that she was afraid of him. He'd been too drunk on her softness to realize it until he saw the wide, helpless terror in her eyes. He fought to breathe normally. He'd lost control. That was a first.

He stared at her, his expression slowly reverting to its usual impassivity, his eyes startlingly black. "That's what you've been asking for," he said in a cutting, harsh tone as he fought for sanity.

"No!" It was a cry from the heart.

"You wanted me," he spat. "Why else do you keep coming here?"

"I love you," she sobbed, shaken into telling the truth as she stood hugging her arms over her breasts.

"Love!" His eyes glared hotly at her as a visible shudder ran through his powerful body, still aroused and hurting. "All right, if you love me, come here. Prove it, you icy little tease," he added with a mocking smile that hid overwhelming frustration.

Her heart went cold, like the tears on her face. She looked at him with anguish. "I can't," she whispered. "You...you hurt me!"

Her fear infuriated him. It was Jane all over again, hating his lovemaking, taunting him, her sarcasm vicious and unforgiving. "No?" he asked coolly. "Then if you won't give out, get out," he added. "All I wanted from you in the first place was sex. My God," he ground out involuntarily as she shrank from him, "why not me? Surely to God you've had others...!"

Her eyes were as big as saucers, her flushed face red, her body shaking. And it dawned on him, too late, that there hadn't been any others. She couldn't look like that, even with him, if she were experienced.

He felt a surge of horror. "Tess, are you a virgin?"

She thought she might faint at the expression in his eyes. She couldn't look at him after that. She grabbed her purse and ran from the apartment. Without a word Dane watched her leave. He didn't go after her; he didn't call later to apologize. It was, he told himself, the only out he was likely to get. Let her think he'd done it deliberately. She made him vulnerable. He had nothing to offer her. It would be a kindness, in a way. He turned back into the apartment, his eyes as cold as he felt inside. He'd never trust a woman again as long as he lived. Not even Tess. A virgin. How could he have not known? He hoped he hadn't left too many scars....

He'd tried to consider it a lucky escape. Eventually, his pretended indifference and hostility had crushed the spontaneity right out of Tess, so that now she was quiet and polite and even a little shy when they were together. After her father died, Dane had offered her a job as a secretary. She had had nobody except him, and he'd wanted to help. It had worked fine, but only when he made her angry did he see any traces of the old Tess. Perhaps, he confessed silently, that was why he kept goading her.

Angrily, he started the car and drove to the office, to be met by the whole staff the minute he walked in the door. It shouldn't have surprised him that his employees loved Tess. She was forever doing things for them.

"Will she be all right?" Helen got in first, her big dark eyes worried.

"She's fine," he assured them. "Still drowsy from the anesthetic, but there won't be any impairment. She has to heal."

"When does she come home?" Helen persisted. "She can stay with me. She'll need looking after."

"She'll stay with me," he said, shocking all of them, including himself. "I'll take her down to the ranch. José and Beryl can take care of her when I have to be in the office. Did you get a temp for the next week or so?" he asked Helen.

"She'll be here any minute," she agreed. "Good typing and dictation speeds and her agency says she's discreet. No worries about loose lips sinking ships."

"Good." His eyes went involuntarily to the desk where Tess worked. It wounded him to see it empty.

"See if you can make any sense out of her appointment book, will you?" he asked irritably, glancing at Helen. "I don't even know what I have on my calendar today."

"You're having lunch with Harvey Barrett," she reminded him. "That's on the extortion case. This afternoon you were supposed to see a couple who want you to find their daughter—the Allisons—and a man who wants his wife watched."

"And this morning?"

She stared at the appointment book and shook her head. "Nothing urgent."

"Good. I'm going to the apartment to change and then I'll be at the hospital until lunch."

Helen frowned. "I thought you said she was okay."

He moved toward the door without answering. "If there's anything important, you can reach me in her room." He gave her the number.

"Okay, boss. Tell her she's missed."

He nodded. His mind wasn't on what was going on around him. It was on Tess.

Chapter Two

Tess moaned in her sleep as the pain caught her un-
awares. She'd been dreaming. Probably about Dane,
she thought drowsily. She never dreamed about anyone
else. That was almost comical, considering how badly
he'd hurt her.

A sound penetrated her semiaware state. She opened
her eyes in time to see Dane sitting down in the chair
beside the bed.

"What are you doing back?" she asked, her body
going rigid. "It's a workday."

"I'm working," he said. "Looking after you."

The wording brought back unbearable memories of
the time that *he'd* been shot—and what had followed.
She closed her eyes on a wave of pain. "Please go
away," she whispered huskily.

He took a slow breath. The anguish in her face made
him uneasy. "You don't have anyone else."

That was true. Her grandmother had died a year ago.

Her eyes met his, and there was nothing in her face
to betray what she really felt. "You're just my boss,

Dane,'' she said quietly. "That doesn't require you to look after me.''

He sat up, his forearms across his knees as he stared at her. "I've never asked. Maybe I need to. How much damage did I do that day?''

She flushed and averted her eyes. "I don't know what you're talking about,'' she said stiffly.

"Don't you?'' he asked on a cold laugh. "We've waltzed around it for three years. I can't get near you, even to apologize.''

"Why should you care?'' she replied. "You wanted me out of your life. You got it. I wouldn't come near you now for a handful of diamonds!''

"Me or any other man,'' he said out of the blue.

She pulled the sheet closer, her eyes on the window, not on him. "Don't you have something better to do than bait me?''

"I'm taking you down to the ranch to recuperate.''

She went white. She sat up in bed, her eyes like saucers in a face drained of life.

"Oh, my God, don't!'' he said harshly. "Don't look like that!''

Her hand trembled on the sheet. "No,'' she whispered, choking on the word. "Not in your house, with you. Not ever!''

His eyes closed. He couldn't bear the way she looked. He got up jerkily and went to the window, lighting a cigarette as he stared out at nothing at all. He drew in a harsh breath of pungent smoke and let it out.

"I didn't realize you were a virgin,'' he said curtly. "Not until it was too late and I'd frightened you half to death. Don't you think I know why you don't go out with men?'' He turned, pinning her shocked eyes with his. "Don't you think I care about what I've done to you?"

She swallowed, dropping her gaze to her cold, nervous hands on the sheet. "It was a long time ago...."

"It might as well have been yesterday," he said heavily. "God in heaven, stop pushing me away!"

She flushed. "I haven't."

He turned, moving back toward the bed, his face as drawn as her own. He paused beside her. "Tess, I know you're afraid of me physically. I'd have to be blind not to be aware of it. I'm not going to hurt you. I just want you where you'll be taken care of until you're back on your feet again. Beryl will be at the ranch if I'm not."

"I don't know Beryl. Helen says I can stay with her...."

"When Helen isn't at work, she's at ballet class. If she has any free time at all, she's eating pizza with her friend Harold. She means well, but you'd be alone most every evening, and all day while she's at work."

"I'd be all right by myself."

He moved closer, hating the way she stiffened. "Listen," he said through his teeth. "You saw a drug deal go down. You'll have to testify. The policemen didn't actually see the drugs being passed, do you understand? You're the only witness who actually *saw* them. One man is still loose, and he almost certainly knows who you are by now. Do you get the picture?"

"You can't mean what I think you do," she said slowly.

"The hell I can't! I dealt with this kind of vermin for ten years. I know what lengths they'll go to. You aren't going to be safe until they apprehend the second man and bring them both up for trial. I want you where I am, where I can take care of you. When I'm not home, my ranch manager is. He was a ranger back in the forties, and he's almost as good a shot as I am.''

She put her face in her hands. It was agonizing to have to agree to what he wanted. She'd almost rather have taken her chances with the drug dealers.

"Hate me, if it helps," he said. "But come with me. Don't throw your life away."

She smoothed back her long, disheveled hair. "What kind of a life do I have?" she asked miserably. "Work and television don't add up to much."

"You're twenty-two," he said. "Years too young to be that cynical."

"Oh, I learned from an expert," she said, lifting her face. "You taught me."

Her expression made him uncomfortable. "I've never had anyone of my own," he said shortly. "My father left when I was a boy. He couldn't take the pressure of responsibility. I worshiped him, but my mother hated him, hated me because I looked like him. Jane said she loved me when we were first married, but she walked out on me and didn't look back." He leaned over her, his eyes black as coals. "You wanted to love me, and I wouldn't let you. I hurt you, made you afraid of me. Don't you get it, little girl? I don't know what love is!"

"You needn't look at me as if I'm any threat," she said defiantly. "I gave up on you years ago."

"Yes. I know."

She averted her eyes. "I don't love you. I had an inconvenient fascination for you that you put into perspective for me. You won't have to fight me off ever again."

His lean hand went to her face. He touched her cheek

lightly, catching her chin when she tried to jerk away. His eyes probed hers relentlessly.

"That goes double for me," he said. "I won't ever touch you that way again."

She watched him, too aware of the warm fingers on her softly rounded chin. "You would have forced me," she choked out.

His face contorted. He wanted to deny it, but he couldn't. He'd been out of his mind. "You don't understand," he said bitterly.

She stared at him as if she didn't quite comprehend. He sounded tortured, haunted. "Dane?" she whispered.

He wouldn't look at her. "You were a virgin," he said huskily. "But I wasn't. I'd had women. You were soft and vulnerable and loving, and I wanted you in a way I...couldn't handle."

Wheels turned in her mind. Men were vulnerable sometimes; even in her innocence she knew that. She'd avoided the thought for years, but a part of her had realized how desperate he was for her that day, how hungry. "You scared me out of my mind," she laughed nervously. "Every time I went out with a man, I was afraid he might become like that, and I wouldn't be able to get away in time."

"That isn't surprising," he replied. "Will you believe that it hasn't been easy for me, either? You can't imagine what it does to me when you cringe every time I come close to you."

Her chest rose and fell slowly. She searched his eyes. "It was a long time ago, wasn't it? I suppose I blew it up in my mind until it was nightmarish."

He saw the faint softness in her eyes and hesitated. "Tess, is it only fear that you feel when you're with me?" he asked. His eyes fell to her mouth, to the helpless parting of her lips under the intent stare. His thumb moved slowly, the nail just lightly tracing the moist inner surface of her lower lip in a movement that made her breath catch. "Or is there something more, in spite of the way I frightened you?"

She pulled back frantically, oblivious to what he'd said at the last in her desperation to get away from that maddening touch. Her eyes widened and her heartbeat became rushed.

He had to drag his eyes back up to hers. His own breathing was uneasy. So it wasn't all terror. Something inside him thawed a little, even as he watched her futile attempts to hide what he'd aroused in her with that sensuous little brush of his hand. Amazing that in all his thirty-four years, he'd never thought of touching a woman's mouth exactly like that.

"No," he said, almost to himself. "It's a little more complicated than fear, isn't it?"

"Dane…"

"Your doctor says you can leave in the morning. In the meanwhile, there's a uniformed officer outside the door. He's been there since you were brought in, and he'll be there until I take you home."

She watched him nervously as he put out his cigarette.

He caught her scrutiny and his dark eyes slid to meet hers. "You make me want to be gentle. That's a first," he said quietly. He studied her thoughtfully. "Maybe I could make you want my touch, if I tried."

Cold chills worked down her spine. "No," she whispered huskily. "I won't let you touch me. Not the way…you did that day!"

"I've never been with a virgin, little one," he said, his voice deep and slow. "I've never been a gentle man, either, I guess, but I set new records on wildness with you. It made me take a long look at myself. I didn't like what I saw.''

Her hands linked together and she looked at them, not at him. ''I don't want to talk about it, Dane.''

He had to search for the right words. ''Haven't you realized by now that most men...that a man who loved you would want to be gentle? That it wouldn't be like that with someone who loved you?''

''How do you know if someone cares?'' she asked with bitter cynicism. She looked up at him. ''I thought you did,'' she said huskily. ''I thought you liked me, at least, but you made me afraid of you so that I wouldn't be a threat to your privacy. My father didn't want me, either. He landed me with my grandmother because he didn't want me.'' She shivered. ''Nobody ever wanted me....'' She lay back against the pillows, looking ten years older than she was. ''Please go away, Dane. I'm too tired to fight anymore.''

Why hadn't he known how she felt? After all these years, he still knew next to nothing about her. Of course she'd felt rejected when her father left her with her grandmother; more so because of all his affairs. And then he'd planned to marry Dane's mother, further isolating her. She'd wanted someone to love, and she'd had the misfortune to pick a man who didn't even know what it was, who'd known nothing but resentment and dislike all his life, a man with a failed marriage behind him and a crippled body to boot.

He grimaced at the defeated expression on her face. He felt responsible for her anguish, as if he'd caused it. Certainly he'd added to it.

''Do you like horses?'' he asked.

''I'm afraid of them.''

"Only because you don't know much about them. When you're up to it, I'll teach you to ride."

Her eyes met his. "Don't do this to me," she said unsteadily. "Please don't. I don't need pity."

He started to speak, but he didn't know what words to use. He drew in a long breath.

"I'll see you tomorrow. Try to rest."

She nodded. Her eyes closed, blocking him out. She wasn't going to let him get to her again. No matter what she had to do to protect herself, he wasn't getting a second shot at her!

Chapter Three

The Lassiter Bar-D was a working cattle ranch. Besides José Dominguez and Hardy, who were horse wrangler and cook, respectively, Dane employed a ranch manager, Beryl's husband Dan, and half a dozen cowhands and other assorted personnel necessary to keep the place running. One man did nothing but look after the purebred bulls. Another took care of the tanks used to water the cattle. Still another was a mechanic.

Tess hadn't really wanted to let Dane spirit her out of the hospital and down to his ranch, but she hadn't been strong enough to fight him. He'd cleared it with the doctor, had had her bags—packed by Helen—already in the car, and the minute she was released, had headed straight down to Branntville.

Tess was uneasy about the prospect of several days in Dane's company. He was acting strangely, and she was nervous—much more so than usual.

He'd never been much of a talker unless he had to socialize as part of his job, so the trip down to Branntville was undertaken in silence. Tess stared out the window, buried in her own thoughts and occupied with the twinges of pain she was still feeling from the wound in her arm.

"Is that a ranch?" she asked when they reached the outskirts of Branntville, her eyes on a huge white-fenced property with a black silhouette of a spur for a logo.

"Yes. Cole Everett and the Big Spur are known all over the state. Cole married his stepsister, Heather Shaw. They have three boys, all teenagers now."

"It's very big, isn't it?" she asked.

"Except for the Brannt Ranch, it's the biggest north of the King Ranch."

"Brannt Ranch? Is Branntville named for the people who live there?"

He nodded and indicated a ranch house far in the distance. "King Brannt owns the spread now. Talk about a hard case," he murmured. "King makes up his own rules as he goes along. He married a beautiful young girl, a model named Shelby Kane, daughter of the movie star Maria Kane. Nobody thought he'd ever marry. He says Shelby came up on his blind side." He smiled mockingly. "He'd do anything for her."

"Did she take to ranch life?" Tess asked curiously.

"Like a duck to water. She and King have a son and a daughter. The daughter, I understand, is sweet on one of the Everett boys."

"What a merger that would be," Tess said.

"They're young yet. And marriage isn't always the end of the rainbow," he added with faint bitterness.

"I guess it has to have common ground, doesn't it?" Tess asked absently, staring out at the horizon. "Two people need more than physical attraction to make a marriage."

He glanced at her. "Such as?"

"Respect," she said. "Shared interests, similar backgrounds—things like that."

"And no sex?"

She shifted uneasily, her eyes on the windshield. "I guess if they wanted kids…"

His eyes darkened. "Children aren't always possible."

"I suppose not." She glanced at her hands. "Maybe some people don't mind intimacy."

"Tess," he said heavily. "You don't have a clue, do you?"

She flushed. "Don't I?"

His dark eyes played over her profile, and the fire in his blood kindled. She knew nothing of men and women. It was his fault that she had such hang-ups. He'd hurt and frightened her. Now he wished he'd been different. If he could learn tenderness, it would be sweet to lie with her, to share the beauty of a man and a woman together with her. His body tautened as pictures danced in his mind. Tess, loving him. He could have groaned out loud. He'd thrown away something precious. Ironic that it should have taken a bullet to bring him to his senses, when it was a bullet that had robbed him of them in the first place.

"Here's the ranch."

He turned in between two rows of barbed-wire fences where red-coated cattle grazed. "I share a purebred Santa Gertrudis stud bull with the Big Spur," he explained. "We'll have to replace him pretty soon, though. We've been using him for two years, and that's enough inbreeding."

"I don't understand."

"Are you interested in ranching?" he asked suddenly.

"Well, I don't know much about it," she faltered, her gray eyes darting up to his. "I guess it's complicated, isn't it?"

"Sometimes. But it isn't as difficult a subject as it sounds. You don't ride, either."

"I guess...I could learn," she said hesitantly.

He smiled to himself as he rounded a curve, and suddenly they were coming up to a sprawling one-story white wooden frame house with beds of flowers all around it and tall trees.

"How beautiful!" she exclaimed.

Dane's heart swelled at her delight in it. "It belonged to my grandfather," he told her. "He left it to me when he died."

"Oh, it's charming," she said breathlessly. "And the flower beds! I'll bet they're glorious in the spring!"

"They are Beryl's contribution to beautifying the landscape. There are magnolia trees and azaleas and camellias, all sorts of blooming things. She can tell you, if you're interested."

"I love to garden," she confessed. "I've never had anyplace to do it, except in my apartment window, but I used to do all the yard work at my grandmother's house."

He pulled up at the steps and turned off the engine, staring at her quietly. "I don't know you," he said, his voice soft and deep. "I don't know a damned thing about you, Tess."

"Why would you want to?" she asked evasively. "Look, is that Beryl?" A short, white-haired woman had come onto the porch.

"That's Beryl."

"It's about time you got here!" the woman muttered. "Late, as usual. Is this her?" She stopped in front of Tess and looked her over. "Thin and sickly, she is. I'll take care of that with some good home cooking. How's that arm, lovey?" she asked gently. "Still hurt?"

Tess smiled, at home already. "It's much better."

"If you're through running your mouth, I'd like to get the walking wounded into the house," Dane drawled. "She isn't going to get better standing out here in the cold."

"It's not that cold at all," Beryl scoffed. "Why, in little more than a month there'll be flowers everywhere!"

Tess could picture that, but she wouldn't be around to see it, she thought wistfully. She let Dane help her inside, unable to stop herself from stiffening at the feel of his lean arm around her.

"Don't panic," he said curtly as Beryl went ahead to lead the way to the guest room. "I won't hurt you."

She colored involuntarily. "Dane…"

Her reticence made him irritable. "Relax, can't you? You're among friends."

"You were never that," she said stiffly.

"I'm thirty-four years old," he said as they moved down the long hall. "Maybe I'm tired of being alone. You said once that neither of us has anybody else."

"And you said once that you didn't need anyone."

He shrugged. "I've spent fourteen years being a cop. It isn't easy to change perspective."

The mention of his profession made her uneasy. She didn't like thinking about the drug dealers she'd seen or what Dane had said about her being the only witness.

"What's wrong?" he asked.

"I was thinking about the night I got shot," she confessed. "About those men..."

"You're safe here," he said. "Nobody is going to hurt you."

"Of course not," she agreed, and forced a smile.

Beryl settled her in while Dane went out to check on some new cattle that arrived shortly after they did. It was several hours before he reappeared, after Beryl and Tess had gotten acquainted. But the man who walked into the bedroom wasn't the man she thought she knew.

Dane was wearing the garb of a working cowboy. He was in a striped blue western-cut shirt, long-sleeved with pearl snaps, and worn blue jeans under equally worn batwing chaps held up by a wide, silver-buckled belt. He wore black boots with spurs and a battered black Stetson pulled low over one eye. Tess stared curiously. She'd never seen him dressed like that.

"You look like you've been dragged through a brush thicket," Beryl grimaced.

"Not far wrong," he said, nodding. "We had to flush some cows out of the draws. No job for tenderfeet, that's a fact. Are you settling in?" he asked Tess.

She nodded.

He cocked an eyebrow at her. "Well, why the wide-eyed stare?"

"You look...different," she said, searching for a word to describe the change in him.

"I don't have to keep up a businesslike and impeccable image down here," he said with a faint twist of his lips. "This is home."

Her eyes slid away. *Home.* She had an apartment, but she couldn't remember ever having a home where she felt comfortable. Her grandmother's house had been elegant but untouchable. Her memories of the time when her mother was alive were very dim and stark.

"What are we eating?" he asked Beryl, uncomfortably aware of Tess's apparent indifference to him.

"Beef," she replied. "And potatoes. What else is there?" she added with a grin.

"For me, nothing. I'll get cleaned up."

Tess watched him go. Her eyes were more expressive than she realized as she wrapped her arms tightly around herself and almost shivered, remembering the day he'd cured her of hero worship. She'd wanted so desperately to love him, but he wouldn't let her. Now he seemed to want to mend fences. Didn't he realize that it was years too late?

Beryl was giving Tess a curious stare after he left. "You're afraid of him," she said unexpectedly, her expression incredulous. "Honey, he wouldn't hurt a fly!"

Probably not, she thought, but he had hurt her in ways she could never confess to Beryl. "He never liked my father very much," Tess said evasively. "Or me. He's been kind to me since I got shot, but I still feel safer across town from him."

"He isn't like that." The older woman tried again. "Sharp, yes, even hot-tempered, but he isn't vengeful. I've known him all his life. He was a sweet child until his father left. His mother took his father's desertion out on him. I spared him as much as I could, but she was never much of a parent."

"Neither was my father," Tess confessed.

"See, you've got something in common."

"Right. We're both human beings."

Once she got used to the new routine, Tess found the ranch fascinating and the pace relaxing. She insisted on helping Beryl as much as she could. Her arm was sore, but as she told Beryl, the doctor had said it wouldn't hurt to exercise it, to prevent it from becoming stiff. She set the table at mealtime and did what she could to lessen the strain of her presence, and she enjoyed the warmth of the other people who lived on the ranch.

But she carefully kept her distance from Dane, to his dismay. There was always some reason why she had to leave a room once he entered it, why she had to be unavailable if he was in the living room after dinner, instead of in his study working.

In the office, their relationship was strictly professional. She took dictation, answered the phone and kept things running smoothly. But here, where he was in his element, he was a different man. She had trouble adjusting to him on a personal level. Even when he'd been shot, he'd been the professional lawman, except for that once. And it had happened at the apartment he kept in town, not here at the ranch. If he had an inner sanctum, this was it. This was the first time she'd seen it; he'd made sure of that.

Here, away from the world, he was relaxed and not so severely on his guard. He limped a little because of the primarily physical work he did on the ranch, and his temper was more noticeable than at the office, but he was also less driven and stoic. That fact was what made Tess so nervous. She was vulnerable here, away from prying eyes. Beryl never intruded. Neither did any of the ranch hands. It made her uneasy to be totally at Dane's mercy.

He noticed that she avoided him and became impatient with it. And finally, three days later, he confronted her while she was helping feed a stray calf in the barn.

He was angry. The set of his jaw and the glitter in his eyes would have told her, even without the taut stance of his body.

"Stop avoiding me," he said without preamble, his very tone intimidating.

She looked up at him nervously. She was wearing jeans and a denim coat over her blue blouse, with her hair plaited at her nape. She looked very pretty, even without makeup, something Dane noticed.

"I'm feeding the calf...." she said hesitantly, indicating the bottle she was holding to the calf's mouth as she balanced its small head on her knee.

"That isn't what I mean, and you know it." He whipped off his Stetson, the quick action unnerving, and knelt beside her. He was in working garb, too. His jeans and boots were much more disreputable-looking than hers, his batwing chaps stained and worn. The cuffs of his long-sleeved chambray shirt were speckled with mud and blood, like the sleeves of his open shepherd's coat. He looked up, catching her eyes in a look she couldn't break. "I've tried to tell you that I regret what I did that day," he said roughly.

She flushed. Her heart was beating her to death. She didn't want to analyze why.

"I thought you were more experienced than you turned out to be, or I wouldn't have taken it that far, that fast."

"You said so before," she faltered.

"You didn't listen before." He ran his hand through his thick, damp hair. "You go out with men occasionally. You must know by now, at your age, that intimacy can be rough."

She looked down at the calf. She didn't answer him.

"Right?" He caught her softly rounded chin in his lean fingers and tilted her face up to his. "Tell me."

"There hasn't been...anybody," she said unsteadily. "Not...that way."

His face changed all at once. He frowned slightly, his eyes falling to her parted lips and then back up to her eyes. "How deep are the scars I gave you?" he asked quietly.

Her thin shoulders moved restlessly. "Pretty deep," she said with a humorless laugh. "Dane, I have to finish this."

He withdrew his hand, draping it across his knee as he watched her. Her reaction to him was damning. He made her nervous. He could see her hands shaking, and he hated that part of the past that was responsible for her helpless fear.

"You kept coming, no matter how hard I tried to push you away. You got closer than anyone else ever had," he said without meeting her eyes, his fingers tracing a streak of mud on the knee of his jeans as the involuntary confession escaped him. "I got in over my head before I knew it. I didn't really want a woman in my life."

"But you were married once, before you got shot," she said.

His eyes met hers and he smiled with pure mockery. "I started dating Jane because my mother didn't like her. Then I married her because she wouldn't sleep with me any other way. But she only suffered me in bed for one reason," he said, without elaborating on the reason. His face hardened. "Eventually she went looking for a man who could give her everything she needed. I assume she found him when we were divorced. She's remarried and has a child."

"Oh." She frowned, her eyes searching his curiously as she tried to get up enough courage to ask a question that was gnawing at her.

"You want to know why she didn't like sleeping with me," he said, nodding. "Do you really need to ask?"

He was like a bulldozer, in every way. Perhaps the ardor he'd shown her that long-ago day was how he made love naturally. She hadn't considered that likelihood.

It opened her mind to new possibilities. She lifted her face. "Was it…were you that way with her? Like you were with me that day?"

His jaw tautened. "I've never liked a woman enough to care whether or not she enjoyed me in bed," he said bluntly. "I wanted Jane. I thought if she loved me, preliminaries wouldn't matter."

Her breath escaped in a sigh. She was innocent on certain subjects, but she seemed to know more about than he did.

"But…but you can't just…just…" She colored. "Dane, women aren't like men," she said helplessly. "A woman has to have time, tenderness."

"How would you know?" he asked insolently. "Didn't you just practically admit to me that you're still a virgin?"

The blush got worse. She glared at him. "Being innocent doesn't make me stupid. I watch movies and read books, you know. I do have some idea of what a woman is supposed to feel with a man she loves."

"You loved me," he said darkly. "And you felt nothing except fear."

"I was infatuated with you," she corrected, shivering inside at the knowledge that she'd been so transparent. At nineteen, she'd known nothing about how to keep her heart hidden. "You hurt me, and not just emotionally."

"That wasn't deliberate. I was…hungry for you," he said hesitantly. He sounded almost vulnerable. "You were sweet and loving, and I thought…" He cursed under his breath. "What does it matter?" His eyes darted up and slammed into hers. "You didn't want me."

"You were so violent," she whispered weakly.

His fist clenched on his knee. "I don't know any other way with a woman!" he said stiffly. His eyes narrowed as they met hers. "I was a late bloomer. My mother was the only woman I'd been around much and she hated men with a vengeance. In fact, she hated me, too. I got my first taste of women when I was a rookie cop. The kind of women you meet out on the streets in police work are every bit as tough as the men, because they have to be. The only encounters I ever had were rushed and unemotional." His eyes were unconsciously intent on her face. "The way I was with you that day… is the only way I know."

"Dane," she whispered, her voice soft with unwilling compassion. "I'm so sorry!"

His dark eyes met hers. "What?" he asked absently.

She wondered if he realized what he'd told her, how much of himself he'd revealed. She reached up, for the first time voluntarily touching his lean cheek. Her fingers were cold.

He jerked back from her, his eyes glittery, and closed up like a clam. "I don't need pity, honey," he said mockingly. "I don't need a damned woman, either."

He got up and stomped off down the aisle, leaving a shocked, puzzled Tess behind.

For the next two days, it was Dane who avoided her, almost as if his confession had embarrassed him. Tess found herself less nervous as she considered how his attitude toward women had stifled his ability to feel tenderness.

Tess had never really liked his mother—Nita Lassiter had been very brittle, very flighty. When Tess's father wasn't around, she was all but hostile toward Tess, and even more so toward Dane.

Dane's ex-wife hadn't seemed much of a prize, either, judging from that one dinner Tess had spent with Dane and her. Her sullen, resentful behavior had convinced Tess that the woman had never loved Dane, and he himself had said that it was the uniform that had attracted Jane more than the man inside it. Jane had struck Tess as being just as much a man-hater as Dane's mother.

She frowned thoughtfully. Didn't they say a man unconsciously looked for women who reminded him of his mother? Or that men sometimes, equally unconsciously, chose women who lived down to their image of them? Dane had spent his time around women of questionable character in his youth, so perhaps he thought sex was only permissible with women who had no softness, no vulnerability.

It was a sobering thought. But she had no time to work on the theory, because Dane announced suddenly that he'd been away from the office long enough and had to get back. Naturally, Tess agreed to return to work, too, because her arm was back to normal, even if a little soreness remained.

He packed and drove them back to Houston, silent and unapproachable, after Tess had said her goodbyes to Beryl.

"I'm going to post a man outside your apartment, and I'm having you followed," he said curtly when he deposited her suitcases in her apartment an hour later.

She looked up at him irritably. "I don't need a watchdog. I'm perfectly capable of calling the police if I need to."

"No, you aren't," he replied. "You don't know these people. I do."

"Mr. Policeman." She nodded, eyes flashing at him. "I'll bet when you were a beat cop, your badge was sewn to your skin!"

He smiled, a sensual twist of his lips that made her heart race. "I loved the job," he agreed. "It was, and is, the only place I feel comfortable, apart from the ranch. Detective work isn't so different from what I did. Especially when I take a criminal case."

That was a fact. During the time she'd worked for him, she'd known him to track down murderers and bank robbers, to subdue them and bring them in, all as part of the job. Returning fugitives for worried bail bondsmen was a big chunk of the agency's income. Tame cases he left to the skip tracers and operatives. He took the dangerous ones—he and Nick, his protegé.

"It's the adrenaline," she murmured. "You're addicted to the danger."

"Am I?"

"It would explain why you won't slow down," she said. Her eyes slid down the muscular length of him, over the scarred shoulder and chest she knew were hidden under his clothes.

"You wouldn't want to look at me after the damage

the bullets did,'' he said quietly. ''It would make you sick.''

Her eyes jumped back to his. ''I was thinking about how it happened,'' she said. ''Not how it would look.''

He relaxed a little, but not much. He always seemed as if his spine were glued to a wall. He walked tall, never slumped or slouched. His posture, like his character, was arrow-straight.

''All the same, I'll never be anyone's idea of a pinup in a bathing suit,'' he said with a faint smile. ''Not that I was before I got shot.''

Her unblinking stare was involuntary. ''I've never seen you in a bathing suit,'' she remarked absently.

He didn't move, but his eyes darkened, became intent on hers. ''I wouldn't be caught dead in one, now. Not in public, anyway.'' His chest rose and fell heavily. ''I'd let you look at me, I guess. But no one else.''

Her body stilled as she looked up at him. ''Why me?'' she asked softly.

''Because you wouldn't make me feel like less of a man,'' he said simply. ''Some women have a knack for putting a knife in a man's ego. It makes them feel superior. When a man does the same thing to a woman, they call him a chauvinist. Some double standard.''

''All women aren't like that.''

He moved a step closer to her. When she didn't tense or move back, he took another step, and another, until he was close enough to smell the faint scent of violets that clung to her skin. She was wearing a soft gray pantsuit with a heather-colored jacket. Her hair was loose and she looked young and pretty and very vulnerable.

He caught a handful of her hair a little roughly and

pushed up at her nape to lift her face to his narrow, darkening eyes.

"Teach me," he said huskily.

Her lips parted on a rush of breath as her heartbeat ran wild. "Wh-what?" she whispered.

His eyes fell to her mouth and he bent toward it, his own mouth parting just as it touched hers. "Teach me how to be gentle...."

He spoke the words into her mouth. She stiffened at the moist, hot pressure, the smokey warmth of his own mouth so intimately touching hers. She could breathe him, smell the tang of cologne, feel the strength and power of his body almost touching her.

His eyes were open, and she looked into them just as his lips brushed hers.

"What do you like, Tess?" he whispered. His teeth opened and closed with exquisite tenderness on her upper lip, while his tongue softly tasted its moist inside. "Tell me."

Her hands were on his chest, under the tweed jacket, against his white shirt. Under the material, she could feel a thick cushion of hair over hard, warm muscle. "Dane, you can't," she began shakily.

"Why?"

His mouth was easing her lips apart. The contact was making her knees weak. "You hated...me," she whispered.

"I hated my mother," he corrected, his eyes searching hers while he played with her mouth, that steely hand at her nape still clutching her soft hair, "I hated my ex-wife...I hated half the world. But I never hated you." His heavy brows drew together in something like pain. "Never, Tess...!"

She felt him shudder as his mouth came down completely over hers, capturing it in a silence that danced with tension, with impossible desires.

For an instant, it was like the past again. But his arms weren't bruising. She could feel the restraint in him, the determination to go slow, to not rush her. Because of it, and because of what she'd learned about him, the panic began to recede. She let him hold her. And for the first time, she allowed herself to feel his mouth, to let herself taste it as he kissed her with exquisite softness. The contact was more pleasurable than she'd ever dreamed. His lips were firm, and he tasted of coffee. She liked the way he tasted.

As the pleasure grew, she felt a sudden heat in her lower body, a faint trembling in her legs. "Dane…" She heard her voice sobbing against the pleasure of his mouth, but like lightning striking, his hand contracted and he ground her lips apart under his, so that his tongue could ease between her teeth and push softly inside the sweet darkness of her mouth.

She remembered the one time she'd shared a deep kiss with him and gasped.

He lifted his head slowly, his heart pounding with a heavy beat. He looked down into her shaken eyes for a long moment, fiercely satisfied with what he saw there. She wasn't afraid; she was aroused. Amazing, that tenderness could make such a difference. It enhanced his own pleasure.

But he read the hesitation she couldn't disguise. "You don't like deep kisses with me, do you?" he asked huskily, his eyes glittering with desire. "My tongue pushes inside your mouth, penetrates it, and you shiver because of the images it produces." His hand loosened on her hair, smoothing it. She stood quietly against him, not protesting, as his deep, soft voice held her captive. "It's very much like another kind of penetration," he breathed, nibbling at her mouth. "Intimate, and urgent, and very, very deep...." He whispered into her mouth, suiting the action to the words as his tongue probed slowly.

She cried out and suddenly lifted her arms convulsively around his neck, at almost the same moment that the telephone jangled noisely in the heated silence.

Her body jumped, and her wounded arm throbbed, even as his head lifted with a faint groan. Her eyes were wild, frightened all over again. She was trembling, but this time not because of fear. She was clinging to him, not fighting him. He'd aroused her. The knowledge made his heart slam at his ribs.

She couldn't stand. Her knees gave way when he let go of her.

"It's all right," he whispered, lifting her in his arms. "I've got you."

She laid her cheek against his jacket, clinging to him weakly as he carried her to the sofa and sat down with her in his lap before he answered the telephone.

"Yes, she's back. Yes, she's all right. No, you can't speak to her. I'll have her call you later," he said tersely.

He hung up. "Helen," he murmured dryly, looking down into her dazed eyes. "Checking to see if you were home."

"That was nice of her."

"Yes, it was, but her timing stinks," he said huskily. His eyes fell to her mouth. "I'm glad that I can make you want me, Tess."

"That's conceit..." she began.

His mouth covered hers, parting her mouth, making her cling to his strong neck. He didn't increase the pressure or deepen the kiss. He stroked her mouth with his for a few aching seconds and then lifted his head. He looked at her with pure hunger until she flushed and averted her gaze to his throat.

"I've never kissed anyone like this," he whispered after a minute.

"Neither have I." Her cheeks flushed with heat. "The things you said to me…!"

"Turned you on so much that you gasped," he murmured, his eyes glittering. "I've never said things like that to another woman. They seem to come naturally with you."

"You didn't hurt me."

His jaw tautened. He looked at her mouth until his body began to ache. He was getting in over his head here. He had to stop, now, while he still could. "No," he returned deeply. "I didn't hurt you." He'd never tried to be gentle. Tess made him want that. Made him want things he resented wanting. "I couldn't hurt you now. Not even if I wanted to."

He nuzzled his cheek against hers with rough affection and hugged her close for an instant before he made himself put her gently away and get to his feet. "I'd better go. Keep the door locked. Get some rest. We'll try to restore order to the office in the morning, if you're sure you feel up to a day's work."

"Of course I do," she stammered. Her hair was disheveled, and her mouth tingled. She stared at him helplessly as he straightened his tie. "Why?" she whispered.

He was still getting himself back together. He'd never felt such a weakness for a woman, such a raging need to please, to pleasure her. He hadn't thought he was still vulnerable, but he was. He wanted Tess as he'd never wanted another woman. He couldn't afford to give in to it. Not now. Not yet.

His dark eyes pinned hers. "Remuneration for past sins?" he asked, lifting an eyebrow as he smiled mockingly.

Her face fell. "Oh."

Her naked vulnerability took the sting out of his hunger for her. He took a long breath. "Hell!" He laughed harshly. "I'm a loner, have you forgotten? None of this is easy for me." He pulled a cigarette out of his pocket and lit it with a flick of his lighter. "I wanted to know that I could arouse you, that I could make you stop being afraid of me, all right?" he asked irritably.

"Only that?"

"No. You know, you must know, that I want you so much I can hardly bear it." His eyes dropped to her mouth. "Don't let me get that close again, for your own sake," he said finally, turning away. "There's no future in it. Let's just say that I wanted to see if tenderness had any selling points."

"Does it?"

At the doorway he turned, the knob already in his hand. He didn't answer the question. He looked at her with quiet desperation. "Tess, I'm set in my ways, too jaded and hard for a little puritan like you. I'll probably always want you, but I don't want commitment. That being the case, you can't let me seduce you. Let's keep some distance between us, okay?"

She forced a smile. At least he was honest. And some of those old scars were smoothing out, because of what had just happened. "Okay. Thanks for taking care of me, when I needed help."

"I'll always be around if you need me, baby," he said gently.

The casual endearment made her pulse race. She couldn't hide her reaction to it from him.

"You remember the last time I called you that, don't you?" he asked quietly. "Despite the way I just was with you, in bed I'm rough and quick and my pleasure comes first," he said with brutal honesty. "Virgins aren't my style, and I'm sure as hell not yours." He drew in a slow, regretful breath and his lips twisted. "So let's quit while we're ahead. Good night, Tess."

He went out and closed the door. She went to it, her fingers touching the doorknob with exquisite care, as if she could still feel the warmth of his hand there. He'd just walked out on her for the second time, except that now she wasn't afraid of him anymore. She was back in her old rut, teetering on the knife-edge of love, with no way to go but down.

Chapter Four

Dane hadn't relented on the subject of Tess's bodyguard. One of the operatives, a free-lancer named Adams, was two steps behind her all the way to work.

Helen grinned when she came into the office. She sang a few lines from "Me and My Shadow" and did an impromptu tap dance.

"Oh, shut up," Tess grumbled. "Dane thinks I'll be killed in broad daylight, I guess."

"He can't take the chance," Helen whispered, wiggling her eyebrows. "Think of the damage it would do the agency's reputation if our own secretary bit the dust with us guarding her!"

Tess burst out laughing. "You raving lunatic." She hugged the other girl warmly. "It's good to be back to work."

"We missed you," Helen asserted. "Nobody hid under my desk all week."

"I don't hide under your desk."

"You would have, but there isn't room, what with my feet and the trash can I keep under there. I'm really sorry I forgot to tell you about that stakeout," she said with a grimace. "Dane in a temper is a sight to behold, isn't he?" She sighed. "Although sometimes I think it's too bad I'm committed to Harold. I could go for Dane in a big way." She frowned thoughtfully. "He hasn't dated anyone since his ex-wife left him, has he? Do you think it's because he got shot?"

"What do you mean?" Tess asked curiously.

"I mean, he limps sometimes," the other girl replied, careful to make sure they weren't being overheard. "It might cramp his style in bed."

Tess cleared her throat. "It doesn't cramp it on a horse," she said. "He was out helping round up new calves while I recuperated at the ranch."

"Good point." Helen shrugged. "Maybe he thinks he's unsightly. Or maybe he just hates women. What a waste of a good man. If only he didn't have that textbook police officer's face. He hardly ever smiles, and everything is always business with him." She shook her heard and turned away. "I wonder if he's like that with a woman."

Thinking about how Dane was with a woman made Tess's knees go weak. The things he'd whispered to her when he kissed her weren't dry as dust, for a fact. He might be rough, but he was sensual, and she was just discovering—as he seemed to be, too—that he could be very tender....

"Catch me up, will you?" Tess asked as she uncovered her computer. "I feel as if I've been away for a month."

"I don't doubt it. Arm okay?"

"A little stiff." She grinned at Helen. "No need to worry. We tough, dedicated professionals can take the odd gunshot in our stride."

"Rub it in," Helen groaned. "Now, everybody in the *office* has been shot except me. Even the secretary!" she added with a hot glare at Tess.

Tess raised her hands. "Not my fault. I swear I didn't invite those men to point a gun at me, not even to get one up on you."

"Oh, yeah?" Helen propped her hand on her hip. "How do I know that?"

The office door opened and Dane glared at them. "On company time, you work. Get busy."

"Yes, sir," Helen said demurely.

Tess couldn't quite meet his eyes. She sat down at her desk. "Helen was going to catch me up."

"Make sure it's business, not play," he said tersely.

She glanced at him. "You look tired."

"I didn't sleep." He ran a hand through his dark hair, letting his eyes dart off hers without lingering. "When Andrews calls, have him drop by the office about lunchtime. I've got an assignment for him. I'll be in conference with the skip tracers. Hold my calls until I'm through."

"Will do."

His dark eyes slid over her face and down to the rounded neckline of the red blouse that went with her cream-colored suit. Her hair was in a chignon and she was wearing only a trace of makeup. "You look very elegant this morning," he said unexpectedly. "Lunch date?"

"No." She fiddled with the keyboard. "I didn't want to disappoint my shadow by dressing like a boring office girl. I thought he might be more impressed if I put on my Mata Hari outfit."

He cocked an eyebrow. "Wrong genre. We're detectives, not spies."

"It wouldn't be the same if I wore a trench coat and an Indiana Jones hat."

"Maybe not." He stuck his hands in his pockets. There was something preoccupied in his manner.

She hadn't missed the black scowl. "What's wrong?"

He let out a hard sigh. "Your assailant jumped bail. He's out on the streets and nobody knows where."

Her arms felt chilled. She didn't have to ask why that worried him. It was disturbing and frightening to know that she was the only witness to a drug deal. What she'd seen could send two men to prison. If they were desperate enough to silence her, her life wouldn't be worth a plug nickel.

"Adams had me in sight constantly this morning," she said.

He nodded. "He's one of the best. But having you in sight won't be enough. He can't sleep with you."

"You could teach me how to use a pistol."

"It takes years of experience to shoot one properly," he reminded her. "And it isn't the same when you're in a desperate situation, as when you're on the practice range."

He would know, she thought, watching him. He'd been in enough desperate situations over the years. "I could move in with Helen," she suggested, as she had once before.

He took his hands out of his pockets and sat on the edge of her desk, leaning forward so that none of the others in the office could hear him. He stared at her intently. "Don't take this the wrong way. I'm not making improper suggestions. But I want you to move into my apartment until we catch your assailant."

"Live with you?" she asked hesitantly.

He nodded. "It's the safest way. I'd let you move in with Adams, but his girlfriend wouldn't like it," he murmured dryly, trying to lighten the moment.

She hesitated.

"Tess," he said quietly, "if you're worried because of what happened last night, there's no need. I told you that I don't want commitment. I won't seduce you. And you must know by now that I won't force you, either."

She bit her lower lip. "Yes, but it wouldn't look right."

"No one will know except the office staff," he promised her. "And they know why. It isn't as if I'm asking you to have an illicit affair with me."

"I know that." She stared at her pink fingernails. The thumbnail was chipped. She picked at it nervously.

He tilted her chin up and smiled faintly. "I won't walk around in the nude or watch football games for the duration."

She smiled in spite of her fears. "Do you normally watch football games?"

He shook his head. "But I do normally walk around nude. I'll have to buy a pair of pajamas while you're in residence. And a robe."

"I like pajamas, too," she said.

"I'll pick you up tonight at seven and take you home with me," he said. "Until then, Adams can keep an eye on you."

He got up from the desk. Tess felt more uncertain than she ever had before. Living with him was going to be one big test of her immunity to his attraction.

With a frown she watched him go back into his office. Why was he doing it? To prove to himself that he really didn't want her? She wished she knew. But she was much too afraid of the consequences of staying by herself to argue with him. Over the years she'd learned how cheap life was to people who used and sold narcotics. Dane was a trained policeman, an ex-Texas Ranger who knew more about means and methods of protecting people than she had time to learn. She was glad he had that knowledge. Now, her very life might depend on it.

The day turned out to be a quiet one, thank goodness. She left at five with Adams on her heels, and when she got home, packed enough for a few days. She didn't like leaving her apartment, but she really had no choice.

Dane buzzed the apartment at seven sharp, and she opened the door.

"Ready?" he asked.

"I've just got to get my coat," she said, looking around. She had a single suitcase.

"Is that all you're bringing?" he asked with a frown.

"Well, it's enough for a few days," she began.

"Tess, this could take weeks," he said shortly. "I don't want to alarm you, but you may be with me for some time."

"I—I can come back and get what I need, can't I?"

"I suppose. Did you pack a gown and a robe?"

"Yes." She flushed. "Well, pajamas and a robe."

He smiled gently. "You'll have your own room. It's a big apartment."

"I remember," she said absently, and then regretted dragging the memory up when he glowered.

"Let's go," he said tersely.

She locked up. He carried her case down to the garage, his eyes watchful and alert to any sign of danger. She noticed with quiet resignation the faint bulge under his jacket. He carried a .45 automatic pistol on the job.

He had a permit for it, and it was registered. A tool of the trade, he called it. But to Tess, it was a painful reminder of the ever-present danger of his profession and the realization that he could be killed pursuing it.

He helped her into the car before he put the case in the trunk, and he examined the engine and every inch of the frame before he started the vehicle.

"Is that necessary?" she asked.

He nodded as he backed out of the parking space. "Part of the routine, honey. Don't worry about it. You're in good hands."

"I know that." She leaned back against the seat. "Why did I have to leave the office late?" she groaned. "If I'd gone home when I should have that night, I wouldn't have seen anything."

"I was busy calling you on the carpet," he reminded her with a glance. "I get to share the blame."

"I deserved it, blowing the stakeout that way."

"In fact, you saved it," he murmured reluctantly. "The storekeeper had grown suspicious of our people outside. When you waved to Helen and asked about Harold's nephew, he grew careless. They collared his son five minutes after you left."

Her jaw dropped. "You didn't say!"

He glanced at her sternly. "You could have done a lot of damage by being careless. So could Helen. You both deserved a scare, and you got it."

"Slave driver."

He chuckled, a rare sound that was pleasant in the dark interior of the car. "Next time you'll be more careful, won't you?"

"My job isn't dangerous." She glared at him. "You won't let me do what I really want to," she accused.

"Which is what?" he asked as they stopped at a red

traffic light. He laid his arm over the back of the seat and looked into her eyes. "Sleep with me?"

"Of all the conceit," she gasped.

He smiled at her. "You want me."

She averted her eyes. "The light's green."

"Change the subject," he invited as he pulled ahead. "But you'd better stay out of my bed at night," he said matter-of-factly. "It won't do any good to plead with me," he added when she opened her mouth. "My bedroom door will be locked, in case you feel like trying it for yourself."

She stared at him, dumbfounded. He didn't sound like the all-business detective she knew.

He arched an eyebrow. "Sorry to disappoint you," he said. "I'm just not modern enough for casual affairs."

"Dane, do you feel all right?"

"Yes, and don't come an inch closer to see for yourself how I feel," he cautioned sternly. "You can keep your hands off my leg. I'm not that kind of man."

She burst out laughing as his words finally got through to her. She hadn't realized he even had a sense of humor. Presumably, he'd kept it hidden over the years.

"I feel absolutely dangerous," she mused.

"Most women are," he agreed. "I'd put sex-starved virgins at the top of the list, too."

"I'm not that!" she protested.

"How do you know?" He pulled into the parking lot of his own apartment complex. Since most of his business was in Houston, it took too long to commute back and forth from the ranch, so he maintained an apartment in town. He glanced at her as he parked the car. "These urges tend to creep up on women like you.

One minute you're blushing and nervous. The next, you're panting and ripping a helpless man's clothes off.''

Her eyes twinkled with laughter. "I promise to control my...urges," she assured him.

"God, I hope so. And no peeking when I'm in the shower," he added darkly.

The repartee took all the fear out of the new experience. She followed him up to his second-floor apartment without a qualm.

The room he gave her was decorated in blues, from wallpaper to carpet to curtains. She felt right at home, as she had at the ranch. All it needed was Beryl fussing over them.

"I'll cook, if you like," she volunteered. "I love it."

"No argument from me," he nodded. "I can cook, but I hate it."

She opened the freezer. It was well stocked. So was the refrigerator. "How about a steak and salad for supper?"

"Suits me." He kicked off his shoes and collapsed on the sofa with his jacket half-off.

She went into the guest room and changed into jeans and a sweatshirt, walking around in socks but no shoes. He was apparently as shoes-prejudiced as she was, because he left his off, too.

When she got back to the kitchen, he was out of his jacket and tie, his shirt half-unbuttoned down the front. She studied him covertly, curious about his body in a way she never had been about any other man's. His chest, what she could see of it, was covered in thick black hair. He was deeply tanned from his face down to what she could see of the taut muscular flesh above his belt buckle, and it didn't look like the type of coloring gotten from the sun.

"It's natural," he murmured, surprising her by reading the question in her eyes. "I tan in the summer, but this stays with me year-round. One of my grandfathers was Spanish."

"I didn't mean to stare."

He took the package of steaks out of her hands and tossed it to one side. His lean hands tugged until she fell against him. In his reclining posture against the counter, the contact was total, all the way up and down, and she stiffened unconsciously.

"No surprises," he promised. "Just this. Watch." His voice was deep and sensuous. He held her waist loosely with one hand while the other slowly worked buttons out of buttonholes and finally tugged his shirt free of his slacks, disclosing a broad, muscular chest that was almost completely camouflaged by thick, curling black hair. "Now, look at me," he said quietly.

She did, helplessly. She'd never seen anyone quite as masculine or as sensuous. He even smelled male, a scent that worked on her senses fiercely as she stood against his long, powerful legs and stared at the expanse of bare flesh he'd uncovered for her.

"Your eyes are very expressive," he said, his eyes darkening, glittering. "Giving away secrets."

"What kind of secrets?" she asked huskily, lifting her face to meet that hungry gaze.

"You'd be surprised." He bent and bit at her mouth roughly. The contact was swift, and then she was free. "Keep those sultry eyes to yourself. They're more dangerous than you realize."

He moved lazily toward the bedroom. Tess had barely recovered her balance and her good sense by the time he'd changed into tight jeans and a white T-shirt. The clothing fit him like a second skin, outlining a body that most men would have killed for. He was tall, but not thin. His broad shoulders tapered down in a wedge, over a muscular chest to lean hips and impossibly long legs. He was built like a rodeo rider. Tess had to drag her gaze back to the steaks.

"Like coffee?" he asked, smiling with pure delight at the way she was watching him.

"Yes."

"I'll make it."

The kitchen was too small for two people. That was probably why, she thought breathlessly, he was constantly brushing against her in the most arousing way as he brewed the coffee.

He finished, but he didn't go away. In his sock feet, he was still taller than she was, and his relaxed manner of dress made her much too aware of him as a man.

"I disturb you," he mused.

She started to deny it, then thought better of that. He might be compelled to prove it if she did. "Yes," she said instead.

He leaned back on his hands against the counter, smiling with his eyes in a way that made her knees weak.

"Why don't you come over here and do something about it," he challenged softly.

She wanted to groan. She shouldn't have been vulnerable. The last time she'd been in this apartment, he'd hurt her, scarred her, almost savaged her. How could she feel so wanton now?

"Dane," she protested, her eyes lifting to his.

"I can feel you tremble," he whispered deeply, his eyes narrowing with desire. "I can hear you breathing,

Tess.'' His eyes fell to her breasts, which were shuddering under the thick sweatshirt. ''Think how it would be, if I eased up the hem of that sweatshirt and slid my lips over your breasts, took the nipple in my mouth and made it tight and hard....''

''Dane!''

She was shaking. She barely saw him move the frying pan off the burner and turn off the stove. His lean hand snaked out and caught her wrist, pulling her within reach. Both hands went to the sweatshirt and bunched it, clutched it, while his dark eyes probed hers.

''Inch by inch,'' he whispered, moving it up to her rib cage. ''Inch by aching inch, with my hands on your bare skin...''

Her face burned. Her body burned. She gave in quite suddenly, closing her eyes with a shaky breath, arching her back to ease his way. She felt his hands spread over her rib cage, warm and faintly rough, as he pushed the fabric up farther. He bent and she felt the hot moistness of his lips touch her. She shivered and moaned harshly, her voice unrecognizable.

''Lean on me so that you don't fall,'' he whispered. His tongue eased out against her bare flesh, teasing it, spreading over it until she shuddered, the hem of the sweatshirt rising with his hands to the very edge of her breast in its soft lacy casing. His nose rubbed against the lower band of the bra and she clutched at his shoulders to keep her balance, so overwhelmed that tears of tense pleasure were stinging her eyes.

She hung, waiting, yielding, totally submissive to anything he wanted to do to her. Waited...waited...

''Tess!'' His voice exploded into the silence. His hands contracted suddenly and his head jerked up while he fought for breath. ''My God, I'm sorry...!''

He pulled the sweatshirt down and left the kitchen without looking at her. She couldn't move for several long seconds. She was dimly aware of water running somewhere, but even that didn't immediately register. She finally managed to stand up and turn her attention back to the steaks. They were done, but not burned, thank God. She put them on a platter with shaking hands.

She'd set the table, served the food, and poured the coffee by the time he rejoined her. He was wearing a shirt over his T-shirt now, and it was buttoned. His hair was damp, as if he'd just come from a shower. Probably he had. She wouldn't have minded some cold water, either. She was still on fire for him. Incredible, that kind of hunger, when only days before she'd been afraid of him.

"It's all right," he said quietly, noticing the way she avoided looking directly at him while they ate. "Nothing happened."

Nothing? She almost said the word aloud. She couldn't manage to look at him. Not that he was paying her any attention. His eyes, like his mind, were forcibly concentrated on his steak.

"This is good," he said. "I can't ever get it medium rare. Either it's raw or leather."

"It's the heat," she faltered. "You have to be sure the pan's hot enough."

"You can teach me, while you're here."

"Yes, all right."

He looked at her then, finally, his eyes dark and oddly wary. "Why so embarrassed, Tess?" he asked quietly. "I didn't even touch you intimately."

"You did," she protested. "With words..."

His expression was unreadable. Intense and faintly

threatening. "Things went too far, too fast. I was playing with you," he said cruelly. "Until you melted into me like that…"

Her heart felt as if he'd kicked it. Perhaps that was how he meant it to sound. "I get the message," she said, forcing her voice to sound light and unconcerned. She looked up, surprising an odd expression on his face as he stared at her. "I'm as guilty as you are."

He leaned back in his chair, his coffee cup in his hand as he looked at her openly. "Fair enough. But before you get any ideas about why it happened, it's mostly abstinence, Tess," he said tautly. "I haven't been intimate with a woman since the shooting. Maybe I'm more desperate than I realized."

So that was it. Hope died hard, but he was forcing her to realize that it wasn't undying love that had motivated him. All the same, he puzzled her. She couldn't stop the question slipping out. "Why hasn't there been a woman?" she asked.

He stared at her, shocked. "Because of my leg," he said involuntarily.

"Because it's still painful?"

"Because of the way it looks. The way *I* look, with my leg shot to pieces." He frowned. "And maybe because of you," he added reluctantly, searching her eyes. "Sex…hasn't appealed to me much since you ran from me that day." He averted his eyes. "Call it a lack of self-confidence."

"You were different then," she began slowly. "Tonight… Well, you didn't frighten me at all."

"So I noticed," he said tersely. He stared at her until she blushed. "Don't trust me, Tess. If I'd gotten my mouth as far as your breasts, I honestly don't know what would have happened. Do you understand, little one?'' he asked, his eyes narrow with concern. ''I want you. God, Tess, I want you so damned much!'' he whispered huskily.

It was true. She'd gotten under his skin in the past few days. He'd never been as tender, or as aroused, in his entire life as he'd been with her lately. Her responsiveness went to his head, made him careless and vulnerable.

''But you don't want to, do you?'' she asked softly. She searched his dark eyes.

''You're a virgin,'' he said stiffly. ''You tell me if I want to.''

He was more open than he'd ever been. It was obvious that he was afraid of commitment, of loving, of being deserted again. He didn't trust women, or like them. But his body was starved for physical satisfaction, and Tess was innocent and handy. She had to keep the situation in perspective.

''If I weren't innocent—'' she began.

''If you weren't, we'd already be lovers,'' he said heavily. ''You're afraid of me like that, but you want me just the same.'' His dark eyes narrowed on her flushed face. ''The first time might be pretty uncomfortable,'' he said, his voice almost choked with feeling. ''I might not be able to help hurting you, since it's been so long for me. But the second time...'' His high cheekbones went ruddy as he looked at her. ''The second time, I'd pleasure you until you cried. I'd be tender. So tender. I'd love you the way I just did in the kitchen, slowly and softly. I'd put my lips all over you. And by the time I joined your body to mine in that intimate way, you'd be sobbing under my mouth....''

He cursed under his breath and got up, running a

rough hand over his face. "God," he breathed unsteadily. "I've got to get out of here!"

Tess watched him leave the room, trembling with desire that he'd kindled so unexpectedly. She could hardly believe that he wanted her so much. All the years he'd denied it, been hostile, kept her at arms' length had been a sham. With shocking clarity, she saw right through him to the vulnerability he was trying to hide. He cared. He cared deeply. Maybe he always had, and her reaction to his ardor had hurt him. She hadn't known anything about him, really. Hadn't totally understood that he'd been savaged by two women he cared about, persecuted by one and deserted in his time of need by the other. He was afraid to love, but he did. Tess caught her breath. He loved her. It was the only possible explanation for the way he was with her lately, for the tenderness that he was learning to give her, for his protective attitude.

He didn't know it, or wouldn't admit it. But the realization made Tess feel warm all over. The trick was going to be making sure he didn't find out that she knew. In the meantime, her heart almost burst with joy. He was hers; he belonged to her now as surely as if he'd given her a solemn vow.

He came back a few minutes later, smoking a cigarette and looking totally uninvolved.

"Want some more coffee?" she asked gently.

"Please."

She poured it while he watched her, averting his eyes when she noticed. They drank coffee in tense silence.

"I'll get used to having you here," he said after a minute, "and we'll manage. I can't let you go home until the dealers are caught and the court decides how to dispose of them."

"I know. I'll try not to be too much trouble," she added with a smile. She got up and brought out a pudding she'd made for dessert, serving it with no conversation at all. When he touched her, he was vulnerable. But the minute he moved away, the wall came back, reinforced. Except that now she knew why he kept building it, and she wasn't hurt by it anymore.

Dane was fighting his feelings tooth and nail. He could go crazy for her if he let himself. That couldn't be. Tess was an old-fashioned girl, with old-fashioned ideas about life and men, courtesy of her grandmother, who'd been responsible for most of her upbringing. He couldn't take her to bed and forget about her. So he had to forget about her physically. In order to accomplish that, as much as he hated to, he was going to have to push her away and keep her there.

He studied her downcast face with eyes that wanted her, but he averted his gaze the minute she looked up. Boss and employee, he told himself. Surely he could manage that.

Chapter Five

Tess enjoyed living with Dane. She hadn't expected it to be so sweet, even just being with him while they watched television at night. He liked to sit around in his white T-shirts and jeans, in his sock feet, and sprawl over his armchair while he drank beer and watched old movies. Tess found herself relaxing with him, now that she had a good idea how he felt about her. The way he watched her was exciting, like the evasive tenderness in his eyes when she smiled at him.

He was a loner by nature, a very private man with any number of hang-ups that she discovered quite by accident. It embarrassed him to discuss his feelings, so he never let conversation between them get personal. They talked about the job, about everything except themselves.

A few days after she'd moved in, she was watching a program about birth. He came into the room during it, having been working in his study.

As if it disturbed him to see the embryo being shown at that moment on the screen, he turned to leave.

"I can change the channel if you don't want to watch this," she offered.

He hesitated, his eyes going reluctantly back to the screen. They were showing a delivery room now, a very explicit delivery.

"Sorry." She pushed the Off button on the remote control and laid it down. "I was curious," she confessed. "I never learned much about sex and reproduction at home, and school courses are very brief. I wanted to know how babies...how they grew."

"How they got made, you mean," he corrected, watching her face color. "But they didn't show that, did they?"

She cleared her throat. "Not really."

"I've got a book," he said slowly. "You wouldn't want to read it with me here, I know, but you might find it interesting. It shows how people make love without being graphic or offensive."

Her eyes searched his averted face. "I didn't think men were curious about things like that. I mean, you know it all already, don't you?"

He lit a cigarette, pausing in the doorway. "I know how to have sex with a woman," he corrected. "I...wanted to know how to make love."

The words made her warm inside. He looked frankly embarrassed. She watched him quietly. "Because I ran from you?"

His eyes glowered at her. "Don't get personal."

She smiled. "That was why, though, wasn't it?"

He drew in an irritated breath and took another draw from the cigarette. "Maybe it was. So what?" he asked belligerently. "It isn't as if I'll ever need to know for your sake. I'm not going to make love to you."

Her eyes fell to the irregular rise and fall of his broad

chest. "I wouldn't be afraid of it now," she said softly. "You're very sexy. I didn't want you to stop that time in the kitchen."

His heart shuddered in his chest. "Talking like this is dangerous," he whispered. "You don't know how dangerous."

She looked up at him, her eyes adoring his lean, hard face. "Dane, have you ever thought about having a child?" she asked huskily.

His face exploded with color. He moved jerkily and turned away from her to pull nervously at his cigarette. "No," he said curtly.

"You don't want children?" she persisted.

He fingered the cigarette, staring at its glowing orange tip with eyes that barely saw it. "It wouldn't have made any difference, Tess," he said after a minute. He looked down at her, his expression reluctant. "I can't father a child."

Her mind wouldn't absorb it. She heard the words without comprehending them.

He turned, his eyes dark and quiet as they searched hers. "Jane wanted to get pregnant," he said slowly. "She was obsessed with it. Maybe that's why I couldn't be gentle with her. She demanded, raged at me when she didn't conceive. I felt like some gelded bull by the time she gave up and stopped offering herself to me." He sighed wearily. "I couldn't make her pregnant. Eventually, I couldn't even make love properly." He bent over to put out the cigarette, only half-smoked. "You think you've got scars because of what I did to you. I wish you could see mine."

He turned and started to leave.

She got up, too, and went to him, her eyes big and

soft. "There are a lot of reasons why women don't conceive."

"She had a child by her new husband barely ten months after they married," he said curtly.

"That wasn't what I meant. You like jeans, but they create a climate that sometimes prevents men from being fertile...." She flushed as she realized what she was saying.

He lifted an eyebrow. "You're a virgin, I believe?"

"That program I was watching mentioned it," she hedged.

"I don't wear jeans all the time," he reminded her. "Well..."

His gaze went slowly down her body and back up. She was wearing jeans herself, with a floppy, button-up green shirt. Her hair was up in a disheveled knot on top of her head. She looked young and pretty and very sexy.

"Go away," he said softly. "If I touch you, I won't stop. I can't stop. I'll go every inch of the way."

She searched his eyes and the flush got worse. It was as intimate as a kiss, the way she looked at him. "I know, Dane," she breathed.

His jaw tautened. His breathing changed suddenly, sharply.

She looked down, and her eyes triggered a reaction he'd been trying desperately to avoid. She didn't look away, even then. She found him fascinating. Her expression told him so.

"You're afraid of me," he reminded her with choked passion in his voice. "Hold that thought."

"If you were gentle, I wouldn't be afraid," she said. She lifted her eyes to his and searched them, her body tingling with new sensations, new needs. He loved her.

She knew it all the way to her bones, and if she could let him see how it would be with someone who cared, really cared about him, he might change his mind about commitment.

He was sure he was going to die from what he was feeling. He felt near to bursting with it.

Tess felt his tension, sensed how limited his control was. It wouldn't she thought, recklessly, take very much to break through his restraint.

In fact, it didn't. She took one step toward him, and his will collapsed.

He bent and picked her up, managing her slight weight easily, even with his bad back. He didn't look at her as he carried her into his bedroom and kicked the door shut.

He placed her in the center of his bed and stood over her, looking down at the soft contours of her body, his face like rock.

Her hands were beside her head on the beige coverlet, her lips parted, her eyes yielding and submissive, like her body.

"It will hurt," he said tersely.

"I know," she whispered.

His hands trembled as he took off his T-shirt and dropped it onto the floor. He stood, fighting for control. "If you change your mind after I've touched you, I won't be able to stop," he said hoarsely. "Don't you understand?"

"I love you, Richard," she whispered, using the name he never let anyone use, the name she'd always wanted to call him because nobody else did. "I love you with all my heart. I never stopped, even when I was scared to death of you."

He winced. "Tess...!"

"Teach me. Love me," she said gently.

His eyes closed. His fists clenched at his sides and he shuddered visibly. "I don't want this to happen," he ground out. "God in heaven, you're a virgin...!"

"I love you," she whispered again.

He looked at her, his face quietly resigned as he registered the enormity of the gift she was offering him. "I'll try to give you tenderness," he said slowly. "If not at first, afterwards. I won't...hurt you deliberately, you understand?"

"Yes."

He sat down and leaned over her, his eyes moving possessively down her relaxed body. He touched her lips with a tentative brush of his fingers, an action that made her ripple with pleasure.

"There is no more precious gift than what you're offering me," he said huskily. "You can only give your chastity once."

"Shouldn't it belong to someone I love more than my own life?" she asked gently.

He framed her face with unsteady hands. "I...can't love you," he said bitterly. "Tess..."

Her fingers touched his mouth. She knew that he was denying how he felt out of fear. The very hesitancy in his actions told her more than words could how much he cared for her.

"I won't ask you for anything," she promised. "Not even for you to love me. I want to belong to you completely, just this once. I want to know how it feels with someone I love."

He bent to her lips, stumped for words. His mouth trembled as it settled on hers. He opened it, gently, and his hands slid under her nape, to lift her face, tilt it to the gentle assault of his mouth and then his tongue.

Tess smiled under the slow loving as his lips whispered over her face, learning its contours, so tender that they made her warm all over.

His hands slid down, under her back, and he lay down beside her, lazily bringing her body to his as he slid one long leg between both of hers and began to kiss her with slow hunger.

She tangled her hands in his thick, cool hair and drifted while his hands found their way under her blouse, against the soft skin of her back. He kissed her until her mouth was gently swollen, then carefully unfastened the bra so that he could caress her breasts. Their hard tips dragged abrasively against his palms and she began to breathe raggedly as his expert touch kindled fires within her.

"I've never looked at you, even if I have touched you like this before," he whispered, his hands coming back to the buttons that secured the shirt. "Now I'm going to."

She sat up while he divested her of everything she wore above the waist. But when she started to lie back down, his hands prevented her.

He held her there, his lips teasing hers while his knuckles played with exquisite tenderness against her taut nipples. She shivered, and he lifted his head to look at her eyes.

"This is exciting," he said unsteadily. "I've never done this."

"Neither have I," she confessed.

"I want you…in my mouth, Tess," he whispered jerkily, bending his head.

She arched back over his arms as he opened his mouth on her breast and began a warm, moist suction against the nipple. It was like flying, she thought shakily. She felt a burst of heat in her lower body, a surge of ecstasy that startled a cry from her lips.

"Yes," he said, nuzzling the softness his mouth was exploring. "Yes, little one."

She went from plateau to plateau in the minutes that followed, so dazed and helpless from pleasure that she lay almost lifeless while he removed her clothes. Then she watched him take off his own, afterwards noticing the way he hesitated with his back to her.

"It won't...matter," she said, her voice thick and unsteady as she realized why he was hesitating. She could see the deep scar the bullets had left near his spine. She knew there were worse ones on his chest. "I love you!"

He turned. Her eyes went to the core of his masculinity with awe and wonder before they reluctantly moved to his scarred chest and shoulder and leg. There were white streaks and an area that was graphic evidence of a shooting, but to Tess, who loved him, they were only faint imperfections in a body that nature couldn't have improved on.

She shifted on the coverlet, a tiny movement of her hips, her long legs, as she looked up into his eyes and shivered. Woman at the mercy of man and her own aching need of him.

"You are the most beautiful human being I've ever seen," he said hoarsely, his eyes on her body.

"So are you," she whispered.

He eased down beside her, trembling from his years of abstinence and his raging hunger for this one woman. "I want you, baby," he whispered against her warm belly, feeling her jerk under its intimate touch. "Feel how much."

He slid over her, against her, while his lips touched

hers in tender teasing, his powerful, hair-roughened body hard and sensually abrasive against hers as he drew it over her trembling warmth. The evidence of his need was blatant and awesome.

"Let me fill you," he whispered at her open mouth. He positioned her carefully as his tongue teased around her lips and slowly, slowly, past her teeth into the soft, sweet darkness of her mouth. "Open your mouth...for me."

Incredible, she thought in the flash of blind pain that accompanied the words and his slow movement. Incredible, that he could make her want him so much....

His lean hand was on her thigh, curling around it, pulling her upward. It contracted, but what she felt was his tongue sliding into her mouth, the fullness of it warm and welcome. The pain came again and she shivered.

"I'm sorry that I have to hurt you like this," he breathed, nibbling at her mouth. He lifted his head and looked into her eyes. His were dark as night, blazing, glazed. His hand contracted again and pulled. "Let me watch you become a woman," he whispered, his eyes holding hers as he slowly pushed his hips down against hers.

Her nails curled into his shoulders and she gasped, shuddering.

"Tell me," he whispered huskily as he moved. "Share it with me."

"It...burns," she choked. "Like...fire!"

His breath was hot in her mouth as he looked at her and moved again. "Don't cry, little one," he said huskily. "Only a few more seconds..."

She moaned and shivered. His remorseful eyes held hers and he took a long, shaky breath. His hand contracted. "You're going to fight me now, because it's going to hurt like hell. But I have to finish it," he whispered, and the muscles in his hips bunched. His eyes dilated as he felt the barrier give. His face flushed with the knowledge, even as he heard her cry out and saw her eyes dilate with pain.

He didn't stop. She pushed at him frantically, but he didn't stop. Her head went back and she sobbed. Then, when she thought she couldn't bear it, the pain all at once eased.

He let out the breath he'd been holding. He didn't move, his body poised against her, his eyes holding hers. He smiled.

Her eyes were bright with tears. He bent and kissed them, sipping the wetness away, his cheek sliding against hers as his lips pressed with aching tenderness all over her face and he whispered husky words of endearment and praise.

Her hands relaxed on his shoulders and her body followed suit. She felt his possession of her increase with the tiny movement and she flushed as she met his eyes.

He smiled tenderly, through his own raging need. "Now I can make love to you, Tess," he said softly. "It won't hurt anymore."

His teeth caught her upper lip and nibbled at it softly as his hips lifted and pushed, lifted and pushed, in a slow, tender rhythm that made her gasp and jerk with sudden, stark pleasure.

He watched her react to it with an excess of male pride. "You were very brave," he whispered as he increased the pressure and rhythm, feeling her body begin to echo his slow movements. "Very, very brave. You didn't even cry out."

"Dane?" she cried, frightened.

"Let me pleasure you," he whispered, bending to her mouth as the silver ripples worked up his spine. "I'll teach you now. I'll teach you, baby."

Instinctively she knew he'd never done this before, never loved anyone the way he was loving her. It was as if he, too, were a virgin all over again. She clung to him, sobbing as he'd promised she would, begging for fulfillment at the last. He gave it to her unexpectedly, completely, lifted his head and watched her convulse, and smiled through his own fierce excitement before it caught him up in its vortex and made him cry out harshly with the sheer joy of ecstasy.

He held her for a long time afterward, drying her tears, kissing her undemandingly, soothing her torn, exhausted body. He got up and got a cold beer from the refrigerator, sharing it with her while he had a cigarette. He wasn't thinking about tomorrow. There was only tonight, only the joy of loving, the beauty of her whispered love for him, the sweet anguish of fulfillment.

He put the half-finished beer on the bedside table, and crushed out his cigarette. Then he eased her over onto her back and slid up beside her.

"I'm going to take you again, now," he whispered as he moved between her long, trembling legs. "This time, it will be very slow, very gentle. This time, you'll feel it so intensely that you'll cry out, as I did earlier."

"I...love you," she whispered frantically, her body so perfectly attuned to his that the first hard thrust of it brought a cry of ecstasy from her parched lips.

"Already?" he asked huskily, moving fiercely against her.

"Now," she groaned. "Now, now, now...!"

He thought that never in his life had he felt such

sensations. He convulsed almost immediately, feeling her body surge under him, hearing her hoarse cries as he fulfilled her once, twice, three times. He shouldn't have been capable of this, of endless potency, of tireless arousal. But he was. Perhaps the abstinence, or what he felt for her, or even her unexpectedly sweet sensuality triggered it. Whatever the reason, by the time he finally rolled away from her, too exhausted to even kiss her swollen mouth one last time, he was asleep before his head even reached the pillow.

The next morning, she kissed him awake. He opened his eyes and saw her over him, saw the light in her eyes, and he groaned softly as he levered her instantly onto her back and rolled onto her body.

"No," she whispered quickly, blushing when he loomed over her with virile intent. "I'm sorry," she said miserably. "But it hurts...."

He breathed slowly until he could calm his blood. His hand smoothed over her soft breast. "I took you four times," he whispered, lifting his eyes back to hers. "I hurt you."

"No," she said, shaking her head. "Oh, no, you didn't hurt me."

He brushed his lips over hers, and then over her eyes. "But I would if we made love now?"

"I'm afraid so."

He sighed and rolled onto his back. "I should have thought about that. I'm not properly awake. Do you want some coffee?"

"Yes. I'll make it."

She started to get up, realized she was undressed, and pulled the sheet demurely to her breasts.

He glanced at her, following her embarrassed gaze to his own body. He made a sound and threw his legs over the side of the bed, carelessly tugging on his briefs and jeans and socks while she watched.

"You can dress while I shave," he said. He didn't look at her.

She watched him with soulful eyes that he didn't see. *I love you,* she wanted to say. But he wouldn't have said it back, even if he had made love to her like a man out of his mind with it. He loved her. She was certain of it now, and her eyes adored him.

"Get a move on," he said from the doorway. "We'll be late for work."

"Oh. Of course."

He didn't mention what had happened. Not by word or inference did he refer to it. He was all business.

Tess had expected resistance. She wasn't surprised by his attitude. He was a man afraid of emotion, and he had every reason to be. He couldn't be sure even of Tess. She knew that, and wasn't offended.

"Helen said I could go with her at lunchtime to that stakeout," she began as they finished toast and coffee.

He glared at her. "No."

"Let me finish, please," she said quietly. "I'm going to be the decoy. While people are watching me, she's going to be following them."

"You'd be too vulnerable," he said shortly. "Helen isn't being stalked by dope peddlers. You are. No, ma'am. You'll be where I can see you, all the time. I'm not trusting you to anyone except me."

She blushed. "All right."

He scowled darkly. "And don't get any ideas about what happened last night. That was a one-off, do you hear me?"

Her eyebrows lifted. "A one-off?" she asked.

His cheeks went ruddy. She looked surprised that he

could refer to something so profound in such a way. He was surprised at himself. He glared at her, his heart racing. "What did you expect me to say?" he asked coldly. "That it was the closest I'll get to heaven without dying?"

"Not really," she agreed. "But it was. For me, I mean."

"I hurt you."

Her eyes lifted, searching his. "At first," she agreed. Then she smiled.

His breathing went ragged as the memory of the pleasure they'd shared washed over him. Just looking at her aroused him. He got up from the table, slamming his napkin down. "Let's get out of here," he said roughly.

She went along without an argument, wrapped in acres of dreams and delight because she was loved. He would fight it. That was inevitable. But in the end, he was going to lose. He couldn't resist her any more than she could resist him, but she had to give him time. She couldn't rush him. Not with so much at stake.

Her only regret was that a child couldn't come of the beauty they'd created together. She would have loved a child so much.

Once they got to the office that morning, problems claimed their attention immediately, and for Dane, it seemed to be a relief. He got into the thick of it without a backward glance, leaving Tess to sort out schedules and appointments.

The past few days had been so eventful that Tess had all but forgotten the night she'd been shot. Her arm was a little sore, and it had gotten a workout last night. She flushed and smiled, remembering Dane's mouth on the healed wound. She'd touched his scarred back and shoulder and leg with equal tenderness, stroking it while he made love to her, whispering that it was a badge of honor, a war wound. It had increased the pleasure. She could still hear his voice as he cried out, almost sobbing as the force of ecstasy lifted him over her and shook his powerful body like a whip.

She caught her breath. Could he really believe something that beautiful was only explainable as a "one-off"? She knew better. He did, too, but he'd been hurt so badly that he couldn't accept it just yet.

Her attention was diverted by the telephone, but as the day wore on her body reminded her of the unusual activity it had been subjected to the night before. It was difficult to sit, though she didn't dare mention it in case someone became suspicious.

At lunch, she watched the operatives who were in the office leave; watched with a wistful smile as Helen disappeared. Dane was at a luncheon, so she was in the office alone. He probably hadn't realized she would be by herself when he'd refused to let her go out with Helen for the noon meal. Well, she'd walk up the street to the fast food restaurant and get chicken and biscuits. It was better than nothing.

She put on her coat and locked the office behind her. Her mind was on Dane instead of on where she was going. The sudden shock of a man's hand clamping over her mouth surprised her into stunned immobility.

"Here you are, pretty thing," a rasping voice said harshly. "Right on schedule. When I'm through with you, you won't be in any hurry to tell a jury what you saw!"

Chapter Six

Tess couldn't remember ever being quite so afraid. The man had her in a half nelson, and he was slowly dragging her to the front door of the building, where another man was sitting in a running car.

This couldn't be happening, she told herself. She couldn't let it happen. A knife was being held at her ribs, and she felt the certainty of death like black ice on her tongue.

If she let him get her into the car, she didn't have a prayer. She would die. They'd carry her off and then certainly kill her. Desperate men, desperate deeds. The car the other man was driving was an expensive brown sedan, and they were both wearing suits. These were no run-of-the-mill street people, no lower-rank mules. These were men who made millions on the despair and desperation of weak people, and they certainly wouldn't mind killing anyone who stood between them and their livelihood.

Dane had known that. But Tess hadn't realized it until now, when it was too late.

There was a chance, only a brief one, that she might get away before the men got her into the car. When he opened the door at the front of the building, he was certainly going to have to take that knife away from her rib cage for an instant. If she was quick and kept her head, she might get away.

Her heart raced madly. She was shaking all over, but she couldn't give way to panic and fear. She kept telling herself that, going over everything she'd learned from the operatives, the slick little moves they'd taught her about how to get away from a potential attacker. She'd listened and learned. Now those lessons were going to pay off.

She went along with him, acting terrified to throw him off guard. She pleaded with him tearfully to set her free. All the time her mind was working, going over and over the one move she was going to employ when the time came.

It was working. She felt him begin to relax his painful grip. He laughed. He was enjoying her fear. The front door was a foot away. He moved toward it, the knife lifting as he raised his arm to push open the glass door.

Just as he raised it, Tess brought her elbow into his diaphragm with a vicious jab. As his chin came down, she brought the back of her fist up to meet his nose, and felt blood on it. Reacting swiftly, she tore away from him while he was doubled over and ran up the side street toward the crowded main street. It was noon, and people were everywhere. Thank God! The men wouldn't dare risk taking hold of her with a crowd around her. She ran, panting, not daring to look back.

She merged quickly into a group of people waiting for a red light to change. Out of the corner of her eye, she spotted a car speeding up the side street toward her. They wouldn't, she thought feverishly, they wouldn't...!

"Tess!"

She looked. It was a Mercedes, and Dane was at the wheel.

"Dane!" She ran across the side street and scrambled in beside him, throwing her arms around his neck and shivering.

He brought her close for an instant, barely aware of his surroundings in the stark terror he'd just experienced. He'd rushed back to the office, hoping to get there before the operatives left. He'd seen Tess running and the other car suddenly speed away. His choices dwindled immediately to getting to Tess or giving chase. That was no choice at all.

His mouth crushed down over hers for one long instant before he dragged it away and turned the car down the wide street into traffic. He didn't let go of Tess. He couldn't.

"They almost had me," she whispered breathlessly. "One of them grabbed me as I started out of our office. He had a knife at my ribs...."

"God," he groaned harshly, pulling her closer.

"Helen taught me how to defend myself against somebody holding me from behind," she said. Her cheek moved against the soft fabric of his jacket. "I remembered it. I caught him off guard and got away." She grinned, now that it was all over. "It was very exciting," she said, her eyes sparkling as she looked up at him. "I can see why... Dane?"

He pulled off the street into a parking space and sat, white-faced, his hands trembling on the steering wheel. He didn't speak or look at her.

"It's all right," she said softly. She moved, reaching up to draw his head down to hers. She kissed him slowly, nibbling at his lips, his nose, his closed eyes. Her arms slid around him and she pressed close, her face finally sliding against his hot throat and resting there. "It wasn't your fault," she whispered. "You forgot that you'd told me I couldn't go with Helen."

"I didn't forget," he said unsteadily. "I left in plenty of time to get back before the office emptied. But I had a flat on the way."

"Dane?" she murmured.

"Let me hold you, Tess," he said, his voice torn. "Don't talk. Just let me hold you."

She did, sighing as the peace of the embrace finally got through to him and calmed him. He felt guilty, she supposed, although God knew why he should. She didn't blame him. She smiled against his throat and kissed him just below his Adam's apple. She was about to say that for a man who didn't love her, he was certainly excitable. But she thought better of it. He was vulnerable. He wouldn't like having her point it out.

He drew in a rough breath, and she glanced up at him. His eyes were frightening. He touched her face with warm, hard fingers. "Did he hurt you?"

"No," she assured him. Her eyes sparkled. "But I hurt him. I think I broke his nose."

He whistled softly. "I'm going to have to talk to Helen."

"You wouldn't teach me," she said defensively.

"Thank God she did. I'll treat Helen and Harold to the biggest damned anchovy pizzas they can eat," he mused.

"That's nice." She laid her forehead against his chin. "Can I have one, too? I'm hungry."

"Poor little scrap, you haven't eaten." He put her back in her own seat and fastened her seat belt, his hands brushing against her body accidentally and setting her tingling. "You can have a pizza if you want one."

Her eyes melted into his, adoring, acquisitive.

He bridled at that look, at his own vulnerability. He didn't like having her see him when he couldn't hide his disturbed state from her. She might think he was emotionally involved. Ridiculous, of course. All the same...

He bent and put his mouth softly over hers, kissing her gently. "From now on, if I have to leave the office, I'll make sure someone's with you. I'm sorry, Tess. Damned sorry."

She smiled. "I told you, it wasn't your fault." She stared at his mouth dizzily. "Kiss me again."

"Too public," he murmured, drawing back. He indicated throngs of passersby.

"We could eat at the apartment, couldn't we?"

"No, we could not," he said gently, reading her expression all too well for his peace of mind. "In the first place, you'll need days to recuperate from what I did to you last night. In the second place," he said, his expression growing sterner by the second, "from now on, you're going to sleep in your own bed, not mine. I won't let that happen again."

"Why not?" she asked softly.

His thumb rubbed slowly over her chin and he looked worried. "Because I don't want commitment," he reminded her. "I won't ever forget how it made me feel to be your first lover. But you want forever after. I don't believe in it anymore. I've had my illusions shattered."

"You might change your mind," she said. "I might grow on you."

"You already have. But I can't marry you," he said bluntly. "Listen to me, Tess. You think you love me, but you don't have any experience of men except what you've learned with me. One day, sex won't be enough for you. You'll want a child."

"I love you, Dane," she said simply.

His cheeks darkened and his eyes seemed to kindle, but he fought down the fever those words initiated. "You don't know what love is," he replied quietly. "You think it's two bodies in bed."

Her eyes searched his. "What we did together last night was much more than two bodies in bed. We made love, Dane," she said. "Made it so beautifully that I can't imagine ever letting any man but you touch me as long as I live."

His eyes closed. He felt that way, too, but he couldn't tell her. His feelings were locked up, chained.

"It was sex," he said coldly, forcing his eyes to open and stab into hers. "And you're damned lucky I'm sterile or you'd really have a problem."

"I wouldn't have thought so," she said, smiling.

He gazed out the window blindly. "Anyway, it's a moot point," he said. He started the car. "We have to report this to the nearest precinct. Assault with intent is a felony. I'll have that—" he employed some old ranger language "—in jail by sundown, and he won't get out this time, not if I have to call in a few markers and have some old friends help me surround the courthouse!"

She could picture a throng of cold-eyed Texas Rangers holding a courtroom at gunpoint. She laughed gently.

"How can you laugh?" he demanded. "God in heaven, don't you realize how close you came to being killed?"

"Nerves," she told him. "Reaction. Yes, I realize it. I remember thinking I wouldn't see you again," she added, adoring his face with her gray eyes. "It made me sad."

He looked away. He'd had too many shocks lately, all of them to do with losing her. He put the car into gear and pulled out into traffic. He lit a cigarette and didn't say another word all the way to the police station.

Helen gloated later when she found out that Tess had used her instructions to foil a kidnapping. Dane was in a black temper that lasted all day, even if he did unbend enough to give Helen a bonus for teaching Tess how to survive an assault. But he watched Tess openly, his mind on the dope peddlers. He'd never felt so homicidal.

While the office was full of armed operatives, he made his way back to the police station, to talk to the sergeant who was handling the case.

"Nothing yet," Sergeant Graves told Dane when the two men were in the former's office. "We've got feelers out, but those two rats have gone down a hole somewhere. They probably knew we'd pull out all the stops after what they did. Your secretary was damned lucky, do you know that? Tomby, the man who tried to abduct her, got off once on a murder charge for lack of evidence. I don't doubt he'd have killed her if he'd gotten her into his car."

"Neither do I," Dane said stiffly. He didn't want to think about that. He'd go crazy. "I'm volunteering my staff to help find them. I can't risk having Tess at their mercy again.''

"We'd appreciate the help," Graves replied. "With your background in police work, you know how much there is to do and how inadequate our staff is. People don't realize the time it takes to run down felons, or the bureaucracy that stands between law enforcement and the justice system.''

"God, I do," Dane said heavily. "You try being a ranger. You'll get an eyeful.''

The older man smiled wistfully. "I did try. Couldn't pass the oral exam. God, those old-timers are thorough!''

"And damned mean, some of them." Dane chuckled.

"They have to be. Everyone remembers the story of the single Texas Ranger who got off the train after he was called to put down a full-scale riot. The townspeople were astonished that one man was expected to accomplish all that. The ranger just drawled, "Well, you've only got one riot, haven't you?''

"One man was usually enough," Dane replied.

"I've got a hunch about these two men we're after," Graves said suddenly, after the laughter diminished. "They're high-class suppliers. There's a man named Louie on parole for distributing. He has some ties to the same underworld element these two are involved with. I'd like to lean on him a little, unofficially.''

Dane smiled slowly. "Got an address?''

The other man returned the smile and scribbled something on a piece of paper. "You don't know where you got this," he cautioned.

Dane nodded as he got to his feet. "It was in my

pocket when my jacket came back from the cleaners,'' he promised.

"Good luck."

"We could both use a little of that."

Back at the office, Dane gave the address to Adams with some instructions. At closing time, he made sure Tess was with him every minute until they got back to his apartment.

He threw off his jacket, an action she watched with possessive familiarity. Living with him had her spoiled. She loved being with him. Once the men who'd assailed her were caught, she'd have to go home. Her face paled at the realization.

He turned, rubbing a hand around the back of his stiff neck, and caught her expression. "What is it?" he asked gently.

"When they catch those two men, I'll have to go home."

He frowned slightly. He didn't want to think about that, either. It made him feel empty. The past few days with her here had been magic, and not just because they'd become lovers. He enjoyed being with her.

"You'll probably be glad," she said, trying to brighten up. "No more lingerie drying in the bathroom, no more shoes under the couch...."

"That isn't quite true," he said. "I'll miss you. I think you'll miss me, too. But we adjusted to being apart a long time ago."

She searched his eyes. "You mean, just after you got shot and I took care of you."

He nodded. "We were almost this close then, until I made a dead set at you and scared you off."

She smiled tenderly. "I'm not scared anymore," she reminded him, and her face colored.

He moved closer, pulling her against him. His head bent over hers and he rocked her gently. "It has to end," he said bitterly. "I told you, I don't want commitment."

Her arms slid under his and she lay her cheek on his broad chest, against his warm white shirtfront. She didn't argue because there was no use. She drew in a breath, savoring every second she had with him. The memories would be sweet, at least. "Can I sleep with you tonight?"

He stiffened. "I want that," he said huskily. "But, no. It will only make it worse when you have to leave."

"That's like not driving a car because it will be irritating when it breaks down."

He chuckled despite himself. "I suppose so." He lifted his head. "It isn't a good idea to get any closer than we already have," he said finally. "It's going to hurt like hell as it is."

She started to speak, but he put his thumb over her lips.

"I know you think you love me," he said. "That will pass, once you're back in your own apartment and resuming your own life. This will seem like a bad dream."

"Last night won't," she replied.

"I know." He kissed her forehead with breathless tenderness. "But it was only one night. You'll forget, in time."

"Will you?"

He let her go and stretched, pretending he didn't hear her. "Who cooks, and what?" he asked. "I feel like a hamburger. Several hamburgers,'' he amended. ''That slice of pizza at lunch wasn't filling.''

''Hamburgers it is. I'll cook,'' she volunteered.

''You always cook. That isn't fair division of labor.''

''It is, considering how you cook hamburgers,'' she said under her breath as she went toward the kitchen.

''Female chauvinism.''

''Contradiction in terms.''

He made a huffy sound and went into the bedroom to change.

She made hamburgers and sliced some Swiss cheese to go on them, along with chives and onions and mustard and mayonnaise. Dane stared at his suspiciously when she put it before him.

''Try it before you say terrible things about it,'' she coaxed.

He narrowed one eye and glared at it. Eventually, he picked it up and tasted it, and his eyebrows arched. ''Different,'' he said.

''Kit taught me,'' she said. ''She learned from her boss.''

''The office has missed them,'' Dane said dryly as he washed down bites of hamburger with rich black coffee. ''Logan Deverell is one of my biggest accounts. His mother, Tansy, keeps me in the black.''

She laughed. ''She's a wild woman, isn't she? Always into something, mostly trouble. We spend a lot of time looking for her. Mr. Deverell worries too much.''

''Not really,'' he mused. ''Not since she got arrested in Mexico for drug trafficking.''

''But she wasn't,'' she argued. ''She bought a colorful purse from a vendor who mistook her for a mule.''

"Mistaken identity has landed saner people than Tansy in jail," he reminded her. "If Logan could tie her to a post, he'd stop worrying."

"Yes, but we'd lose his business," she pointed out.

"Perish the thought."

"I miss having lunch with Kit," she sighed. She glanced at him. "She'd have a flying fit if she knew we were living together."

"We aren't," he pointed out.

"We are so. Temporarily, anyway," she replied.

He finished his hamburger and made himself another one. This time he sliced onions and spread mustard on one bun and catsup on another.

"Purist," she muttered.

"I'm conventional," he explained as he sat down again. "I like a downtown hamburger."

She laughed. Her gray eyes sparkled as she looked at him, so enthralled by the sight of him across a table that she couldn't hide it. Even in an old T-shirt and jeans, he was something to see.

"I don't guess we could go down to the ranch for the weekend?" she asked wistfully.

He shook his head, his eyes wary. "We can't risk it."

"Because of the drug dealers." She nodded.

"No, Tess," he replied quietly. "Because we've been lovers. Beryl isn't blind. The way we look at each other would give the show away."

"Oh."

"She's old-fashioned in her attitudes." He grimaced at her blush. "I know. So are you. So am I, for that matter." His eyes darkened. "And despite that, it made me feel ten feet tall to know I was the first. I'll treasure that night as long as I live."

"So will I," she said softly, searching his eyes. "You said you'd never been tender with anyone. But you were patient and gentle, and I know you didn't feel like being that way. You wanted me very badly."

"I wanted to cherish you," he said huskily. "I wanted to give you a sweet memory, something to wipe out the fear I'd kindled in you the first time I kissed you." He shrugged. "Maybe I wanted to know if I was capable of tenderness, as well."

She cleared her throat. "I don't think there's much doubt about that anymore," she said demurely.

His eyes softened as he looked at her. "You were everything I used to dream you would be," he said quietly. "Soft and loving, gently abandoned in my arms. I exhausted you because I couldn't manage to stop. I couldn't get enough of you."

She colored, remembering. She wrapped her hands around her coffee cup and sipped the hot black liquid. She met his eyes evenly. "I'm not sorry," she said. "Not if I died of it, I wouldn't be sorry!"

His jaw tautened. He had to drag his gaze back to his hamburger. He could have said the same to her, but he was getting aroused all over again. "I've got some work to do in the study. Can you amuse yourself?"

"There's a *National Geographic* special on," she replied. "About lizards. I thought I'd watch it."

His eyebrows arched. "Lizards?"

She shrugged. "I don't know why, but I've always been fascinated by them. Especially the Komodo dragons. Have you seen pictures of them? They're huge, and they have forked tongues...."

"And a very well developed Jacobsen's organ," he added, smiling at her surprise. "They interest me, too. So does most wildlife."

"You like cattle and horses. I guess wildlife is wild-life," she mused.

"I'd have liked taking you back to the ranch," he confessed, searching her face quietly. "But Beryl would make you feel uncomfortable."

She looked down at the empty plate. "Is there such a thing as happily ever after these days?" she asked.

"For some people, maybe. I can't forget how my marriage failed, Tess. Maybe it never had a chance, but in the beginning, things were bright for Jane and me. Somewhere along the way, we stopped caring about each other." He looked up. "There aren't any guarantees. If I could give you a child, I might think differently. But I can't. I don't think we could make it work. I'm afraid to take the chance, can you understand that?"

"You think I'm too young," she sighed. Her eyes coveted him shyly. "I don't know whether to be flattered or insulted. I loved you when I was nineteen, and I love you now." She smiled sadly. "How do I stop, Dane?"

His teeth clenched. He couldn't handle questions like that. He swallowed the last of his coffee and put the mug down. "Leave the dishes," he said as he rose. "I'll take care of them, since you did the cooking."

"I don't mind...."

"This is my apartment," he reminded her coolly. "I'm used to doing dishes. And cooking. I've lived alone for years."

He went off in the general direction of the study and she got up after a minute and cleared things away.

"You really must feel like you have a shadow," Helen remarked a couple of days later at work. "Dane never takes his eyes off you, and if he has to be out of the office, it's Adams or me or Nick. You poor thing, I know you'll be glad when this is finally over. Living with Dane must be pure hell. It's a good thing you don't have a social life, or you'd be screaming.''

Tess controlled her expression, just barely. ''I suppose so.''

''Dane would have been your stepbrother, wouldn't he?'' Helen asked. ''Everyone knows that your respective parents were going to be married. I don't suppose it feels funny to you at all, being that close to him. After all, he's almost family.''

She murmured her agreement, but it was a lie. Dane wasn't family. He was the light of her life, except that she wanted something he didn't. She wanted marriage and togetherness. Dane was afraid that she'd turn out like Jane, harping on his inability to make her pregnant, making his life hell.

She wouldn't, though. It was a disappointment, surely, that he couldn't give her a child, but it wasn't the end of the world. She cared about him too much. If it could be only the two of them for fifty years, she'd have leaped at the chance. She couldn't bear to even think of how life was going to be without him, now that she'd known him so intimately.

He didn't seem to be having similar problems. If he was worried about their relationship, his expression gave nothing away. In the evenings, he was pleasant and kind, but he never looked at her too long or came too close. He spent most of his time in his study, working, and when he wasn't in there, he was in bed.

Tess was alone these days at the apartment, and the distance between Dane and herself was growing. He was determined to put her out of his mind. She fought to keep the wonderful closeness they'd attained, but she did it with no help from him.

"Tess, come in here a minute, please," he said the next morning, motioning her into his office.

Nick Reed was in there, too, tall and blond and carelessly attractive. He was Helen's brother, an ex-FBI agent whom Dane had coaxed away from the government agency, and if Tess hadn't been so hopelessly in love with Dane, she'd have gotten weak-kneed every time she saw Nick. He had that kind of good looks. He smiled at her as she sat down on the sofa and waited for Dane to close the door.

"We're going to force their hand," Dane told her abruptly. "Nick's been to see a man I got a tip about. He got some information we can use, and I had him deposit a few clues about your movements in the process. We're going to set you up, honey, and let the bad boys come after you."

"Thanks," she sighed. "I always knew you loved me, really."

Nick chuckled at what he thought was a joke. Dane didn't. His face closed up.

"You'll be quite safe," Dane told her. "We're going to back you to the hilt, the whole damned staff and two off-duty cops. It's the only way I've been able to find that wouldn't give them the advantage. We can't sit and wait until they try for you again. It's too dangerous."

"What do you want me to do?" she asked calmly.

"First they shoot you, then they try to nab you, and you break free and evade them," Nick murmured. "Pity Dane won't let you on the staff, Tess, you're a natural."

"Tell him, tell him," she muttered, pointing at Dane. "He thinks I'm hopeless at detective work."

"Getting shot doesn't require ability as a detective," Dane informed her.

"No, but getting away from a potential killer does," Nick told him. "Some of our best operatives wouldn't have been able to manage—"

"Let's keep to the topic at hand," Dane said tersely, glaring at Nick. "Tess, this is what we want to do," he began.

He told her when, where and how they were going to set the trap. She was afraid and nervous, but she reminded herself that she'd been both when she evaded the men in the first place. She could keep her head under fire. She knew that now. It would be all right.

At least she'd be out of danger when it was over. She'd be out of Dane's life, too. He seemed to be in a hurry to accomplish that, even if she wasn't. What did they say about a quick cut being kindest in the long run? Maybe she could get her life back together when she was out of Dane's, but she'd never be the same without him. Nothing was going to change that.

That weekend at the apartment, Dane was unusually restless. He couldn't sit still long enough to watch television.

"Let's go out," he said tersely, glancing at her. "Put something on."

"I've got something on," she began, indicating her jeans and T-shirt.

"Then add a jacket and some sneakers to it. I feel like riding."

"Where?"

"At the ranch," he muttered. He saw her flush. "It's

Beryl's day off," he told her. "Even so, we manage the facade in public. Helen actually asked me if I'd ease up on you. She thinks I've been giving you hell."

"Haven't you?" she asked pertly.

He turned away. "Come on. Sitting around here all day isn't going to do a thing for us."

Probably not, since he wouldn't touch her, she thought bitterly. But a whole day in his company wasn't anything to sneer at. In the years to come, every minute would be a precious memory.

She grabbed her denim jacket, slipped into her pink sneakers and followed him out the door.

It was a cool day, and she was glad of the jacket when she and Dane rode across the lower part of his ranch, which lay along the boundary of the Big Spur. Her efforts to get on the horse had amused Dane, bringing a rare smile to his lips. The old mare he'd given her to ride was gentle, though, and after a while she felt quite at home on the animal. It wasn't nearly the ordeal she'd thought it would be, learning how to ride. She was enjoying it.

She stared curiously at the red-coated cattle in the distance.

"They're the same color as yours," she remarked, nodding toward them. "Are they the same breed?"

"Santa Gertrudis," he agreed. He eased back in the saddle, grimacing a little.

"Is your back all right?" she asked with concern.

He glance at her with a wry smile. "It was until a few nights ago."

She actually gasped out loud.

He chuckled helplessly. "My God."

"Do you mind?" she asked breathlessly, her color flaring.

"My back is all right," he assured her "A little stiff, but it gets that way from routine work. I can assure you," he added in a soft tone, "that I'd much rather have a stiff back from what we did together than from going on stakeout."

She cleared her throat. "I see."

"Coward. You were the one who brought it up last time." He caught her hand in his and brought it to his mouth. "Thank you for the gift you gave me that night."

She really colored then. She couldn't manage words.

He stopped his horse, and hers, and clasped her hand against him until she looked his way.

"I felt like a whole man," he said slowly. "Even if I couldn't give you a child."

She winced. "Dane, a child isn't the only reason two people marry."

"Perhaps not," he said wearily. "But it can destroy a marriage." His face went hard. "God knows, it destroyed mine."

"I'm not Jane!" she cried.

He looked at her hungrily. "There's no doubt about that," he said quietly. "She could barely suffer having me in bed." His high cheekbones went ruddy. "You didn't, though. My God, you…" He couldn't even find the words. He pressed his mouth hard into her palm, his eyes closed on an anguished scowl. "I've never had it like that," he said in a rough tone.

She flushed, too, at the unfamiliar emotion in his deep voice. "I thought it was always good for the man."

His dark eyes caught hers. "I all but passed out in your arms," he said huskily. "Just thinking about how it was arouses me."

Her lips parted. It aroused her, too. She sensed his vulnerability, and just for an instant she thought he might be weakening.

The sudden sound of approaching horses distracted him, too soon. He let go of her hand and his eyes narrowed under the wide brim of his hat.

"Two peas in a pod," he mused, watching two tall riders approach.

Tess shaded her eyes. "Who are they?"

"Cole Everett and King Brannt." He kicked his boot out of the stirrup and looped his leg around his saddle horn while he lit a cigarette. He grinned as the two men galloped up beside him and stopped. He knew they'd seen him with Tess and had moved in for a better look. It was, as they knew, unusual for him to bring a woman to the ranch.

"Nice day," the older of the two remarked, his narrow silvery eyes appraising Tess's flushed face.

"Good weather, too," the other man agreed, his dark eyes twinkling in a lean, formidable countenance.

"Her name is Teresa Meriwether," Dane told them with exaggerated patience. "Tess for short. Her father was going to marry my mother until the wreck, so she's…family. She's my secretary at the agency."

Cole Everett pushed back his creamy Stetson and eyed Dane curiously, his silver eyes quiet and steady. "Do tell." He glanced at Tess. "Nice to meet you," he said, smiling. He had a warm smile, not sarcastic or mocking.

"Same here," King Brannt agreed. He was pleasant enough, but he had a cutting edge to his personality that intimidated Tess. She smiled shyly in his direction, wondering absently how his Shelby had ever gotten up enough nerve to marry such a wildcat.

Everett, too, had an untamed look, but he was older than the other two men, graying at the temples.

"How's Heather?" Dane asked Cole. "Still teaching voice?"

"And writing songs," Cole replied. "She sold one last year to a group called Desperado, based up in Wyoming, and their lead singer won another Grammy with it. Heather was over the moon. So were our boys." He chuckled. "They're just at the age where they like pop music."

"My kids like it, too," King mused. "Dana's got a keyboard and Matt has drums." He held a hand to his ear. "Shelby spends a lot of time working in the kitchen garden while they practice. They're all in high school. His three hang out with my two," he muttered, glaring at Cole. "God knows, I'll go insane one day and start howling at the moon from the noise."

"I send them over to his house so that we can have some peace and quiet at ours," Cole explained dryly. "Shelby told Heather that she wished she had more than two kids of her own." He pursed his lips at King. "You aren't too old yet, are you?"

"Speak for yourself, Grandpa," King returned. He glanced at Dane curiously. "Ever think of marrying again?" he asked bluntly.

Dane didn't bat an eyelash. "No. Anything in particular you wanted, besides a look at my houseguest?" he added with a meaningful stare.

"We could use a new bull," Cole reminded him. "King's got one he's ready to sell, and he needs a new one of his own. Since you and I are ready to unload...er, sell...that bull of ours, King thought we might work out a trade, when you've got time to discuss it.'' He grinned at Tess, ignoring King's dry glance in his direction. ''Not today, of course.''

Dane chuckled at the blatant excuse. He saw right through them. ''Okay,'' he said. ''I'll come over next weekend and we'll talk about it.'' By then, he thought, he'd have sprung the trap on Tess's assailant and she'd have moved out. The thought depressed him.

''Suits us,'' King said. ''As for unloading your bull on me,'' he added with a mocking smile at Cole Everett, ''that'll be the day.''

''You watch too many reruns of old John Wayne movies,'' Cole pointed out. ''You're starting to sound like the character he played in *The Searchers*.''

The younger man cocked an eyebrow. ''All the same, you won't slip a worn-out bull under my nose.''

Cole looked insulted. ''Would I do that to a business partner?''

''Sure,'' King said pleasantly. ''Like you tried to land me with that gelding last year when I wanted a new stallion for my stud.''

''It wasn't my fault. I swear to God I had no idea he'd been to the vet—''

''Like hell you didn't. He was in on it with you,'' he added, nodding toward Dane. ''You gave it away when you started snickering into your hat.''

''Yes, but the joke backfired, didn't it?'' King mused. ''I bought the animal anyway and he turned out to be one of the best stud horses I've got. The vet pulled a fast one on both of *you*.''

Tess was laughing out loud by now. ''I thought you people were friends!'' she burst out.

''Oh, we are,'' King agreed. ''But friends are much more dangerous than enemies.''

''I'll drink to that,'' Dane murmured.

"Yes, well, it pays not to turn your back on these two," Cole returned. "Are you staying at the ranch long? Heather would enjoy getting to meet you, I'm sure. I imagine your job is pretty interesting. *He* never talks about it." He jerked a thumb toward Dane.

"That's how *he* keeps his clientele," Dane returned easily. "We're leaving in a few minutes, but maybe I'll bring her over another time."

"You do that. Well, we'll see you next weekend, then."

"Nice to have met you," King added to Tess. He wheeled his mount and started up. Cole Everett smiled and followed suit.

Tess watched them ride away. "Have your friends been married a long time?"

"Years and years," he replied. "Their kids are all in their early teens now." *Kids.* His face hardened. "We'd better get back."

She put her hand on his upper arm as he gathered the reins in one lean hand. "Don't let it wear on you like that," she said softly. "Dane, children aren't everything...."

"They are if you can't produce any," he said tersely. He looked into her eyes with pure malice. "Tell me you don't want a baby, Tess," he challenged coldly.

Her eyes clouded with mingled anguish and compassion, but he didn't read it that way at all. He cursed under his breath and rode quickly ahead of her, leaving her to follow behind him with her heart in her shoes. She knew then that he was never going to give in. He wouldn't marry again, because the specter of not having children was too much for him to bear. He'd never be convinced that she could be happy without them, so no matter what his feelings for her were, marriage was out of the question. He'd made that clear just now, without saying a single word.

She was sore and shaky when they got back to the barn. Dane saw her grimace and reached up to help her down. But, as always, the feel of her body triggered helpless longings in his own.

He let her slide down against him, his hands firm on her waist, his eyes holding hers.

"I like your friends," she whispered huskily.

"So do I." He had to fight to breathe normally. He looked down at her soft mouth and all but groaned. "We have to go back."

She drew in an unsteady breath. "I enjoyed the ride."

"Sore?"

She nodded and smiled. "I'm not used to horses, but I think I could learn to like riding."

He searched her eyes slowly. "I could learn to like a lot of things, if I let myself." His face hardened. "I want you so," he whispered roughly. "But I can't have you."

"Dane…"

He let go of her and moved back. "No. In a day or two, we'll wrap up your problem. Then we'll get on with our lives."

He turned to lead the horses into the barn. He had shut her out. Just that easily, he turned his back on what had happened, on any future that contained both of them. As they drove back to Houston, Tess thought she'd never felt quite so alone.

As long as she and Dane were communicating, she'd been able to push what had happened with the attempted kidnapping to the back of her mind. That, and the trap they were going to set the following Monday night for the men. Now she worried over it until her hands were twisting nervously in her lap. If anything went wrong, she could die this time. She glanced at Dane and wondered if losing her would hurt him at all. That was unfair, she thought. Of course he'd care if she died. He was a caring man, despite his misgivings about her role in his life.

He saw her worried face. "What's wrong?" he asked quietly.

"I was thinking about the trap," she said, surprising him. He hadn't let himself consider the upcoming event, because it disturbed him so much. Now he was forced to think about it, and to worry about what might happen if something went wrong.

His chest rose and fell heavily. "Try to remember that Nick and I are fairly competent at what we do for a living," he said after a minute, his voice deep and slow. "We'll take good care of you, little one. We'll get them."

She smiled wanly. "Okay."

She didn't sound convinced, but he couldn't dwell on that. He had to hope that the scenario would play as he and Nick had rehearsed it. Once the assailants were in custody, he could decide what to do about Tess. One thing was certain. He had to get her out of his life before he weakened and let her stay. For her own sake, that couldn't happen. He cared too much to let her settle for a barren marriage, even if it was going to kill him to let her go.

Chapter Seven

The darkness outside the windows was dismal. Rain had begun to pepper down. It was a cold rain. Tess wrapped her arms around her body, because even the gray sweater she was wearing over dark slacks and a blue-and-gray-patterned blouse didn't spare her from the chill. Behind her, Dane was smoking a cigarette, waiting.

Out of sight were Nick and Helen and Adams, along with two of Sergeant Graves's best men. Some subtle investigative work had revealed that the office was being watched. Tonight, the office staff was going to take advantage of that surveillance to spring a trap. Dane and Tess were apparently working late. The rest of the office staff had left earlier, with a great deal of noise, so that anyone watching would see them. Once out of sight, they'd parked their cars several blocks away and had crept back into position, as planned.

Dane checked his watch. He was uneasy. He hadn't wanted to do this, but he had no choice. He couldn't let it drag on, let Tess be constantly in danger. He might not be quick enough the next time. The drug lords had already gotten to her. At least this way, he had a good chance of success in catching them once and for all.

He didn't want her threatened. He couldn't keep her, but he couldn't bear to see her hurt, ever.

"Scared?" he asked gently.

"Terrified," she confessed. "That's normal, isn't it?" she added, turning. "It isn't lack of fear that creates heroes. It's going ahead, doing what you have to when you're so frightened you can hardly stand on your feet."

He nodded. "That's it, exactly. I've been in gun battles more than once. Every time, I could taste the fear. But I never ran."

She smiled. "The adrenaline surge you get from danger is powerful," she remarked. "Once I was away from the drug people and running, I could have flown."

He scowled. "It's addictive," he said quietly. "That's why I'd never let you work as an operative. You'd have taken to the danger without hesitation. It would have put you at risk constantly."

"You're at risk constantly," she pointed out. Her eyes slid over his hard, lean face. "But you won't quit, either."

"I don't have anyone to leave behind," he said. His expression dared her to argue. "This isn't a married man's—or woman's—occupation, not the way we operate. The demands of the job can kill the best of relationships. Jane hated my work when I was a ranger. I was never home."

Her eyes softened. "Dane, if you'd loved her, really loved her...wouldn't you have been?"

His face went expressionless. He turned his wrist and glanced at his watch. "It's time." He put out his cigarette. She asked questions he didn't want to answer. "You know what to do."

"Yes."

He picked up his attaché case, hesitating as he passed her. His dark eyes caressed her face. "Don't take chances. If it goes down unexpectedly, scream, break a window, do anything to get my attention. I won't be out of earshot, no matter what."

"All right." She swallowed. Her mouth was dry, her palms sweaty. Her heartbeat was racing, but she couldn't let him see how frightened she was. It would only make things worse.

"You've got plenty of backup," he added. "It's going to be all right. After tonight, it will be over."

"They can make bail again...."

"Not in this case. If it's permitted, we'll make sure it's set high enough that they'll never raise it."

"It's still my word against theirs."

"After tonight it won't be," he promised. He touched her lips with his forefinger. "Chin up, lover," he breathed. He bent his head and nipped her lower lip hard, making her mouth open so that he could take it hungrily. But before she could reach up to hold him, he was out the door.

She was alone. The office was suddenly cold and frightening. She paced nervously. Dane had had time to get to the parking lot, get to his car and put the attaché case in the trunk. From there, he was going to light a cigarette and then start back toward the office. It would look as if he'd just stepped out for a minute, not as if he was deliberately leaving Tess alone—that would have been a dead giveaway to anyone watching that it was a setup.

In those few minutes, a dark brown sedan had purred

to a stop down the street and two men had emerged. From the shadows, they'd eased along the side of the building, keeping Dane in sight until he rounded the corner at the parking lot.

They'd seen their opportunity and they took it. Darting into the building and then into the elevator, they went up to the floor where the office was located. When the elevator stopped, they were already drawing their weapons. This time they were taking no chances. None at all.

What they didn't know was that Dane had seen them. Wasting no time, he'd darted around to the back of the building and the service elevator. There was a back way into his office. He had his .45 automatic out, cocked, and in his hand when the main door to the office began to open. Tess had turned automatically to look when she heard the sound. The flash of the first man's gun burned into her consciousness, leaving her rigid, unable to move. She wasn't going to make it. She knew that no operative was going to have time to get to her before the shots hit her. Remembering the pain she'd known before, she stared at the pistol with blank, terror-filled eyes. *Dane,* she thought in anguish. Her last conscious thought was of him.

"Duck!"

The voice commanded and she obeyed, falling to the floor even as the sound of automatic gunfire shattered the silence.

Dane hit the floor near her, rolling to escape the bullets with all his ex-policeman's skill. He had only one instant to aim and fire, but he was an expert shot. He had one clear shot at the first man with the small Uzi in his hands, and he took it. The drug dealer's gun discharged again and suddenly flew out of his hands seconds before he caught his shoulder and went down, crying out as the bullet hit him. The second man whirled and ran. Dane leaped to his feet with fluid grace, his face set in lines Tess had never seen, his eyes black fires in a stony countenance as he spun the wounded man onto his belly and searched him with quick, deft motions. He always carried handcuffs. He snapped them onto the man's wrists and left him, coming back to Tess, who was by now on her knees and shaking from the experience.

"The other man," she gasped.

He took her arm and pulled her to her feet. "Nick will have him by now."

"Get me a doctor, damn you!" the downed man cried. "This is inhuman! I'm bleeding!"

"So was Tess when you shot her," he replied, adding a few adjectives that turned Tess's face ruddy.

"Are you all right?" she asked Dane, her hands unconsciously searching his arms for wounds. "He didn't hit you?"

A corner of his mouth tugged up. "I've spent most of my life dodging bullets," he reminded her. "I used to get paid for it. Are you all right?"

"I am now," she said, and leaned against him weakly, her cheek on his chest. She stared at the downed man, who was curled up, groaning. Blood stained his elegant jacket. The Uzi he'd brought with him was dangling from one of Dane's lean hands.

"Tess!"

Helen's voice echoed loudly as she leaped from the elevator with Nick right behind. "We heard shots..." She stopped, staring at the downed man briefly before she studied Dane and Tess. "Everybody okay?"

"We're fine. How about his cohort?" Dane asked, nodding toward the wounded man.

"I handed him over to Sergeant Graves's men," Nick said, reholstering his automatic. He gave Helen a dark glare from eyes almost as black as Dane's. "No thanks to my sister, Miss James Bond, here," he added. "She actually walked into the line of fire."

"I did not!" Helen raged. "You came out of nowhere! Why is it always my fault anytime something goes wrong?" she demanded. "Don't you ever make mistakes, Mr. Perfect?"

"No," he said with a pleasant smile.

Dane had to stifle a grin at the expression on Helen's face. "Cut it out," he said. "Call an ambulance for our victim there," he instructed, handing Helen the Uzi.

"Careful, don't get fingerprints on it," Nick said with deliberate sarcasm.

"I know how to hold a gun," she said smugly. "You taught me yourself! Are you okay?" she asked Tess.

"I'm fine, thanks," Tess said breathlessly.

"Damned detectives," the downed man spat. "Damned detectives!"

Dane lifted an eyebrow and drew Tess closer. "Come on," he said gently. "Let's get you out of here."

It was a long night. She had to give a statement, wait until it was typed and read back to her, then sign it. The wounded man was taken to the hospital under police guard. Later he'd be removed to the county jail pending trial. The other man was booked and jailed and his lawyer was telephoned.

No bail, Dane had promised. Tess breathed easily for the first time.

She slept without being coaxed, right past the alarm

clock. When she woke, there was a note from Dane, telling her not to come to work that day, that she needed the rest.

Probably she did. And she needed the time to pack, she thought miserably. He hadn't said so, but then he'd barely spoken to her the night before. He'd been kind but impersonal, and he hadn't offered more than cursory comfort. He'd sent her to bed, insisting that she needed sleep more than conversation.

But what he really wanted was to see the last of her. She didn't need a crystal ball to understand that he wasn't going to let her into his life on any permanent basis. Probably, now that she was out of danger, he wasn't even going to want her in the office anymore. Her very presence would be a painful reminder of his vulnerability, of the night he'd given in to his need of her and let himself love her.

He *did* love her. That was the only certainty she had. But he was going to fight it, and he might win. That was the chance she was taking by complying with his wishes; by going away without argument. She had to draw back and let him think it out for himself. Only by giving him freedom of choice did she have any chance of convincing him that they could have a future together.

She packed her things and had them ready when he came home that evening. She was sitting on the sofa, dressed in neat gray slacks with a white bulky-knit sweater, her hair in a braid down her back, her coat next to her.

She looked up as he entered the apartment. He paused at the sight of her suitcases, scowling.

"I thought you'd prefer it like this," she said quietly.

"No fuss. No trouble." She stood up. "Can you drive me home, please?"

He drew in a slow breath. She was right. It was better this way. But he'd expected to find her curled up on the sofa, as she'd been so many evenings, watching television. The stark reality of her departure hit him like a body blow.

"Come on," he said, his voice as stiff as his posture. "I'll do that before I get comfortable."

"Thank you."

She put on her coat and followed him out of the apartment. She didn't look back. It would have broken her heart.

"You don't have to worry about your assailants," he told her. "I have assurances that they won't get out again. You'll have to testify. Graves will notify you."

"So he said." She concentrated on the streetlights and didn't speak again. She was too choked up for that.

When they arrived at her apartment, it was cold. She turned up the thermostat while Dane unloaded her suitcases and brought them in. He stood there, elegant in a vested navy blue suit, his posture arrow-straight.

"Will you be okay?" he asked.

"Of course. I'm safe, now—right?" she added nervously. "They don't have friends who owe them favors, or anything?"

He shook his head. "Fortunately, these two are jump-ups—renegades who poached on another pusher's territory. Nobody loves them enough to make you pay for their arrest."

"Thank God."

He studied her quietly, with faint sadness in his expression, in his eyes. "You don't have to come in tomorrow if you don't feel like it."

"I won't mind getting back to work." She wrapped her arms around herself and looked up. "If you won't mind letting me stay...?"

"My God, that would be gratitude, wouldn't it?" he asked harshly. "Turning you out on the streets when you took a bullet on my account!"

"It wasn't on your account. I saw something I shouldn't have. I never blamed you."

He drew in a rough breath. "Well, I do. I blame myself for a hell of a lot of things."

"I'm a big girl now," she told him bravely. "I made my own choices, Dane."

"Did you?" he asked, his dark eyes narrowing as they searched hers. He watched her blush. "Maybe you think you had a choice. I'm not sure you really did. I seduced you."

She smiled sadly and shook her head. "I'm afraid it was the other way around."

He lit a cigarette, his shoulders slumping a little as he smoked it, watching her quietly. "You'll get over this," he said, searching her sad eyes. "You don't think so, but you will. God knows, people can get over any kind of pain eventually."

"Jane hurt you badly, didn't she?" she asked. "I wouldn't, but you can't be sure of that, because you don't trust emotions. Do you really want to be alone for the rest of your life, Dane?"

"Yes," he said curtly. He averted his eyes so that she wouldn't see the lie in them. He wanted Tess, but getting out of her life was the kindest thing he could do for her. When she was happily married, with children, she'd forget him.

Tess didn't know how to answer the stark statement he'd just made. She couldn't convince him. Words wouldn't be enough. Her body wasn't enough to tempt him to stay with her. She had nothing left, except the fact that she loved him, and he didn't believe that. With one word, he'd robbed her of every convincing argument she had.

"Then there's nothing left to say."

"Nothing," he agreed. His eyes searched around the small apartment and then went back to her, lingering only for an instant. He turned then, and opened the door. "I'll see you in the morning."

"In the morning," she whispered, fighting tears.

His back stiffened as he heard her choked tone. He didn't look at her. It would have been fatal. "Take care of yourself."

"I'll do that. You, too." She hesitated. "Dane?"

"What?"

"Thank you for saving my life. If you hadn't been in the office, I wouldn't be here now."

His eyes closed. A wave of nausea washed over him. He couldn't think about that. He couldn't bear the pain of remembering how close she'd come to death, twice now. "Good night, Tess," he said tightly. He went out and closed the door, only then lifting his hot face to the cold night air, swallowing down the sick lump in his throat.

There was rain, and more rain. He walked back to the car, but he didn't get into it. He turned and leaned against it, his eyes on the lighted windows of Tess's apartment complex. He was always on the outside looking in, he thought bitterly, always standing in the cold rain and looking at warm windows. If he could have given Tess a child, he might have been inside even now, holding her, loving her. But he couldn't give her that, and he'd be cheating her if he gave in to his own feelings.

He finished his cigarette and threw it to the pavement, watching it fizzle out in the puddle of rain. He felt like that, as if a fire inside him had been coldly quenched. He turned and got into the car and drove away into the night.

When they were back at work again, Tess expected coldness from Dane. What she hadn't expected was total indifference. Dane treated her like he did the computer. He extracted information from her, replaced it with other information, and left her sitting in the office without a backward glance when he went home. It was boss-employee now, all the way.

She went through the motions of working, but her heart wasn't in it. Dane didn't want her around. She knew he hated even the sight of her at her desk, but she couldn't make herself do what he really wanted her to. She couldn't resign.

"Want to go out and have a pizza with me?" Helen offered, grinning. "Now that I'm a heroine, with my name in the papers," she added, because the arrest had made headlines, "the pizza-parlor owner thinks I'm the berries. He gives me anything I want." She snapped her fingers. "Even double cheese and mushrooms and anchovies."

"You'll start melting one day," Tess cautioned. "All that pizza will turn your poor insides into mozzarella and you'll ooze all over the floor."

"Not as long as I eat enough anchovies to keep me solvent." The older woman grinned. "Come on. Come home with me. You look dismal these days, all pale and worn. You need cheering up."

"I don't feel like going out," Tess said. "I get sleepy with the chickens these days. Residue from all the pressure," she added with a smile. "I still have to go to court next month when the trial comes up." Her assailants had since been arraigned and a trial date had been set.

"The vultures," Helen muttered. "I hope they get life."

"Unlikely," Tess replied. "But they'll very probably spend some time in jail. I hope I'm living in Antarctica when they get out," she added, shivering.

"Haven't you heard?" Helen asked. "I thought Dane would have told you that they've been implicated in the murder of a rival drug lord. He was shot with an Uzi, and ballistics matched the fatal bullet to the Uzi that wild man was shooting in here the night we apprehended them. It isn't you they'll be doing time for assaulting—the DA's going for murder one and two counts of possession with intent to distribute. He figures that's more than enough, even without your assault charge, although they may use it if they think they need to."

"Dane didn't mention that." Tess didn't add that Dane only spoke to her when it was absolutely necessary, or that he avoided her like the plague most of the time.

Helen's eyes narrowed. "He doesn't look much better than you do," she remarked. "Poor guy, he lost a lot of sleep while you were in danger. I don't suppose he's caught up yet, and he's taken on a double caseload since the arrest. I suppose he's trying to use up some of that nervous energy."

"I suppose so." Tess yawned. "I wish I had some of it. I'm so tired!"

"Maybe you do need an early night at that. Come have a pizza with me. It'll cheer you up, and I'll get you home so you can catch up on your beauty sleep."

"Thanks, but really, I don't want anything spicy, anyway. My stomach's been queasy for a couple of days. I'm afraid it's that stomach bug Adams had. He breathed on me."

"Harold's got a cold. I'll bring him to the office and have him breathe on Adams for you," Helen offered.

"You're a real friend," Tess said fervently.

Helen grinned. "Don't I know it."

After work, Tess went home and went to bed. The virus was potent, she thought as she lost her breakfast the next morning. She called in sick and curled up in bed again, listening to the pouring rain outside with vague pleasure as she went back to sleep.

Dane came by after work to check on her. She was astonished that he bothered. His attitude in the office had convinced her that he'd put her completely out of his mind.

"How are you?" he asked at the doorway.

She was disheveled and pale, clad in a worn cotton gown and a thick, red chenille bathrobe that covered her from head almost to bare toes. "I've just got Adams's virus," she said weakly. "Shoot him for me, will you?"

"Can I get you anything?"

She shook her head. "Thanks, but I've got frozen yogurt. It's keeping me alive."

He hesitated. "Maybe you should see a doctor," he said with a frown.

"For a stomach bug? Sure." She held the door open pointedly. "I need to lie down, Dane. Thanks for coming by, but I'll be okay in a couple of days. You can get a temp while I'm out, can't you?''

"We had one today.'' He hesitated. "She's very good. Her dictation skills and typing speeds are on par with yours.''

"If you want me to resign, you only have to say so,'' she told him softly, her eyes meeting his. She caught a look on his face that confirmed her suspicions. "Talk to her and see if she'll agree to stay,'' she told him. "If she will, and you'll let me go without proper notice…''

"You can't leave until you've got another job to go to,'' he said through his teeth.

"Short Investigations will hire me in a minute. You know that. Mr. Short said once when he was collaborating with you on a case that he'd love to have me work for him.''

Mr. Short was in his forties and good-looking, a widower with style and daring. Dane's eyes narrowed as he thought about Tess in the same office with that man.

"I don't think so.…'' he began.

"Dane, you don't want me around,'' she said wearily. "Let's stop pretending. Since you slept with me, I'm a perpetual thorn in your side. You look at me like you can't stand the sight of me. I understand. It's just as hard for me to work with you, knowing you feel that way. Let me go. I'll be all right.''

He winced. "Don't look like that,'' he said huskily. "You make me feel two inches tall.''

"I don't mean to.'' She leaned against the wall beside the door, her eyes loving him unconsciously. "Maybe I can forget, if I don't have to see you everyday,'' she said weakly.

"You'll find someone else," he said through his teeth.

"I know," she said to placate his conscience. Not that she believed it. Love like hers didn't wear out. She forced a smile for him. "Goodbye, Dane."

"It couldn't work, honey," he said, his voice so tender and anguished that she could have cried. "We'd have two strikes against us from the beginning. I don't want marriage."

"I know," she said softly. "It's all right."

His chest rose and fell heavily. "No, it's not. I miss you. I'm alone. Nothing is the same anymore."

Tears filled her eyes,threatening to spill over. "Please go, before I make an even bigger fool of myself," she pleaded.

"It isn't love you feel for me!" he ground out. "Don't you see? It's just physical!"

She couldn't answer him. Her eyes, in her thin, pale face, were tragic.

"It's for the best. You'll realize it eventually. You'll marry and have a houseful of kids...." He turned away before his voice broke. He couldn't bear to think about that. "Goodbye, little one. I'll have Helen bring by your severance pay. You can tell her you can't bear the memories of the shooting. She'll believe it."

"I'll do that," she choked. *Please leave,* she was thinking frantically, *please leave before I break down and go to pieces!*

His shoulders squared. "If you ever need me…"

"Thank you. Good night."

He didn't look back. He started to, but his control was precarious.

He went out and heard the door close behind him. It broke his heart to walk away and leave Tess, but he had nothing to give her. She didn't really love him, he told himself. It was just physical attraction. And marriage was impossible and unfair to Tess. He kept telling himself that all the way home.

But when he was back in his empty apartment, the only thing that registered was that he was totally alone.

Chapter Eight

Mr. Short did indeed want Tess to work for him. The following Monday, when she was feeling a little better, she went in for an interview.

The tall, distinguished man had an office full of people, just like Dane. This office was less rigid, though, and Desden Short's operatives were a little more haphazard than Tess liked. The position he was offering her was that of skip tracer, not secretary, and she was delighted.

"I never expected…!" she exclaimed.

"I haven't forgotten how you moaned about being only a secretary at Lassister's agency," he chuckled. "Skip tracing isn't as dangerous and demanding as being a full-fledged operative, but it might satisfy your thirst for stealth and excitement. We'll see."

"I can't thank you enough!"

"Yes, you can. Work hard and make me proud." He stood up and shook hands with her. "If you can stay today, Mary can explain the job to you and help you get acclimated. She doesn't leave until next Monday, so that gives you a week to familiarize yourself with the operation before you have to start work.''

"Fine," she agreed, smiling. "I'll enjoy it, I know I will. I'll work hard."

"What puzzles me is why Dane let you go," he said with a curious smile. "You were practically related."

"It was the shooting," she lied. "The office has such bad memories for me now that I get cold chills just sitting in it."

His curiosity faded. "I see." He smiled. "Well, we'll do our best not to let you get shot here."

"Thanks," she murmured dryly.

Mary Plummer was thirty, a blonde like Tess, and vivacious. "You're going to love this," she said, introducing Tess to the tools of the trade. "It's a plum job, and I'll even give you the names of all my contacts at the public agencies. You can pump them for information when you're really stuck. This," she said, picking up a thick book, "is something you've probably seen plenty of times at Lassiter's.''

"Yes," Tess agreed. "It's Cole's—the directory that gives names and addresses for telephone numbers. Dane said once that no detective agency could operate without one."

"Amen. It's the most important book I own. Here. It's yours now. Take good care of it, and it will take good care of you."

"You're a real friend."

"That's what my fiancé says. We're getting married Saturday, and by Monday, I hope to be sailing in the Bahamas, never to return. He's filthy rich." She sighed. "But I'd love him if he were a pauper."

Tess knew how that felt. Not a day went by that she didn't think of Dane and wish she could be back with him again. That might never happen. She'd resigned herself to the fact that it was highly unlikely he'd willingly come after her now. He'd convinced himself that she was only infatuated with him and that she wanted things he could never give her. She'd been so certain that he loved her, but as time passed without even a word from him, she grew depressed and unsure of herself.

"You look very pale," Mary observed. "Are you sure you're over that virus?"

"Of course I am," Tess replied.

But weeks went by and she didn't get appreciably better. If anything, her stomach problems grew worse. She convinced herself that it was an ulcer. With all the pressure she'd been under—being shot, being stalked, losing Dane, changing jobs—no wonder she was having problems.

She settled into her new job, though, determined not to let her bad health get her down.

Helen insisted on meeting her for lunch a month after she'd left the agency. She'd tried before and Tess had refused, but this time Helen wouldn't be put off, so Tess gave in.

"You really do look bad," Helen said without preamble, frowning as they sat eating cheddar-cheese soup in a sandwich shop.

"It's all the pressure, I think," Tess told her. "So many changes in so little time."

"You've lost weight. You're pale."

"Nerves. Mr. Short is a great boss, but I'm doing a job I've never tried before."

"I suppose so." Helen wasn't convinced. She watched the younger girl with narrowed eyes. "Dane is—"

"How about some ice cream for dessert?" Tess changed the subject, forcing a smile.

Helen didn't speak for an instant. But she got the message. She smiled. "Okay. Point taken. Ice cream it is."

Tess enjoyed the meal after that, but she didn't enjoy the memories it brought back. She'd actually kept Dane out of her mind for a whole day just recently, until Helen came along and opened the floodgates.

Tess went back to her apartment that night and cried herself to sleep. She was so hungry for Dane that even the sound of his name on someone else's lips made her heart beat faster. She'd told herself that she could live without him, but doing it was proving impossible. She couldn't go on like this. She couldn't bear it!

The next morning, she got up and started to leave the apartment, and fainted dead away.

When she came to, it dawned on her that something was very wrong with her. It had been weeks since she'd left the agency, six since she'd left Dane's apartment. That was over a month with the strange virus that had assailed her, ruined her appetite, made her tired. She had all the symptoms of cancer, she told herself, and it was stupid not to see a doctor. Having only an ulcer would be a blessing. Being scared to death was no excuse for hiding her head in the sand. Knowing the truth was always best.

She called for an appointment, and got in that very morning for an examination with the local family practitioner she'd been going to. They must have thought she was terminal, she thought with bitter humor as she phoned the office to tell them she was going to be late.

It was a routine examination until she explained her

symptoms to Dr. Reiner. He sat down on his stool and stared at her.

"I have to ask you something you aren't going to like," he began quietly. "Have you been intimate with a man in the past several weeks?"

Her heart jumped wildly. "Yes," she blurted out. "Once. Well, one night…"

"That would do it," he said on a sigh.

"But he's…sterile," she faltered. "He said…that he couldn't father a child."

He cocked an eyebrow. "When was your last period?"

She thought back; she hadn't realized that she'd missed one. She swallowed and told him her best guess.

"We'll run tests," he said. "I'm sorry, Miss Meriwether, but I think you're pregnant. The symptoms certainly fit."

It was like a blow to the solar plexus. She touched her stomach with wonder, her eyes wide and wild-looking.

"It isn't the end of the world," he said quietly. "There's a clinic nearby…"

"No!" She paled, gasping, her hand flattening protectively over the child she might be carrying. "Oh, no, not ever!"

"You want it, then?"

"With all my heart," she whispered. "I've never wanted anything in my life as much!"

"And the father?"

"I'm afraid he probably won't believe it's his," she said sadly. "In any case, he doesn't believe in marriage, so it's not something I need to bother him with. Not now. When I'm sure…I'll make the decision then."

"Very well. I'll send Nurse Wallace in and we'll get started." He patted her shoulder absently. "Don't worry about it."

Not easy to do, she thought. She couldn't help worrying. The thought of being responsible for a tiny human being was almost as terrifying as a fatal illness. She'd get over it, though, she told herself. People had been having babies for thousands of years. Presumably every mother was afraid of the responsibility at first.

They ran tests and Tess spent a long, sleepless night worrying about it. She hadn't told anyone at the office what the doctor suspected. But when she answered the phone at work, and she heard the nurse's calm voice telling her that she was, indeed, pregnant, she had to struggle to not fall over. She numbly thanked the woman and hung up, without waiting to schedule her next appointment or talk about referral to an obstetrician. That, she decided vaguely, could wait one more day.

"You've gone white," Delcy, the other skip tracer, said worriedly. "Tess, are you all right?"

"All right." Tess nodded.

"Want some coffee?"

"No. Yes. I don't know. Thank you."

Delcy began to laugh. "What *was* that phone call? A proposal from a boyfriend?"

Tess fought to pull herself together. "Sorry," she said, flushing. "No, it was the doctor's office telling me that I'm going to be all right."

"Thank goodness. You've had us all worried."

"Me, too," Tess confessed. She sat back in the chair, her hand resting protectively on her stomach. She was carrying Dane's child. He wouldn't know. He probably

wouldn't even believe it was his. But she knew, and
the thought of having a child was suddenly magical,
awesome.

For the rest of the day, Tess did her job mechanically. A big part of a detective agency's routine was
finding missing people: deserting spouses, runaway
teens, felons skipping out on bail, people trying to outrun debtors, even adopted children trying to find natural
parents for one reason or another. Usually, a good skip
tracer could find a missing person in under an hour,
with some help from contacts at public agencies and a
little careful conversation. It wasn't exactly deductive
reasoning on the order of Sherlock Holmes's, but it
served a purpose and it could be rewarding. The day
before, when she'd gone to work after visiting the doctor, Tess had located a runaway teenage boy who was
trying to make enough money to go home to his frantic
parents. The ensuing reunion had earned Tess a tearful
phone call of gratitude from parents and son. She'd
gone home feeling a little less brittle than usual, feeling
useful again.

Today was less successful, probably because she was
preoccupied. She succeeded in locating a man whose
wife was tracking him down to recover a year's worth
of child-support payments. She was glad the man didn't
know who at the agency had found him, but all the
same Mr. Short was on the receiving end of some nasty
language and a veiled threat.

"I'm really sorry...." Tess began when he hung up.

He laughed with real delight. "Tess, it goes with the
job," he said. "I'll bet Dane got his ears burned every
day. People in trouble don't like being found. That's
human nature."

Mention of Dane made her uncomfortable. She nodded.

"You're just nervous because of what happened to you," he guessed. "That was a once-in-a-lifetime thing, having a felon try to hurt you. You'll never be in the line of fire here, okay?"

"Okay."

He paused by her desk, his eyes narrow and speculative. "I don't usually mix business with pleasure, but how would you like to have dinner with me tonight?"

She was shocked by the suggestion. Dane was in her past now and she was pregnant, but it was as if she'd been asked to commit adultery just by going out with a man.

"Thank you very much," she said genuinely. "but I can't, if you don't mind. I'm...getting over someone."

"Ah. I see." He smiled. "Time does heal wounds, you know. I'll ask again, one of these days."

She nodded, but she didn't encourage him. She had enough upheaval in her life at the moment.

Houston was a big city, and because she was confined to the office, she didn't see much of it. That was good. There was very little chance of running into Dane. But as a month became two, and then three, Kit came home. And life became tedious.

Tess wanted so badly to call Dane and tell him about the baby. But he'd said, over and over, that he didn't want to marry again, that he didn't want commitment. She couldn't tell him she was pregnant because he'd feel obliged to marry her. Even if he wanted the child, how could she put him in such a position? And what if, heaven forbid, he didn't believe it was his? He'd told her he was sterile. He might accuse her of being with another man.

There was, as well, one really good reason why she shouldn't say anything just yet. She was having some pain and a good deal of spotting. She knew those were bad symptoms, and so did her doctor, who promptly made an appointment for her with the obstetrician when she described them to him. She had to find out exactly what was wrong. If she was in danger of losing the child, telling Dane would be the worst thing she could do.

In the end, her muddled mind simply avoided thinking about the problem. But it didn't go away.

"*Why* can't you come and have lunch with me today?" Kit moaned. "I'm just home from Italy! Mr. Deverell is giving me fits! I want to assassinate him. I've got to talk to you!"

She couldn't go have lunch with Kit because Kit worked just down the street from the Lassiter Agency, and the restaurant where she ate was one that Dane frequented. But she couldn't tell Kit that.

"You could drive over here...."

"I don't understand any of this," Kit said heavily. "If it wasn't for Helen, I wouldn't even have known how to get in touch with you. I come home from one little trip and you've changed jobs and moved across town."

"It was necessary."

"This isn't like you, to desert your friends," Kit muttered. "It's something more, I know it is."

"Look, you could come over tonight and I'll tell you all about it."

"Lunch would be quicker."

There was a long pause. Tess tangled the telephone

cord in her hands, wary of being overheard. "I can't have lunch at the restaurant. I don't want...to run into Dane."

There was a longer pause on the other end. "I had a feeling that might be the case. There's a restaurant that specializes in fish between your office and mine— know where it is?"

"Yes."

"I'll meet you there at noon. Fair enough? Neutral ground?"

"Fair enough."

The restaurant Kit had chosen was busy, but big enough to serve a large lunch crowd. Even though it was miles from Dane's office, Tess's gray eyes slid around nervously until she saw tall, elegant Kit walking toward her. Kit had thick dark hair that curved toward her pixie face, with sparkling blue eyes under long, silky lashes. Tess was tall, but Kit was taller, and thinner at the moment.

The older girl stared at Tess and frowned. "You've gained weight, haven't you?" she asked, indicating the loose, white knit sweater Tess was wearing. Her charcoal slacks were two sizes larger than she normally wore, to accommodate her expanding waistline. Her face was fuller, too; more radiant.

"I've gained a little," Tess confessed. "There's an Italian restaurant near the agency."

"I hear you're working as a skip tracer now," Kit said, shaking her head. "It took you long enough to decide to fight Dane's influence. He'd never have let you do anything like that while you worked for him. He's hopelessly overprotective."

Tess was stiff, unusually so, as they were seated and given menus.

Kit stared at her intently. "You might as well tell me. I'm not going to give up until you do."

"I'm pregnant," Tess blurted out, her lips trembling.

Kit became statue-still, as if she'd stopped breathing. "Dane's?" she asked finally, letting out a slow breath.

"Yes."

The older girl began to smile, her eyes quietly compassionate. "And he doesn't know," she said.

Tess nodded, dropping her eyes to the menu. She could hardly see it for the mist in front of her.

"His marriage failed," Kit said gently. "He's running scared. Everybody knows. Not only that, he lost the job he loved, along with his mother, and he's not as able physically as he used to be. It's natural that he'd fight getting involved again, especially with someone as vulnerable as you." She touched Tess's cold hand. "You're going to tell him, aren't you, eventually?"

"Eventually. Not now."

"Why?"

Tess hesitated. "I've been having some problems. I've got an appointment to see my obstetrician tomorrow morning." She grimaced. "His nurse didn't sound very encouraging when I gave her my symptoms." She looked up worriedly. "I've got one of those all-purpose medical books. It could be early signs of a miscarriage," she said nervously. "Kit, what will I do? I can't lose it now, I just can't! It's all I've got…!"

Kit clasped the cold fingers firmly. "Get hold of yourself," she said, her voice reassuring. "It's all right, Tess. It's all right. Take a deep breath. And another.

That's it. Listen to me—you've got to stop this. Don't start thinking negatively. It's dangerous.''

"But what will I do—'' She stopped in midsentence and her face became drained of color as she saw who was coming in the door.

"Dane,'' Kit guessed before she turned around. She winced. "He never comes here!''

Not only was he there, his eyes were searching the restaurant as if he were looking for someone. When his gaze found Tess, he started visibly. His face tautened and he made a beeline for her.

"No,'' Tess whispered huskily. "He can't…!''

But he did. He paused by the table, his dark eyes sliding with quiet desperation over Tess's wan face, as if he couldn't get enough of just looking at her. "We haven't seen you in weeks,'' he said curtly. "I thought you might at least stop by once in a while to say hello. Or don't you care enough?''

That was a strange question from someone who'd as much as admitted that he couldn't bear the sight of her.

"I work across town,'' she said, schooling her voice to remain calm even though she was shaking inside. "It's difficult for me to get away.''

"Yes. I understand that you're doing a skip tracer's job now.''

She lifted her chin. "Yes. It's nice to do a little real detective work for a change.''

He searched her gray eyes slowly, and she saw shadows in his that she couldn't define. She couldn't know he'd been starving for her. The apartment was empty, his job was empty, his life was empty. He'd never thought he was capable of missing someone so much. The fact that she'd gone away and stayed away made him vicious. She'd sworn undying love, but she didn't seem to be dying without him. She couldn't be bothered to phone the office or visit, not even to see Helen or have lunch with her friend Kit.

"Detective work is dangerous," he said shortly.

"Yes, I know. I got shot, didn't I?"

He drew in a slow breath, ramming his lean hands into the pockets of his gray slacks. He looked worn. "You might at least call us once in a while, so we know you're still alive."

"I'll try to do that," Tess replied. She averted her eyes to the table. "I suppose Helen does miss me."

His jaw clenched. His hands curled into fists. Yes, Helen missed her. But not like he did. He wanted to tell her how much, but she acted as if she wouldn't have believed him. Her whole attitude was one of indifference. *How, Tess?* he thought bitterly. *How can you be like this, after what we shared that night?*

It didn't help him to remember that her departure had been his idea. He hadn't wanted commitment, he'd told her. But that was before he'd tried to face life without her beside him. He hated going home at night, because Tess wouldn't be in the apartment when he got there. He hated his very life, empty and cold and unsatisfying because she was no longer part of it. His dark eyes caressed her bent head and he sighed. He'd sent her away. Now he couldn't get her back. He didn't know what to do. Had he killed every shred of feeling she'd had for him?

"Don't you want to join us, Dane?" Kit asked when the silence grew tense and prolonged.

"No," he said absently. "I have to get back to work. Tess?"

She looked up, wounded by the false tenderness in his deep drawl. "Yes?"

He searched her drawn face quietly. "Are you all right?" he asked gently. "You look…" He wasn't sure how she looked. Sick. Worried. "Have you been ill again?"

The color surged back into her cheeks. She averted her face. "Winter brings on plenty of colds, you know," she replied evasively. It hurt her to look at him. She didn't dare do it for long, or everything she felt would rush into her eyes and betray her. She was carrying his child under her heart, and she couldn't tell him. It hurt…!

She gasped as a stab of pain went through her. It was a familiar pain—one she had every time she did a lot of walking just lately—and the reason she'd called the obstetrician's office for an appointment.

"Tess!"

Dane was beside her, kneeling, his hand grasping hers, his dark eyes full of concern. "What is it, little one?" he asked quickly. "Are you all right?"

"I think I have an ulcer, that's all," she hedged. The touch of his hand was driving her mad, sending waves of helpless pleasure through her body. She lifted her eyes and met his, and the world stopped. Everything stopped. She looked at him and her heart broke in two inside her body.

His face contorted. His eyes were tormented. "Tess," he groaned, his voice as haunted as his eyes.

She took a slow breath and shivered at the need for him that still consumed her. "I'm okay," she whispered. "Really, Dane."

His hand was clutching hers bruisingly. He realized it and loosened his grip. Neither of them noticed Kit, who was sipping coffee and trying to be invisible.

"See a doctor, will you?" he asked tightly. "Don't take chances with your health."

"I'll do that," she promised. Her eyes slid to his mouth and she forcefully levered them back up to his. "Are *you* all right?" she asked softly.

Her voice made him warm all over. His cheeks went ruddy as he looked at her, and his heart raced. "No," he said huskily. He drew in a sharp breath, fighting down the need to beg her to come back. "Maybe I miss you, pretty girl," he drawled, his smile faintly mocking.

"Maybe beans walk," she returned, smiling back.

His broad shoulders rose and fell. "You could do skip tracing for me, I guess," he murmured reluctantly.

"You've got three skip tracers already," she reminded him, although the offer made her tingle. He had to miss her a little, even if he didn't want to.

"I'll fire one," he offered.

She laughed. "No. I'm happy with Mr. Short, Dane," she said after a minute. "It wouldn't work out."

"You could give it a chance," he said slowly, with an expression in his eyes that she couldn't understand.

"The job?" She faltered.

He hesitated. He wanted to say, *No, not the job, me.* He wanted to ask her to pack a suitcase and move in with him, live with him, sleep with him. Nothing could be as bad as life without her. Perhaps if she cared enough, they could build some kind of marriage even if children were impossible. God knew, he wanted her enough to risk it. She'd loved him once; he knew she had. There might still be time....

But she laughed suddenly again, hiding her own feelings. "I don't want to come back, thanks all the same," she said, sparing him the embarrassment of knowing she was still hopelessly in love with him. She didn't want his pity. "I'm very happy, Dane. I like what I'm doing, and Mr. Short even asked me out. Who knows where it might lead?"

Dane's eyes went black, glittery. "Short's in his forties," he said through his teeth. "Too old and too much of a philanderer…!"

"Is that the time?" Kit interrupted, seeing danger signals ahead. "Gosh, I've got to go, Tess!"

"Yes, I'll be late, too," Tess said, staring pointedly at Dane, who was blocking her exit.

He got to his feet slowly, vibrating with anger. Short, with his Tess! He felt like hitting something.

Tess got to her feet slowly and clasped her bag while Kit left the tip. "It was nice to see you," she said hesitantly.

Dane didn't speak. He looked at her blindly, anger in every line of his tall, fit body. All at once, he frowned. His eyes went over her like hands and the scowl grew worse.

"You've gained weight, haven't you?" he asked suddenly.

"A little." She avoided his piercing gaze. "Too many doughnuts."

"No. No, it suits you," he said hesitantly.

She bit her lower lip almost hard enough to draw blood. She wanted to tell him. It was killing her not to tell him. She had no idea how he'd react, and it would probably be a bad thing, with the problems she'd been having. But it was his right to know. Committed, she raised her eyes to his and opened her mouth to speak. But before she could form a word, a passerby recognized him and stepped forward, hand out, grinning.

"Dane Lassiter! I thought it was you!" the man said enthusiastically.

While Dane was fielding his acquaintance's greeting, Tess darted around him and followed Kit out of the restaurant. It had to be fate, she told herself, her heart racing as she realized how close she'd come to blowing her cover. She shouldn't tell him yet. Not until she'd seen the doctor. After she found out what was wrong, she could make decisions.

"I'll bet he followed me," Kit mused as they went to their respective cars. "He isn't a private detective for nothing. He misses you, Tess. A blind person could see it."

"Missing and loving are two different things," she sighed.

"He had to have cared a little bit. After all, it took two for you to be in that condition," the other girl began.

"I seduced him," Tess said, flushing. "I had some crazy idea that if I could convince him of how deeply I loved him, he might start believing in commitment again. But it didn't work. He couldn't shoot me out of the door fast enough."

"He doesn't look as if he likes having you out the door."

Tess shrugged. "It still isn't enough. I can't go back to work for him. I'd eat my heart out. Especially now, I don't need to be around him. He isn't stupid. Eventually, my condition will become obvious."

"Forgive me, but it's already getting there. He's bound to find out," Kit said.

"I know. I'll deal with that when I have to. Right now, I have to get back to work. Not a word to Helen," she cautioned.

"Not a word to anybody. You know me better than that." Kit frowned. "Tess, I'd do anything I could to help you. I hope you know you can depend on me."

"I do. You're the only friend I have."

"That works both ways. Keep in close touch, okay? And let me know what the doctor says."

"I will." Tess got into her small foreign car and waved as she started it and drove back to work. She felt unnerved, and she wondered if it was only because she'd unexpectedly seen Dane. She was uneasy for the rest of the day, without knowing why.

Chapter Nine

Tess was thirty minutes early for her appointment with Dr. Boswick. She hadn't slept or eaten much since the day before. The unexpected pains she'd had in the restaurant had frightened her. Dane had been beside her, holding her hand, and the pain had dissipated much sooner than usual. Mystical, she thought, as if the child had heard its father's voice and had felt compelled to survive. No doctor, she was sure, would subscribe to *that* theory.

Dr. Boswick was right on schedule, so she didn't have to wait long. But the tests he performed told him something she didn't want to hear. He called her into his office and sat down behind his desk, poring through test results, having had her come back after work to talk to him.

He laid down the open file folder and looked at her over his glasses. "How badly do you want this baby?" he asked abruptly. "I know you're single, and not well-to-do, so think carefully before you answer."

She didn't understand what her financial situation

had to do with it, but the question was easily answered. "I want him more than anything in the world," she said simply.

He smiled gently. "I'm glad you put it that way, because you've got some hard times ahead and no guarantees even then." He swung forward in the chair and leaned his hands on the desk, aware of her taut, worried expression. "You have a rather rare condition—one we sometimes see in the second or third trimester—where the placenta partially or completely covers the cervix. The placenta stretches, sometimes tears. There can be frequent bleeding and the danger of spontaneous abortion."

"Oh, no!" she ground out.

"It happens to some degree in only about one out of every two hundred pregnancies," he continued. "We found an abnormal placement of the placenta in the ultrasound we did earlier. It usually occurs in women who have had multiple pregnancies, and later than this. You're not that far along. Your case is unusual, but this does happen."

"Is there anything I can do?" she asked frantically. "Anything at all?"

"Yes. You can quit your job and stay home until your pregnancy advances sufficiently that we can ascertain whether or not the placenta is going to detach itself from the cervix. That will probably be until you deliver—a normal delivery, I hope, but sometimes a C-section is mandatory. In the meantime, you won't be able to do a lot of walking, and working at a job isn't advisable, either. For God's sake," he added, "don't take aspirin during your pregnancy."

"I'll remember that." Her face felt tight. She had very little in her savings account. She had monthly bills and she needed the job. But he was telling her that she might sacrifice her child if she didn't stay at home.

"As I said, there are no guarantees. You could still lose the child. There's another reason that you shouldn't be alone. Later on, there's a potential for massive bleeding with this condition. I don't want to frighten you, but you could hemorrhage. If there's any bleeding at all, I want to see you, night or day. That will mean complete bed rest until the bleeding stops. Perhaps hospitalization. You see what I meant when I asked how important this child was to you?"

She nodded, her fingers painfully entwined. "I live alone."

"There's no chance that the father might become involved in the pregnancy?"

She hesitated. Then she shook her head. "He doesn't know."

"He should be told."

"Yes, sir." She wasn't going to tell Dane, but it was easier to agree with the doctor than to argue.

"Good girl. You're going to need help. This won't be easy. Meanwhile, I'll have Bertha set up another appointment. You'll need to come fairly regularly. Don't worry about the bill," he added with a grin. "I trust you for it. We'll work something out. All right?"

"All right." She asked as many questions as she could, finding that knowledge was better than ignorance in such a situation. Then she went home and did what came naturally until her eyes were as red as her nose.

She laid her hand on the slight swell of her stomach and smiled through the tears. "Okay, buster, it's just you and me. I can't do it alone so you're going to have to help me. I want you, little one," she added with breathless tenderness. "You don't know how much! So will you try to stay alive, just for me?"

She laid her head back against the sofa and stared into space, her mind whirling with possibilities. No walking. No lifting. No strain of any kind. A quiet lifestyle, good food, no stress. That was pushing it for a single woman with no income, she mused. But she'd manage somehow. Women did, all over the world.

Telling Dane was out of the question, though. Even if he believed the baby was his, it would look as if she expected him to support her. It would mean living with him, letting him assume full responsibility for both of them. She couldn't do that to him. He didn't want commitment, he didn't want marriage. He'd said so forcefully when he'd thrown her out of his life, and she'd gone willingly. This was no time to open old wounds.

Someday, perhaps, she'd tell him, when she was back on her feet and no longer needed help. That way, she could go to him on an independent basis and let him decide if he wanted any part of the child's life.

That decided, she went and made herself a bowl of soup. There were all sorts of agencies to help expectant mothers, she knew. She'd just have to find one or two.

She quit her job the next day. Mr. Short was stunned. She explained that she had a bleeding ulcer—as good an excuse as any other lie, she thought miserably—and that her doctor had advised her to stop working for a couple of months. He was sympathetic and insisted on giving her two weeks severance pay, which was very good of him considering that she couldn't give notice and had left him shorthanded. She apologized profusely and went home to her apartment. She'd never felt so scared or alone in her life. Not that the baby wasn't going to be worth all the sacrifices, she assured herself. The baby would be her whole world!

She spent the next few days getting used to a new routine. She found a part-time job doing telephone sales from the apartment, which brought in a little income. She had enough money to pay the rent for three months, which she did to insure that she wouldn't get thrown out during the first part of her confinement. Since utilities were included in the rent, that was taken care of as well. One of the government agencies provided coupons for milk and cheese, to give the baby enough protein, and she arranged to make regular payments on Dr. Boswick's bill from what she brought in from telephone sales.

Meals were precarious. She made plenty of stews and casseroles to stretch her food budget, and took her prenatal vitamins regularly. The worst of it was being totally alone in the daytime. Her neighbors all worked, so there was no one she could call for help if she got into trouble.

She lost weight because of the strain and worry. There were still periods of spotting, when she had to call Dr. Boswick, and every episode meant days in bed until the bleeding stopped. She had to take extra iron tablets to compensate for the loss of blood. She was tired all the time.

Kit came to see her, bringing tasty things to tempt her appetite. Tess had sworn her to secrecy, and she stopped answering the phone so that nobody from Dane's office could reach her.

But if she thought those measures would discourage anyone from checking up on her sudden retirement from work, she was mistaken.

She woke to the sound of the doorbell being jabbed

repeatedly early one rainy morning two weeks later. Morning sickness still plagued her. She'd just returned from the bathroom and another bout of nausea. She was bundled up in her thick red bathrobe over striped pajamas, her hair tousled and needing cutting badly. She looked terrible. When she opened the door, annoyed at the repeated buzzing, she came face to face with Dane. He was more startled than she was.

"My God!" he swore slowly, his breath catching as he looked at her.

"Thanks, you look wonderful, too," she muttered weakly. "You'll have to let yourself in. I have to get back to bed before I fall down."

"Wait. I'll carry you."

He closed the door and picked her up before she could protest, hefting her easily against his chest. He frowned as he carried her into the bedroom. His back protested for the first time in memory, but he didn't let on to the fact. "You've gained weight again, or is it swelling from the ulcer?" He laid her gently on the bed and started to remove the robe.

She couldn't risk having him see her body, so she caught his fingers. "I'm cold, leave it on," she said huskily.

"Okay." He pulled the covers over her and sat down beside her, his eyes dark with concern. "Short told me you'd quit. Are you getting treatment, for God's sake?"

She stared at him, feeling alone and frightened, a sense of hopelessness in her eyes. He looked very successful in his charcoal gray suit, with a red-and-black striped tie and a matching handkerchief in his watch pocket. By comparison, she looked like something the cat had brought in.

"Treatment?" she asked absently. She grimaced and

tears gathered hotly in her eyes. "There is no treatment," she whispered huskily. "The doctor's already done all he can do."

He scowled. "For a bleeding ulcer?"

"It isn't a bleeding ulcer," she said dully, closing her eyes.

He stilled. "Then what is it?"

"Nothing that can be cured with a pill, I'm afraid," she said tiredly. "Dane, I'm so tired...!"

"What do you have?" he asked with concern he couldn't hide. He looked pale, she thought. Then she realized what he must be thinking.

"Oh," she said, her mind finally grasping what he thought. "No, it's not cancer. I'm not dying. Really I'm not. I don't have anything terminal."

He let out a heavy breath and fumbled in his pocket for a cigarette. "God, you scared me to death," he ground out. "If it's not that, and not a bleeding ulcer, what did you mean there's nothing they can do?"

She hesitated. Now that he was here, she wanted to tell him. She was afraid and alone, and she wanted to lean on him, to be taken care of, protected. She wanted him to know about the child. But would it be fair to tell him? Now, when she was so close to losing it?

He saw the tormented look in her eyes without understanding it. He touched her dull hair curiously. "You look terrible," he said. He studied her narrowly. "Are you going to tell me what's the matter with you, Tess?"

She nibbled on her lower lip. "I don't know if I should," she said honestly. "You may not believe me. Even if you do, I'm not sure it's fair."

He looked at her with quiet contentment. Even when she was half-dead with illness, he felt at home with her.

At peace. He smoothed her hair away from her fore-head. "All the color is gone, did you know?" he asked quietly. "I get up, I go to work, I go home and I lie awake at night. I don't care about the job, or much else. You took the joy out of living when you went away."

"You sent me away," she said softly.

He searched her pained eyes. "Yes. I didn't want anything permanent...."

"I haven't asked for anything permanent," she interrupted. "You don't have to worry that I would. I'm not asking for anything now, although it might sound like it, I guess."

He scowled. "Explain that."

She took a deep breath and met his eyes reluctantly. "Dane...I'm pregnant."

The look on his face might, in other circumstances have been comical. He stopped with the cigarette an inch from his mouth and stared at her like a man who'd been bashed in the head with a shovel.

He lowered the cigarette very slowly and without thinking dropped it into a glass of water on the bedside table. "You're what?" he asked in a choked tone.

"I'm going to have a baby."

Something in his expression made her nervous. He looked ill. His eyes glittered in a countenance that seemed carved out of stone. Slowly, slowly, his gaze moved down her body. He reached out, drawing the covers away. His hands found the tie of the robe and loosened it. He pulled the thick red fabric away from her body and unsnapped the catch of her pajama pants before she could protest. Then he peeled them back from the slight, swollen softness of her stomach and sat staring at it like a demented man.

"You didn't tell me," he said roughly.

''I didn't know how,'' she groaned. Her anguished eyes searched his face.

Slowly, he stretched both his lean, warm hands toward her belly and touched it. There was something reverent about the way he did it, about the hushed rasp of his breathing. He lifted his dark eyes to hers and his cheekbones flushed with building temper.

''I thought I couldn't father a child. You knew that. God in heaven, how could you have kept it from me?''

She hesitated. ''I'm sorry,'' she said, too shaken by his reaction to try to explain her reasoning.

''Sorry...!'' He bit off what he was going to say as the enormity of her condition got through to him. ''When is he due?'' he asked, glaring at her. ''How soon?''

She managed to meet his stormy eyes. ''Five months.'' She hesitated, indecision tearing her apart. His face was livid with his discovery, with the pleasure he couldn't hide of knowing that he'd fathered her child. How could she destroy his peace of mind, now? But she had to give some excuse for staying home, for her inactivity. She bit her lip. ''Dane...'' She swallowed. ''I have to stay at home until I deliver. I can't work.''

''Why?'' he asked curtly.

She hesitated. Her eyes adored him involuntarily. She loved him far too much to tell him how dangerous the pregnancy was, how much risk was involved. Fear for the child would drive him mad.

''I'm having a lot of morning sickness,'' she hedged.

''I see.'' Obviously relieved, he let out a sigh.

He got up from the bed and turned away, running a restless hand around the back of his neck as he stared blindly at the wall.

"You don't have to feel responsible," she said help-lessly.

"Don't be absurd. It's my baby." He turned, his face slowly changing with dawning wonder as he looked down at her. "My baby," he repeated slowly, his eyes on her stomach. He smiled faintly. Then his dark eyes cut at her. "And you weren't even going to tell me, damn you!"

She cringed at his tone. But it was either let him believe that, or force him to share her quiet terror. He'd been through so much in the past few years. His mother's death, his horrible injury in the shooting, the loss of his job. No, she thought with helpless compassion, no, not this, too. She lifted her face bravely. "You said you didn't want commitment, remember?" she asked coolly. "You wanted me out of your life. If I'd told you about the baby, you'd have thought I was try-ing to trap you," she said instead.

The accusation made him feel guilty. She didn't know how he really felt. She looked indifferent, and he wasn't confident about revealing his emotions right now. He'd told her he didn't want commitment, sure, but that was when he thought he couldn't give her a full marriage. Now he could, but she didn't seem to want him anymore.

He drew back into himself. It was the child he had to be concerned with now. Later, he and Tess could sort themselves out. First things first. "Things have changed," he said quietly.

"You mean you didn't want me, but the baby is another matter."

Her expression kindled his temper. "Of course," he said with a mocking smile, lashing out at her.

She stared at him with a breaking heart, but she

didn't dare let him know how much that flat statement had hurt.

"Did you ever plan to tell me?" he persisted.

"Yes," she said. "Eventually."

"When?" he drawled, his black eyes accusing. "After he started school? Well, you don't need to tell me now. I know." He stuck a lean hand in his slacks pocket and stared at her, refusing to let his emotions show. Her treachery in hiding her condition from him, when she knew he thought he was sterile, was going to take some forgiveness, but that might come in time. "I'll take you down to the ranch," he said, thinking out loud. "You'll have Beryl for company."

"No," she murmured, averting her eyes. "I—can't go there."

He frowned. Then he remembered what he'd told her about Beryl. They weren't married and she was pregnant.

Inside, he brightened. Now he had a concrete reason for marrying her, one that spared him from revealing his real feelings. Let her think it was only because of the child.

"We'll work out something." He flicked his cuff back and looked at his watch, his mind churning. "I'll be back in a few minutes."

"Dane, we have to talk," she began.

"Later."

He glanced at her again with quiet possessiveness, but he didn't speak. He left the apartment and Tess lay back, disturbed and saddened by the way he was acting. He'd admitted that the child was all he wanted. She'd hoped he might have missed her, wanted her back, but that was daydreaming.

If his appearance in her life had been a shock, what

he came back with three hours later was devastating. He dragged a strange man into the room with him, handed her a pen and a sheet of paper and indicated where she was to sign it and how. He didn't even give her time to read it before he laid it on the table and sat down beside her, taking her hand in his.

"Go ahead," he told the man.

The man produced a small book, smiled, and proceeded to read a wedding service. Tess was so shocked that she was barely able to answer when called upon. Before she knew it, Dane was sliding a plain gold band—two sizes too big—on her finger, and she was married.

"Dane…!" she protested.

He got up and shook hands with the man, let him sign the paper, handed him a wad of bills and escorted him to the door with profuse thanks.

When he'd let him out, Dane moved back to the bed and looked down at Tess. She was his wife now. She belonged to him—she and the baby. His baby. His chest swelled with raging pride.

She looked at the ring on her finger dazedly, trying to equate it with the odd look on Dane's face, the glittery darkness of his eyes.

"It takes three…three days to get married…." she stammered.

"It takes one if you threaten to shoot a judge," he said pleasantly. "Don't worry, it's perfectly legal." He frowned thoughtfully. "I don't know about the kidnapping charge, though."

"What kidnapping?"

"The probate judge who just married us didn't know he was going to," he explained. "I appropriated him at the courthouse and brought him with me."

She laughed. Then she cried. It was so unlike Dane to be impulsive like that.

He cursed under his breath. "All right, I'm sorry I had to spring it on you without any warning," he said stiffly. "But we had to present Beryl with a fait accompli when I take you there tonight."

"It isn't fair that she has to be responsible for me," she whispered. "Or you, either, for that matter."

He lifted his head. "You have my baby inside you," he said, his eyes darkening as he searched hers. It took all his willpower to keep himself from lifting her into his arms and kissing those tears away. "The baby is all that matters right now. My God, it's everything!" he breathed huskily.

He certainly did want the child, she thought sadly. She stared at his tie, wondering how he was going to feel if she lost it, if he ended up married to her for no reason. It would be so much worse, because she hadn't told him the truth. But how could she?

"Stop brooding," he said. "I'll take care of you, Miss Meriwether." He hesitated. "Mrs. Lassiter," he corrected. The name had a new sound, a different sound from when it had been used for Jane. "Mrs. Teresa Lassiter," he murmured.

She lifted her sad eyes to his. "You really do want the baby, don't you?"

His face went hard. "You know that already. Hadn't you realized how I felt, thinking that I couldn't father a child? Didn't it matter to you?"

She stiffened miserably. "Yes, it mattered...." She choked and shifted. "I didn't want you to feel trapped, or that you had to marry me," she said finally, giving him the only reason she felt safe disclosing. "I knew you didn't want to marry again. You'd said so half a dozen times.''

He only looked at her, his eyes narrow and probing. That had been true, until he'd made such long, sweet love to her. After that, she'd become his world. The baby was a bonus, a big one, but it was her he'd wanted. He hadn't wanted to marry her and have her grieve for lack of a child. Jane's obsession to get pregnant had left deep scars on his emotions. They'd influenced his attitude toward Tess. Now, all he wanted was Tess. He wanted his child, too. But she'd meant to keep her conception a secret, and he didn't think it was because of the flimsy reason she'd given him. Did she hate him now—was that it? Had his treatment of her killed what she'd once felt for him? Uncertain, he withdrew behind a camouflage of anger.

''Whether or not I wanted to remarry is a moot point now, isn't it?'' he asked, more harshly than he'd intended. ''The child has to have a name. We'll get by, somehow.''

That wasn't what she wanted to hear. She wanted him to say that he loved her desperately, that he'd want her even if she wasn't carrying his child, that he'd missed her and needed her. None of that was realistic, though. The truth was that he'd done very well without her. If not for the baby, he'd never have come near her again.

His presence in the restaurant that day was puzzling, though. Why had he been there? Kit had hinted that he'd wanted to see Tess. She didn't believe it. Dane knew where she lived. He could have seen her anytime. No, Kit was wrong. It had only been a coincidence. She'd looked bad and he'd felt sorry for her. She drooped a little, worn out from the emotional strain of the day.

"I want you to change clothes, if you can manage. Then we'll get your things together and go down to the ranch. I guess morning sickness can be pretty debilitating."

"Yes," she said evasively. "It can. I'd like to have a bath first," she said weakly.

"Are you up to it?"

She nodded. "The nausea is the worst when I first wake up. I'll be all right."

"Tell me what to pack and where to find it. I'll take care of that. If you need me, I'll be within earshot."

She did, amazed at how quickly he'd taken over. It was nice to have everything arranged, to be looked after. She was too weak and sick to take care of herself. She wouldn't think about his motives. If she did, she'd go crazy.

An hour later, bathed and dressed, she let Dane lead her out to the black Mercedes. He'd already talked to the landlord—God knew what he'd said—and her bags were packed and in the car.

She worried all the way to Branntville about what Beryl was going to say. Dane talked to her about work, about Helen and the staff, but she barely heard him. She was too upset to listen.

She needn't have worried. Beryl came out to the car to meet her, looking motherly.

"You poor child," she said gently, opening the door for her. "Don't you worry about a thing," she said sternly. "It's going to be all right. When Dane can't be here, I will. I won't let anything happen to you."

It was too much, after all the worry. She broke down, letting Beryl cuddle her while she cried her heart out.

"Here, this won't do," Dane said finally. He drew her away from Beryl and lifted her against him. "I'll carry you inside. You need to rest. It's been a long day."

"I'll warm up some of the nice chicken soup I made," Beryl promised. "You'll like it. It will be good for the baby," she added, her eyes twinkling as she went ahead of them.

"You told her?" Tess asked Dane.

"Yes." He searched her eyes. "Everything's all right. All you have to do is rest."

She nodded. But she was thinking that life wasn't that simple. It seemed suddenly very much harder than it had been, with the man she loved most in the world both so close and so far away, and her baby under constant threat. She wondered if she might go quietly mad.

Chapter Ten

Dane had his evening meal in the room with Tess. Beryl had helped her into a pair of clean pajamas and a matching robe, and had tucked her up in the big antique four-poster bed, sympathizing with Tess's incapacitating nausea. Tess felt guilty letting Beryl and Dane believe it was only that. But she'd have felt worse telling them the truth.

This wasn't the same bed she'd slept in the last time she'd been at the ranch, and it was in a different part of the sprawling house. She hadn't asked Beryl why she was in here, or if it was near Dane's room. She'd been too shy.

"Eat," he told her firmly, watching her toy with her spoon.

"Sorry. I was just wondering whose room this was."

"It's mine," he said quietly, watching her start. He nodded grimly. "That's right. You're sharing it with me."

She stared at him wildly. They couldn't be intimate, but how was she going to tell him that without telling him everything? "Dane..." she began worriedly after she'd lifted a spoonful of hot, delicious chicken soup to her mouth.

"I know that sex can be unpleasant for a pregnant woman," he said unexpectedly. "I want you with me at night, that's all. If you need me, I'll be close by."

His concern touched her, even as the flat statement about no intimacy reassured her. "Thank you."

He hated her look of relief. It made him feel unwanted, but he disguised his reaction. "Have you thought about names? Do you hope it's a boy or do you want a little girl?" he asked.

She'd been afraid to hope, but he couldn't know that. "No. I don't care if it's a boy or a girl."

"Neither do I," he replied. "As long as the baby's healthy, that's all that matters."

She nodded. "You were an only child, weren't you?" she said, desperate to change the subject.

"Yes, but my mother didn't really want me," he said bitterly, his eyes going dark with remembered pain.

"This baby will be wanted," she said softly.

His eyes lifted. He looked at her, sitting there so vulnerable and pretty in his bed, her blond hair soft and curling, her big gray eyes watching him. "He certainly will."

"Was your father an only child?"

"I don't know," he said. "He never talked about his family. He vanished when I was young, and I didn't hear from him again. My mother had two brothers, but they died in Vietnam, both of them."

"You and your mother never got along, even when you were a child?" she asked.

"No." He closed up. "Eat your soup."

She grimaced and went back to the nourishing liquid. He had a knack for closing doors, she thought.

They'd eaten fairly late. Dane took time to check with his ranch foreman before he came back into the bedroom and began stripping off his clothes.

Tess tried not to watch, but she couldn't help it. He was the most magnificent man she'd ever seen. Her eyes lingered on the deep scars on his back and shoulder before he turned, and then her attention was captured by the powerful lines of his arms and chest. She was so preoccupied that he'd taken off everything he was wearing before she became aware of it—and the fact that she was staring. She went scarlet.

He smiled faintly as he moved to turn off the lights. "You'll get used to me," he said, ignoring her scarlet blush. "I wore pajamas for your sake at the apartment, but we're married now. I've slept this way since I was a boy. Old habits are hard to part with."

"I don't mind," she said as he climbed in under the covers beside her. "It's your bedroom, after all."

"Know where the controls are for the electric blanket? It's spring, but the weather still turns cold sometimes at night."

"Yes, I found them earlier." She lay quietly under the soft warmth of the sheet and electric blanket, her eyes on the dark ceiling, trying not to move around and disturb him. This was familiar, because she'd slept with him once before. But then it had been new and exciting and she'd slept because of exhaustion. Now, it was difficult to get used to having someone beside her in the darkness. Not only that, she could feel his resentment, his displeasure.

His hand suddenly slid over her stomach and pressed there, making her jump.

"Don't have hysterics. I want to feel him. Does he move yet?"

She swallowed. The feel of his hand was comforting as much as disturbing. "Little flutters," she managed. "He'll start to kick soon."

"Are you going to nurse him, Tess?"

Her heart skipped. She thought about it, about the advantages of it that she'd read about in magazines. "Yes. I want to, very much."

She held her breath, hoping that he might pull her close and cradle her in his arms while she slept. But he didn't. He removed his hand and she felt him turn away form her. It was like a harbinger of things to come. It made her nervous.

She didn't know that he was concealing an explosion of emotions he didn't want her to sense. He felt like a magician when he thought of her pregnancy. He'd never wanted anything as much as he wanted this child; anything, except Tess herself. That was something he couldn't quite admit yet. His emotional scars were hurting. He'd thought he could trust Tess because she loved him, but she'd denied him the one miracle of his life— the knowledge of his paternity. If he hadn't gone looking for her, she wouldn't have told him. It didn't bear thinking about.

He closed his eyes with a rough sigh and finally slept.

From that night on, the distance between them grew. Tess became quiet and shy around him. At night he had to reach for her. She never went to him voluntarily, never teased him or played with him or looked at him with love in her eyes as she had months before. The baby began to kick, and she longed to share it with

him, but she was too subdued to invite that intimacy.
He never touched her these days. He talked about the
future sometimes, but the conversation was always
about the baby, never about Tess and himself.

Tess grew depressed. They seemed not to be able to
communicate anymore. Tess helped Beryl work in the
flower beds during the warm afternoons, but Dane soon
noticed that she seemed to do nothing strenuous at all.
She never exerted herself. That disturbed him, because
exercise, he'd been told, made the delivery all that
much easier.

"You don't do enough," he said one evening after
he'd come home from work. "You sit around all day.
I want you to start walking. No arguments," he said
firmly when she started. "This inactivity isn't healthy
for the child. Tomorrow when I get home, we'll take a
nice turn around the ranch."

"Dane," she began nervously.

He glanced at his watch. "I'm on stakeout tonight.
We'll talk later, Tess. Don't stay up too late. It isn't
good for the baby."

She could have screamed. Everything he said or did
was with the baby in mind. She was only the incubator,
it seemed. Not that she wasn't concerned about her
child; she was all too concerned. She hadn't told him
the truth, and now things were going to get dangerous
if he insisted on her walking. It could cause the bleeding to come back again.

She'd felt a revival of good health since she'd been
with him. The pain had stopped, and the bleeding had
stopped, too. She felt optimistic for the first time. But
what he proposed could cost her the child. She worried
all night about how or if to tell him the truth.

Fortunately, his stakeout extended for the next several days, and Tess learned to lie. Beryl went to help out an elderly neighbor an hour a day, and during her absence, Tess told Dane, she made sure that she walked.

He froze up, disturbed that she seemed to be making sure that he spent no time at all with her.

"Is my company that distasteful to you?" he demanded coldly, his smile no smile at all. "You can't bear having me near you, so you go walking when I'm not around, is that it?"

"No!"

"Well, don't sweat it, honey," he said icily. "It's the baby I'm concerned with, not you."

He'd lashed out in a moment of fury, but Tess didn't know that it was because she'd hurt him. She winced at the anger, at his flat statement that she didn't matter to him. It was no more than she'd expected, but it left a deep wound.

She turned away, her face lifted proudly. "I'll make sure the baby isn't harmed by my life-style."

"See that you do. Mrs. Lassiter," he added with venom.

She looked up at him, her eyes quietly accusing. "If I hadn't been pregnant, you'd never have married me, would you?"

"Didn't you know that already?" he agreed unsmilingly. "You're treacherous, Tess, like the rest of your sex. My mother drove my father away. She broke him, because he loved her. Jane very nearly did the same damned thing to me with her obsession to become pregnant, her distaste for my job. You were the last person in the world I'd have expected to put a knife in my back. My mistake. You won't get a second chance. Just be sure you don't harm my child," he said with cold authority.

"I didn't hide it from you to hurt you," she blurted.

He ignored that. "I'll be late for work."

"Why won't you talk to me?" she ground out. "You can't even be bothered to come home at night anymore. You're always gone."

He couldn't admit how hungry he was for her. He stayed away because the mask slipped sometimes when he looked at her, because he cared too much. "What is there to say?" he asked evasively. "You seduced me into your arms the night we made the baby. I gave in, because I wanted you. But it was only desire. You understand? Only that. Nothing more."

A light went out in her. "Yes, Dane," she said. "I understand."

She left the room, tears blinding her. He couldn't have made it any more plain than that.

He slammed his fist down on the dresser top in impotent rage. He hadn't meant to say that, to belittle the exquisite loving they'd shared. He didn't trust her. He couldn't. She was like his mother, like Jane. She was going to sell him out. In fact, she already had, by hiding her pregnancy. She didn't love him now. She avoided him, never looked at him. The baby was all she seemed interested in. He had to remember that and not weaken again. But it was hard. He adored her, never more than now, as she blossomed with his child. It should have been a time of sharing, of unequaled closeness. But he withdrew, because she pushed him away. Nothing had ever hurt quite so much.

Weeks turned to months. Dane and Tess lived like polite strangers. He'd long since moved her into another bedroom, with the excuse that he was disturbing her sleep with his late hours. It wasn't true. Her silence, her depression was disturbing him. She looked at him with an expression he couldn't fathom, as if she were hurting and hiding it. He felt guilty every time he saw her and he didn't know why. Being near her and unable to touch her, to hold her, was killing him. He sat and stared at her when she wasn't looking, like a lovesick boy. His work suffered because he couldn't keep his mind off her. She grew bigger and paler, and one day, after she'd been to see her obstetrician, she took to her bed and stayed there. That disturbed him, and he said something about it.

"Are you all right?" he asked her that evening, his eyes concerned.

"Of course," she replied, her face schooled to disguise her terror. She'd had a lot of bleeding and Dr. Boswick was worried. He didn't say so, but his expression hadn't been reassuring. She was scared and she wanted to tell Dane, but it was far too late for that. "I'm just tired. There's so much of me to carry around," she added impotently.

"I told you before," he said quietly, "that I don't want you lying around the house. You have to get enough exercise. I'm sure the obstetrician's told you that."

She felt near panic. It was fall now and good walking weather, but she didn't dare! Dane was still irritable since she'd refused to go to natural childbirth classes with him. She was too afraid of the trips to and from the hospital where they were given, because what Dr. Boswick had told her about the final trimester unnerved her. He had said the method might help, but he hadn't pressured her to attend the classes. He knew how afraid she was.

Her visits to the obstetrician had been very close together lately, and fortunately, Dane didn't know why. She'd managed to keep her secret, despite his cold indifference to her feelings. She'd protected him from the fear. She knew all too well how much a child would mean to him. She wanted him to have his son—Dr. Boswick had told her that it would be a boy.

She looked up at Dane from her reclining position on the bed, propped up by pillows because she was so big now, in her eighth month.

"I'll go walking tomorrow," she promised. "It's so hard these days. I'm heavier than I've ever been."

His dark eyes narrowed on her wan, pinched face. He felt guilty all over again, just looking at her. "Why is it that I never see you walk?" he asked. "You always arrange to do it when no one is here except you."

She colored and averted his eyes.

"I know you're heavy. But, Tess, laziness is no excuse," he said quietly. "This is for your own good. Tomorrow, you walk. I'll make sure of it."

"No," she replied wearily, tired of the deception. "No, I can't do that." She took a deep breath. "Dane, there's something I haven't told you, something you need to know…. Oh!" She gasped at the wrenching pain that caught her unaware and lifted her straight up on the bed. She cried out piteously.

"The baby!" he exclaimed harshly. "Tess, is it the baby?"

"Yes…!" She wept because the sudden contractions were so fierce. Even as she felt them, she felt a terrifying gush of wet warmth beneath her and her face went stark white. "You have…to get…an ambulance! Call Dr. Boswick…!"

"It may be false labor. You're a month early. I'll

take you in the car," he began tersely, and threw back the covers.

He froze. Every drop of color ran out of his face, every sign of life. His black eyes glittered like diamond fragments. "Oh, my God!" he exploded.

"Call…an ambulance!" she cried.

He grabbed up the telephone by the bed, galvanized into action. Beryl came running while he was talking to the hospital and, seeing the situation for herself, went running to get towels.

Assured that an ambulance was already in their end of the county and could be there in five minutes, he dialed Dr. Boswick.

"I think there's something wrong. She's in pain and bleeding badly," Dane said, his voice cold but unsteady. "The ambulance is on the way."

"The placenta has detached," came the terse reply. "When I examined her today, I warned her that it could happen any time. The baby is near enough to term that it has a chance, but we could still lose both of them," he said, and Dane's heart stopped. "She hasn't been exercising today?"

Dane's fingers shook on the receiver. "No."

"Thank God for that. I'm sure she's told you how dangerous her condition is, so that you wouldn't allow her to exert unnecessarily. I'll be at the emergency room when they bring her in, and we'll gear up for a transfusion." He told Dane what to do, to help contain the bleeding. "Tell those paramedics that every second counts."

Dane hung up, tossing orders to Beryl. He looked down at Tess with anguished realization.

"Something went wrong a long time ago, didn't it? It's been there all along. It wasn't morning sickness that kept you home at all," he ground out, his voice tormented.

Her lips were white as she compressed them, trying not to scream from the pain. "You wanted...the baby...so much," she panted. "I only wanted...to spare you," she whispered weakly. "Not...your fault!"

"So you took the risk and the worry all alone, and I gave you hell.... Oh, God, Tess...!" His voice broke. He touched her face with unsteady fingers, as she arched and cried out again from the force of the pain.

"Where the hell is that ambulance?" he cursed.

A faint sound of sirens was barely audible as Tess caught her breath. "Hold on, little one," he said huskily, motioning for Beryl to stay with her. He went out of the room as the sirens approached, so shaken that he could hardly speak at all.

Tess was barely conscious on the long drive to the hospital. Dane sat beside her in a terrified posture while the ambulance attendants kept watch on her and did what they could to stem the profuse bleeding. Dr. Boswick was waiting when they wheeled her into Branntville General.

"She comes first," Dane told the doctor, white-faced. "No matter what, she comes first, do you understand?"

"We'll do everything we can," Boswick assured him. They rushed her to the operating room and, minutes later, took the baby.

She was drifting through layers of pain and drug-induced drowsiness when she heard a voice at her ear.

"It's a boy," Dane whispered. "Can you hear me, sweetheart? We have a little boy."

She barely made sense of the words. "John Richard," she whispered with difficulty.

It was the name they'd both chosen for a boy, on one of the rare evenings when he'd been home on time and they'd talked. He touched her mouth with his. "John Richard," he whispered. "How do you feel, darling?"

That couldn't be Dane calling her darling. She must be delirious. "Hurts," she said weakly.

"They'll give you something else. The nurse is bringing a shot for you. He's so beautiful, Tess," he said unsteadily. "So beautiful."

Her eyes opened, glazed with pain. She looked up at him. "Love…you," she managed. "Whatever happens…always remember."

His eyes were wet. She couldn't see them clearly, but she heard the rough sound he made.

"You're going to be all right," he said harshly. "They said so. Don't talk like that!"

Her eyelids were so heavy. She felt them close. "Take care of him," she said weakly. "You wanted him…so much."

"I want you!" He leaned close, his voice in her ear. "Listen to me, you silly child, I lied! I've been lying all along! I didn't think I could give you a child—that's why I didn't want to marry you! It was for your sake, not mine, that I let you go! Tess, it's you I want! You! God in Heaven, I almost went out of my mind when Dr. Boswick told me about your condition after they took the baby. Open your eyes, Tess. Open your eyes!"

He sounded urgent, almost desperate. She forced her eyelids open again with an effort and tried to focus. His face was white. Stark white.

"Don't you die on me!" he said through his teeth. "Don't you dare! You're going to live and help me raise our baby. I'm not going to try and live without you again! I can't. Listen to me—I can't make it without you!''

"Only...the baby...you want," she managed.

"No."

Nothing he said was getting through the pain. "Yes. You said..."

He realized that she wasn't comprehending any of it. He had to make her listen, make her understand, while there was still time! "Look at me. Tess, look at me. Look at me!"

She swallowed, forcing her eyes toward his face.

"I love you." He said each word deliberately, forcefully. His eyes were blazing like black coals in his face. "I love you!"

That was nice. She tried to say so, but darkness fell on her like a wall. She closed her eyes, and the anguished sound of his voice slowly became indistinguishable. She slept.

Chapter Eleven

Dane sat beside her all night without sleeping. He couldn't bring himself to leave her, not even to see the son he'd thought he'd never have.

Her face was pale and she cried out with the pain, even with the sedatives they were giving her. He watched her suffer, and suffered with her. It devastated him to know what she'd gone through in such silence, sparing him from the worry that had haunted her all these long months. He'd accused her of betraying him, when she was in fact protecting him. She'd loved him and he'd failed her at every turn, when he loved her more than his own life.

But she didn't know that. He'd said so many cruel things to her. She might not be able to forgive him, but she had to stay alive. She had to!

Daylight was streaming in the windows and the hospital was bustling with activity when she finally came back to consciousness. She was weak and still in pain.

She opened her eyes. "Dane?" she whispered. "My baby...?"

He looked terrible, she thought dimly. His face was unshaven and starkly lined.

"Do you want the baby now?" he asked gently, bending over her. "They'll bring him whenever you like. Right now, if you want."

She swallowed. "I want to see him."

He pushed the buzzer and called the nurse, asking for John to be brought in. The cheerful voice promised instant compliance. Sure enough, barely two minutes later, a nurse came into the room with a small bundle in her arms.

"Here he is, Mrs. Lassiter," the nurse said cheerfully. "I'm glad to see you awake. You had us worried for a little while. Look what I've got."

She laid the bundle down beside Tess and pulled the blanket away from the baby's face.

Tess looked at him and saw Dane. She caught her breath. "He looks like my husband," she whispered. "Oh, he looks like you, Dane!"

He leaned over her, touching the baby's head gently. "He has your eyes," he disagreed. "Big and soft."

"I'll bring his bottle—" the nurse began.

"No," Tess protested. She looked up. "Please. I want to feed him myself. Dr. Boswick said—"

"All right." The nurse smiled. "We'll bring the bottle, too. You're very weak. You lost a lot of blood, and you may not have enough milk yet to satisfy him."

The nurse went out and Tess fought pain to sit up against the pillows with the baby in her arms. "Help me, please," she whispered, tugging at the neck of the gown.

He found the ties and helped her ease the gown away. She brought the baby to her breast and gently nudged the nipple into his mouth. He began to suckle at once, his tiny hand clenched against her breast.

She caught her breath at the pins-and-needles sensation, and then she laughed. She looked up at Dane, but he wasn't laughing. His face was rigid and ruddy with color as he watched. His jaw clenched.

"My God," he said unsteadily. "I didn't realize it would look like that." He moved closer, his eyes helplessly riveted to the baby. He reached down and lightly touched the small head before he looked into Tess's eyes. "Does it hurt you?" he asked.

"No," she said. "It's uncomfortable just at first, that's all. My stomach feels awful," she grimaced. "The stitches pull and it hurts."

"They can give you something else when you're finished with John Richard."

"You aren't at work," she said, frowning.

"I couldn't leave you, honey," he replied quietly. "You scared me."

"Scared you?"

He hesitated for a long moment before he spoke. "You sounded as if you meant to go away," he said. His hand touched her mouth. "I was afraid you didn't want to live."

"I don't remember."

"It could have been the drugs, but I couldn't take a chance." He bent and kissed her gently. "You mean the world to me," he said huskily. "I can't lose you now."

She didn't trust her ears, or her mind. She only smiled, certain that it was the first flush of new fatherhood talking. Whatever he felt, he wanted John, and since there was no other woman in his life, presumably he'd decided that they might as well stay married.

She'd take a chance on him, she decided. After all, he might learn to love her one day.

A week later, she and John were released from the hospital. Helen and Kit came to see the baby, raving over him while Tess smiled indulgently.

Dane was always somewhere nearby, although he went back to work with a vengeance. Tess was aware of his irritation that she wouldn't listen to him when he tried to talk to her. She couldn't help it. She didn't want him making confessions of love. He'd been upset about her condition once he found out about it, and the labor had been a nightmare. Now he was feeling elated with his new son and relieved that Tess was out of danger. He was happy. But Tess didn't want any false promises. She wanted him cold sober and completely over the experience of her pregnancy before they talked again.

Meanwhile, she had her son to take care of. It was six weeks before she could get around enough to feel like her old self. She doted on the baby, adored him, cosseted him, spent every free second with him. The baby was her life.

He was Dane's, too, but as Tess lavished attention on the child, she denied it to him. He began to feel alone, unwanted, and his temper became hot and unpredictable. He loved his son, but he couldn't seem to make Tess notice that he needed her, too. She'd withdrawn into a world of her own, where her child was the only other occupant.

She was feeding John early one Saturday afternoon when Dane came down the hall, his gloves clenched in one hand, his chaps making leathery sounds against his powerful legs as he walked. His battered gray Stetson was cocked low over one eye. He wasn't working today, so he'd been out with his men on the ranch. He looked out of sorts and viciously irritable.

Dane paused in the doorway, hesitating as he saw Tess in the rocking chair in their bedroom, nursing the baby.

"I have to talk to you," he said tersely.

"I'll be finished in a minute," she replied.

He sat down on the edge of the bed, his eyes calming as he watched their child nurse. Pride softened his expression, and he smiled. "I never get tired of watching that," he said quietly. "You look like something out of a dream with the boy at your breast."

She smiled shyly. "He's growing, have you noticed?"

"Tess, how long are you going to nurse him?"

The question startled her. She looked up, idly brushing away a loosened strand of blond hair. She seemed so young in her green gingham dress, so vulnerable.

"I hadn't thought about it," she said. "Does it matter?"

He hesitated. "He's tied to you as long as you feed him," he said. "You can't be away from him for more than a couple of hours at a time."

Her face paled. Her eyes went huge in her face. "You want me to leave?" she asked huskily. "Is that why you want me to stop nursing him, so that you can get a nurse for him...?"

His breathing checked. "God in heaven, no!"

She shivered, her expression torn between relief and fear.

He closed his eyes and reopened them. He got up and went to the window, slapping his gloves into his palm as he stared angrily out at the autumn landscape.

"I guess I've given you plenty of reason to think I wanted the baby and not you. But I'm not such a monster that I'd take your child away from you."

"I know that," she said, faintly shy of him. The baby finished pulling at her breast, his eyes drooping. She burped him and got up to put him in his baby bed against the wall, gently settling him on his side and covering him with a light blanket. She tiptoed out of the room, leaving Dane to follow.

"Don't run off again," he said tersely, glaring at her. "You've avoided me ever since you've been home."

"I want to sit on the porch," she said evasively.

"It's too cold."

"No, it isn't. I'll ask Beryl to watch out for John."

He gave in. "All right." He waited until she talked to Beryl, then he followed her out the back door and sat down beside her on the warm concrete stoop that overlooked the outbuildings.

She glanced at his batwing chaps. "You've been working."

"I bought some new horses," he said. "I've been watching the vet work on them."

He lit a cigarette and she stared out over the pasture.

"Tess, I've been trying to get you still long enough to apologize. I said some harsh, cruel things before the baby came. Things that haunt me now."

"You didn't know about what was wrong with me," she said simply. "I only wanted to spare you. You didn't think you could even have a child, and you were so excited about him." She smiled wanly. "I didn't want to spoil it for you."

His eyes closed and he groaned. "And what about you, you little idiot? Worried to death, and all you got from me was a cold shoulder and accusations about being lazy. Lazy!'' He jerked off his hat and tossed it aside, running a restless hand through his hair. ''I can't bear to remember the way I treated you. I've given you nothing but heartache, Tess.''

She searched his profile quietly, her eyes soft and loving. ''That isn't quite true. You gave me John.''

He glanced down at her. ''I never thought of precautions,'' he said slowly. ''Because I didn't think I needed to. If I'd known the risk…!''

''But you didn't. Neither did I. But I would have taken the risk, even if I had known, Dane,'' she said with quiet conviction. ''I'd do it all over again.''

He searched her eyes slowly. ''It wasn't just the baby I wanted,'' he said huskily. ''It was you. I wanted you, needed you, so I…would have married you even if there hadn't been a child, because my world collapsed when you walked out of it. Sending you away was the single worst mistake of my life.'' His expression was vulnerable then, so loving that it knocked the breath out of her. ''That night… I never knew what love was until then. I was afraid of it, terrified that I was wrong and it wouldn't last. But it has. It will. God, Tess,'' he whispered, ''I'll love you until I die.''

She shifted a little away from him and averted her eyes to the horizon. She couldn't believe him. She didn't dare. ''You don't have to pretend,'' she said gently. ''It's all right. You love John, and maybe you're fond of me. That will be enough.''

He crushed out the cigarette and stood up. He glared at her. ''No, it will not. You want me to love you.''

She flushed and averted her gaze to the distant horizon. ''I know how hard relationships are for you.…''

He caught her gently by the shoulders and she stood up. ''My mother warped my outlook. Jane savaged my pride. By the time you came along, I was an emotional basket case. I was afraid of you,'' he said. ''Didn't you know?''

''I think part of me did.'' She lifted her eyes to his. ''I tried to make you see that I'd never hurt you. But you wouldn't trust me.''

''I couldn't.'' His hands slid down to clasp hers. ''I told you that I didn't know how to love, how to be gentle.'' He leaned closer. ''I had to learn those things. I learned them with you, Tess.''

''You're proud of John,'' she whispered, glancing down, ''and you felt responsible for the trouble I had. You don't have to say these things....''

He caught her chin between his thumb and forefinger and lifted her face, made her look at him. ''I love you,'' he said. ''How many ways, how many times, do I have to repeat it before you start believing that I mean it?''

She winced. Her eyes narrowed worriedly. ''It might be so many things besides love, Dane.''

''It might. But it isn't. You know it, you little coward.'' He smiled as he bent his head and gently took her lips with his. ''But maybe it's time I proved it.''

He kissed her softly, teasing her mouth until she began to relax, her mouth answering his in the warm silence of the afternoon. He caught his breath and groaned when he felt her arms go around him, felt the soft trembling of her body as she gave in. His lips probed her open mouth, his tongue teasing and then thrusting, so that she moaned hoarsely and tried to get closer to him.

His lean hand contracted at the base of her spine, rubbing her hungrily against his fierce arousal.

''I want you,'' he ground out. ''Are you able?''

''Oh...yes,'' she whispered dazedly thorugh swollen

lips, her body already throbbing wildly from the contact.

He groaned. "Where the hell can we go?" He lifted his head, looking so haunted that she almost smiled. "Beryl's upstairs with the baby."

She glanced toward the barn. He shook his head. "No," he said unsteadily. "It's far too unsanitary."

"They do it in books," she moaned.

"That is fantasy," he whispered. He nuzzled his face against her full breasts and then back up to her mouth. "And what I feel right now isn't a quick lust that I need to satisfy. I love you. I want to make love with you, be a part of you."

"I want that, too," she said huskily.

He pulled her closer, kissing her again, his mouth slow and sensuous, loving. "Tess," he breathed into her mouth, and he shuddered. "Tess, I love you...!"

The back door suddenly opened, breaking them apart, and Beryl came out wearing a sweater. "John's sleeping soundly. Would you two mind if I ran down to see about Mrs. Jewell? I'll only be an hour or so...."

Tess could have hugged her. She probably knew that the two of them would have killed for some time alone together, even with a sleeping baby nearby. "You go right ahead," Tess said softly.

"Thanks. Mrs. Jewell looks forward to our afternoons," Beryl assured her. She left, smiling secretly to herself.

They waited until the car pulled out of the driveway before Dane escorted her upstairs with undue haste and locked the bedroom door behind them.

He lifted her quickly and carried her to the bed, easing down onto it with her. "Don't be noisy or you'll wake the baby," he breathed into her mouth. "God bless Beryl...."

"The door..." She choked.

"It's locked. Tess, it's been so long!"

He kissed her with aching hunger for a long time until the fever burned too high to contain. He smiled sensually as he proceeded to remove every stitch of fabric from his powerful body. Tess watched him unashamedly, her eyes wide and curious. He was beautifully made, she thought, scars and all. The most perfect man she could ever have imagined.

As she thought it, she said it, whispered it to him. He smiled as he eased back down beside her and removed her dress and underthings between soft kisses.

She was a little self-conscious about her own scar, but he kissed it gently and smiled. It was, he murmured, like a battle scar that she'd earned with exceptional courage. She relaxed then and smiled back, lifting her face for his kiss.

She couldn't have imagined the tenderness of his possession. It was slow and thorough and breathlessly gentle. In between kisses and erotic caresses, he told her that he loved her, that he needed her, that she was the most important thing in his life. The magic they'd shared in his apartment was still there, intensified. He touched her and she felt boneless, anguished with her need of him.

Her arms clung to his neck when he moved over her and hesitated.

"Wait," he whispered. He paused and removed something he'd stuffed under a pillow, taking time to put it in place. She stared at him shyly. "No more babies just yet, sweetheart," he whispered softly. "I won't let you take that risk again."

"I'm all right," she said unsteadily. "It was a rare thing, Dane, and it might never happen again."

"We'll talk about it another time. You're weak and vulnerable right now. I have to take very good care of you, Mrs. Lassiter," he whispered against her mouth. "I love you far too much to risk losing you twice." He moved over her, easing her body to accommodate him. Then he began to join his body to hers with exquisite slowness and tenderness.

She was uncomfortable at first and he had to pause, to give her time to absorb him.

"You're like a virgin all over again," he said huskily, shivering with the restraint he was exercising for her sake. "Relax. Relax, little one. Yes." He sighed and let his hips slowly merge with hers.

She moaned as he completed his possession, her arms clinging as she lifted to him. "Oh, Dane," she gasped, "it's been almost a year...."

"I know," he said with a heavy groan, and his body began to move with helpless urgency.

She laughed in spite of the pleasure and kissed him hungrily. He caught her hips in his hands, and in seconds she was incapable of laughter or speech.

It was like the night they'd made the baby. She wept in his arms as the rhythm built in her body and in her blood, his possession of her so achingly complete that she went rigid with pleasure and stopped breathing altogether when the first heated contractions shook her under his weight. He cried out as she went over the edge, and her eyes opened at that instant, misty with her own helpless fulfillment. She saw him arch and his face clench just before her senses exploded, and she heard her own voice shattering....

She knew they'd never achieved such pleasure before. She lay heavily against his warm, damp body when they were coherent again, listening to his steady heartbeat, feeling him breathe against her breasts.

"You love me," he said with shaky humor. "I'd know it now even if you hadn't said it twenty times while we were loving just now."

"You said it several times yourself," she gasped.

He drew her closer and kissed her tenderly. "I mean it," he said. "Do you believe me now?"

She looked up into his soft, dark eyes. "Oh, yes," she agreed breathlessly, and blushed as she remembered the way it had been.

He bent and kissed her again with tenderness and possession. "I'd love to show you again, and again, and again," he whispered huskily. "But I hear the beginnings of a small thunderstorm."

She closed her eyes as he kissed her eyelids. "A small what?" She smiled lovingly.

"Listen."

A tiny sound exploded suddenly into a wail of pure fury in the quiet bedroom.

"Are you hungry again?" she asked, aghast. She threw her dress back on and got up to look at little John, who was waving his tiny fists and turning puce. "Or are you wet?"

"Better check for yourself," he murmured dryly from the bed. "As smart as he is, I doubt he's mastered enough English to answer you just yet."

She stuck out her tongue and proceeded to change a very wet diaper. As she was working on that, the telephone rang and Dane reached lazily across to answer it.

"No, I'm not coming in today. Why?" he asked. He frowned. Then he burst out laughing. "You don't mean it? When? Is she going to be all right?'' He shook his head. ''My God, of course I'll tell Tess. She'll die laughing. Tell her we'll be along to see her tonight, and for God's sake, confiscate her piece before she manages to do it again!''

''What is it?'' Tess asked the minute he hung up.

''You'll never believe this,'' he said. He got up and pulled on his jeans, still chuckling. ''You remember Helen was complaining that she was the only person in the office who'd never had a brush with a bullet?''

Her hands hesitated on the diaper she was fastening. ''Yes.''

''Well, it seems this afternoon she grabbed the wrong way for her pistol and shot herself in the foot.''

''Oh, the poor thing!'' Tess exclaimed, and ruined her sympathetic remark by bursting into helpless laughter. ''I'm sorry, it isn't funny. She'll be all right?''

''Only a flesh wound. By the time she gets through embroidering it, she'll have had near-gangrene. They're keeping her overnight at the hospital just in case, so I told Nick we'd drop by to see her.''

''I'll take flowers,'' she said. She grinned. ''And a medal if we can find one.''

He went to stand beside her as she finished changing the baby and lifted him into her arms. His eyes as he looked down at the two most beloved people in his life were stormy with happiness and love.

''He really does look like you,'' she said softly.

''Like both of us,'' he corrected, sliding a loving arm around her. His eyes twinkled. ''Happy?''

''I never dreamed of being so happy.'' She reached up and kissed him. ''You're not sorry it worked out this way, that you had to marry me?'' she asked worriedly.

"I never *had* to marry you," he corrected with lazy tenderness. "I was only looking for an excuse, or did you really think I just happened into that restaurant the day you were having lunch with Kit?"

"You followed her!" she said, laughing. "She said you did."

"I followed her, all right. I'd brooded all morning about what I was going to do. Tess, I was going to ask you to come back with me," he confessed. "To live with me, marry me, to take a chance on a life without children."

She touched his face. "Oh, Dane!" she breathed.

"Then everything went wrong," he murmured. "And I got interrupted too soon."

"I was going to tell you about the baby," she replied, "and that man who approached you cost me my nerve."

He groaned. "All that time, wasted." He scowled suddenly. "You were having problems that day. It wasn't the ulcer, it was the baby."

"Yes," she said quietly. "But when you held my hand, the pain went away. I thought later that it was as if the baby knew you were his father, and he was responding to you."

His eyes darkened as he looked at her. "I gave you a hard time. I'm sorry, about everything."

"I loved you," she whispered. "I thought you might learn to love me, if I didn't rush you. I didn't want you to worry, or I'd have told you about the baby as soon as I knew. I didn't realize how hungry you really were for a child."

"Not for *a* child. For *our* child. Part of us." He bent and brushed his lips tenderly over the baby's temple, then he lifted his eyes back to hers. "You don't know how I missed you when you moved out of the apartment, or how afraid I was for you when those drug dealers were after you. For a long time, I thought I didn't want marriage. And then you wanted me to show you what lovemaking was.'' He groaned. ''I didn't think it was possible to feel so deeply. I'd have done anything to get you, except sacrifice your need for a child.'' He searched her eyes. ''It makes me humble, thinking of how much you were willing to sacrifice for me.''

''Didn't that work both ways,'' she whispered.

He kissed her softly. ''I like learning about love with you. I must be an apt pupil, because you sure make a lot of noise when we're in bed together.''

She flushed, and he chuckled at her embarrassment. He grinned, bending to kiss her nose. ''The baby gave me the best excuse in the world to marry you and take you home with me, without having to tell you how desperately I loved you. I thought I'd killed everything you felt for me.''

''Silly man,'' she said lovingly. ''Love doesn't die that easily.''

''So it would seem. You had a hard time carrying John. Next time, we'll plan the baby, and I'll be with you every step of the way.''

''That sounds like you want me to stop seducing you,'' she remarked.

''Heaven forbid!''

She smiled. ''I wanted you so badly that night. I loved you. I thought if I gave you all I had to give and asked for nothing in return, you might learn to trust me, maybe to love me.''

''I loved you, all right,'' he said huskily. He drew her closer with her precious bundle in her arms. ''My

God, we've had a rocky road. I hope things will be a little smoother for us now.''

She reached up and kissed him with aching tenderness. ''Stand back and see how smooth. I'll love you to death,'' she whispered huskily.

He actually flushed, his darkening eyes almost a statement of intent.

''Want me to try?'' she murmured provocatively, parting her lips to draw his eyes to them.

''Are you serious?'' he asked unsteadily. ''Come here.''

But before he could get further, their son let out a wail and went searching for the rest of his lunch.

Tess laughed as he found it, smiling at the ferocity of her son's furious expression. She looked at Dane, and the love in his eyes made her warm all over.

''It seems that my son has priorities,'' he mused, fighting down the surge of desire. ''But there's always tonight.''

''Yes. I love you,'' she whispered.

''I love you, too, little one. So much!''

She nibbled softly at his lips. ''When John starts school, how would you feel about letting me go back to work?''

He lifted his head. ''As a skip tracer for Short?'' he asked.

''As an operative for *you*,'' she corrected.

He pursed his lips. ''Keeping it in the family, I gather?''

''Until John is old enough to look good in a trench coat,'' she agreed.

He hugged her close and drew his fingers lovingly over his son's head. He hesitated, but she looked determined. Well, if he taught her, and watched the cases she took, he could keep her safe. It wouldn't hurt to let her feel independent. At the same time, he wouldn't really mind having her underfoot half the time. He smiled at just the prospect. "Okay. But you'll start out as a skip tracer, and no Mike Hammer stuff, got that?"

"Of course!"

She leaned her head on his chest and smiled at their son. But behind her back, where she was sure he couldn't see them, her fingers were crossed. Seconds later, his smile almost a declaration of love, he reached slowly behind her. And uncrossed them.

* * * * *

THE CASE OF THE
CONFIRMED BACHELOR

To Diane, Sydney and my Roz.

Chapter One

It was a lazy day in late spring. Nick Reed was feeling restless again. Working for Dane Lassiter's Houston detective agency had been exciting at first, and he'd enjoyed the work. But wanderlust called to him through the open window from the park across the way.

He watched a particularly trim young woman strolling along with a small furry dog and he smiled, because her pert figure reminded him of Tabby.

Tabitha Harvey. Shades of the past, he mused, leaning back in his chair. He'd deliberately avoided thinking about her over the past few months, because of what had happened when he and his sister, Helen, had flown back to their childhood home in Washington, D.C., on business. The trip had been right before New Year's, and Tabby had been around. That was natural, because she and Helen had been friends forever. They'd all been invited to a party together.

Nick had noticed that Tabby was watching him with unusual interest that night. She'd gone back to the punch bowl several times, as he had himself. But the punch had been spiked and Tabby hadn't known. She'd cornered Nick in a deserted room and started kissing him.

He could still feel her fervent, if untutored, mouth trembling under his lips. For a few seconds, he'd returned her kisses with everything in him. But he'd stopped her then, and demanded an explanation.

Fuzzily she'd explained that she knew he'd come all that way just to see her, that she knew he was finally ready to settle down. They'd be so happy, she said dreamily, smiling through an alcoholic haze.

Nick had no idea where she'd come up with those wild statements. If he'd ever thought of Tabby romantically, it had been years ago. Her remarks had come right out of the blue, and he'd reacted with shocked anger. He'd said some cutting and sarcastic things about her confession, which had sent her running. He'd gone back to the house with Helen and packed to leave D.C. He'd never told Helen exactly what happened, but he imagined Tabby had. He and Tabby hadn't had any contact since. Not that he wasn't sorry for the things he'd said; apologies were just hard for him.

He was scowling over the memories when Helen tapped at his office door and let herself in.

"Have you thought it over?" she asked eagerly.

He glowered at her, swinging his chair back around with a long, powerful leg. His blond hair gleamed like gold in the light from the window. His eyes, as dark as her own, had a hard glitter.

"Yes."

"You'll do it?" she asked with a grin, pushing her long hair back from her elfin face.

"Yes, I've thought about it, and no, I won't do it," he clarified.

Her face fell. "Nick! Please!"

"I won't," Nick said firmly. "You'll have to get your information some other way."

"Blood is thicker than water, remember," Helen Reed persisted hopefully. "I'm the only sister you have. There's only the two of us. Oh, Nick, you've got to!"

"Not really," he said with maddening indifference and a grin.

There were times, she thought, when he'd look really good hanging from a long rope. But then she'd be alone in the world except for Harold, to whom she was engaged.

"You're the only ex-FBI agent we've got at the Lassiter Detective Agency," she reminded him. "You've got contacts in all the right places. All you have to do is make one little-bitty telephone call," she persisted.

And she fixed her big brown eyes on him in their thin elfin face in its frame of long, straight brown hair. Except for his blond hair, they looked very much alike. Same stubborn chin, same elegant nose, same spirited dark eyes. But Nick was much more introverted and secretive than she was. He'd been that way all their lives, since they'd grown up in Washington, D.C.— where she attended college and he worked for the FBI.

Over the years, he'd done a lot of traveling, and she hadn't seen him for months, sometimes years at a time, until he'd received the offer of work from Richard Dane Lassiter. He'd met Dane on a case just before the Texas Ranger had been shot to pieces. When Lassiter began his own private detective agency, he coaxed Nick away from the FBI and Nick volunteered Helen as a paralegal, with her two years of business college giving her an edge over the competition. She'd come hotfoot from Washington to be with her brother. Their parents had been dead for some time, and she'd liked the idea of being near the last of her kin.

She did miss Tabitha Harvey very much at first, because she and Tabby had been friends since they were children. They still corresponded, although Tabby was very careful not to ask how Nick was. Obviously her memories of Helen's brother were painful ones.

"No," he said again. "I won't call the FBI for you."

She grinned at him, her slender hands together. "I'll tell."

"You'll tell what?"

"That you were out with that gorgeous blonde when you were supposed to be on stakeout for Dane," she said.

"Go ahead and tell him. She was my contact. I don't play around on the job."

"You do play around, though," Helen said, suddenly serious. "You never take women seriously."

He shrugged. "I don't dare. I'm not made for a pipe and slippers and kids. I like traveling and dangerous work, and the occasional pretty blonde when I'm *not* on stakeout."

"Pity," she sighed, smiling up at him. "You'd look nice covered in confetti."

"Who'd have me?" He grinned.

She had to bite her tongue to keep from mentioning Tabby's name. She'd done that once, and he'd gone right through the ceiling. He hadn't seen Tabby since New Year's Eve, when he'd gone with Helen to see about their parents' house in a small Washington suburb called Torrington. Tabby's father had died two years before, but she was still living in his house. It was next door to the Reeds. Nick had never discussed what happened when he and Tabby had talked one night while they were in Torrington, but it had caused him to bristle at the mention of her name ever since.

"The renters have moved out of Dad's house, you know," she said suddenly. "I can't fly back there and take care of it this time. Can you?"

His face hardened. "Why can't you?"

"Because I'm engaged, Nick," she said, exasperated. "You aren't. You're due for a vacation anyway, aren't you? You could kill two birds with one stone."

"I suppose I could," he said reluctantly, and his eyes darkened for an instant. Then he looked over his sister's head and his brows shot up. "Here comes the boss. Better vanish, before you become another statistic on the unemployment rolls."

"I wish you were on a roll. Filleted!" She chuckled.

He sauntered off, leaving her to Dane.

"Problems?" Dane asked, his eyes going from Nick back to Helen.

"Not a single one, boss," she assured him. "Nick and I were only discussing food."

"Okay. How about the Smart investigation?"

She grimaced. "I need one piece of information I can't dig out," she said miserably. "I can't get anybody to talk to me about Kerry Smart's brief stint with the FBI."

"Didn't you ask your brother? He has contacts over at the FBI office."

"That's why I'd like him filleted on a roll," she said sweetly. "He won't call anybody."

"Well, I can't order him to," he reminded her. "Nick's very secretive about his FBI days. He never talks about that period of his life. Perhaps he doesn't want any contact with the agency."

"I guess. Well, I'll trudge over to see Adams. He used to have one or two confidants."

"Good."

"How's our Tess, and the baby?"

"She's great, and the baby never sleeps. The doctor says he will one day," he added wistfully. "Meanwhile, it's just one more thing we can do together—sitting up with baby."

"You know you love it," she reminded him.

"Indeed I do. I could live without breathing much easier than I could live without my family."

"And there you were, a confirmed bachelor." She shook her head. "How are the mighty fallen!"

"Watch it," he threatened, "before you become redundant."

"Not me, boss. I intend to be even more valuable than Nick, if you'll just give me a few days off to work for the FBI so that I HAVE SOME CONTACTS I CAN USE WHEN I NEED THEM!" she said loudly, so that Nick heard her. But it didn't work. He made her a mocking bow and went out the door.

"One day, he'll deck you, Reed," Dane mused. "Sister or not, he's all for woman's lib. Equal opportunity, even in brawls, was how he put it."

"That's how I trained him," she said, tongue-in-cheek, and got a laugh for her pains.

"I'll tell him you said so."

"God forbid!" she said with a mock shudder. "You can't imagine what he told Harold the other day about what I did when I was two."

"You'll have to make sure he and Harold don't meet too often."

"That's what Harold says!" she confided mischievously.

She got her things together and wished she had the time to go and see Tess and the baby. But now that Tess had married Dane and they had a child of their own, it had put some distance between the two women. They still had lunch together occasionally, but Tess was closer to her friend Kit than she was to Helen.

Helen went to see Adams, who actually did have a contact in the FBI office. He made one telephone call and got her the information she needed.

"Quick work! Thanks!" she said enthusiastically.

He cleared his throat. "If Harold isn't treating you to pizza I'll buy you a beer," Adams offered. "Just casual, you know. I know you're engaged."

She smiled. He was nice. Big and burly and a little potbellied, but nice. "Thanks, Adams," she said sincerely. "Rain check?"

"Sure," he said easily. He grinned and went out the door. He always seemed to be by himself. Helen felt a bit sorry for him, but he was the kind of man who got attached to people and couldn't let go. She was afraid of that kind of involvement. Well, with anyone except Harold.

"So, what did you talk to Adams about?" Nick asked from behind her as she went out the door.

She gasped and then laughed. "I didn't hear you!"

"Of course you didn't," he said pleasantly. "I'm a private detective. We're trained to sneak up on people without being noticed."

"Really?" she asked, smiling. "I didn't know that."

He glared at her. "Nice to know you love me. What were you doing over there," he gestured toward Adams's now-deserted desk. "Warding off Adams?"

"No! I like Adams."

"Sure. I do, too, but he's a tick. If you ever get him

attached to you, you'll have to stick a lighted match to his head to make him let go.''

She burst out laughing. ''You animal!'' she gasped.

''You know I'm right. He's not a bad dude, all the same.''

''Neither are you, once in a while.''

''Get what you needed?''

She nodded. ''No thanks to you,'' she said.

He shrugged indifferently. ''It's no bad thing to teach you to be self-sufficient. I won't always be around.''

The way he said that worried her. ''Nick...'' she began.

''I'm not dying of something,'' he said when he saw her expression, and he smiled. ''I mean I'm getting restless. I may be moving on sometime soon.''

''Wanderlust again?'' she asked gently.

He nodded. ''I get bored in the same place.''

''Go home,'' she said. ''Take a vacation. Relax.''

''In Washington?'' His eyes widened. ''Funny girl!''

''You'll find a way. It's a quiet street. No drug dealers, no shoot-outs. Just peace and quiet.''

''And your friend Tabby right next door,'' he said icily.

''Tabby's dating a very nice historian at her college,'' she told him, enjoying the way his eyelids flickered. ''I think it may be serious. So you won't have to hide from her while you're there.''

''She wasn't dating anybody when we were there earlier in the year,'' he said. He sounded as if he thought she'd betrayed him.

''That was then,'' she reminded him. ''A lot can happen in a few months. Tabby's twenty-five. It's time she married and had kids. She's settled and has a good job.''

He didn't answer her. He looked hunted. He *felt* hunted. So he changed the subject without appearing to be evasive. "Did you get your information from Adams?" he asked her again.

"Yes. I had to have it to finish my case," she said. "Dane was just asking me how far I'd gotten earlier. The client needs the background information. He hopes it may help him avert a court case."

"I see." His fingers traced a teasing line down her nose. "I don't suppose it occurred to you that I might have a damned good reason for not wanting to talk to people I used to know at the agency?"

Her dark eyes searched his curiously. Her handsome brother had bone structure an artist would love—from his high cheekbones to his straight nose and perfectly chiseled masculine mouth.

"You're staring. And you haven't answered me," he said.

"I was just thinking what a dish you are," she said with a grin. "You look just like Dad. No wonder women threaten to leap off buildings when you throw them over. You never talk about the time you spent with the FBI, and I never knew why. I thought maybe you missed it."

"Sometimes I do," he confessed. "Not often. But it's never a good idea to open up old wounds. Sometimes they bleed."

"Yes," she said absently, "I suppose so."

"All right. Have a sandwich with me and we'll talk about what we're going to do with the house. I'm tired of renting it out. Too much hassle. I want to talk to you about selling it."

"Sell our legacy?" she burst out.

He sighed. "I figured you'd react that way. Come on. Let's eat. We can fight over dessert."

He took her to a nice seafood restaurant. She'd been expecting a hamburger, and she paused self-consciously at the door, nervous in her old black skirt and black-and-white checked blouse, her hair loose and unkempt.

"Now what's the matter?" he asked impatiently.

"Nick, I'm not dressed for a place like this," she said earnestly. "Can't we go someplace less expensive?"

"I beg your pardon?"

"A fast-food place," she explained. "Plastic cartons? Paper sacks? Foam cups?"

"Nonbiodegradable litter." He frowned. "No way. Come on." He took her arm and forcibly led her inside. He chuckled as he seated her, very elegantly, at a table. "I hope you aren't really that mad for pizza. They don't serve it here."

She smiled. "Harold and I are sort of tired of it, if you want the truth," she confessed as he sat down across from her. The table had a burning red candle in a glass chimney. The lighting was cozy, like the atmosphere with its classical music playing unobtrusively overhead.

"I like service," he said. "Old-fashioned service, and good food. They have both here."

Even as he spoke, a slender blonde paused beside the table and presented them with menus. Her eyes lingered on Nick's face while he ordered coffee, to give them time to decide on a choice of entrée.

"Thanks, Jean," he said warmly.

The woman smiled back and with an envious glance at Helen, went on her way.

"She likes you," she said.

"I know. I like her, too. But that's all it is," he added, his face very serious as he met Helen's curious stare. "Stop trying to play matchmaker. You only complicate lives."

He sounded incredibly bitter. "Are you trying to tell me something?" she asked quietly.

"You threw me together with Tabby at that New Year's Eve party the last time we were home. You didn't mention that you'd told her I flew all the way from Houston just to take her out."

He hadn't talked about this before. She felt guilty and apprehensive at his tone. "I didn't think it would hurt," she began.

He cut her off. "She had some crazy idea that my feelings had changed and I wanted a relationship with her," he said curtly, his eyes accusing. "I wasn't expecting it and I overreacted. She cried." His face went harder. "In all the years we've known Tabby, I've never seen her cry. It really got to me."

Helen knew Nick well enough to guess what happened next. "You lost your temper," she guessed.

"I told you, I wasn't expecting it. One minute she was telling me about some new find they were studying in the anthropology department, the next she was off on a tangent about the future."

"The punch was spiked," she said. "I didn't know. I poured her two cups of it."

"I finally figured out for myself that she was three sheets to the wind, but that sudden burst of affection knocked me off balance," he replied. He rammed his hands into his pockets and looked uncomfortable. "I panicked. Tabby's a sweet woman, but she's not my type."

"Who is?" she challenged. "You make confirmed bachelors look like old married men. You could do a lot worse than Tabby."

"She could do a lot better than me," he countered. "A little cottage with a picket fence isn't what I'm saving up for. I want to sail around the world. I want to go exploring. In the meantime, I like being an investigator, even if this job is beginning to wear on me."

"Tabby's an investigator, did you know? She searched for the solutions to ancient mysteries. That's what anthropologists do—they discover the cultures of ancient civilizations and how they worked."

"No two-thousand-year-old mummy is likely to sit up in his sarcophagus and pull a gun on her, either," he argued.

"Probably not," she conceded. "But digging for the truth is something you both like to do."

He ran an angry hand around the back of his neck. "I didn't like hurting her that way," he said abruptly. "I said some harsh things."

"Well, that's all in the past now," she reminded him. "She's dating someone and it sounds serious, so you won't have to worry about any complications while you're deciding what we should do about Dad's house."

"I suppose not," he said, but he wasn't looking forward to seeing Tabby again. His treatment of her wore on his nerves, and she wasn't going to be pleased to see him. Tabby, like Nick himself, deplored losing control. Her lack of pride was going to hurt her as much as Nick's sharp words, and she wouldn't like being reminded of their confrontation any more than he did.

"It will be all right," Helen said gently.

"Your favorite saying. What if it isn't?"

"For goodness' sake, think positively!" she chided. "Buy a plane ticket and go to Washington."

"I guess I will. But I still have my doubts," he said.

Two days later, with Dane Lassiter's blessing, Nick was on his way down Oak Lane to his father's old house in Torrington.

It looked just the same, he thought as he wheeled lazily along in the rental car. The oaks were a little older, as he was, but the street was quiet and dignified, like the mostly elderly people who lived on it.

His eyes went involuntarily over the flat front of the redbrick home where he and Helen had grown up. There were blooming shrubs all around it and the dogwood and cherry trees were green now with their blossoms gone in late spring. The weather was comfortably warm without being blazing hot, and everything looked green and restful. He hadn't realized before just how tired he was. This vacation was probably a good idea after all, even if he had fought like a tiger to keep from taking it.

It was Friday, and not quitting time, so he didn't expect to see Tabby at her family's house next door. But in his mind's eye, he saw her—long brown hair down to her waist and big dark eyes that followed him everywhere as she walked by the house on her way home from school. She was tall, very slender, with curves that weren't noticeable at all. That hadn't changed. Her hair was in a bun these days, not long and windblown. She wore little makeup and clothes that were stylish but not sexy. Her body was as slender as it had been in her teens, nothing to make any man particularly amorous unless he loved her. Poor Tabby. He felt sorry for her, angry at Helen because she'd engineered that meeting at New Year's Eve and made Tabby think he cared about her.

He did, in a sort of brotherly way, mainly because that was how he'd always interpreted Tabby's attitude toward him. She'd never seemed to want a physical relationship with him. Not until New Year's Eve, anyway, and she had been intoxicated. Perhaps this colleague she was dating did love her, and would make her happy. He hoped so.

Life in a garret wasn't for him. He was already thinking about applying to Interpol or as a customs inspector down in the Caribbean. A tame existence appealed to him about as much as drowning.

He pulled into the driveway of his father's house and sat just looking at it quietly for a long time. Home. He hadn't ever thought about what it meant to have a place to come back to. Odd, with his need for freedom, that it felt so wonderful to be in his own driveway. Possession was new to him, like the feeling of emptiness he'd had since the Christmas holidays. Loneliness wasn't something he'd experienced before. He wondered why he should feel that way, as if he were missing out on life, when his life was so full and exciting.

As he unlocked the front door and carried his suitcase inside, he drank in the smells of wood and varnish and freshener, because he'd had a woman come in and clean every week since the house had been vacant. His parents' things were neatly kept, just as they'd been when he and Helen were children. Nothing changed here. The smells and sights were those of his boyhood. Familiar things, that gave him a sense of security.

He scowled, looking toward the banister of the staircase that led up to the three bedrooms on the second floor. His long fingers touched the antique wood and fondled it absently. Selling the furnished house had seemed the thing to do. Now, he wasn't sure about it.

As the day wore on, he became less sure. The power had been turned on earlier in the week, and the refrigerator and stove were in good working order. He found a coffeemaker stashed under the sink. He went shopping for supplies, arriving home just as a small blue car pulled in next door.

He paused on the steps, two grocery bags in one powerful arm, watching as a woman stepped out of the car. She didn't look toward him, not once. Her carriage very correct, almost regal, she walked to the front door of her house, inserted the key she held ready in her hand, and disappeared out of sight.

Tabby. He stared after her without moving for a minute. She hadn't changed. He hadn't expected her to. But it felt different to look at her now, and it puzzled him. He couldn't quite determine what the difference was.

He went inside and started a pot of coffee before he fried a steak and made a salad for his supper. While he was eating it, he pondered on Tabby's lack of interest in his presence. She had to have seen the car in the driveway, seen him go to the door. But she hadn't looked his way, hadn't spoken.

He felt depressed suddenly, and regretted even more the wall he'd built between them at New Year's. They were old friends. Almost family. It would have been nice to sit down with Tabby and talk about the old days when they'd all played together as children. He didn't suppose Tabby would want to talk to him now.

After he'd finished his meal and washed up the dishes, he sat down in the living room with a detective novel. The television wasn't working. He didn't really mind. It was like entertainment overkill these days, with channels that never shut down and dozens of programs to choose from. The constant bombardment sometimes got on his nerves, so he shut it off and read instead. Nothing like a good book, he thought, to cultivate what Agatha Christie's hero Hercule Poirot called the "little gray cells."

He was knee-deep in the mystery novel when the front door knocker sounded.

Curious, he went to open the door.

Tabby stood there, unsmiling, her hair in a neat bun, her glasses low on her nose, her expression one of strain and worry. She was wearing a neat suit with a white blouse, and she obviously had worn it all day. It was nine in the evening and she hadn't changed into casual clothes.

"Hello," he said. His heart felt lighter and he smiled.

Tabby didn't return the smile. Her hands were folded very tightly at her waist. "I wouldn't have bothered you," she said stiffly, "but I don't really know any other detectives. It seemed almost providential that you came home today."

"Did it? Why?" he asked.

She swallowed. "I'm under suspicion of theft," she said. Her lower lip trembled, but only for an instant until she got it under control. Her head lifted even higher with stung pride. "I haven't taken anything, and I haven't been formally charged, but only I had access to the artifact that's disappeared. It's a small vase with cuneiform writing that dates to the Sumerian empire, and they think I stole it."

Chapter Two

Nick's dark blond eyebrows rose curiously. "You, a thief? My God, you walked two blocks to return a dollar old man Forbes lost when you were just sixteen. People don't change that much in nine years."

She seemed to relax. "Thanks for the vote of confidence, but I need proof that I didn't do it. If you're going to be in town for a few days, I want to employ you to clear me."

"Employ for pete's sake!" he growled. "Honest to God, Tabby, you don't have to hire me to do you a favor!"

"It's business," she said firmly. "And I'm not a pauper. I don't need to impose on our old friendship."

"You can't imagine how prissy you sound," he mused, his dark eyes twinkling as they searched hers. "Come in here and talk to me about it."

"I, uh, I can't do that," she said, glancing uneasily around her as if there were eyes behind every curtain.

"Why not?"

"It's quite late, and you're alone in the house," she reminded him.

He gaped at her. "Are you for real?" He scowled and leaned closer, making a sniffing sound. "Tipsy, are we?" he asked with a wicked gleam in his eyes.

"I am not!" she said stiffly, flushing. "And I wish you'd forget that. I was drunk!"

"Absolutely," he agreed. "I've never seen you with a snootful. Your mask slipped."

"It won't ever slip again like that," she told him. "I hope I didn't embarrass you."

"Not really. Why can't you come inside? I almost never have sex with women in suits."

The color in her cheeks got worse. "Now cut that out!"

He shrugged. "If you say so." He folded his arms across his broad chest. His shirt was unfastened at the collar, where a thick golden thatch was just visible. It seemed to disturb Tabby, because her eyes quickly averted from it.

"I thought, if you had time, we might meet for lunch tomorrow and I'll fill you in."

He sighed with mock resignation. "There's not really any need for that." He reached beside him and turned the porch light on. Then he escorted her down the steps and neatly seated her on the middle step, lowering himself beside her. "Here we are, in the light, so that everyone in the neighborhood can see that we aren't naked. Is that better?"

"*Nick!*" she raged.

"Don't be so stuffy," he murmured. "You're living in the dark ages."

"A few of us need to or civilization as we know it

may cease to exist,'' she returned hotly. ''Haven't you noticed how things are going in our social structure?''

''Who hasn't?''

''Drugs, killer sexual diseases, streets full of homeless people, serial killers.'' She shook her head. ''Anything goes may sound great, but it brings down civilizations.''

''Most people don't know about ancient Rome,'' he reminded her. ''You might start wearing a toga to get their attention.''

She glowered at him. ''You never change.''

''Sure I do. I'd smell terrible wearing the same clothes over and over again.''

She threw up her hands. It was just like old times, with Nick cracking jokes while her heart broke in two. Except that now it wasn't just her heart, it was her integrity and perhaps her professional future.

He touched her chin and turned her to face his eyes. The mockery was gone out of them as he asked, ''Tell me about it, Tabby.''

She drew back from the touch of his hands, so disturbing to her peace of mind. ''There was an old piece of Sumerian pottery that I was using to show my students while I lectured on the Sumerian Empire. It was a very unique piece with cuneiform writing on it.''

''You've lost me. It's been years since I took Western Civilization in college.''

''Cuneiform was an improvement in the Sumerian culture, one step above pictographic writing,'' she explained. ''In cuneiform, each wedge-shaped sign stands for a syllable. There are thousands of pieces of Sumerian writings contained on baked clay tablets. But this writing,'' she continued, ''wasn't on a tablet, it was on a small vase, perfectly preserved and over five thousand years old.'' She leaned forward. ''Nick, the college paid a small fortune for it. It was the most perfect little find I've ever seen, rare and utterly irreplaceable. I was allowed to use it for a visual aid in that one class. None of us dreamed that it would be lost. It cost thousands of dollars…!''

''Only the one artifact?''

''Yes,'' she agreed. ''It was on my desk. I had to tutor a student in the classroom and I was going to put it back under lock and key afterward. I wasn't gone more than five minutes, but when I came back, it was missing. There was no one around, and I can't prove that I didn't take it.''

''Can't the student vouch for you?''

''Of course, but not about the artifact. She never saw it.''

He whistled. ''No witnesses?''

She shook her head. ''Not a one.''

''Anyone with a motive for stealing it?''

''A find like that would be worth a fortune, but only to a collector,'' she admitted. ''Most students simply see it as a minor curiosity. Only a few members of the faculty knew its actual value. Daniel, for one.''

''Daniel?''

''He's a colleague of mine. Daniel Myers. We…go out together. He's honest,'' she added quickly. ''He has too much integrity to steal anything.''

''Most people who steal have integrity,'' he said cynically, ''but their greed overrides it.''

''That's not fair, Nick,'' she protested. ''You don't even know Daniel.''

''I guess not,'' he said, angered by her defense of the man. Who was this colleague, anyway? His dark eyes whipped down to catch hers. "Tell me about Daniel."

"He's very nice. Divorced, one son who's almost in his teens. He lives downtown in Washington and he's on staff at the college where I work."

"I didn't ask for his history. I said tell me about him."

"He's tall and slender and very intelligent."

"Does he love you?"

She shifted uncomfortably. "I don't think you need to know anything about my personal life. Only my professional one."

He sighed. "Well, you don't have anyone to look out for you," he reminded her. "I always used to when you were in your teens."

"That was then. I'm twenty-five now. I don't need looking after. Besides, you're only five years older than I am."

"Six, almost."

"Daniel wants to marry me."

"What do you get out of it if Daniel doesn't love you?"

"Will you take the case?" she asked, changing the subject abruptly.

"Of course. But Daniel had better not get in the way."

"Oh, he won't," she said, but with unvoiced reservations. Daniel tended to be just the least bit superior. He wouldn't like Nick, she decided. Worse, Nick already didn't like him. It was going to be a touchy situation, but she was sick with worry. She had to have someone in her corner, and who better than Nick, who was one of the best detectives in the world according to his sister Helen.

''I'd like to come around to the college tomorrow and get a look at where you work.''

''Tomorrow is Saturday,'' she stammered.

''Classes won't be in session,'' he reminded her.

''Daniel was going to take me shopping…''

''Daniel can buy his clothes some other time.''

''Not for clothes, for an engagement ring!''

His eyes narrowed. He hated *that* idea. Hated it, for reasons he couldn't put a finger on. ''That will have to wait. I'm only going to be in town until next Friday.''

''I'll phone him tonight.''

''Good.''

She got up, smoothing her skirt, and Nick rose with her, his face solemn, concerned. ''Don't they know you at all, these colleagues?''

''Of course. But it does look bad. My office was locked at the time. Nobody else has a key.''

Nails in her coffin, he was thinking, but he didn't say it. ''Try not to worry. We'll muddle through.''

''Okay. Thanks, Nick,'' she said without looking at him.

''No need for that. I'll call for you about eight in the morning. That too early?''

She shook her head. ''I'm always up at dawn.''

''Just like old times,'' he recalled. ''I hope you don't have plans to climb the drain pipe, just like old times, and climb in a bedroom window.''

She caught her breath. ''It was only once or twice, and it was Helen's room I climbed into!''

''You were such a tomboy,'' he mused. ''Hell with a bat in sandlot baseball, the most formidable tackle we had in football, and not a bad tree climber. You don't look much different today.''

She grimaced. "Don't I know it." She sighed. "No matter what I eat, I can't put on a pound."

"Wait until you hit middle age."

"That's a few years away," she said with a faint smile.

"Yes. Quite a few. Get some sleep."

"You, too. Good night."

He returned the sentiment and watched her walk to her front door. Old times. He thought back to warm summer evenings when he'd bring his dates home and they'd all sit on chairs on the lawn and watch Helen and Tabby, who were a few years younger, chase fireflies on the lush lawn. He supposed Tabby would watch her own children do that very thing one day.

He didn't want to think about that. He went back inside and tried to pick up his mystery novel again, but he'd lost his taste for it. He put it down and went to bed, hours and hours before usual.

Tabby was dressed in a floral skirt and white knit blouse when he called for her the next morning just at eight. He wasn't much more dressed up than she was, comfortable in slacks and a red knit shirt. He scowled down at her.

"Must you always screw your hair up like that? I haven't seen it long in quite a while."

"It's hot around my neck," she said evasively. "I only let it down at night."

"For Daniel?" he asked sarcastically.

"Do we go in your car or mine?" she asked, ignoring the question.

"Mine, definitely," he said with a disparaging glance at hers. "I like having room for my head."

"The seat lets down."

"I can't drive lying on my back."

"Nick!"

"Come on." He led her to the big sedan he'd rented and helped her inside. "Direct me. It's been a long time since I've driven here."

"Not so long," she replied. "You didn't leave until you quit the FBI. That's only been about four years ago."

"It seems like forever sometimes."

"I guess Houston is a lot different."

"Only when it floods. Otherwise, it's a lot of concrete and steel and pavement. Just like every other city. It's Washington with a drawl."

She laughed softly. "I suppose most cities are alike. I haven't traveled much. And when I do, it's to places that seem pretty primitive by modern standards."

"To digs, I gather?"

"That's right. I went out to the Custer battlefield in Montana a few years ago to help archaeologists and other anthropologists identify some remains. Then I had a stint in Arizona with some Hohokam ruins and once I flew down to Georgia where they were excavating an eighteenth-century cabin."

"How exciting."

"Not to you," she conceded. "But it's life and breath to me. I want to investigate aboriginal sites in Australia and explore some of the Greek and Roman ruins they're just beginning to excavate. I want to go to Machu Pichu in Peru and to the Maya and Toltec and Olmec ruins in Mexico and Central America." Her eyes sparkled with excitement. "I want to go to Africa and to China... Oh, Nick, there's a world of mysteries out there just waiting to be solved!"

He glanced at her. "You sound like a detective."

"I am, sort of," she argued. "I look for clues in the past, and you look for them in the present. It's still all investigation, you know."

He turned his attention back to the road. "I suppose. It depends on your point of view."

She studied him briefly. "You aren't smoking. Helen said you'd quit."

"Five weeks, now," he replied. "I only had the jitters once Lassiter asked us all to give it up, to help him. Tess made him quit," he said with a grin. "Imagine, old Nail Eater being led around by a woman."

"I doubt she's leading him around. He probably loves her and wants to make her happy. He'll live longer if he doesn't smoke."

"We're all going to die eventually," he reminded her. "Some of us might do it a little quicker, but we don't have much choice."

"The law of entropy."

He cocked an eyebrow. "I beg your pardon?"

"That's what scientists call it—the law of entropy. It means that everything grows old and dies."

"As long as we're scientific about it," he said mockingly.

She adjusted her glasses, pushing them back up on her nose. "No need to be sarcastic. Turn here." She pointed.

He drove into the parking lot and pulled into a space marked Visitors. "Why here?"

"You don't have a sticker that permits you to park here," she reminded him. "If you park in a student's spot, you'll be towed. I know you wouldn't like that."

"It's not my car," he reminded her.

"You rented it. You'd have to liberate it."

"I love the way you use words," he chuckled as he got out of the car and helped her out.

"Nice manners," she said, tongue-in-cheek.

"You opened the door for me back when I broke my leg in your senior year of school. Drove me back and forth to work every day, too, on your way."

"Wasn't I sweet?" she asked wistfully. "Ah, those good old days."

"You were less irritating then."

"So were you," she tossed back. She cocked her head and studied him. "Footloose Nick," she murmured. "I suppose you'll end up in a shoot-out with spies somewhere and they'll mount you on a wall or something."

He grinned. "Lovely thought. How kind of you."

She gave up. "My office is on the second floor."

She led him into the big brick building, past the admissions office and up the staircase that led to the history and sociology departments.

"I'm down the hall. The historians have this wing. The sociology department here is rather small, although we offer some interesting courses."

"Anthropology is sociology," he remarked. "I took one course of it in college myself. Sociology and law go hand in hand, did you know?"

"Sure!" she said, unlocking her office. "That's the biology lab down the hall. They're only up here temporarily while their facilities are being remodeled. They have snakes in there," she said with a shiver.

A primal scream echoed down the hall with its high ceilings. "Is that one of them?" he asked.

"Snakes don't scream," she muttered. "No, that's Pal."

"Who? Or should I say what?"

"Pal's a what, all right. He's the missing link. That's what we call him up here. Australopithecus insidious."

"Greek."

"Latin," she corrected. "Pidgin Latin. What I mean, is that Pal is too smart to be a monkey. We have to lock him up. He likes to rip up textbooks. And if you ever leave your keys lying around when he's on the loose, you'll never see them again."

"Isn't he caged?"

"Usually. He picks the lock." She laughed. "The last time he got out, the administrator and several members of the board of trustees were having a catered meeting in the conference room. Pal got in there and started pelting everybody with melon balls and rolls."

"I'll bet that went over well with the guests."

"Guest," she corrected. "It was a senator from Maryland. We never did get that funding we needed for a new research project."

"Why doesn't that surprise me? Out of idle curiosity, what were you going to research?"

Her eyes brightened. "Primate social behavior."

He burst out laughing. "It seems to me that you're doing enough of that without funding."

"That's exactly what our president said. Here." She opened the door to a Spartan office with a desk, a chair, and a bookcase jammed full of reference books. On her desk were stacks of paper and a college handbook. "Like most everyone else here, I'm a faculty advisor. In my spare time, I teach anthropology."

He stood looking down at her with open curiosity. "You were always a brain. I used to feel threatened by you sometimes. No matter what I knew, you seemed to know more."

"Brains can be a curse when you're a young girl,"

she replied with faint bitterness. "But they last a lot longer than a voluptuous figure and a pretty face," she added.

"There's nothing wrong with you," he mused. "Except that you need feeding up."

"Oh, I'll spread out one day. This is where the artifact was lying when it vanished."

She pointed to a central spot on the desk.

"How long ago did it walk off?"

"Yesterday afternoon."

He nodded and pulled a small leather-bound kit out of his pocket. "Go and read a book or make a telephone call for a few minutes while I do a little investigating."

"What are you going to do?"

"Dust your desk for fingerprints and look for clues, of course. Has anyone been at this desk except you since the artifact was taken?"

She shook her head.

"Good. That narrows it down a bit."

She started to ask him more questions, but he was knee-deep in thought and investigation. She shrugged and left him there.

Minutes later, he straightened, irritated by the lack of fingerprints. The desk had a rough surface, which made it hard to find a full print. But a tiny piece of what looked like hair lay on a white sheet of paper, and that he took with him, securing it with a pair of tweezers and sticking it in a tiny plastic bag that he then sealed. It wasn't much, but if it was human hair, the lab over at the FBI could tell them plenty about it. It was amazing how much data one strand of hair could provide. It was strangely coarse. He dismissed it instantly when Tabby came in the door, his eyes watchful as they skimmed over her. She made him feel as if he'd only just come back from a long journey. It was a very pleasant sensation. When he was with her, his restlessness seemed to go momentarily into eclipse.

"Anything?" Tabby asked hopefully.

Her question diverted him. "Not much," he said. "I couldn't get a full print...."

He stopped as a tall, unsmiling man appeared in the doorway behind Tabby.

"This is Dr. Daniel Myers," she introduced the newcomer, who was wearing a dark blue suit with a white shirt and conventional tie. On a Saturday, he was dressed like a preacher, which gave Nick a pretty accurate picture of his meticulous personality.

"Nick Reed," Nick said, introducing himself. He didn't offer his hand. Nor did Daniel, he noticed with some amusement.

"You must be discreet," he cautioned Nick. "I'm sure you understand what a theft like this could do to the image of Thorn College."

"Certainly," he agreed. "As aware as I am of what it could do to Tabby's future."

"Tabby?"

"Her family and mine have been close all our lives," Nick told the man.

"It sounds like something one would call a cat, don't you think, darling?" he asked Tabby, and slid a long arm over her thin shoulders.

Nick just stopped himself from leaping forward. Incredible, he thought, how his mind reacted to the sight. Tabby was like a sister to him. Perhaps he only felt protective. That had to be it.

He pocketed the sealed plastic envelope. "I'll run this over to the lab. I have a friend there."

"Will he be at work on Saturday?"

"Since I phoned him at home last night and asked him to meet me there, I do hope so," he replied.

"That was kind of him," she said.

"I'll drop you off on my way to FBI headquarters," he offered.

Daniel seemed to grow two feet. "That's hardly necessary," he said stiffly, and his arm drew Tabby closer. "Tabitha must have told you that we're to shop for an engagement ring today."

"Yes, I hear you're planning to be married," Nick said.

"A very sensible move, too," Daniel said carelessly. "I live alone and so does Tabitha. She had that huge house and lot, where we can live, and her car is paid for." He hugged her close. "She likes keeping house and cooking, so I'll have plenty of time to work on my book."

Nick was going to explode. He knew he was. "Book?"

"Our book," Tabby inserted with a glare at Daniel. "It's a new perspective on what I found at the Custer battlefield after the fire."

"And includes information I dug out about its history," Daniel added quickly. "Tabitha could hardly do it without my help on the grammar and punctuation."

Nick's eyebrows jerked up. "You think Tabby needs help with those? Are we talking about the girl who was school spelling champion in seventh grade and won a scholarship to Thorn College?"

Daniel shifted on his feet. "I have a master's degree in English." His watery blue eyes made mincemeat of Nick. "What was your field of study, Mr. Reed?" he asked with pleasant sarcasm, as if he considered that a detective probably had less than a high school education. In fact, an FBI agent was preferred to have a bachelor's degree in accounting or a law degree. Nick had a law degree. It wasn't something he'd ever boasted about. He wasn't going to now, either, if that careless, mocking smile he gave Daniel was any indication.

"Oh, I know a little about the law," Nick said. "I am, after all, a trained detective."

"Like a police officer." Daniel nodded, looking superior. "They're only required to have a high school education or its equivalent, I believe?"

Nick stiffened. But before he could explode, and he looked close to it, Tabby stepped in.

"We really have to go, Daniel," she said. "Thanks again, Nick. I'll talk to you later."

He murmured something and Tabby moved Daniel out into the hall with unusual dexterity.

"I don't like that man," Daniel said angrily as they walked down the hall.

"I know," she said, soothing him.

A loud screech sounded as they passed the temporary biology lab. "I don't like that monkey, either."

"Yes, Daniel. Let's go."

A door opened at the end of the hall and a small man with a moustache came out, pausing as he saw Daniel and Tabby. He looked uncomfortable for an instant. "Uh, the missing artifact," he said to Tabby. "Found it yet?"

"No. But I've engaged a private detective to look for it," she began.

Dr. Flannery stood very still for a moment. "Detective?"

"Just to look for the pottery," she said.

"Of course. Of course." He turned and moved off

down the hall, stopped suddenly, turned and went back the other way with a mumbled goodbye.

"Flannery is a flake," Daniel muttered as they left the building. "He spends too much time with those monkeys. He's beginning to act like them."

"Primates," she corrected. "They're very nice when you get to know them. Even Pal. He's intelligent, you know, that's why he gets into so much trouble."

"Maybe Flannery took that piece of pottery," he said speculatively. "Did you know that his house was repossessed just recently? He's in financial trouble. Some collectors would pay anything for a find like that."

"Yes, I know. But it couldn't have been Dr. Flannery," she said stubbornly. "My goodness, he's a biologist, not a thief!"

"Desperate men do desperate things," he said. He slid his hand into hers. "You are going to marry me, aren't you? We're very compatible, and this will certainly be a successful book. Probably the first of many." His eyes had a faraway look. "I've always dreamed of being in print."

"Daniel, you aren't marrying me so that we can write a book together, are you?" she teased.

He cleared his throat. "Of course not. Don't be silly."

She wasn't being silly. Daniel kissed her only when he had to, and not very enthusiastically. He'd never tried to step over the line, to be amorous. He never sent her flowers or phoned her at midnight just to talk. He only ever talked about writing. She sighed. Marriage was what she'd always wanted, but this wasn't how she'd envisioned it. Not at all like this.

Her dreams had been passionate ones, full of Nick.

Dreams died hard, and hers never had. Now that he was back in her life, she'd have to start all over again forgetting him. Perhaps, she thought, it would be easier when he left. Meanwhile, all she had to do was live through the next week, and hope that he could clear her name. If he couldn't, she thought with real fear, she might not even have a job much longer!

Tabitha couldn't find a ring she liked. Honestly, she wasn't that interested in marrying Daniel at all. He seemed bent on using her, while she was hitting back at Nick in the only way she knew. It was ridiculous to promise to marry one man just to show another that someone found her desirable. As if Nick was fooled! He'd seen right through Daniel's motives for the engagement. Probably through Tabby's, too. She flushed.

Daniel had taken her to a nice restaurant for lunch. She was nibbling dessert while he went to the bathroom.

Her mind was far away from the strawberry short-cake she was eating. It was on that fatal New Year's Eve party.

She'd felt as if anything was possible that night. She'd been wearing a black dress with spaghetti straps, her long hair around her shoulders. She'd left her glasses off—despite the fact that she was nearly blind without them—and put on much more makeup than usual. Helen had told her that Nick was finally ready to settle down and that it was Tabby he really wanted. That bit of encouragement had been just enough, along with the alcohol, to make her act totally out of character.

Nick, gloriously handsome Nick, had been leaning against a door frame sipping punch. Tabby had stared at him with her heart in her eyes, drowning in the sight of him. She'd loved him for, oh, so long!

Putting her punch on a nearby table, she'd walked a little unsteadily to where he was standing in the shadows of the room while sultry blues music played from the stereo nearby.

"All alone, Nick?" she'd asked, with pouting lips.

He'd smiled indulgently. "Not now," he mused. "You look nice, Tabby. Very grown-up."

"I'm twenty-five."

"That wasn't what I meant. You aren't very worldly."

"I'm working on it," she purred. "Want to see?"

She noted the faint surprise on his face as she suddenly stepped close to him, smoothing her slender body completely against his.

"Tabby!" he exclaimed.

"It's all right," she'd whispered nervously. "I only want to kiss you, Nick. And kiss you…and kiss you…!"

She'd reached up while she was speaking and looped her arms around his neck to draw his shocked face within reach. She knew little about men and less about kissing with her mostly academic background, but she loved him and she put her heart into it.

She seemed to shock him. His body froze for a few seconds. Then his dark eyes closed and his mouth hardened, and all at once, it was Nick who was doing the kissing. His steely arm clenched around her and jerked her into his body, one powerful leg moving just enough to let her slim figure intimately close while the kiss went on and on. His lips lifted while he breathed unsteadily.

"Is this what you want?" he asked roughly.

"Yes," she breathed, coaxing his mouth back to hers. "Do it again," she whispered against his hard lips.

He obliged her. The glass of punch found its way onto a table. They were hidden from the rest of the partygoers by a large potted plant and an alcove, but Tabby was beyond knowing where they were. She let her hands slide up and down his long back, gave her mouth to him totally even when he deepened the kiss far beyond her meager experience. She began to moan softly when she felt Nick's thighs against her.

That was when he jerked back and pushed her away with a vicious motion of his lean hands.

"What the hell are you doing?" he demanded harshly, his dark eyes blazing. "You're no drunken floozy out for a cheap roll in the hay, are you? Or is that what you do want?" he added with an insolent laugh. "Do you want me, Tabby? There's probably a room upstairs that we could use. Or as a last resort, we could go out on the patio into a dark corner and pull up your skirt..."

She'd cried out at his remarks. "No! Nick, I want to marry you," she'd blurted. "I know you're ready to settle down. I want to have children with you. Isn't that why you came back?"

His face had actually paled. "I came back to check on my father's house. Nothing more."

"But... But I thought..." She swallowed and went deathly pale. "I thought you wanted me."

"A dried-up spinster with a computer for a brain and no breasts to speak of?" he asked arrogantly. "My God, did you really?"

She ran. She turned and ran out the door and went straight home—blind and deaf to the turmoil she'd created in the face of the man she'd left behind. Helen had come after her and she'd cried on her friend's shoulder until dawn, only then swearing Helen to secrecy about her anguish.

She hadn't touched a drop of liquor since, and the shame lingered. But Nick would never know how badly he'd hurt her. All she required now was his help to clear her name. And then maybe she would—and maybe she wouldn't—actually marry Daniel.

Having Nick come back was slowly clearing away the desperation and madness of the past few empty months. She could see what she'd been doing, trying to substitute Daniel for the man she wanted. She couldn't have Nick, but she didn't need to make herself and Daniel miserable by trying to replace him with someone who would never be more than second best.

That decided, finally, she smiled at Daniel when he came back and managed to keep the conversation on just a friendly level for the rest of the afternoon.

Chapter Three

Nick had always been fascinated by the forensics lab at FBI headquarters. It had a reputation second to none for being able to put together evidence from almost nothing. A human hair with its DNA structure could yield a pattern as individual as a fingerprint. The tread of a tennis shoe involved in a murder could be traced to the person who purchased it. A scrap of cloth could yield an incredible amount of information about its owner. And the FBI boasted the largest file of fingerprints on record anywhere. It was an agency to which Nick had been proud to belong. Leaving it had been a wrench, too. A woman with whom he'd been involved had been killed while he'd worked there. She, too, had been a special agent, infiltrating a counterfeiting ring. She'd been spotted and eliminated. That was how the supervisor had put it. Nick had been inconsolable and he'd quit the agency.

He wondered now if it hadn't been a case of simple loneliness and pity. The woman had needed someone at a time in Nick's life when he was feeling hopelessly alone. He'd almost turned to Tabby. But at that time, she'd been shy and introverted and he'd been sure that she would back away from any advance he made. She'd seemed to see him in only one light—that of a protective, affectionate older brother.

Obviously she hadn't seen him like that at the New Year's Eve party. His blood still ran hot at the memory of how eager she'd been for him. Now, having had time to adjust to seeing her in this unexpected way, he'd regretted pushing her away.

But years ago, he'd wanted Tabby. It had been because of that that he'd pursued the woman at work in the first place, out of a need to prove to himself that any woman would do. He didn't need a shy, nervous young woman who didn't even see him as a man.

Sometimes he thought Tabby was a bit afraid of him. The first move she'd ever made toward him had been at that party, when she'd had too much to drink. Apparently he was only palatable to her if she was too tipsy to think properly, and that was hardly flattering. If she'd ever wanted him in the old days, it had never shown. He was defensive toward her because it hurt his pride to think that he couldn't even attract a backward egghead like Tabby. Good God, she wasn't even pretty, and her figure left plenty to be desired. Why, then, he wondered angrily, did the memory of her body against his keep him awake at night? Why did her kisses haunt him?

Momentarily diverted when the elevator stopped, he strolled into one of the huge laboratories that peppered the building and grinned at the elderly form bent over a microscope. That familiar sight had greeted him every time he'd come here during his tenure as a special agent.

"Hello, Bartholomew," he greeted.

The old man looked up, and smiled with delight. "Nick! How nice to see you! Can you stay a while?"

"At least long enough to let you identify something for me," Nick teased. He shook hands with the amused laboratory chief. "How are you, Bart?"

"I've been better. When you get to my age, even arthritis is encouraging. It means you're still alive enough to feel pain!" He chuckled. "Why are you in town? Come home, are you? We could use a good special agent…"

"No. I'm on vacation. I'm working as a private detective these days. It's a little less fraught than working for the agency," he added with a chuckle.

"You look as if it agrees with you. What can I detect for you?"

"This." Nick pulled out the small plastic bag with the strand of hair. It looked odd now that he was out of the influence of Tabby and her snobbish boyfriend, and he scowled as he handed it over to Bart.

The older man lifted an eyebrow as he opened the bag and took out the sample. "Losing your touch, aren't you?"

Nick let out a sharp breath. "I must be. My God, that isn't human hair!"

"Bingo." Bart studied it and shrugged. "Animal fur. Someone has a dog, right?"

He wasn't sure if Tabby had one or not, but she'd mentioned going into the biology lab on the way over to the college. Probably she'd picked it up there, where they kept rats and mice and dogs and cats and such, and it had come off on her desk.

Nick took the sample back. "A dog or a rabbit or

some such thing," he agreed. "Funny I didn't notice that it wasn't human."

"I can run it for you and tell you exactly what it is, if you like."

He shook his head. "No need. I'm getting careless, I guess," he said with a rueful smile.

"Something on your mind?"

"Yes. A lady," Nick replied. His broad shoulders rose and fell. "I'm sorry to have bothered you. There's been a theft. Nothing major, to my mind, but I'm trying to help a friend catch the culprit."

"If you come up with anything tangible, come back," Bart said with a twinkle in his eyes. "I don't get a lot of work these days. My eyes, you know. These younger boys and girls are taking over my old stomping ground." He stared at the test tubes and beakers and microscopes with a loving stare. "Don't get old, Nick."

"I'll do my best," he promised. He shook hands with the older man. "It was good to see you again," he said. "Sometimes I miss the old days."

"Don't we all. I didn't expect to hear from you again, after your own tragedy," he added sympathetically.

Nick nodded sadly. "It was a blow, losing her that way to a bullet. But I don't know that we'd ever have made a go of it. We were both career-minded, and she loved her work." He remembered the woman who'd filled the gaping hole Tabby had left in his life with fondness. He'd never loved Lucy, but he'd been fond of her. Her death had haunted him for years; now, he was finally able to face it.

The older man saw the bad memories in Nick's eyes and quickly changed the subject. "Say, remember that redhead who gave you fits when you first came here, the one who was transferred to Miami and we all got down on our knees and gave thanks?'' he asked.

Nick chuckled. ''Yes. What was her name…Cynthia something?''

''That's right. Well, she's chief agent in Miami these days,'' he told Nick. ''Doing a helluva job, too. Married to one of her agents and has two kids.''

''Imagine that,'' Nick said, shaking his head. ''Funny, I never thought of her as a marrying woman.''

''Neither did I. Sort of like you and me, Nick. I never found a woman I could live with. It doesn't look as if you ever did, either.''

''I suppose some of us are born loners,'' Nick replied. Then he remembered Tabby's mention of Daniel as her fiancé and his eyes glittered with anger. He felt as if something was being taken from him. Ridiculous, of course. Tabby wasn't his.

The thing was, he couldn't get her out of his mind. All the way back to the college, he had her in his thoughts. It wouldn't do; it really wouldn't do.

Tabby wasn't in. He went by the admissions office and picked up a catalog. It gave some pretty detailed information about the faculty, and he could put that to good use. He strolled up to the floor where Tabby worked on the pretext of looking for her and got an earful from a janitor who was cleaning the hall. By the time he drove back to his parents' house, he had plenty of information to get him started on suspects.

He phoned the agency, and asked for his sister. She could get what he needed without involving any of the skip tracers. He didn't want everyone in the office knowing about his private life.

''What's up?'' Helen asked.

"Tabby's career, if we don't find a thief," he said, and explained what he meant.

"But they wouldn't fire her, would they?" Helen asked worriedly. "I mean, she has tenure."

"That won't matter if that artifact doesn't turn up," he assured her. "I've got a list for you. Right at the top is her new 'fiancé.'"

"Daniel?" she asked pointedly, hiding a smile when Nick hesitated before confirming the guess.

"Do you know him?" he asked.

"Sure. He's my age, you know. He and Tabby and I were friends when we were all in college together. He's a bit of a stick in the mud, and I wouldn't call him exciting company. But he's nice, and settled. He'll take care of her."

"More than likely, she'll do the nurturing," he said shortly. "I don't like him. He's a prissy, self-centered snob."

"That, too," she agreed without heat. "It's Tabby's life, Nick. She's entitled to marry the man of her choice."

"Even if he's a rank idiot?" he asked coldly.

"Even then. Give me those names, will you, and I'll start checking. But you won't find anything shady in Daniel's past. He's much too straitlaced to have ever robbed a bank or anything."

"You never really know people until you dig deep," he assured her. "You know that. Got a pencil?"

"Yes. Go ahead."

He gave her the list of names and read her the appropriate information from the college catalog. "Get everything you can," he told her. "And phone me the minute you have anything concrete on any of these people."

''You can count on me, Bro,'' she agreed. ''You might get some input from Tabby. Ask her if she suspects any of them,'' she said easily.

''That was my original idea,'' he said. ''But I can't get her in the house. She's afraid her reputation will be ruined if people see her go into a house alone with me,'' he said irritably.

''She lives in an old-fashioned world,'' she told him. ''She's not modern.''

''I suppose not. It's so damned silly...''

''Humor her,'' Helen said. ''Probably she's still raw about New Year's Eve. Tabby never drinks, and I really fouled things up for her by telling lies about your intentions,'' she added with quiet regret. ''I was only trying to be a good scout, but I made her life miserable. She's probably embarrassed to be alone with you at all, in case you think she frequently gets drunk and throws herself at men.''

''I know she isn't going to let history repeat itself, for heaven's sake,'' he said angrily. ''She doesn't have to avoid me.''

''Tell her.''

He sighed roughly. ''Maybe I should.''

''Good man. Go to it. I'll get busy in the meantime. I'll give you a call when I find something. Bye.''

She rang off and he put the receiver down. He wondered how long it would take Tabby to get home.

As it was, her car didn't pull into the driveway until dark. Nick watched her out the window, angry that she'd taken so long to come home, that she'd been out with her idiot fiancé. Tabby deserved better than that stuffed shirt. She was too good for him.

He went out and strolled over, just in time to open

the door for her as she climbed out of her car with an armload of books.

"Oh. Thanks," she faltered. She hadn't expected to see him twice in the same day. Maybe he'd found out something. "Anything new?" she asked hopefully.

He shrugged. "Nothing yet. I'm working on it." He lifted the glass to his lips and caught her eyes on him. "It's whiskey and soda. Want some?"

She made a face. "I hate whiskey."

"You didn't mind it New Year's Eve. Did you?"

She flushed and turned toward her front door. "I have to get inside."

He caught her arm and held her back, so that her shoulder touched his broad chest in its thin shirt. She could feel the warmth, the maleness of him, and it made her ache.

"Don't, Nick," she pleaded gently.

"You did all the running that night," he accused at her ear. "Primped and swanned around me until all I saw was you. Then you plastered yourself against me in that black dress that fit you like a second skin and started kissing me." His body tautened with the memory. "I had to do something, quick, so I pushed you away and read you the riot act. But it was for your own good. You have to understand that it wasn't malicious on my part."

"I know that," she said, almost choking on wounded pride. "I'm engaged..."

"Oh, hell, he isn't an engagement, he's an ego trip. You only took up with him to prove to me that I was off the endangered list. Okay. I get the message. You don't have to shove it down my throat."

She turned, the heavy books clasped close to her breasts. "Nick, I'm not marrying Daniel to...to prove anything to you. I'm twenty-five. I want to settle down and have kids. Daniel is settled and he doesn't smoke or gamble or...drink,'' she added averting her eyes from his drink.

"I don't drink, either, as a rule,'' he said quietly, "and never to excess. I'm not driving, you notice,'' he added mockingly.

"Good thing,'' she murmured, grimacing at his breath. "You could probably fell an oak tree if you breathed on it. For heaven's sake, don't light a match.''

"Funny girl,'' he said without humor. His eyes slid down to her vulnerable mouth and lingered there. "You still don't know how to kiss, do you?'' he asked conversationally, ignoring her embarrassed start. "I should have taught you years ago, but you were afraid of me.''

"I was not,'' she said defensively.

"You ran every time I came close,'' he challenged. "Once, I tried to ask you out. When you saw me coming, you left through the back door.''

"I didn't know you wanted to take me anywhere,'' she said, avoiding his piercing stare. "You told Helen I was a pest and you wanted me out of your life. I got out.''

He stood very still. "When was this?''

"That night you came over and asked to see me, when I was eighteen. I figured you planned to warn me off. I had a feeling that someone had told you how I, well, that I had a crush on you, and you were going to tell me it was no use. I didn't want to hear it, so I ran.''

He hadn't known about any crush. Helen hadn't told him anything. "Did Helen tell you that she'd said any such thing to me?'' he persisted.

"Oh, not Helen. She wouldn't have been so cruel. No. Mary Johnson told me. She said Helen had confided it to her. I was too embarrassed to say anything to either of you about it. I thought everything would be all right if I just kept out of your way. And it was.''

''I didn't tell anyone that you were a pest,'' he said through his teeth. ''And I never knew about the crush. Maybe you don't know that Mary Johnson had an outsize yen for me and I had to slap her down, hard. She was one of your circle of friends, I recall.''

She stared down at her books. One of them had a creased cover. She traced it with her fingernail. ''I thought she was my friend.''

''Apparently she was jealous of you.''

''Without cause.'' She sighed. ''She said you hated the very sight of me, that I was too plain and dull to appeal to you.''

He didn't reply to that. He was trying to take it all in. So pretty little Mary had been the culprit who'd sent Tabby running from him all those years ago, passing lies to Tabby and keeping her at bay. What a travesty. Not that it would probably have mattered, because he wasn't any more ready for marriage then than he was now.

''For what it's worth, all these many years too late, I never thought of you as plain or dull. You had—still have—a keen, analytical mind and more than your fair share of intelligence.'' He smiled slowly. ''You're not bad on the eyes, either. Not that you couldn't use a few more pounds.''

''I don't eat much. I work hard.''

''So do I.'' He drained his glass and stared at it. ''Why Daniel?''

''Nobody else wanted me,'' she said involuntarily, and then felt stupid for having said such a thing. ''I have to go in now, Nick,'' she added quickly. ''I've got all this research to do for Daniel.''

''Damn Daniel,'' he said carelessly. ''Come home with me. I've got a new blues album we can dance to.''

''You like blues?'' she asked.

''Sure. Old-time blues, what they used to call torch songs.''

''I like those, too.''

''So Helen mentioned.'' He put his glass on top of her car and took the books from her grasp, despite her protests. He stuffed them back into the car, retrieved his glass, caught her by the hand and led her over to his house.

''It's dark. I can't,'' she began, pulling against his grasp.

He ignored her. A minute later, she was behind his closed door with him.

''I won't seduce you,'' he promised wickedly. ''Not without fair warning. Come and have a drink with me while I put on the music.''

''I don't drink and I'm not a good dancer...''

He ignored that, too. He put on the music, poured her a soda with a little whiskey in it and handed it to her. While she sipped it, he pulled her against his tall, fit body and began to move lazily to the rhythm while he drank from his own glass.

''You smell of gardenias,'' he said with lazy pleasure in the feel of her body against his. ''I gave you a corsage of them once, remember?''

''When you took me to a class dance in college.'' She nodded. ''I was the envy of every girl there, even though you only did it because Mary got Helen to ask you to.''

He frowned. ''She didn't.''

"Mary said…" she protested.

He held her eyes. "Mary lied. Haven't you caught on yet? She wanted me. She was jealous of you."

"She was pretty."

"Plenty of women are. But I'm selective. Very, very selective. Right now," he murmured, bending close to her, "I have a raging hunger for tall brunettes with bow mouths."

She turned her face away and stiffened. "Don't tease me, Nick, please."

"You tasted of whiskey New Year's Eve night," he said huskily, his eyes still on her mouth. "You slid between my legs and moved on me as if you were born to be a siren, and I thought it was going to kill me to let you go. It damned near did. I wanted you."

"You didn't!" she protested, stopping to glare up at him. "You said horrible things to me!"

"It was that or take you to bed, and I wanted to," he said shortly. His eyes kindled. "You don't know how much I wanted to, Tabby. I could feel your body burning under those layers of cloth and I wanted to strip you down to your skin and make a banquet of you with my mouth."

She cleared her throat. "Shouldn't we sit down? It's rather warm in here."

"Isn't it, though." He moved her toward the mantel. Placing his glass on it, he took hers from her nerveless fingers and put it beside his. "Now," he said quietly.

He lifted her in his embrace as his mouth glided down to possess hers, its movements comforting, slow, encouraging a response that she'd rather have died than give him. But she couldn't resist. He tasted of whiskey and lime and his tongue was in her mouth, probing and teasing and withdrawing like a living thing. She moaned, trying to pull back while she still could.

"Don't fight it," he breathed. "Don't fight me. Open your mouth. Let me teach you how."

She tried to argue, but the motion of her lips only accommodated him more. She felt her body begin to sway toward him. He took instant advantage of that weakness, his hands pulling her hips gently into the thrust of his while he kissed her more and more deeply.

"Don't be afraid," he whispered as he bent and lifted her clear off the floor, his lips touching hers as he spoke. "I won't hurt you."

"Nick," she moaned weakly. But her hands were clinging, not fighting, and her body was on fire for him. It was the old need again, only this time he was giving her what only dreams had provided before. He was loving her, even if only physically.

"There's…Daniel," she tried to speak.

"Damn Daniel," he breathed roughly. "Make love to me."

She felt him place her on the long leather sofa. She felt his weight settling over her, pressing her down, consuming her. He was heavy and warm, and she loved the way he was kissing her, the way he was holding her. Daniel would never have presumed to touch her in such a way, to disregard the rules of conduct that she'd always expected.

Nick's hands accepted no restrictions. They smoothed over her taut breasts as if they had every right. They possessed her, made her ache with their expert caresses. His thumbs eased over the hard nipples and rubbed at them insistently, and he lifted his head to watch her reaction.

She gasped. He liked that, so he did it again. She trembled.

"Move up," he said quietly. When she did, he held her eyes while his knee insinuated itself between her thighs.

She stiffened, but he shook his head. "It's all right, Tabby," he said softly. "I'm only going to move a little closer. It isn't dangerous. I promise you, it isn't. Let me lie over you completely, little one. I can spare you most of my weight, like this…" He rested on his elbows as he eased down, and when she felt the intimacy of the movement, the arousal of his body, she cried out in mingled excitement and fear.

"This is overdue," he whispered unsteadily as his hips lowered. "Long, long overdue. Lie…still!"

Her last sane thought was that she was going to lose her chastity on a sofa. After that, nothing seemed to matter except pulling Nick as close as she could get him to the raging ache in her lower body. It gnawed so that it made her ache and cry out in her need. She'd never known sensations so urgent, so violent, that they pulsed through her like fire.

"Rock under me," he whispered quickly. "Yes. Yes! Lift up to me, Tabby…!"

She tried to, but her body was weak with need, with hunger. Her arms clung to him, gave in to him, while his mouth devoured hers with long, slow kisses that gave no relief at all.

His hand went under her, to force her hips up into the cradle of his. He moved rhythmically, feeling her body jerk as she accepted the intimacy, accepted the arousal of his body in an embrace he'd never meant to offer her.

"I want to have you," he said into her mouth, his

body stiff and unsteady. "Are you protected? Is there a risk that I could make you pregnant?"

Risk. Pregnant. She opened her dazed eyes and looked at him. She was twenty-five and engaged to be married, and this man had already devastated her life once with his rejection. How had she managed to forget all that?

He moved involuntarily, and she remembered. Her face flamed as the intimacy they were sharing penetrated the delight he'd kindled in her.

"Nick?" she whispered unsteadily.

He lifted himself a little and looked down at her, at the position she was lying in beneath him. Her long legs were wrapped around his thighs and she was holding him low down on his back.

He smiled through his desire. "My, my," he said huskily. "I think you're getting the hang of this, Tabby."

She followed his gaze and abruptly moved her legs, pushing at him. "Let me go!"

"That isn't what you said five minutes ago," he replied lazily as he complied with her plea.

She tore out of his arms and got to her feet. Her legs would barely support her. Her hair was askew and hopelessly tangled. Her mouth was swollen. So were her breasts. He'd touched them through the fabric and they were tender. She felt…as she'd never felt in her life, and she didn't know how to handle it.

She stood over him, looking down at the length of his powerful, visibly aroused body and suddenly averted her gaze to his amused face.

"I'm not going to spare you by trying to hide it," he said. "I want you."

"I'm not…in the market for a love affair," she choked. "This isn't why I came home with you!"

"Isn't it?" he asked. He sat up lazily, his eyes acquisitive as they lingered on her soft body. "Are you going to try and pretend that you didn't feel anything?"

"I'm not that good an actress. I expect you could arouse a rock, with your experience," she said shortly. "But I'm not fair game. I'm engaged."

"Not for long," he said, "Not after I tell Daniel what we were doing on the sofa tonight."

"You wouldn't!" she exclaimed, horrified.

"I was having a good time until your conscience reared its ugly head," he said. "God knows why your body is living back in Victorian times when you have such a sensuous little mouth."

"Let's leave my sensuous mouth out of it," she said stiffly. "I have to go home. I've got work to do."

"You could come up to bed with me instead," he coaxed, his eyes soft and coaxing. "I could undress you and love you all night long. By morning, you couldn't remember Daniel's last name if your life depended on it."

"By morning, I'd be suicidal and you'd have a hangover and a guilty conscience that you led me on," she said coldly. "Just like New Year's Eve, when you accused me of everything from seduction to blackmail."

"You weren't ready for me then," he said quietly. "Now you are. That's the difference. I can give you something Daniel never will. I can satisfy you."

"I don't want you to satisfy me, thank you very much," she said stiffly. "I appreciate you helping me clear my name, but my body isn't going to be in lieu of salary. I hope that's understood."

"It is, but it's a hell of a shame," he sighed. "Money

isn't half as sweet as you are when you let yourself go, Tabby.''

"You were kidding, weren't you?" she asked at the door. ''About telling Daniel, I mean.''

He stared at her for a long moment. ''Was I?'' he asked softly.

She got out, quickly. He watched the closed door for one long moment before he poured himself another drink and went upstairs to take a long, very cold shower. Even so, it was hours before he finally slept. He hadn't realized just how potent Tabby would be. Now that he knew, he wondered if he was going to be able to forget.

He tossed and turned as the sensations he'd felt with Tabby racked his body. He slept nude, and the softness of the sheets was so much like the softness of her skin that he groaned out loud.

He got up finally and went to get himself a drink. It might not help, but it wouldn't hurt.

As he sipped it, he stood at his bedroom window and looked over at Tabby's house. He smiled slowly. Her bedroom light was on, too, so apparently she wasn't sleeping any better than he was.

She was such a contrast to Lucy. He could finally think about her without flinching. Lucy Waverly had been small and spicy and she'd liked to take risks. She liked long lovemaking sessions on the floor of his apartment, and she knew how to use her body as Tabby had never learned. Lucy had been exciting and a balm to his wounded masculinity after Tabby's rejection.

But love? No, he hadn't loved Lucy. He might have married her, just because of the excitement she gave him. But a bullet put paid to that proposition.

He'd gone to Lucy's funeral with dead eyes, and part

of him had never been the same. He'd blamed himself for not marrying her and making her give up her job. Then, after a year, he got realistic and came to the conclusion that he could no more have deprived her of the job she loved than she could have deprived him of it.

Lucy was gone and he had to face the world without her. But he thought about the way she'd died, and the risks of his own job. That had kept his later liaisons brief and unemotional.

Tabby was changing all that. She was winding herself around him with her eccentric little ways and her soft, sweet mouth. She was killing him with remembered pleasure.

He wasn't sure what was going to happen, and he didn't want any commitment. But he did want Tabby. If he could induct her into the modern world, and get her out of her Victorian attitudes, what an affair they could have! He had erotic visions of Tabby's eager body in bed with him while he took her from frightened virgin to sated woman.

The prospect was so delicious that he barely slept the rest of the night for dreaming about it.

Chapter Four

Nick was drowsy and out of sorts when he dragged himself from the bed. He felt hung over from frustration as well as alcohol. He, who seldom drank, had certainly made some inroads into the meager supply of scotch whisky he kept at the house.

It was Sunday. He hadn't been to church in some years. Now he felt the need to go again, to be with Tabby. That need sent him right back to bed, and he slept without interruption until midafternoon.

Eventually he drank enough black coffee and took enough aspirins to get his mind back together. He phoned Helen to see if she'd had time to find out any morsel of information. He half hoped she hadn't. He didn't relish the thought of seeing Tabby after the fool he'd made of himself the night before. He seemed to have this crazy compulsion to lead her on, when he had nothing, not a damned thing, to offer her. He didn't want her permanently. Why couldn't he manage to leave her alone? It would be in her best interests, and certainly in his. But every time he thought of her, his toes curled.

He really wouldn't tell precious Daniel what they'd done together the night before, but it did serve to keep Tabby guessing when he threatened it.

She'd been so sweet wrapped around him like that. He remembered her long, silky legs sliding against his and his body violently protested the memory.

He got up and paced the floor, trying to calm the heat in his loins. Nothing seemed to work. Bedtime finally came. He'd wasted a whole day being miserable. He wondered if Tabby had, too, or if she'd had other things on her mind. He noticed a strange white car in her driveway for most of the afternoon and knew without being told that it had to be Daniel. Damn Daniel, he thought as he went up to bed. The man was driving him crazy.

So was Tabby.

He got up early the next day and went over to Tabby's kitchen, knocking on the door as soon as he saw the lights go on.

Tabby opened the kitchen door sleepily. She was so sleepy, in fact, that she didn't seem to realize she was standing there in a thigh-length soft cotton nightshirt that revealed every line and curve of her body. With her hair long around her shoulders and her face flushed from sleep, she was enough to arouse a statue—which Nick wasn't.

She realized suddenly what she'd done, but it was too late. Nick moved toward her with intent.

Quickly she got a kitchen chair between them and held it there, blocking him.

"Now, Nick," she said, laughing nervously. "You

just remember that you're a confirmed bachelor. Repeat it several times.''

"I have. It doesn't help. Move the chair, Tabby," he said huskily.

He did look sexy with his shirt half unbuttoned, his sleeves rolled up. His hair was just disheveled enough to give him a rogueish look. His dark eyes twinkled with amusement and frank desire as he tried to go around the chair.

She blocked him again. "No good, Nick," she commented. "I'm a dried-up spinster living in the cobwebs. Isn't that what you told Helen after you left here at New Year's?"

He stopped dead. "She wouldn't have said that to you," he began.

"She thought she was doing me a favor, actually," Tabby replied, and she looked faintly wounded. "I'd cried all night long and she thought I was going to die eating my heart out for you, if she didn't tell me the truth. In the long run, it was best, Nick."

"I never knew how you felt about me when you were in school," he said, his voice deep and quiet in the kitchen. The only other noise was the faint whirr of the washing machine on the utility porch. "You ran the other way so much that you bruised my ego."

"I'm sorry. I was shy of you," she said. "Much too shy to do anything or say anything blatant." Her face lifted proudly. "But that's all in the past, Nick. I'm engaged to Daniel. I'm going to be married."

His dark eyes narrowed. "You don't love Daniel."

"I respect and like him," she said. "At my age, that's no bad thing. I can live without passion. It's like flashfire—easily kindled and just as easily put out."

He got the message at once. "And what you felt with me on my sofa last night was just flashfire?"

She nodded, schooling her face not to give her away. "Just that. Overdue passion, a residue from my hero-worshiping days. I wanted to know how it would feel if you made love to me. Now my curiosity is satisfied."

"Not completely," he said, his face arrogant and hard. "Why don't you go to bed with me and get a complete picture?"

Her face flooded with heat, but she shook her head. "Too drastic. A taste was enough."

"That was more than a taste."

She cleared her throat. "Nick, I have to get dressed and get to work."

Work. He remembered that he was supposed to be working, too, and on her case. He'd allowed himself to get sidetracked the night before because of his hunger for her. He couldn't afford the luxury today.

"Yes. So do I." His eyes ran down over her body. He wondered what her breasts looked like under that cotton. They seemed to rise without support, and he remembered how warm and firm they'd felt in his hands the night before. "Take it off and let me look at you," he said huskily, catching her gaze. "I want to see you without your clothes, Tabby."

His voice was as seductive as his eyes, but Tabby had enough will to save herself from that final humiliation. Nick wanted her. Men could be devious when their needs were involved. But once he'd actually possessed her, it would be the end because he couldn't make a commitment. She'd be agreeing to nothing more than a delicious but quickly forgotten one-night stand on his part. The thought made her sad.

"I'm sure you've said the same thing to half a dozen

other women over the years, Nick,'' she replied. ''Sorry. I don't do striptease work. Just anthropology.''

''Ancient work does rather go with ancient attitudes, doesn't it?'' he asked sharply.

She shrugged. ''I wasn't raised to be licentious. You weren't either, but I guess your early education didn't take, did it?''

He glared at her. ''I'm not locked up in outdated myths and morals.''

''To each his own,'' she said without heat. ''Go home, Nick. I'm busy.''

''You still look a little hung over this morning,'' he told her dryly. ''Wouldn't Daniel have a screaming fit if he knew why?''

''Daniel wouldn't have a screaming fit if I had sex with a martian on my front lawn,'' she replied imperturbably. ''He's an intelligent man. He'd understand.''

''Think so? We could find out.''

''Why bother?'' she asked with a faint frown. ''Nick, you don't want me, really. You've discovered years too late that I had a crush on you, and maybe you were as curious as I was. But that's all it is. You don't have the slightest temptation to settle down and have children.''

He stuck his hands deep in his pockets and his eyes grew thoughtful as he stared at her. ''No,'' he said honestly. ''I don't. But if I ever did want a family, I think I'd want it with you.''

She smiled. ''I'm very flattered.''

He shrugged. ''I'm footloose. I don't suppose I'll ever be able to stay in one place very long. I like detective work, police work. I like the challenge and the danger. That doesn't really mix with a settled life-style. And I can't imagine watching you go out of your mind

wondering when I might end up in a hospital somewhere because I poked my nose into the wrong pot.''

"If you loved me, I might risk it," she said. "But
love isn't a word you know."

"It never will be," he said. "Dodging bullets is one
thing. Being at the mercy of a woman is another."

She knew what he was telling her. He never intended
letting a woman close enough to hurt him. She'd heard
rumors about his lady love at the FBI getting killed,
and that he'd never gotten over it. Helen, and Mary,
had told her. He probably never would get over it. She
couldn't go on tormenting herself with hope that he'd
care about her one day. Helen was right on that score.
It was better to go ahead and marry someone and settle
down.

"You're independent," she said. "I know how that
feels. But I'm tired of living alone and depending on
myself. Daniel and I get along very well. We'll have a
good life together."

"Sure," he said easily. "As long as you don't have
to suffer him too often in bed."

She colored. "I beg your pardon!"

"Don't sound so starchy. If Daniel could satisfy you,
I wouldn't have had such an easy time of it last night.
You were ready for me the second I touched you. You
don't want him at all, physically, do you?"

"Sex isn't everything!"

"Marriages stand and fall on it, or so I'm told," he
countered. "If you don't want him, Tabby, your life is
going to be hell. He'll know it, and hate you for it."

She couldn't admit that Daniel already found her
stiffness unappealing. Her lack of response to his in-
frequent kisses irritated him.

"I'll get used to that part of it."

"Get used to it! My God!"

"I'd rather have a man I can talk to...Nick!"

He'd torn the chair out of her hands while she was still speaking. Seconds later he had her back down on the kitchen table, and his mouth was on hers.

She couldn't struggle. The slick Formica top made her position precarious, so that if she moved she was in danger of sliding off. Nick held her down with one big, lean hand while his mouth ravaged hers. She gave in helplessly, almost hating him for the ease of his conquest.

His hand slid down over her breast to her stomach and then to the top of her thigh. He eased the hem of her nightie up, very slowly, making her all too aware that there was nothing under it.

All the while, she looked up at him with wide, shocked eyes that couldn't see beyond the intense pleasure his mouth had given her, the feel of his warm, deft hand on her body.

His fingers trailed up her silky thigh. She caught her breath and shivered. She should catch his hand and stop it. She should protest. But all she did was lie there, at his mercy, waiting.

His dark eyes slid down to the hem of the nightshirt. Under it, his hand had found the soft apex of her hip and her thigh and was resting there.

She felt the caress in every pore of her body. Her legs felt boneless, her heart throbbed. Her lips parted as the lingering touch made her ache and swell.

"You aren't wearing briefs," he whispered. "Do you always sleep like this?"

"Yes," she whispered huskily.

"And always alone?"

"Always."

His hand flattened on her body, teasing, tormenting. If he moved it a few inches, it would promote an intimacy she'd never experienced. Part of her wanted that, wanted to know passion. Another part was afraid, shy, inhibited.

"You're tense," he said softly. "So tense. It isn't necessary. I wouldn't hurt you for anything in the world. Don't you know that?"

"Yes."

His hand moved slowly up her body until it found the taut, high swell of her breast. He touched her there, feeling her stiffen and catch her breath. His thumb and forefinger drew circles around the taut nipple, making her squirm.

"I've already seen you in my dreams," he whispered. Both hands went to the bottom of the nightshirt. "Now, I'm going to make them come true for both of us."

He eased the fabric up her body until it came to rest, finally, bunched up under her chin. He looked at her and caught his breath, while she lay there, flushed and hungry under his eyes.

"My God," he said through his teeth. "Tabby, you're exquisite!"

His eyes told her that she was desirable, even before his head bent and his mouth worshiped her breasts. She arched upward, welcoming his warm lips, his tongue, his teeth as he made a meal of her. His mouth was pressing down hard on her belly when the telephone rang and kept ringing.

He lifted his mouth from her body and stared at her, not quite rationally.

"It's the telephone," he said huskily.

"It isn't stopping," she murmured dazedly.

He gave her one long, last look. His lean hands smoothed over her body with possession, leaving a trail of pleasure where they touched. "I thought you were thin," he whispered ruefully. His mouth teased around her breasts and kissed the hard tips with a warm, torturous suction that made her pulse with new hunger. "I want to make love to you," he breathed. "I want you to lie under me and let me take you."

"Nick!" she wailed.

He stood erect all at once, his eyes dark and possessive for several seconds before he pulled her off the table and jerked her nightshirt down to cover the body his mouth had explored so tenderly.

"You'd better answer it," he said curtly.

She picked it up with trembling hands. "Hello?"

"Tabby, it's nine o'clock," Daniel said impatiently. "Your class is waiting for you."

She gasped. "Daniel, I'm sorry! I…overslept," she said with a flushed glance at Nick. "I'll be right there. Can you sub for me for a few minutes? I'm going over physical anthropology and its technical terms—you know those as well as I do."

"All right," he said. "You're lucky my next class isn't until ten."

"Thank you! You're a lifesaver!"

She hung up and pushed back her disheveled hair.

"Forget the class and come to bed," Nick said, his body still throbbing with hunger.

"I can't," she whispered. "Even if I didn't have a class. Nick, you have to stop doing this to me! I can't handle it!"

He smiled slowly. "You want me."

"Of course I want you! But there's no future in it!"

His broad shoulders shifted as he leaned against the

table. "We could still enjoy each other, while it lasted," he said seriously. "I wouldn't hurt you."

"I'm engaged," she repeated.

"To a fool," he scoffed. "He's only using you."

"What are you trying to do?" she exclaimed.

He didn't like the way that sounded. "If you want to put it like that, we'd be using each other. I need a woman. You need a man. We've got a long past behind us, and we like each other."

"You're describing what I have with Daniel as well," she said stiffly. "I'd like you to leave, Nick."

"No, you wouldn't," he replied, his eyes going like homing pigeons to her sharp-tipped breasts. "You're still as hungry as I am."

"But I'm back in my right mind now," she said. "I won't be unfaithful to Daniel."

"That comes after marriage, not before."

"Not in my world," she replied. "I haven't become cynical, Nick. I still have my golden ideals. I believe in happy marriages and long relationships."

"Relationships don't last. You're as big a fool as your Daniel if you don't know that by now."

"All I know is that I've got a better chance for happiness with Daniel than I have with you," she said, exasperated. "Please go."

"If you insist." He pushed away from the table and opened the back door. "I've got Helen doing some checking for me. The offices were closed yesterday. She'll have something for me later this morning, I hope." He stared at her. "I'll need access to your office today. I have a couple of people I want to interview."

"You won't start any trouble?" she asked nervously.

"I'm a trained private investigator," he said angrily. "I have a degree in law."

"Sorry."

"I know you're nervous about being accused of something you didn't do, but if it takes stepping on a few toes to clear you, I don't mind doing it."

"I just don't want to make any more enemies than I have to," she said.

"I'm aware of that."

"Nick, how do you know I'm innocent of the charges?" she asked seriously.

"Because I know you," he said, surprised by the question. "I'll see you at the college, Tabby."

Later, he wondered himself why he'd never doubted her innocence. Perhaps it was a form of telepathy, but he was certain that he'd know if she lied to him. Certainly she was lying about her feelings for Daniel. Seeing her with the man had convinced Nick that she couldn't be in love with him. There was no spark between them, no hint of romantic interest, no physical attraction.

Between himself and Tabby, it was a totally different story. He wanted her desperately. After this morning, it was going to be hell trying to keep away from her at all.

She had the most beautiful, desirable body he'd ever seen. He wanted all of it, all of her. But her price was just too high for him to pay.

Nick went to Thorn College and set up his interrogations in Tabby's office while she was teaching her classes. Dr. Flannery, the assistant biology professor, was high on his list of suspects. One of the few things he'd learned about the man was that he needed money, and that he'd been accused of theft while still in his teens. Tabby's fiancé, meanwhile, had been arrested for taking part in an antiwar demonstration back in the sixties and had spent some time in jail. He'd deliberately falsified information on his record to that effect.

The computer in Tabby's office gave out a wealth of information on the faculty. Helen, one of the finer hackers in the Western Hemisphere, had supplied Nick with the password that got him into the college's personnel files. He was having a field day going through them. There was only one other suspicious person on the staff, and that was Dr. Day. Day was over the art department, and something of a professional layabout before, during and after college. He seemed to always have money, but the things he owned didn't jibe with the salary he was paid to teach. The Lamborghini, for instance, was a bit above the average college professor's salary.

Nick narrowed his investigation down to those three men, and proceeded to carefully and warily dig out any information he could about them. He discovered, not to his amazement, that Daniel was the only one of the three whom most everyone on campus disliked. Daniel soon became his number one suspect, but Nick had to keep his suspicions to himself for the time being. Tabby might not even believe his accusations, or she'd attribute them to jealousy.

He couldn't blame her. His behavior had been erratic and unbelievable, even to himself. He'd sworn to keep away from her, but more and more he was getting in over his head with her physically. One dark night, he thought irritably, he was going to steal into her bedroom and seduce her. That would certainly complicate an already impossible situation. She was bent on avoiding him after their interlude at her home. He sighed as he worked. Back to square one. It was no less than he'd expected.

Meanwhile, Tabby was trying to come to grips with her behavior of the morning. Allowing herself to be bent back over a kitchen table and fondled like some harem girl didn't sit well on her conscience. Ever since he'd come back, Nick had gone out of his way to make her aware of him. He'd been almost jealous of her relationship with Daniel, and frankly protective.

That was flattering, but it wasn't love. It wasn't even something permanent. Nick was on a case and she was handy. Perhaps he hadn't had a woman in a long time. She wished she knew more about his late woman friend.

During a slack period during the morning, she called Helen just to talk, because she wanted to do a little prying of her own.

"How's Nick doing?" Helen asked.

"All right, I suppose, he's very close-lipped about what he's finding out. Helen," she added slowly. "Tell me about Lucy."

"Ah. I was wondering if you'd ever ask," the other woman said gently. "Nick started going with her just after you turned down that skiing trip with us."

Tabby's heart skipped. "You asked me…"

"On his behalf. I even told you he'd wanted you along, but I guess he'd rejected you so much by then that you didn't believe anything he said. I'm sorry."

Tabby tangled the telephone cord around her finger and watched it curl. "So am I. Nick said that Mary had told me a lot of lies."

"Mary!" Helen ground out. "Yes, she did, and I knew nothing about it until you'd gone off to college and she laughed about breaking up your crush on Nick. She wanted him herself, but he didn't want her. It was pure malice. I wish I'd known.''

"She didn't get him,'' Tabby said with quiet satisfaction.

"No, she didn't,'' Helen said curtly. "She wound up with a bald banker twenty years her senior and the last time I saw her she looked older than he did. She hasn't had a good life.''

"Poor Mary,'' Tabby said.

"Poor you,'' came the reply. "If it hadn't been for Mary, you might be married to Nick by now.''

"Not likely. He isn't the marrying kind, is he?''

"I don't know. I think he was, before Lucy got killed, but her death frightened him. He learned that it hurt to lose people you cared about, even if they weren't people you loved. He's afraid to risk his heart. Especially,'' she added thoughtfully, "on someone he could love obsessively. He's growled about you ever since we were here the first of the year. But he hasn't been the same, either.''

"I...noticed that he's less brittle.''

"Our Nick?'' Helen chuckled. "Pat yourself on the back. He's been breakable out here.''

"It's the case. I don't flatter myself that it's me. He enjoys a good mystery.''

"Is that all he's enjoying?'' came the bland reply.

Tabby remembered his eyes on her nudity that morning and blushed to the roots of her hair. "What was Lucy like?'' she asked, putting the knife into her own heart with the question.

"Dainty and beautiful and devil-may-care. She burned like a candle flame, and went out just as easily. She was reckless and liked taking risks, just like Nick.''

Helen paused, because she was thinking, as Tabby was, how he liked risk and how easily he put his life on the line. He could wind up just like Lucy with no trouble at all. It was a frightening thought.

"Did he love her?" Tabby asked.

"He was fond of her. I think he found her exciting and sensual, and I'm pretty sure they were having a hot affair. He mentioned marriage, but without any real enthusiasm. I've never said this to him, but I always had the feeling that he would have broken it off in the end. He wasn't committed to her, even if he did find her vividly desirable."

"I suppose…women like that appeal to sophisticated men like Nick," Tabby said dully.

"In bed, sure." Helen laughed. "But not as prospective wives. Nick was raised to believe in all the virtues, even if he doesn't practice them. He'll settle one day, but it won't be with some vivid butterfly who likes the social life. He'll want a pipe and an easy chair and his children on his lap at bedtime to read stories to. You mark my words, he's got all the makings of a family man. He just doesn't know it yet."

"I wish…" Tabby began fervently.

"Don't give up on him," Helen said gently. "I know I tried to put you off him for your own good, but he's changed since January. He really has. Give it a chance."

"He wants me," she blurted out.

"Good. That's a step in the right direction. Just don't give in to him. That's the best way I know to classify yourself with his other women and turn him away."

"I know that. But it's hard," she confessed. "I do love him so, Helen."

"So do I," his sister admitted. "I think he's pretty

special. But, then, so are you, my friend. Keep in touch. And don't brood, about Nick or the spot you're in. It will all work out. Really, this time next year, you'll hardly remember it.''

''I hope you're right,'' Tabby said. But long after she put the receiver down, she remained unconvinced.

Chapter Five

There was a crowd in the halls when Nick came out of Tabby's office after having used the computer at Thorn College.

Shrieks were coming from the biology lab, and the outer door was open. With assumed casualness, he walked in.

Dr. Flannery was trying to calm a violently upset Pal. The man was holding something in his hands that the primate was obviously bent on possessing.

"You can't have these!" he was telling the monkey. "Where did you get them, anyway?"

"What does he have?" Nick asked with amused interested.

Dr. Flannery looked over his shoulder and his pink complexion went even pinker. "Dr. Day's keys," he replied. "God knows where he found them. Dr. Day must have been in here earlier."

"Are you teaching him to steal now, Flannery?" Daniel asked from the door with that maddeningly superior tone that put everyone's back up.

"I am not!" Flannery choked, and went even redder. "Would you give these to Dr. Day at lunch, please?" he asked Daniel, handing him the keys. "I have a meeting."

"Glad to," Daniel replied. "That animal's a born thief. I'd watch him if I were you."

"That's what I'm trying to do."

"This primate project is a waste of time," Daniel muttered. "The only thing you're going to learn about that creature is that he's adept at sleight of hand."

"I believe your field is history?" Dr. Flannery asked pointedly.

Daniel shrugged. "It doesn't take a biologist to recognize an animal with a bad attitude." He glanced with irritation at Nick, who'd been leaning against the door facing, taking in the conversation. "Did you need something, Mr. Reed?"

"Only Tabby," Nick replied with a sensuality in his tone that penetrated even Daniel's thick skull.

Daniel seemed to grow an inch. "My fiancée," he stressed the word, "is teaching her class."

"I know." Nick shouldered away from the wall. "Nice of you to take her class until she got here."

"How did you know that?" the older man demanded.

Nick smiled slowly. "Why don't you ask Tabby?" He turned and walked along the hall, intent for the moment on finding Dr. Day.

The art department was in a separate building, and it took some searching before he found Dr. Day's class. The interested looks he was getting from some of the women students amused him. But lately, the only face he saw was Tabby's. Who'd have believed that she had a body like that, he wondered as he walked along. Her clothes made her look thin and lackluster. But under them... He groaned silently at the memory of how it had been to look at her, to touch and taste her. He wanted her more and more every day, and that wouldn't do.

He found Dr. Day in a corner classroom, just gathering his things together into an attaché case. He was a tall, thin man with thick dark hair, and he looked faintly nervous.

"Dr. Day?" Nick introduced himself and shook hands with the other man. "I hope you don't mind. I'm trying to find out as much as I can about a recent theft."

"You think I'm involved?" he asked, immediately defensive.

"Good heavens, no," Nick drawled. "I wanted to know if you had any idea why someone might stoop to the theft of an ancient relic in the anthropology department, that's all."

Day relaxed, but only a little. He kept shoveling papers into that attaché case, but now his long fingers were trembling. "Why does anyone steal?" he asked. "For monetary gain."

"There are other motives."

He glanced at Nick. "Professional jealousy, I suppose?" He nodded. "Well, just between us, Dr. Daniel Myers has more than his share of that. He and Dr. Harvey were once what you might call serious rivals even though they work in different departments. They're engaged now, though, so I assume that they've settled their differences."

"Dr. Myers has your car keys, by the way." Nick told him after they'd talked for a few minutes. "He'll give them to you at lunch."

"What is Dr. Myers doing with my car keys?" he asked irritably.

"Dr. Flannery's primate research project took them, I understand."

"That blasted monkey! I wish someone would cook and eat him. He's a positive menace!"

"Most of the faculty on his floor would tend to agree with you." Nick frowned. "How did your keys get into the biology lab, if you don't mind my asking?"

"I haven't been in the biology lab in two days," Dr. Day replied seriously. "The last time I remember having my keys was in the audiovisual room. That's in the library, next door to the main building where the biology lab is temporarily located."

"Surely the monkey can't leave the building when he wants to?"

"He can pick locks, didn't you know?" Day scoffed. "The damned thing's almost human. That's what scares me. One morning they'll find him in the dean's office smoking cigars and drinking brandy. Then where will Flannery's precious research funds go?"

He seemed to find that thought amusing. Nick thanked him and made a few more stops on his way around the campus. Then he went back to find Tabby, because it was now nearing the lunch hour.

She and Daniel were in her office, in the middle of a heated discussion.

"It wasn't like that at all," she was saying. "Daniel, you can't believe…!"

"What else can I believe? And isn't his arrival right now a little convenient?" he added narrowly. "My God, you almost drool when he walks into a room! I've had no input from you in days about our book. I can't even get you on the telephone in the evenings. And this morning you're late and he knows that you asked me to take your class. How?''

"Go ahead, honey. Tell him," Nick dared her, pausing in the doorway.

Tabby flushed. "Don't make it sound like that!"

"Why not?" he returned. "It *was* like that." His eyes went to her blouse and lingered until she flushed. "I'm the reason she was late," he told Daniel, and he smiled.

Daniel went scarlet with rage. He glared at Tabby. "So that's what's going on. And you said it was just an old crush. But that's not true. You're lovers, aren't you?"

"No!" Tabby gasped.

"Conspirators, too, probably," Daniel continued angrily. "I don't doubt that you're guilty of that theft after all, Tabitha, and that you did it to discredit me! You know that when Brown retires, I'm in line for a promotion to head of the history department. You can't stand it that I might achieve a higher position than you have in the sociology department, isn't that it?"

"Daniel, you aren't even making sense!" she exclaimed. "Stealing an important find would only discredit me!"

"I'm engaged to you, so it would discredit me as well!" he shot back. "I must have been out of my mind to propose to you!"

He walked out, still fuming. Nick's dark eyes never left Tabby's white face. "I don't think you did it," he reminded her.

She looked limp. "Thanks, Nick. For that," she added, glaring at him wearily, "*not* for making Daniel think we're lovers."

"We'd be lovers if you were a little less rigid," he said easily. "Come on. I'll buy you lunch."

She was too tired to argue. Besides, there was little danger of any more romantic interludes in a public place.

Or so she thought. But Nick had other ideas in mind. He bought a picnic lunch from a fried chicken franchise and herded her into the nearby park, to a secluded area under a sprawling oak tree.

"Isn't this nice?" he asked while they ate warm chicken.

"Peaceful, at least," she agreed. If it hadn't been quite so isolated, she'd have minded less. A stream flowed through and the gurgling of the water sounded quite close, mingled with the singing of birds in the trees around them.

"You could use a little peace after your morning."

"Why did you have to let Daniel know you were with me when he called?" she asked miserably.

"Why try to hide it?" he countered. "He doesn't own you. My God, you don't even want him. He's only using you to further his own career. A blind woman could see that, but apparently you can't."

"Why he wants me didn't matter at the time," she confessed. "I only wanted…"

"To spite me," he said for her, his dark eyes narrowing as he finished a third piece of chicken. He wiped his hands and mouth on a napkin before he took a sip of coffee from a paper cup. "Maybe to show me that you could get married if you wanted to. I slapped you down hard on New Year's Eve. I don't blame you for doing something outlandish."

"I was drunk!"

He looked at her solemnly. "No. You wanted me. And I didn't want you."

"I know that, you don't have to rub it in," she said in a ghostly tone, averting her eyes to her own cup of coffee.

He studied her, approving the way she looked in the prim green-and-white pattern shirtwaist dress she was wearing. Her hair was bundled up on top of her head with a green scarf. She looked younger than usual, and very flustered.

He smiled, lounging back against the tree. He'd removed the sports coat that went with his dark brown slacks, and his tie with it. His white shirtsleeves were rolled up, the throat of his shirt unbuttoned. His hair was windblown and he looked reckless and elegant, lying there.

"I didn't realize how potent you'd be if we ever started kissing, until that night," he continued. "I was curious about you years ago, but every time I made a move, you backed away."

"You never made any moves," she countered.

"But I did. I can remember one particular instance, when I invited you to come up to law school for the weekend and go to a party with me."

Her dark eyes met his. "You were teasing. You laughed even when you said it."

"And you blushed and mumbled something and rushed off," he agreed. "I was serious. I meant it."

"I'm sure you didn't have any shortage of partners," she said stiffly.

"No. But it was you I wanted. You made me ache when you were eighteen, Tabby," he said softly. "I noticed you without any effort at all. But you were painfully shy of me. When I went to work for the FBI,

I tried again, but that was a disaster. I ran to Lucy in self-defense, to prove to myself that I was still a man.''

Her breasts rose and fell heavily with a long sigh. "They said you never got over her death.''

"It was unexpected," he said. "And I was fond of her. We got along well enough. I might have married her eventually." He searched Tabby's sad face. "But she was the consolation prize, nothing more. A substitute for what I really wanted and couldn't have." He sat up suddenly, holding her eyes. "Haven't you worked it out? I've spent years telling myself that you found me too frightening to touch. Then New Year's Eve, you launched yourself on me and started kissing me, and I couldn't get away from you fast enough. I couldn't believe that you really wanted me. I thought it was a drunken aberration.''

"It was!''

He shook his head. "No." He lay back again and opened his arms. "Come here.''

She froze, her lips trembling as she fought the temptation.

"Come on," he coaxed, smiling.

Her eyes widened. "I won't," she choked.

"Not enough temptation for you?" He paused to unbutton his shirt, watching her eyes go homing to the thick pelt of hair on his strongly muscled chest as he tore the shirt away from it and let her look. "Now, come here," he challenged softly, and held out his arms again.

She went to him against her better judgment. He pulled her down on him and found her mouth with slow passion, opening it to the soft probe of his tongue.

She caught her breath and he felt it, and smiled. He eased her over, onto her back and while he kissed her, his hand gently took the soft weight of her breast and caressed her as if she belonged to him.

"Touch me," he whispered roughly.

Her hands slid up and down over the thick hair, the warm muscle of him. She loved the way he felt, the faint throb of his heartbeat gaining strength under her fingertips. The breeze blew gently and bird songs filled the air while she heard her own quick breathing, and Nick's, magnified in the stillness.

She was dazed with pleasure when she felt his hand guiding hers away from his chest, down over the firm muscles of his stomach, until she touched him where his passion for her was most visible.

Her hand jerked away, but he pressed it there, and his mouth became hot and insistent on her parted lips. For one long, exquisite moment, she gave in to her need and his, and let him teach her.

The intimate feel of his body had an unexpected effect on her. She burned with the need to satisfy his hunger, to give him peace. She wanted him to touch her as she was touching him, she wanted him to pull her dress away and kiss her bare body. She wanted to be under him, over him, wanted to absorb him as earth absorbs water...

She didn't realize that she was whispering it to him, telling him all her secrets, her voice breaking as her hand pressed harder against him, learning him.

He groaned and moved suddenly, his weight between her lax thighs, the press of his aroused flesh suddenly intimately demanding. She cried out at the sensations it gave her when she felt him as she'd never experienced a man in her life.

"Nick...we...can't!" she gasped.

But he didn't hear her. The area was completely isolated, deserted. His hands were under her skirt, touching her, paving the way. She heard a faint rasp and then felt him without any hint of fabric in the way.

''Nick!'' she cried out.

''It's all right,'' he choked at her ear. His hands gentled her, trembling, as he eased closer, probing. He caught his breath and groaned helplessly. ''Oh, God, Tabby, let me! Baby, let me, let…me!''

His mouth covered hers with aching tenderness while he pushed down in a feverish, mindless agony of need. She cried out, because it was difficult. But seconds later, she felt him completely possess her, and she gasped at the incredible sensations she felt when he began to move with a slow, deliberate rhythm.

He kissed her while he loved her, his tongue imitating what his body was doing. He rocked over her, his body slow and unsteady, but very expert as he drew pleasure from her. He whispered to her, his voice unsteady, broken with pleasure, coaxing her to move, to lift, to absorb him.

The rhythm was unbelievably arousing. She jerked as the sensations shot through her like swelling fire, made her body wanton, made her brain shut down completely. There was only Nick, and the heat of his possession, the sharp urgency of his movements, the pleasure he was building and building until she tensed with an anguish bordering on madness.

She heard him repeating her name as his movements suddenly became violent. The world exploded around her, inside her. She cried out and began to convulse helplessly in hot contractions that were as frightening as they were ecstatic.

He shuddered and cried out in hoarse ecstasy, his body arching over her, his face clenched with the unbearable sweetness that racked his powerful body. Eons later, he slowly collapsed on her and lay still and spent, shivering with exhaustion even as she reached the most incredible peak of sensation. She couldn't breathe, couldn't bear it! She whispered it brokenly, her nails digging into his hips, pleading with him.

He gathered her closer and put his mouth over hers, rocking on her body until she convulsed again, and again. She cried out and her eyes opened, looking straight into his and his face blurred into red waves of delight.

She came back to awareness a little later, and her body felt cold and sick. They weren't even undressed. He'd only moved the most necessary things out of the way. He'd made love to her, taken her completely, in a public park under a tree where anyone could have seen them. The fact that the park was completely deserted made no difference. It was shameful and disgusting.

She began to cry. Vaguely she heard Nick's apology, felt him rearranging her disheveled clothing, righting his own. He pulled her up and into his arms, and held her cradled against him, his face a study in remorseful anguish.

"I lost it," he said, as if he still couldn't quite believe what he'd done. "My God, Tabby, I lost it! I'm sorry. Baby, I'm so sorry!"

She cried even harder. It wasn't just the loss of her chastity, it was the knowledge that to him it was just another casual interlude. It was also the shame of where it had happened. She was just like those women who walked the streets and sold their bodies, she thought hysterically. She had no morals!

He dried her eyes, but she wouldn't meet his concerned gaze. She drew away from him and got to her feet, surprised at how shaky she felt.

"Do you want me to take you home?" he asked slowly.

"I want to go back to work," she said shakily. "I'll…I'll…"

He caught her shoulders and turned her to face him. "I hurt you."

She tore away from him, horribly embarrassed, and began to run. He caught up with her easily, but she wouldn't look at him. Tears filled her eyes, her world.

"I'll drive you home," he said shortly. "You need a shower at least. Maybe a doctor…"

"I don't need a doctor!"

"All right," he said quietly. "Come on."

They drove to her house in silence. She phoned the college and told them she'd been delayed and would be right back. It didn't matter what they thought. Daniel had as much as said he didn't want to marry her anymore. That was just as well, because she was a loose woman. Nick's woman. Nick's…lover. There was no question of her ever being anything else, because he wanted no part of marriage.

She went quickly to her bedroom and laid out clean clothes, then into the shower. She felt only marginally better when she was wearing slacks and a gray silk top, with fresh makeup. But finding Nick pacing the living room didn't help her morale, or her feelings.

"Ready to go?" he asked stiffly.

So it was difficult for him, too? Good! She gathered her purse and locked the door behind them before she settled into the seat beside him in the car. She winced a little, because he hadn't been gentle and it had been her first time.

He cursed under his breath, not missing the hint of discomfort.

"I'm sorry," he said again, his conscience killing him.

She gripped her purse, staring straight ahead. "It's…part of the process, isn't it? Pain?"

"So they say. I wouldn't know. I've never made love to a virgin."

"That wasn't love," she said through her teeth, coloring. "That was a quick roll in the hay, because you had to have a woman and I was handy!"

He cut off the engine and turned to face her, lighting a cigarette with nervous fingers before he opened the window to spare her the passive smoke. "It was quick," he agreed with stung pride. "But not because you were handy and I needed sex. And as I recall, you didn't have the breath to complain when you were screaming under me to satisfy you!"

She buried her face in her hands with anguished shame.

"My God, I didn't mean that," he said wearily, running a hand through his sweaty hair. "I didn't mean to…Tabby, you were incredible. Really, incredible. I wasn't even sure that I'd be able to satisfy you," he said curtly. "You're more woman than I've ever had before."

She couldn't look at him. That made it, somehow, even worse.

"I couldn't manage to draw back, to make an effort to protect you," he said slowly. He looked at her flat stomach and something terrifying leaped into his mind. "Tabby," he said slowly, "tell me that this wasn't a good time to make you pregnant."

She flushed. He looked terrified by the prospect. That

registered, even through her anguish. "I don't know," she said miserably. "Oh, Nick...!"

She looked vulnerable and very frightened. Probably she was. He cursed under his breath. "That's great," he said icily. "That's just great!"

All her worst nightmares were flowing into the light. She closed her eyes, wished she could go back, wishing she could have a second chance. "You needn't worry that I'll be a nuisance if anything happens," she said through her teeth.

He jerked her around, his face pale. She seemed withdrawn and not quite rational, and fear lanced through him. He hadn't considered her deeply religious outlook.

"We made love, for God's sake!" he burst out. "It's no sin to sleep with someone!"

"Isn't it?" She couldn't look at him. "Then why do I feel ashamed and cheap?"

Her voice had a note that he didn't like. He took her by the shoulders and shook her. "Don't you do anything stupid, do you hear me?" he said angrily.

"I'm not that far gone," she replied tersely. She drew back from him with a long breath. "I want to go back to work, Nick."

He didn't want to leave her like this, but he had no choice. She wouldn't even look at him. He felt alone and uneasy, as if he'd done something unspeakable. He'd never felt like that with another woman in his life. Not that any of his women had ever been innocent.

She wouldn't talk to him. He had to hope she wouldn't go off the deep end. "All right," he said finally. "I'll drive you back." He started the car and drove her to the campus, but he didn't get out when she started to.

"You're through for today?" she asked, with her hand on the door handle, still avoiding his eyes.

"Yes."

She didn't know what to say. She murmured something and scrambled out onto the sidewalk.

Nick watched her go into the building, his eyes dark with worry. He'd fouled up her life and his own with a moment's passion. Now Tabby would avoid him like the plague, and he'd spend the next six weeks worrying himself to death about having accidentally made her pregnant. Why, oh why, hadn't he stayed in Houston and left well enough alone?

Tabby went through the motions of working for the rest of the day, but she felt sick to her stomach. She'd saved up her chastity for twenty-five years to give to the man she loved. Then in a fit of feverish passion, she'd given it to Nick in the middle of a public park.

She groaned out loud and tears stung her eyes. She had to force herself not to cry as she walked down the hall at the end of the day toward the exit. She loved Nick, but that didn't excuse what she'd let him do. Everything she believed in, everything she'd been taught had gone up in ashes in his arms. She'd wanted him, oh, so much. She hadn't been able to hold back, even when she knew what they were doing was wrong. Why, why, hadn't she tried to stop him?

To make matters worse, Nick didn't call or come over. She felt like something he'd used and thrown aside. He didn't even care enough to see if she was all right, if she'd tried to leap out a window or anything. That was proof that he didn't want her, that he didn't care.

But when the doorbell rang, she flew to answer it,

just the same, certain that it was Nick come to apologize.

Instead, it was a contrite, worried Daniel. ''I know you're angry at the things I said,'' he murmured deeply. ''I'm sorry. I could see all afternoon how upset you were. I know you and that playboy detective don't have anything going on. I came to apologize.''

''Oh, Daniel!'' His sympathy and compassion were so unexpected that she threw herself into his arms in the open doorway and cried as if her heart would break.

''There, there,'' he said uncertainly, backing her into the house while he fumbled the door closed.

Nick had been on his way across the lawn, but neither of them saw him. He'd stopped at the sight of Tabby in a bathrobe throwing herself at the historian.

He stormed back into his own house and slammed the door. He'd felt lower than a snake. He wanted to make sure that Tabby was okay, after fighting his conscience all day. He was sick at his own loss of control. She probably hated him.

He didn't know what he'd been about to say when he spotted her in Daniel's arms. It went right out of his head. Now he was confused and hurt and violently jealous. Was she playing some kind of game? Was she going to take Daniel up to bed and give him the benefit of the experience she'd had with Nick?

And he knew then that Tabby wouldn't do it. Not even if she wanted Daniel to the point of obsession. No, she wasn't that kind of woman.

But she was in the man's arms and apparently happy to be there. How did he equate that with the fervent way she'd given in to him in the park? Did she love Daniel? Was what she felt for Nick only physical after all, and now that she'd satisfied it she didn't want him anymore?

He'd never realized that he had so many insecurities. It had devastated him that he couldn't stop in the park. He'd never lost his head like that, stooping to the seduction of a woman in plain view of anyone who might have walked past. And not just any woman, either, but Tabby, who was virginal. He remembered her soft cry of pain, and then her body had accepted him with such warm sweetness that he'd gone right over the edge. He'd taken her there, too, though. He'd given her heaven. He didn't have to be told to know it. He remembered the things she'd whispered to him, things she probably didn't even recall saying. He remembered the desperate clutch of her hands, the soft, aching moans under his mouth. But most of all, he remembered the heartbreaking way she'd cried when he rolled away from her. She'd been ashamed and hurt, and what he'd said to her afterward hadn't done anything to alleviate the situation between them.

She was probably running to Daniel for comfort, and how could he blame her? He'd given her a moment's pleasure that would be followed by months of shame and anguish and possibly even a child that neither of them wanted.

He didn't know what to do next. His instincts told him to march right over there and bash Daniel's head in with a scotch bottle. The trouble was that first he'd have to empty the scotch bottle.

He picked it up and studied it carefully. Good idea, he thought, nodding. He poured some of it into a glass and drained it. It felt good going down. He sprawled on the sofa and had some more.

About midnight, Nick saw a car leaving Tabby's

driveway. It was about time that stuffed shirt went home.

He picked up the phone and punched in Tabby's number. He got two wrong connections. The third time he got Tabby.

"It won't work," he said, carefully enunciating his words. "I am not jealous of Daniel."

"I don't care what you are!" she raged at him. "Go away!"

"Come over and sleep with me," he murmured. "I need you, Tabby."

"I don't need you," she said huskily, her voice thick with tears. "You've been drinking, haven't you?" she asked suddenly as the slur of his deep voice got through her pain.

"Only a bottle or so of whisky," he said reasonably. "Had to empty the bottle. Didn't want to hit him with a full one."

"Hit him?"

"Lover boy," he explained. "I'm going to brain him, Tabby. You tell him to stay away from you. I don't want him touching you. You belong to me."

Her heart raced. But it was only the liquor talking. "No, I don't," she said firmly. "You go away. Leave me alone."

"Can't. Have to—" he hiccuped gently "—solve the case."

"Solve the case then, but you won't get near me again," she said stiffly. "Once was enough."

"No," he murmured. "Not nearly. So sweet, baby. So sweet! Never touched heaven like that before. Only with you, Tabby…"

Flushing, she slammed down the receiver. It rang again, but she ignored it, white-faced, and went to bed.

Never again, she told herself firmly. Oh, no, Nick. Never again.

She pulled the covers over her head and closed her eyes resolutely. She wasn't going to become one of his women. Somehow, someway, she was going to get over him once and for all. If there just weren't any consequences because of her stupidity. She groaned and closed her eyes tighter as she mumbled her prayers. Foremost among them was that she'd have the strength to escape Nick's arms, and that a tiny new life wouldn't be the price of her folly.

Chapter Six

Tabby had to force herself to get up and dress and go to work the next morning. She was sick and sore and her mind wasn't on her job. She taught mechanically, but she knew that the emotional turmoil she was experiencing had to show.

It did. Her mirror told her that. She hadn't talked to Nick again since last night. He was probably at home with a humdinger of a hangover, and she didn't care. She was just glad that he wasn't on campus. Having to see him now would make her sick. How could she have forgotten all her principles and given in like that?

Because she loved him, she thought with bitter resignation. To her, it had been a surrender that was a declaration of love and commitment. But to Nick it had been another interlude, a brief moment's pleasure that carried no responsibilities. He hadn't even offered to protect her. She flushed. Actually, she had to admit, he'd been much too involved to have been capable of it. She didn't even know if that was normal behavior for him, or if he'd wanted her too much to think of the consequences or even where they were. It would make it somehow a little more acceptable to think that cool, calm Nick had gone off the deep end because of a monstrous desire for her.

That was hardly likely, though, a man of his sophistication and experience. He'd known exactly how to bring her to ecstasy, and he'd done it. She'd never dreamed that such pleasure even existed. It was probably addictive, she thought miserably, because even with its soreness, her body ached for him all over again. The memories were vivid and sweet, and her skin was ultrasensitive after having known the touch of his hands and mouth.

She agonized over the thought that she'd cut her own throat. Helen had warned her that giving in to him would only chase him away, and that was already happening. If he hadn't been drunk, he'd never have called her at all last night. He wouldn't even respect her now. He'd add her to the rank and file of his conquests, and forget her just as easily as he'd forgotten the others over the years.

Her mind was in limbo. She'd borrowed a small clay tablet, a document from ancient Sumer done in pictographs, to show her class. She'd do well, she thought, to concentrate on what she was getting paid for.

"This tablet dates to the ancient Sumerian civilization," she lectured, displaying it. "So far, now, we've covered the earliest settlement in Mesopotamia, which was located between the Tigris and Euphrates Rivers in what is now southern Iraq. The Sumerians were the first people to develop a written language. Who can tell me the first language they produced?"

A hand went up and she nodded at the dark-haired young man. "Pictographs."

She smiled at him. He was one of her best students, and he had every intention of one day following in her footsteps as an educator. "Very good, Mike," she said. "Pictographic writing, which used symbols to convey language, came first. Then a more sophisticated form of writing called cuneiform, emerged. This used wedge-shaped symbols to represent individual syllables of the language. It was done on a wet clay tablet that was engraved with cuneiform writing using a wedge-shaped reed called a stylus. The tablet was then baked. Thousands of these tablets were found in ancient Sumer."

"One of them was the Epic of Gilgamesh, wasn't it?" a female student recalled.

"Indeed it was, a series of stories about Gilgamesh, who was a Sumerian king, and his search for immortality. Part of this work involves a certain legend. Does anyone remember which incident in our history it correlates with?"

"The great flood," Mike replied, grinning.

"Yes." She looked at her watch. "That's all the time we have for today. Tomorrow, I'll go over the method of making paper from papyrus reed once more. Don't forget, we have an examination on Wednesday. This one will be an essay examination. If you have problems with any of this material, I'll be in my office this afternoon, or you can make an appointment to see me at a later time."

She watched them leave and wondered if she'd ever been as young as some of these students. There were a number of older ones, though, some even in their forties and fifties. The days of only young faces on campus were over, and perhaps it was just as well. You were never too old to get a degree, she mused, smiling.

She locked the Sumerian tablet in a glass case to give back to Daniel later, and collected her materials and left the office long enough to go to the rest room. On her way back, she noticed Daniel waiting at her door.

Beside him was a tall, thin young man carrying a camera. Daniel looked faintly irritable. Of course, he always did.

But he smiled at Tabby gently, their quarrel of the day before long forgotten because of the tender way he'd comforted her last night. He'd had no idea why she was upset, thinking it was because he'd argued with her. She hadn't told him, either, or broken their engagement. She would have to, eventually. She couldn't very well marry him when she might be carrying Nick's child. But she couldn't do it yet. She had too much on her mind. All the same, Daniel hadn't asked anything of her, content to just hold her while she cried. She'd made coffee and they'd talked about the book and later, he'd gone home. Nick had seen him leave, she supposed, and been too drunk to remember that he didn't give a damn about her.

It was almost funny, in a way, but she wasn't laughing.

He introduced her to the young man, adding, "Tabitha, do you have that clay tablet from Sumer? This is Tim Mathews. He's with the *Washington Inquirer,* and he'd like to photograph it."

She flushed, more out of having to face Daniel and pretend that nothing had changed, on top of the guilt of what she'd done with Nick, than for any other reason. But the flush made her look self-conscious and nervous.

"Of course! I meant to give it back to you. I'll just unlock my door…"

A shriek came out of the biology lab as they passed it, followed by a demanding voice. "Where have you been? You're going to be boiled one day, don't you know that? How did you do this?"

There was more muttering, something about antiseptic. Tabby didn't listen. She was too nervous.

She fumbled the key into the lock. The door opened very easily. She looked down at a mangled paper clip and absently picked it up, wondering which of her students had untwisted it and left it there.

"It's right through here," she said, leading them into the small library that flanked her even smaller office. She stopped dead.

"Well, what a nice touch this is!" the reporter grinned, hefting his .35 millimeter camera on the broken glass of the case. "You said that a clay tablet was supposed to be in here under lock and key?"

"Yes," Daniel said uncomfortably. He glanced at Tabby. "You're sure you locked the door to this room? It wasn't locked when we came in."

"I'm positive!" she said huskily. "I'm positive I did. Daniel, you have to believe me!"

"The tablet's gone, all right. Look at this. Was there something else in here, a fur pelt, maybe?" He held up a tiny sample of hair.

"I don't remember," Tabby said. She felt sick.

"This looks bad, Tabitha," Daniel said quietly.

"I know that," she murmured miserably and leaned against the wall. "Someone's out to get me."

"It does look that way. Here, I'd better take you up to the dean and let you explain this to him," Daniel said.

"Just a quick shot of you, Dr. Harvey, okay?" the reporter said quickly.

Tabby shielded her face and followed Daniel out into the hall. Her heart was rocketing into her throat. The dean would never believe this. He'd be certain that she'd broken the case and taken the artifact, to make it look like an outside job. She was innocent, but nobody was ever going to believe it now.

"I'm sorry," Daniel was saying. "I'm sorry, too, that we had an argument over Reed. I let him get to me. But this, this accusation of theft…I'll never believe it."

"Thank you, Daniel. Honestly, I didn't do it," she told him. "Why is this happening to me?" She broke down and began to cry. Daniel pulled her against him and comforted her as best he could, but she cried as if her heart was broken.

The dean listened quietly to the new development and grimaced. "And there was a reporter in there with you, Myers?" he asked sharply. "That's just wonderful." He threw up his hands. "This is going to be devastating to our reputation!"

"I didn't take it," Tabby said proudly.

"What?" He glanced at her. "Oh. No, of course you didn't, Dr. Harvey. I'm not naive enough to believe you'd risk your job and your reputation by taking two artifacts that would only be of value to a college or a collector."

"Thank you," she said softly. "But nobody else is going to believe me. And the press will have a field day with this, I'm afraid."

"That's true. It isn't going to be pretty."

"What about the trustees?" Daniel asked.

"I don't know. I'll meet with them tonight and we'll see. Go home, Dr. Harvey, and get some rest. We'll talk tomorrow."

She nodded, too tired to argue.

Daniel went out to the parking lot with her, supportive but distant. "The reporter seems to have gone, at least," he murmured. "I really hate this for you, Tabitha."

He didn't know the half of it. In the space of two days, her life had turned over.

She smiled wanly. "I hate it, too."

"Shall I come over again tonight and we can work? Would that help get your mind off your worries?"

"No," she said quickly. She had to break the engagement. What she'd done had made it possible, but she had to find the right way to break it to Daniel. Right now, her mind was in shards.

"I'll see you tomorrow, then," he said easily. "Get some rest, dear."

"Thanks."

She got into the car and drove home. She needed to tell Nick about this new development, but the thought of even talking to him was just unthinkable.

She phoned Helen, instead, on the pretext that she couldn't reach Nick.

"A case was broken into and another artifact is gone," Tabby told her. "Now they'll be sure I did it. The thing was in my office and the door wasn't locked. They'll blame me…!"

"I'll find Nick and send him right over there," Helen began.

"No! I mean, no, I won't be here. I have to leave for a while. Just…just tell him what I told you, all right?"

"I'll tell him. You're sure…?"

"I'm sure. Thanks."

"No problem. I'll be in touch."

Tabby hung up the telephone. Then she went out and drove her car back to the campus, leaving it in an isolated permitted parking space. She hailed a cab and went home, and she didn't turn the lights on all night. Let Nick wonder where she was. Anything was better than having to face him with the memory of the day before between them. Talking to him on the phone, even when he was drunk, was far less traumatic than having him look at her and see her as she had been— abandoned and totally wanton.

Nick had gotten up with a vicious headache and slept late. It was getting to be an unpleasant habit, and he had to get out of it. The scotch was gone, he noted, and didn't replace it. He had to get a grip on himself. Toward that end, he spent the day searching out leads. He made time to dash into the college and pick up a sample of animal fur that he'd found once more in Tabby's office and take it by the FBI lab. After that, he avoided the college for the rest of the day. He'd seen Tabby briefly, but he'd avoided her and she hadn't seen him. He was no more eager to face Tabby than she apparently was to face him.

He got home that evening to find a message from his sister on his answering machine. He called her, and she relayed Tabby's message.

"She couldn't get me, you say?" He looked out the window, concerned. It disturbed him that Tabby might have gone off the deep end over what they'd done together. But her car wasn't there and the lights were all off. More than likely she was at a motel, he thought furiously, so that she wouldn't have the threat of his company to talk things over. Or maybe she was with Daniel again. Maybe she was at his house tonight, trying to patch up things with him. That made Nick even angrier.

"That's what she said," Helen replied. "She sounded funny. Is she all right, Nick?"

He didn't want to think about how she was. "I'll get back to you," he told her, and hung up.

Later that evening, his old friend from the FBI lab phoned him.

"I've got some news for you about that animal fur. You sitting down?" he asked Nick amusedly.

"I am now. Shoot."

Nick listened and began to smile. Then light bulbs flashed on in his head. Could it be that simple? Tabby was going to be shocked and so were a few other people, if his theory proved true. It was a good thing no blame had been placed and no accusations had been made, or there would be plenty of red faces.

He picked up the telephone and called the dean of the college at home. He asked a few questions and made a request, which was immediately granted. He did not reveal his theory.

Now he knew what to do, and how to go about proving Tabby's innocence. It was a matter of setting a trap and springing it, in just the right way and with just the right people to witness it.

But he needed to talk to Tabby. He picked up the telephone and punched in her number, then waited impatiently. He had to know if she was at home, or if she was with her idiot fiancé.

After he was ready to give up, the receiver was picked up.

"Yes?" Tabby asked quietly.

"It's me," Nick said.

Her heart leaped. She almost put the receiver down.

She hadn't spoken to him since he'd called over there drunk.

"Are you still there?" Nick asked irritably.

"Yes. I'm, uh, distracted. Another artifact has disappeared."

"So Helen said," he replied pointedly. "I gather that you can't stand the thought of speaking to me these days? Can't you deal with the situation between us?"

She swallowed and sat down, still holding the telephone. "I...don't know how one deals with situations like this," she confessed. "I've never had to before."

"You don't need to remind me that I seduced you," he replied tersely. "I do have a conscience."

She took a very slow breath. "I should have said no."

"That would have been interesting," he said. "Do you think it would have stopped me at that stage?"

She blushed like a tomato. "I don't know..."

"For the record, it's very difficult for a man to draw back once he's reached that point. Even though I've never personally been that hot, I've heard about men who have."

He was telling her something, but she was too self-conscious to pursue it. She straightened. "Have you found out anything new?"

"Yes. Don't ask, I won't tell you. I have something planned for tomorrow night that will probably clear you."

"You know who did it?" she asked hesitantly.

"Yes."

"Nick...it isn't Daniel?"

"Do you love him?" he asked harshly. "I want an answer," he said when she hesitated. "Right now, Tabby!"

"As you said yourself, if I did, how did I wind up in the grass with you?"

"Sarcasm doesn't suit you," he told her. "I'm sure you've read that lust and love don't always go hand in hand."

"You should know."

"Yes," he said angrily. "I should. But since I've never experienced love, I'm hardly the person to ask for a comparison."

Her eyes closed. He was telling her that all he'd felt was lust. Her stomach flipped over.

His indrawn breath was audible when he realized what he'd said to her. "I care for you," he ground out. "You're part of my life, part of my past. We've been together forever. I wanted you, but it wasn't impersonal lust. If it had been only that, I'd never have lost control so badly that I couldn't protect you from an unwanted pregnancy."

"Unwanted on your part. You've certainly made that very clear," she said stiffly.

"I'm not ready," he groaned. "I'm restless, unsettled. I don't want to have to live in one place yet."

"I haven't asked you to."

"If you are pregnant…!"

"If I am pregnant," she said very calmly, "we'll talk about it then. I won't have an abortion, so you can forget that option right now."

He didn't say a word. He didn't know what to say. The thought of a child of his growing up without him was painful. It would be another person to risk losing. His eyes closed in fear. Lucy had loved him, really loved him, and she'd died. He didn't want anybody else to love him and die. Especially, he thought in anguish, someone he loved as well.

Tabby didn't know what he was thinking. She only knew that he was totally silent. She quietly put the receiver down before he spoke. Afterward she didn't know if he'd have said anything else or not. She told herself she didn't care.

She got out her books and prepared her lesson for the next day. Teaching anthropology was challenging. There had to be field trips, and they usually involved some physical labor. Digs had to be measured and roped off, spaded down to the plow zone, and then very carefully excavated with trowels and screens. It was laborious and challenging, but very rewarding.

The study of man was a delight. She'd become obsessed with it in college and had known very quickly that she wanted to teach it when she finished. She'd obtained her bachelor's degree and then gone straight into graduate school to work for her Ph.D. It had been a long climb, and left her no time for a social life. When she wasn't studying, she was attending lectures, going to museums, haunting exhibitions and collections. She lived and breathed anthropology. It was her greatest love, next to Nick. Now she stood to lose it. She hadn't realized how much it meant to her until it was too late.

If only she knew something about detective work! She had to depend on Nick, because he was the only person who could extricate her from this tangled web. But the sooner he did that, the sooner he'd be on a plane back to Houston. She grimaced. She didn't want him to leave, even if it meant bearing the shame and guilt longer. But she had to be realistic. What would he want with her, now that he'd satisfied his curiosity and his hunger.

She put out the light and went to bed. Perhaps things would be brighter after a night's sleep.

Chapter Seven

Tabby went through the motions of lecturing until her classes were over, but almost three days after her fall from grace, she felt as if what she'd done in the park was visible to everyone she came in contact with.

Daniel came in just as she finished, his expression faintly apologetic.

"I should never have brought that reporter in. I'm afraid I've made things worse for you," he began slowly.

"It's all right," she said without feeling. "It wasn't your fault, Daniel."

He hesitated, searching for the right words. "Listen, Tabby, we looked at engagement rings, but we never decided on one," he said after a minute. "Suppose we go to a different jeweler…"

It was the very opening she needed, and she took it. Reluctantly, but firmly, she turned to look at him. "I can't marry you, Daniel. I'm very sorry."

He scowled. "Why not?"

"I just…can't, that's all." She lowered her head. "It wouldn't be right."

He moved closer. "Tabitha, it can't be because of this theft charge…!"

"It isn't. Daniel, we're really not suited," she said miserably. "I'll still help you with your research, you know I will. But marriage is something I can't agree to. Not now."

"You won't mind helping me with the book?"

She felt even sicker that the broken engagement mattered less to him than his precious manuscript. Just as Nick had said, Daniel had probably only been using her. He was a shallow man, in many ways, with no real deep feelings. This was evidence of it.

"I won't mind."

He smiled, rubbing his hands together. "Well, that's fine, then. I'll phone you later."

He started out. Something seemed to occur to him. He turned, his gaze oddly hesitant. "You and Reed. There's something there, isn't there?"

"Not really," she said, lifting her face. "Nick wants no part of a permanent relationship."

He studied her curiously. "I see. Well, no hard feelings about the engagement. I'll phone you tonight about the research notes for that next chapter."

"Yes. Fine."

Before the last syllable died on the air, he was down the hall, whistling happily.

Tabby gathered her papers and walked listlessly down the hall. On the way out, the dean stopped her.

"I'm sorry to tell you this, but the story is all over the papers and the board of trustees feels that a leave of absence is in order, just temporarily," he said stiffly. "There are reporters all over the place. I was going to suggest that you go home after your last class, but I gather that you're doing it already.'' He cleared his throat, averting his eyes from Tabby's stricken face. ''Under the circumstances, I think it would be best to have one of the other anthropologists take your classes for a few days. Until this matter is resolved.''

''You don't think I did it?'' she asked miserably.

''No,'' he said. ''Try not to worry. It will all work out, you know.''

His smile was as limp as her heart. She nodded. ''I'll not come in until you notify me, then. I'll avoid the press as well. But I'm not guilty,'' she added solemnly. ''If I meant to steal something, it would be one of the gold pieces from the Troy exhibit or a jeweled brooch from the Spanish galleon collection. A piece of ancient pottery…well, it's hardly dear, is it, except to historians and anthropologists?''

He looked thoughtful. ''My dear, I have considered that aspect. Of course, you're right. It would take a collector to appreciate it. But we're under the gun, you see.''

''Yes. I see,'' she said sadly. ''I only wish I'd thought to make that point to the reporter.''

''I'll make sure that I do,'' he assured her.

She went on out to her car, hoping that she could reach it before any of the press found her. She'd never felt quite so bad in all her life. Nick had seduced her, she might be pregnant, and now she was in danger of losing her job. It was enough to make a saint cry.

Tabby was no saint, and cry she did, all the long way home. She was still bawling when she drove up at her own door. For a long time, she let the healing tears roll down her face. When she was finally drained of emotion, she wiped her red eyes and blew her equally red nose and got out of the car.

Nick, meanwhile, was still uncovering leads. Though he had a theory as to the identity of the culprit, he had to keep an open mind. He'd had Helen do some checking on Dr. Day and she discovered that his wife had inherited a small fortune from a deceased relative. That would explain the Lamborghini. Dr. Flannery, on the other hand, was in financial difficulties *because* of *his wife*. She'd just left him for another man, and the skip tracers said that the gossips were having a field day speculating about his relief. His wife had been much younger and not terribly faithful, either. Flannery was hardly heartbroken.

That left Daniel. His falsification of past records still put him at the top of the list of suspects. But why would he take an ancient artifact? It wasn't even from the period he and Tabby were working on. And no background check of his past came up with a record of theft. Only that radical stage.

While he was ruling out suspects, the telephone rang. It was one of the local police officers whom Nick had contacted, and he set up a time and place for a stakeout at the college. He made one other telephone call and talked to another potential witness. So much for witnesses. Now he had to bait and set the trap.

Hopefully Tabby would soon be out from under suspicion. He could go away and let her get her life back together. He put his head in his hands and groaned. God, if only he'd never touched her! Guilt was eating him alive. Sweet, gentle Tabby had never hurt a soul in her life. Her only weakness was him, had always been him. He'd taken what she'd offered, but it gave him no pleasure to remember that most of the enjoyment had been his. She'd barely had anything, even at the last. He hadn't given her even a sweet memory of his lovemaking to carry down the years. He should have waited. It should have been a different place, with all the time in the world to teach her what lovemaking was. He should have been kinder to her. Cursing, he got up and went back to his notes.

His theory was right on the money, especially now that he had the missing evidence. He needed to make a move, but he had to tell Tabby what he was going to do. That wasn't going to be easy. He was asking her to trust him with her academic future. Perhaps she wouldn't want to.

He went to his window to see if Tabby was home. Sure enough, her car was in the driveway tonight.

But he hesitated about going over there. What he'd found out would offer her some consolation, but his headlong rush into intimacy and the aftermath still had him upset. It had devastated Tabby. He hated the memory of how she'd looked afterward. Her puritan ideals were in hell. He knew what a little saint Tabby was. He'd done something unforgivable to her, really messed up her life. Even if she didn't become pregnant, the way they'd made love would haunt her forever.

He knew he'd treated her shabbily, making love to her in the park that way, but he hadn't meant to insult her. He'd wanted her so desperately that he simply lost control. Years of denied hunger had overwhelmed him—and certainly her as well. But he was experienced enough to call a halt, and he hadn't. He hadn't even managed to protect her.

He wasn't certain if it would be kinder to go and talk to her or stay away.

Finally he decided that staying away, giving her

more time to get over her rawness at what had happened, might be the best course of action. But this night, like the previous ones, wasn't pleasant. His conscience and fear that he might have accidentally made her pregnant gave him such fits that he wound up watching all-night movies just to keep his mind off it.

Tabby, meanwhile, had too much time on her hands and she hated the sight of herself in a mirror. The fact that she couldn't go to work and stay busy made it worse. She spent the day cleaning house and letting her answering machine take care of the incoming calls. Most of them were from the press, and she was glad that she hadn't seen a morning paper. Probably it bore a headline that included her.

One call late in the day attracted her attention, because it was from Helen Reed.

She picked up the receiver with shaking hands. "Helen! Am I glad to hear your voice! The phone's gone off the hook all day, and the dean won't let me work…!"

"What is going on out there?" Helen interrupted. "You're in the papers, did you know? It's all here, about the missing artifact and an accusation against you, that you've been temporarily suspended. So that was what that call was all about the other day, wasn't it? Tabby, I know you don't steal things!"

"Well, no," Tabby said. She sank onto the couch, her heart beating wildly. "It's in all the papers, I suppose? Wire services, too?" She groaned. "Oh, Helen, what am I going to do?"

"Nick's there, isn't he? He's supposed to be solving the case."

"Yes, Nick's around," Tabby said stiffly. Her eyes

closed on a wave of sick shame. "He doesn't even have any suspects."

"But he does. Well, only one, really. Dr. Flannery and Dr. Day checked out okay, but your friend Daniel Myers didn't."

"Daniel?"

"I'm afraid so. There's him and some new theory that Nick won't trust me with yet."

"What did you find out about Daniel?"

"Sorry, pet, but that's confidential. Don't you worry, I know Nick's got enough to clear you right now."

"Daniel wouldn't steal an artifact, I don't care what's in his past," Tabby said. "You know him like I do. He's Mr. Straight—the kind of man who lives and breathes law and order. He won't even keep a nickel he finds on the street unless he can't find the person who lost it! Does that sound like a thief?"

Helen hesitated. Nick had said that Tabby didn't care about Daniel, but she didn't sound very uncaring. "No, of course it doesn't," she agreed. "But he was the last suspect left…"

"No. There's another one. There's me." Tabby's lips stiffened. "Maybe I walk in my sleep and steal things. Maybe I'm really the culprit only I don't remember. Maybe I have multiple personalities…!"

"Tabby, do stop it," Helen said gently. "I know you're upset. But you have to keep your head. It will blow over. Nick will prove your innocence. Honest, he will."

"Pigs will fly," Tabby said wearily. "I have to go. I think a reporter is taking photographs through my window."

"Throw a pot at him."

Tabby laughed hysterically. "Then I'd accidentally

kill him and go to prison for murder. That's the way my luck's running.''

"You're just hopeless."

"You don't know the half of it."

"Try to get a good night's sleep, won't you? If you see Nick, have him call me. I may have something else in a couple of hours."

"If I see him." *I hope I don't,* she added silently. "Thanks for calling."

"Call me if you need me, will you?" Helen asked impatiently. "And don't worry. I promise you, everything will be all right."

"The truth will out, in other words?" She laughed cynically. "Yes, but sometimes that takes twenty years. I'll be forty-five."

"Go to bed."

"Okay. Good night."

"Yes. You, too."

She put the receiver down. No sooner was it in the cradle than it started ringing again. More reporters. More questions. If she'd been more lucid, she might have given them a statement. But she felt too miserable to even try. There apparently had been a man with a camera at the window, because her flower bed had footprints in it. Great, she thought. Now they had a picture to print. She closed the curtains, as she should have done much earlier, and turned on the television to drown out her worries.

Her conscience tormented her for the next two days. She didn't look toward Nick's house. She talked to Daniel on the telephone, having discouraged him from coming over. A reporter was camped on her front porch, making coffee on a hot plate using stolen current from her outside electrical outlet. She wondered if she could call a rival paper and make news out of that? It was really amazing that a small stolen artifact could make this much press. It must be a slow week for news....

There was a knock on the door at the end of the third day. She peered out at Nick and reluctantly opened the door.

"I ran off your happy camper," he remarked, nodding to where the reporter had been sitting. "Unplugged his hot plate. He's afraid of starvation without his coffeepot, so he's gone to a local waffle house to get a cup."

"Thank you."

"Are you going to let me in?" he asked, lounging carelessly against the door frame. He looked nonchalant, which was the last thing he actually was. He felt nervous and vaguely ashamed, emotions he'd been gloriously unfamiliar with before.

"I suppose so." She opened the door and he came inside. She was wearing a lightweight blue denim shirtwaist dress, with her hair in a long braid down her back. No makeup, no fussy hairdo. She looked a little plain and Nick felt worse than ever when he saw the dark circles under her eyes and the drawn, pale look about her.

"I gather you've been avoiding me?" he asked.

"You gather right," she replied tersely. "Why did you need to see me, Nick?"

He had to gather his wits again. Her straightforward attack had thrown him. "I've found something," he said quietly. "The thief left a little evidence this time. A tuft of hair and a speck of blood."

"Is the thief a wounded bald man?" she asked.

"Not quite. I took a sample of it over to the FBI lab, had a friend of mine run an analysis of it and I got the results. I haven't even told Helen yet, but I've phoned the police, and I've talked with that reporter who's had you staked out. I've asked them both to come to the college tonight. I want you along as well. We're going to lock ourselves in your office and wait for the thief to strike again. We're even providing some very tempting bait."

Tabby found it difficult to talk to him. She folded her arms across her breasts defensively. "Helen said Daniel is at the top of your list of suspects."

"The last she knew, he was the only one left," Nick replied. His dark eyes narrowed. "That bothers you?"

"Even though we aren't engaged anymore, Daniel is still a colleague and a friend. Yes, it bothers me."

His eyebrows collided. "What do you mean, you're not engaged anymore?"

"I couldn't go through with it. Not after…what happened."

He let out an angry breath and rammed his hands deep into his slacks pockets. "It was just an interlude! Women have them all the time!"

"I don't," she said levelly, meeting his eyes. "And feeling the way I do about it, I can't go to one man when I've been intimately involved with another. Especially now, before I know…"

His eyes fell blankly to her stomach and his teeth clenched. "It doesn't always happen the first time," he said. "There may not be anything to worry about."

"When do you want to go to the college?" she asked, changing the subject.

He couldn't fathom her. His temper was getting out

of bounds. He didn't like the way he felt. His eyes slid over her with new knowledge. He knew what she felt like under that concealing dress. He knew the sounds she made in passion and the silky softness of her body as it grew feverish under his... Thoughts and memories like that would never do, he told himself.

"You can ride in with me tonight," he said.

"No, thank you. I'll go with Daniel."

His eyes flashed. "He wasn't invited."

"Nevertheless, he'll be there. You've made him a suspect. I won't tell him that, but I think he's entitled to share in the solving of the mystery."

"We might as well invite the neighbors, too," he grumbled.

"Fine by me. The more people who think I'm innocent, the better. God knows, I'm probably as notorious as Mata Hari by now." She frowned. "Do you suppose anyone thinks I'm really a secret agent stealing ancient microfilm?"

"Hidden inside five-thousand-year-old artifacts," Nick said, shaking his head. "Only one of those grocery store tabloids would buy that."

"Great idea. Where did you say that reporter went?"

"I'll leave you to it," he murmured, refusing to be drawn in. "We'll meet in your office at six."

"Daniel would never take anything that wasn't his," she said as he paused in the open doorway.

He turned and looked at her. "Any more than you would," he agreed. "Don't worry. It isn't Daniel." He studied her wan face for a long time. "It should have been him, in the park, shouldn't it?" he asked bitterly.

Her composed face showed no emotion. "What difference does it make now?"

He let out a long breath. "None, I suppose. For what it's worth, I'd give anything to take it back."

"So would I," she replied miserably.

He made an oddly jerky gesture and went out without looking at her again.

Tabby took a bath and dressed in a becoming purple silk pantsuit to sit and wait for the thief to show up. It was going to be a time fraught with tension with a policeman and a reporter, and with Daniel and Nick in the same room. Probably there would be a free-for-all before the night was over. Good copy for the press, she thought hysterically, and had to choke back laughter.

Her good name would hopefully be cleared. Nick would go back to Houston. She could go back to work and wait out the days until she knew whether or not there would be consequences from the fiery encounter in the park. And afterward, none of it would matter. Except that she could never marry Daniel or anyone else. Despite it all, she loved Nick more than her own life.

It must have been a curse, she thought, placed on her at birth that she'd fall in love with a hopeless bachelor and never get over him.

She phoned Daniel to tell him what was going on, without mentioning that he'd been even briefly a suspect.

"Reed's caught the culprit?" he asked.

"It seems so," Tabby replied. "I really don't think he'd have the police and the press along unless he was reasonably sure that he could prove his allegations, do you?"

"It wouldn't be intelligent. Not," he added, "that I think police work requires intelligence. It seems to me that very few people in detective circles are highly educated.''

''You might be surprised.''

''Not by your childhood friend,'' Daniel said. ''How are you coming with the new notes I gave you? Have you incorporated them into the book?''

''Yes. I have had little else to do for the past few days, so I've concentrated on it.''

''Good girl! Uh, would you mind bringing it with you when you come tonight?''

So much for her thought that he'd pick her up and drive in with her.

''Yes,'' she told him. ''I'll bring it.''

''Thanks. See you there at six, then.''

He hung up, leaving her holding the receiver with a dial tone on the other end of the line. She seemed fated to get herself involved with men who found her useful but not lovable. She was never going to marry.

But there might be a baby. The thought cheered her, softened her mood. She touched her stomach and allowed herself to dream about what it would be like to hold a tiny human being in her arms.

She'd protect and love it, raise it all by herself. Nick didn't need to offer her support or act as if it were a burden on him. She might not even tell him.

Sure. Great idea, she thought silently. I won't tell him and then I'll spend years hiding the child from Helen every time she comes to visit.

She wasn't being sensible. She picked up her light-weight silk jacket and went out the door.

Minutes later, she unlocked her office. She was early, as she'd needed to be so that she could let the others in. The campus was growing dark, and it was a good thing that no night school classes were held on this floor, or there would have been no use in trying to stake it out.

She put her purse on the desk and sat down. Looking around her, she wondered at the speed of events. Only a short time ago, she'd been engaged to Daniel, working on a book, teaching her classes and going from day to day. She hadn't given Nick a great deal of thought, because after the New Year's Eve party she was certain she'd lost him for good. She'd resigned herself to being Daniel's wife, to teaching classes until she was old enough to retire.

What a joke fate had played on her.

Daniel might take her back, but she couldn't let him without telling him everything that had happened with Nick. That would be unbearable, to have anyone know, much less Daniel, that she'd behaved like some kept woman.

She heard a sound at the door and swung around as two deep voices merged. There was a knock.

"Come in," she called, nervous now.

A uniformed police officer came in with Nick, and a tall young man.

"This is Officer Jennings," Nick introduced the policeman, "and Tim Mathews. Tim has been living on your front porch," he added, "but he's found new quarters. Starting now, he's going to live in your office, instead, and I notice that he's brought his coffeepot with him."

"We've met," Tabby murmured, trying not to laugh.

"Did you know that Tabitha's an anthropologist?"

"Yes. It's interesting, but I'd never be able to be one." Mathews grinned. "I'm not sure I could spell it."

"We're like ancient detectives," Tabby told him.

"We dig up mysteries from the past and try to solve them."

"I do the same in the present," Mathews said. "Sorry I had to give you the hard sell, but news is sacred to me."

"Invasion of privacy isn't," she guessed.

He chuckled. "Sorry. No."

"Tell that to a lawyer," Officer Jennings said with a smile.

"We might as well get comfortable," Nick said. He frowned at Tabby. "I thought you said your ex-intended was coming."

"He'll be along," she said.

"It had better be soon, or he'll blow my stakeout."

"Blow what steak out?" Daniel asked as he peered around the door. "Am I late?"

"Yes, but don't let that concern you," Nick said darkly.

"Oh, don't worry, I won't," Daniel said imperturbably. "Do you want this locked?" he asked as he closed the door.

"Please," Nick agreed.

"Did you bring the information I wanted?" Daniel asked Tabby.

"I'm sorry," she said quickly. "I left it on the table by the door."

"Oh, bother," Daniel grumbled. "Well, I'll stop by later. I need those notes."

"She had other things on her mind," Nick said in her defense. "I'm sure you agree that clearing her name is more important than a few notes."

Daniel cleared his throat. "Well, certainly..."

"Have a seat," Nick invited. He settled back into an easy chair, with the reporter perched beside Tabby on a straight-backed chair and Daniel taking up a place by the closet door.

"Isn't this entrapment?" Daniel asked the policeman.

Officer Jennings cocked an eyebrow. "I wouldn't say so. Mr. Reed would know more about that than I would."

"Because he worked for the FBI, I gather," Daniel said irritably.

Jennings shook his head. "Why, no. Because he's the one with the law degree."

Daniel studied the blond man with new interest. "You never said you had a law degree," he murmured. "From what school?"

"Harvard," Nick said with magnificent disdain.

"Oh." Daniel was at a loss for words. He glanced toward Tabby. "You do look washed-out, Tabitha. You need a rest."

"I couldn't agree more," she said, closing her eyes. "It's been the longest week of my life."

"Don't worry, dear girl, we'll clear your name," Daniel said, smiling. "Then you might reconsider that ring I offered you."

She didn't answer. She smiled, her eyes still closed, so that she missed the flash of anger on Nick's face.

"Better settle down and be quiet," Officer Jennings said. "We may be in for a long evening."

"I hope not," Tabby sighed. "I want it to be over."

"Don't we all," Daniel murmured, but no one heard him.

Chapter Eight

An hour went by, and then another, with nothing happening. The men began to fidget, and Tabby's heartbeat ran wild. What if Nick was wrong? If no thief appeared, her career would be over.

"This is absurd," Daniel grumbled. "We're wasting time!"

"You're welcome to leave, Dr. Myers," Nick said carelessly. "We'll sweat it out without you."

Daniel looked around and grimaced. "Well, I suppose I could wait a little longer," he added when he saw Tabby's unease.

He settled back, his long legs crossed. Nick stared at Tabby, trying to balance his rocking emotions while he discovered that going back to Houston was less appealing than ever before.

A noise at the door made everyone sit up. Nick put a finger to his lips and eased back into the shadows as the others did.

The door was locked, but someone was working the

lock. The noise was loud in the silence, and there was another noise with it, an odd one that was more a grunt.

A minute later, the door opened. It was too dark to see anything. A chair was bumped, and there was a thud, and then the tinkle of glass as a container on Tabby's desk was knocked over.

"Now!" Nick said.

He turned on the lights and the .35 millimeter camera flashed. And everyone stared breathlessly at the image the camera had captured.

There, on the desk, clutching a small cheap plaster statuette that Tabby had put out as bait, was a small hairy biped. Pal, the primate, with a bandage on one hand.

"My God!" Daniel exclaimed. "It's the bloody monkey!"

"Pal!" Tabby gasped. "But he picked the lock, did you see?"

"Yes. And odds are that he's taken his ill-gotten gains to the biology lab and stashed them. Let's go."

They left Pal in the room and followed Nick down the hall to the biology lab. A thorough search of the premises revealed the two missing artifacts and several other more modern things in a large jar that Flannery used to keep large grass plumes in.

"The lipstick I couldn't find," Tabby laughed, picking it up. "My mirror. I thought it had fallen out of my purse. Daniel, here's the pipe stem you thought you lost." She handed it to him.

"What a story this is going to make," Tim chuckled as he snapped photos of the group.

"Shall we take up a collection for Dr. Flannery?" Daniel mused. "He's going to faint when he hears about this. And if the dean doesn't cancel his research grant, I'm a monkey myself.''

''You'll make sure the story gets to the wire services, won't you, so that Tabby's cleared?'' Nick asked.

''Oh, sure,'' Tim told them. ''She's the best part of the story. Pretty teacher victimized by intelligent ape. I can see the headlines now. We'll have him in love with her and taking personal objects as love tokens.''

''Oh, my God,'' Tabby groaned.

''Now, now, Doc, don't take it like that. How about giving us a quote? That way,'' he added with an irrepressible grin, ''I won't have to set up camp on your front porch again.''

''Anything but that! Yes, I'll give you a quote!''

''His hand is bandaged,'' Nick pointed out. ''That was what cinched the case. There was a tiny bit of blood on the fur I found on Tabby's desk. I took the fur to the lab at the FBI building, and the lab tech identified them as primate fur and blood. In fact,'' he added with an amused look at the reporter, ''he gave me the size, weight and approximate age of the monkey. All from that one sample.''

''Amazing, isn't it, what they can do?'' Mathews agreed. ''I watched a program on public TV about those lab detectives. They're really something, especially now with the DNA matching.''

''A lot of that still isn't admissible in court,'' Nick said quietly. ''But it will come. Eventually a perpetrator who commits a crime won't have a legal leg to stand on if there's a DNA match.''

''Don't you believe it,'' Mathews replied cynically. ''There'll be a way to get around it, right up to copping a sample of an innocent man's blood and leaving it at the scene.''

"You reporters," Nick began irritably.

"Don't blame me," Mathews returned, placing a hand on his heart. "I would not for all the world shatter your illusions, sir, but mankind is rotten to the core for the most part."

"Not all of it," Tabby broke in. "There are some good people."

"You have to dig pretty hard to find them, though. If you'll give me that quote, Doc, I'll get out of your hair."

Tabby gave him one, hoping it would be the end of the oddest chapter in the history of her life. Pal's unmasking was enough to take her mind off her own problems, for a while at least. She was grateful for that.

"I'll drop by in the morning and get those notes," Daniel told Tabby, "on my way to school. I, uh, could give you a lift if you want me to."

Tabby smiled. "Thanks, Daniel."

He smiled back. "I'm glad you were cleared." He glanced toward Nick, who was talking to the reporter and Officer Jennings. "I thought for a while there I might be a suspect. You know, back in the early seventies, I marched in an antiwar rally. I didn't put that on my record for fear that they might think me a radical."

"Nothing would be less likely than that," Tabby told him. "And maybe you weren't a suspect," she hedged to spare his feelings.

"All the same, isn't it a good thing this is over?"

"Yes. A good thing." Because it meant that Nick would go back to Houston and she could pick up the threads of her own life. What a dismal fate, she thought silently.

* * *

Nick walked her out to her car after the reporter and the policeman had gone. Daniel was locking up after them.

"You could ride home with me," he suggested. "Daniel can bring you back in the morning to pick up your car. I heard him suggest giving you a lift," he added when she frowned.

"I don't think…"

"Good. Don't." He steered her toward his own car, his jaw firmly set. "It's late and this isn't a safe city at night. I'll feel better if you're with me."

What in the world made him think she was safe with him, after the ease with which he'd seduced her? she thought hysterically. But she didn't say it.

They rode home in a tense silence. Nick didn't pull into her driveway when they reached the neighborhood. He parked the car in his own driveway. It didn't alarm Tabby at first. Not until he locked the car and pulled her along with him toward his front door.

"I won't go in there with you," she said stubbornly.

"Yes, you will," he replied quietly, his dark eyes holding hers as he inserted his key into the lock and opened the door. "We have some serious talking to do."

"We can talk tomorrow…!"

"I'm leaving in the morning."

"Oh."

She went with him, her head bent down, feeling empty and forlorn and totally vulnerable.

"Sit down." He motioned her to the sofa. He took off his jacket and his tie, unbuttoning the top buttons of his shirt. "Will you have something to drink?"

"No. Thank you."

"I mean coffee," he said defensively.

"Oh. Well... Yes, then."

He put the drip coffeemaker on and then came back to sit across from her in an armchair. "Don't look so shattered, Tabby," he said gently. "You've been completely cleared. I'm sure the dean will have his apologies ready in the morning." He smiled faintly. "Along with Dr. Flannery."

"It wasn't really Dr. Flannery's fault. I feel guilty that you had to pry into my colleagues' pasts to clear me, when it wasn't really necessary."

"We didn't know it wasn't necessary. Besides, I haven't told you what I found out. I won't tell anyone else, either," he said curtly. "I'm a private detective. The operative word is 'private.'"

"I know that. But I seem to have made a lot of trouble for everyone," she confided.

He studied her quietly, wondering at how easily she fit into his private life, how she seemed to belong. He was being fanciful, he told himself. He had no intention of marrying her. He wanted her to understand that.

He clasped his hands together between his knees. "I wanted to apologize, again, for what happened. And to tell you that if there are...complications...I want to be told."

"I'll tell you. But there's no need, because I'm not going to get rid of a child just to suit you, Nick, no matter how inconvenient he might be."

He cursed sharply and vividly. "I haven't said...!"

She stood up. "You needn't say anything." Her face colored as she stared at him, remembering how his body had felt against hers.

"You can't handle it, can you, Tabby?" he asked quietly. "Having sex with me is some kind of mortal sin. I suppose having it happen spontaneously and almost publicly like that is what hurts the most."

"Nick…"

He moved close and took her by the shoulders. "You're incredibly naive for a woman your age," he said. He searched her eyes. "And what I hate most is that I didn't even take the time to teach you all the pleasures of lovemaking."

"Please, don't," she said huskily.

"Just this, darling," he said softly, his eyes dropping to her mouth. He felt an anguish of desire as his head bent. "Just a few kisses, little one…" he breathed into her mouth.

He kissed her deeply, his arms bending her body up into the hard curve of his, holding her gently but firmly. She struggled at first, but the need to experience him again was betraying her will.

His lean hands slid down her back to her hips and tugged rhythmically, moving her against the growing arousal of his body.

She caught her breath and he felt it in her kiss. His mouth opened, his tongue probing deeply, insistently. She gave in to him and began to make odd, high-pitched little noises. She relaxed, letting him deepen the intimacy of the embrace. Her hands caught at his shirt and clung.

His head spun. She was his. She couldn't resist him any more than he could resist her.

"You're sweet, Tabby," he whispered. "You're sweeter than honey."

She was breathing unsteadily already. His hands slid around her and up to cup her breasts, caress them into hard passion. She felt him unfastening hooks and buttons, but all she could think of was how to get closer to him. She loved him. Nothing else seemed to matter, not even the fear and uncertainty in the back of her mind.

He touched bare, warm, soft skin, and she arched back. His mouth found her, caressed her, made her shiver with her need.

It was too late to draw back. He knew it almost at once, and when he looked into her misty, half-closed eyes, he knew that she needed him as much as he needed her. He was helpless against his desire for her.

This, then, was passion, Tabby thought dizzily as he picked her up and carried her upstairs. This helpless surrender that heard no reason, knew no resistance, was what kept women and men bound together despite their differences. She wanted him as she'd never dreamed she could, despite the trauma of their first time. She loved him so! And this would be the last time…

She heard a door open, heard it close. She felt the bedspread under her bare back, felt his hands removing fabric, caressing, seducing.

He was whispering to her, things that made her body burn, her mind sing. She felt him touching her in all the ways he'd touched her in the park. Except that this time, he held back. He aroused her to fever pitch and then pulled her gently to him, and held her, shivering, until she calmed. Then he began all over again, light caresses, light touches, his lips on her body, his mouth suckling hungrily at her breasts while his hands teased her into a state of insane desire.

The lights were out. For an instant she was sorry, because she wanted to see it, to see him, to watch as they blended into one human being in their feverish rush toward intimacy.

But there wasn't enough light to make out his face

as he came over her, into her, and she clutched at his hips, crying out as he eased completely down into stark possession.

He poised there, barely breathing, feeling her in every cell of his body. She moved, crying out, pleading, but his lean hand stilled her hips.

"No," he choked. "No. Lie still."

"Please!"

"Trust me," he whispered shakily. "Tabby, lie still and let me…calm down. I want it to last all night, sweetheart," he said into her open mouth. "I want to take you up and bring you down until you can't bear it, and then I want to explode with you into a thousand lights. Help me, little one. Lie still. Yes. Still."

He calmed her. She cried helplessly, but she obeyed. She felt the tension drain out of him. Then he began yet again, his mouth tracing, touching, cherishing, his hands teasing her back into ecstasy. He didn't move, or lift, and she could feel the depth of his possession, the strength and power of it growing by the second. She grew frightened of its power and whispered it involuntarily.

"Shh," he whispered softly. "You're safe. I won't hurt you. I'll never…hurt you…baby!"

He began to move, ever so tenderly, his body a caress in itself as he kissed her and rocked above her in a rhythm that carried her up and over the edge, long before he was ready.

He felt her convulse and begin to cry, great tearing bursts of sound that mirrored the anguished completion he gave to her. He hadn't wanted to bring it this quickly, because he wasn't ready. But it was all right. She was capable of endless satisfaction. He smiled as he let her rest for a few seconds, turned away for a moment, and then began to arouse her again.

It was a long, long time later when his movements became rough and powerful and urgent. She heard the tenor of his breathing change, felt his body coil and begin to vibrate with its terrible tension. When the pleasure took him, he lifted almost completely off the bed, and she saw his head go back as she felt and heard him experience ecstasy.

He cried out her name in throbbing gasps, his body shuddering so violently that she was almost afraid for him. Then he finally pulled slowly away from her and fell onto his back, and the convulsions were still there, only worse.

"At least," he whispered when he stopped shaking, "this time I managed to protect you."

She only dimly realized what he'd done, what he meant. But she was too tired to analyze it. She closed her eyes and slept, exhausted and drained from pleasure.

When she awoke, it was to light coming in the windows. It took several seconds before she realized where she was. She sat up, feeling sore and uneasy, the sheet falling to her bare breasts. She was nude, and very uncomfortable. She realized why at the same time Nick came out of the bathroom with a towel around his hips.

He paused beside the bed, and he didn't smile. His dark eyes went to her breasts and lingered there.

She couldn't manage to pull the sheet back up. Just looking at him made her sing inside. Her eyes went down his perfectly made body, over his hairy chest to his flat, muscular stomach where the towel caught.

"Want to see all of me?" he asked quietly. "I don't mind." And he dropped the towel.

He was beautiful. She'd never seen a sculpture as perfect as he was, and her eyes told him so.

"You're just as devastating to me, Tabby," he replied. He bent down and pulled the sheet away, revealing the body he'd possessed so thoroughly. He loved looking at her. She was every dream he'd ever dreamed.

As he looked, his body reacted. He chuckled ruefully at the instant effect she had on him, and she blushed.

"I suppose you're on the verge of being the walking wounded this morning?" he asked with resignation.

She blushed more. "If you mean, am I sore… Yes."

He nodded. "That's what I meant, little one." He sighed. "Just as well, I suppose. Last night I was able to protect you, but I have nothing but my willpower this morning. At least we had last night. I didn't want to leave without showing you what it should have been like that day in the park."

"Well, you did," she said, sitting up, tugging the sheet around her as the shame came back again, harder. "You showed me very graphically. Thank you for the lesson."

He retrieved his towel and wrapped it around his lean hips, taking longer than he needed to as he tried to manage the right words. "It wasn't a lesson. It was an apology."

"You're very expert," she said lightly. "Maybe one day I'll be able to appreciate that properly."

"You're unworldly," he replied, frowning. "But you'll learn about the real world, outside that shell you've been living in. It's not such a bad world, Tabby.

Men and women make love all the time without guilt or consequences…''

She looked at him, and he colored. "I have to go now. I have classes to teach.''

He shouldn't feel ashamed, he told himself. He had no reason to feel that way! He went back into the bathroom and slammed the door. When he came out again, freshly shaven, Tabby was back in her silk suit and her hair was in its bun. Except for makeup, she looked just as she had before. Almost. There was a new sadness in her eyes, a new knowledge, a shamed lack of innocence.

"Damn it, you wanted me!" he raged. "You wanted me!''

She turned and looked at him, unblinking. "I loved you,'' she said simply. "I don't think I'm telling you anything you didn't already know. I wanted you because of the way I feel about you. If you loved me back, I don't think I could be ashamed of what we did. But you don't,'' she said, almost accusingly. "You need me, physically, but I'm just another conquest to you, another casual lover. That's what makes it so… sordid.''

He was lost for words. Actually lost for them. Tabby had been part of his life forever. Now he was likely to lose her, because he'd precipitated a relationship neither of them was ready for. He might have wished it undone, but his body throbbed with feverish ecstasy at the delight hers had given him even now. He ached to have her again, and again, and again…

If he'd ever wondered before, he knew now that Tabby loved him. It had felt like love, when she wrapped herself around him and gave him such pleasure that he'd all but lost consciousness from it. Love.

A child. Perhaps a son. A little boy. His eyes kindled as he considered for the first time in his life the possibility of creation that day in the park.

Tabby didn't see the smile, much less guess what he was thinking. She went toward the closed bedroom door and opened it. She had to go home in broad daylight and the whole neighborhood would probably see her. But it didn't seem to matter anymore if her reputation was ruined. She didn't deserve to have one anyway, having behaved with the abandon of a loose woman. She was Nick's lover now, not the prim and upright young lady she'd been before he came back to Washington.

"Tabby, don't go yet," he said. "I want to talk."

"Well, I don't," she said, and she didn't look back. She was breaking up inside, but she wasn't going to let him know that. She loved him, but he felt no such emotion for her. It was best not to rake over the ashes.

He cursed roundly and tried to go after her, but she was in her house and gone. He slammed back into his house.

He'd wanted to explain his changing feelings to Tabby, but she wasn't in any mood to listen to him. He'd only planned to kiss her a little, make light love to her. But, just like the last time, he'd lost control completely the moment he touched her. He smiled ruefully at his own vulnerability, and reflected that if Tabby had had any real experience of men, she'd have known that he was as helpless as she was. A man didn't lose control with a woman unless there were powerful emotions at work. But Tabby didn't know that. And she wouldn't stand still long enough to let him tell her.

Well, he'd start working on her. Now that he knew he was capable of commitment, he had to convince her that his playboy days were behind him. At least, he'd cleared her name. That was going to take some of the pressure off her and make her more rational.

After taking a cab to work Tabby lectured her class on the techniques of uncovering a midden—a layer of cultural artifacts—touching on new legislation that required respect for human remains and their reinterment.

"This is a good thing," she commented as she sat on the edge of her desk, watching her students. "For too long, certain members of our profession have paid too little attention to the human dignity we owe those who came before us. Bones have been pushed into boxes or into drawers at museums and universities with no respect for the people they once were. This is changing, and it should."

"I certainly wouldn't want anyone to dig up my great-grandmother and keep her bones in a box at a museum," one student remarked.

"Nor would I," Tabby replied.

Class let out and Tabby had a lonely lunch at the canteen until Daniel came up, rubbing his hands together and sat down beside her with a cup of coffee.

"I've just had a telephone call from the publisher I sent that proposal to," he told her. "They're interested!"

She brightened. "Daniel, that's wonderful!"

"Suppose I come over tonight and we work up the outline for the last three chapters?"

She hesitated because all day she'd felt guilty that she hadn't let Nick talk to her when he'd wanted to. She felt weak and disgusted with herself for the ease of her surrender, but he hadn't acted as if it were some casual interlude. He'd been...different. Perhaps there was a reason for it, but she hadn't let him speak. She wanted to. She had to know if there was any possibility of a future for the two of them.

On the other hand, it wouldn't do to sit home all by herself and wait for him to come around.

"All right," she told Daniel. "I'll look for you around five. I'll make a light supper for us."

"Just like old times," he said, smiling. "Fine, darling."

She finished her day's work, feeling so good as members of the faculty congratulated her on being cleared. So did Dr. Flannery, but he looked distinctly uncomfortable.

"They're going to discontinue my program," he said miserably. "And Pal is going back to the zoo. I suppose I'll do as well studying iguanas, though," he said, brightening. "They're delivering a lovely five-foot specimen next week!"

Iguanas, she recalled, looked like prehistoric reptiles. Five feet? "Do they bite?" she asked nervously.

"They're vegetarians, Dr. Harvey," he said, grinning. "Besides—" he leaned close, looking around them "—he won't be able to pick locks!"

He laughed, and so did she.

Late that afternoon, she took a perfect quiche out of the oven and put it and the green salad she'd made on the table while Daniel poured coffee. They had a quiet meal, like old times, and then sprawled in the living room to work on the manuscript. Daniel took off his jacket and tie and shoes, as he usually did, and unbuttoned the top button of his shirt. Tabby, in yellow shorts and a tank top, with her hair down, looked uncommonly lovely.

He watched her for a long moment, and smiled. "You know, you're very lovely. Just lately, you're...I don't quite know how to put it…you're much more feminine.''

Probably because of what Nick had taught her, she thought sadly, and colored a little. She was a woman now, not a nervous spinster. Nick hadn't called, hadn't come over. He was avoiding her, she reckoned, probably afraid because she might read more into last night than he wanted her to. It was just like old times.

"You look lovely," Daniel was saying, his eyes on her.

"Thank you, Daniel."

"Are you sure you don't want to get engaged again?" he murmured as he eased her onto her back and loomed over her. "It would be no hardship at all to marry you. Tabitha, you're lovely…!"

He bent and kissed her, very gently. She smiled and reached up to his shoulders to push him away.

But that wasn't how it looked to the angry man who'd just opened the front door without knocking, incensed to find Daniel's car in Tabby's driveway when he'd come back from visiting his friend at FBI headquarters.

Tabby and Daniel heard the door open at the same time and looked toward it.

Nick was almost vibrating with fury. His dark eyes flashed, his deep tan reddened as he glared at the two on the floor. His big, lean hand clenched on the doorknob until the knuckles went white.

"You vicious tease!" he accused Tabby. "Is that all it meant to you? I suppose the engagement is back on again?"

Daniel didn't understand the accusation, but Tabby did. She sat up, flushing. "Nick…"

"Well, don't mind me," he said coldly. "You know

where I stand. I've never made any secret of the fact that forever after isn't my style.''

She knew, but she'd hoped. Her eyes narrowed with sadness. ''Yes, I know, Nick,'' she said quietly.

Her reasonable tone made him even more furious. The fact that dear Daniel was rumpled and had lipstick on his mouth sent him right through the roof. ''It was fun,'' he told Tabby. ''But a little too tame for my taste. Maybe Dr. Myers here is more your cup of tea. I wish you both all the best.''

''What are you implying?'' Daniel asked, ruffled, as he got to his feet.

''What do you think?'' he asked, glaring at Tabby, who was scrambling to her feet. ''I thought you weren't the kind of woman to go from one man to another in two days. What a chump I was!''

''Nick, I didn't!'' she cried, astonished at the sudden realization that he was jealous. He thought she was two-timing him. Perhaps the hurtful things he was saying arose out of jealousy in the first place, and he…*cared!* ''Listen to me…!''

''I've heard more than enough,'' he told her implacably. ''Goodbye, Tabby.''

He went back out, slamming the door. Tabby, horrified that she might have made the biggest mistake of her life, ran after him. She opened the door and sprinted across the lawn that separated her house from his.

''Nick, wait!'' she called in exasperation.

''Leave me alone,'' he growled over his shoulder.

People mowing lawns stopped and watched the sight of their very correct neighbor, Dr. Harvey, apparently chasing a man, and dressed in a very skimpy outfit, too. The men stared admiringly at her long, tanned legs. She'd never before ventured off her patio in shorts.

"Nick, I love you!" she cried.

"No, you don't. You love that stuffed shirt!" he raged. "You only used me for sex!"

She gasped as she realized that his deep voice was carrying, and that her grinning neighbors were having a field day. She blushed furiously.

"How dare you!" she yelled at him. "How dare you say things like that to me in public!"

He whirled at his front door, his eyes blazing. "Go back to your egghead over there and see if he can make you scream your head off the way I did in bed!"

She covered her face with her hands. "I'll never forgive you!"

Nick looked around at the neighborhood audience, cold mockery in the smile that flared on his handsome face. "Ruined your spotless reputation, have I?" he asked coldly. "Well, that's what you get for seducing innocent men and then dropping them when someone else comes along!"

"I didn't seduce you!"

"Fudge." He opened his door.

"Will you please listen!" she burst out.

"Sure. Like you listened to me last night." He slammed the door in her face.

She hesitated for a minute. Then she went up to the door and knocked and knocked. He ignored her. She called. He still ignored her. She called again and knocked until her knuckles were raw and her voice was hoarse. Finally she kicked it, with no response. Then she went to the window, to try to get his attention. He pulled the curtains together with a furious jerk.

"Damn you, Nick!" she yelled, tears of angry frustration in her eyes. "I wouldn't marry you if you had buckets of money and covered me in precious jewels!"

The door opened. "I don't marry fickle women," he told her coldly. "You two-timing Jezebel!"

"Look who's talking!" she shouted. "The playboy of the western world!"

"At least I was reformed! You're just getting started!" He glared toward a shocked Daniel, who was standing in the grass getting an earful. "Go marry your writing collaborator. I don't want you!"

"You did!" she threw back.

"Only for one night," he said with cold pleasure when she flushed. "It was nice, but I've had better. And I will again. Go home!"

He slammed the door for the second time. Tabby cursed. She never had in her life, but she cursed steadily at the top of her lungs, while all around her, male neighbors chuckled and began to form groups. Wives came out of their kitchens to see what all the fuss was about. Tabby, who'd always been so correct and proper and self-conscious, didn't give a damn if the whole world heard her. She told Nick what she thought of him, called him every foul name she'd ever heard in English and two foreign languages. Finally, when she was weak from it all, she stormed back to her own house, past Daniel, and into the house.

"Uh, Tabby, it might be a good idea if we didn't work on the book tonight."

She looked at Daniel. "Yes," she said, realizing belatedly that he was actually intimidated by her unfettered temper. Amazing. He seemed so self-possessed, but feminine rage unmanned him. It hadn't fazed Nick. She grimaced. "Sorry about that."

He put on his shoes and his tie and jacket with a rueful smile. "Well, no need asking how you feel about

Mr. Reed anymore. I wish you luck, Tabby. It would be a pity to waste that kind of emotion on me.''

"I'm sorry," she said again, helplessly.

He kissed her forehead gently. "I'll enjoy working on the book with you," he said. He actually laughed. "And I thought you were cold. My, my.''

She flushed. "Good night, Daniel.''

"Good night, Tabby. I'll phone you tomorrow.''

She nodded, watching him go without any real misgivings. She glared at Nick's house. The neighbors were still glancing her way. No more floor show today, folks, she thought, closing the door. Incredible, she mused, that she felt no shame or regret for her rage outside. Nick had certainly changed her, and not necessarily for the better. Being a scarlet woman was invigorating, if nothing else.

The guilt would go eventually, she supposed. Meanwhile, she punched in Nick's number several times over the course of the evening. He wouldn't pick up the receiver. Finally she slammed it down and went to bed. All right, if that was how he wanted it. He could sulk all night. Tomorrow, she'd try again. If he cared about her that much, that he lost every bit of his self-control in temper, then there was definitely hope for them. Even if he was too stubborn to admit it just yet. She was smiling to herself when she went to bed, and she dreamed of babies and Nick reading bedtime stories to them.

Chapter Nine

Tabby tried once more the next morning to get Nick on the telephone or to the door, but he was being stubborn again. With a reluctant sigh, she went to school, taught her classes and was later called to the dean's office early to hear his apology for placing her under suspension.

"You always believed that I was innocent," she replied with a warm smile. "Even though I was the most likely suspect. You only did what you had to do to protect the school."

"There were other suspects, you know," he said surprisingly. "I have to admit that two of the faculty were high on my list, but I'm glad to find that our thief was small and hairy!"

"So am I!" Tabby agreed. "I hope I still have a job...?"

"Don't be absurd," he said, smiling at her. He rose and shook her hand. "You're one of the best educators we've ever employed. I would have been devastated to lose you."

It was a politically correct thing to say, but she knew that he meant it. She smiled back glowingly. "I would have been very sad to leave here. I learned just how much my work meant to me during all this."

"It usually takes a crisis to make us appreciate the value of things we sometimes take for granted," he agreed.

Yes, she thought, remembering Nick's odd behavior. Why hadn't she realized that his loss of control with her, both times, could have had its roots in deep emotion? Her naïveté had kept her from seeing his involvement until it was almost too late. But there was still hope, if she could reach him and make him talk to her. She could have kicked herself for walking away that night he'd wanted to talk.

She'd planned to corner him that night. But when she got home, the house next door was closed up and the rental car was gone. Minutes after she'd fixed herself a sandwich and a cup of coffee, a power company truck arrived to cut off the electricity. She knew then that Nick had gone. Without another word, without a real goodbye, even without a note, he'd faded away and she was alone again. She'd left it too late. He'd closed the door and no matter if she tried to phone him or write to him in Houston, she knew it would do no good. It was over. He'd told her so without a single word.

She was too depressed to do much after that. She ate her meager fare and sat around trying to grade test papers, but eventually she went to bed and cried herself to sleep. Nick had decided that he didn't want her. He'd seduced her and had his fill, and she'd given in and let him. Now he was on his way back to Houston, to his job and his friends. Tabby had been relegated to the faceless crowd of his ex-lovers, just like all the rest.

She stopped thinking about it because she couldn't bear it. But as the days went by, her face began to show the ravages of her nights. She grew wan and pale, and listless. Her enthusiasm for her job dimmed. She went through the motions of living without really caring whether she did or not.

A week later, one worry was dispensed with. She had proof that she wasn't pregnant, and she almost jumped for joy. She wanted children, but not out of wedlock. Love on one side was never enough. She'd thought Nick might really care deeply about her, but if he did, he'd have been in touch by now. He simply wasn't interested. She had to face that.

She debated about calling Nick and telling him there was nothing to worry about, but she decided against it when she didn't hear anything from him. He was obviously not concerned with what had become of her, so let him continue in his oblivion.

Actually, Nick was oblivious only because he was being worked to death. Lassiter, sensing his employee's violent emotional state upon his return, had immediately thrown him in headfirst on a kidnapping case. For the past week he'd been on the road, trying to track down a parent who'd absconded with his four-year-old son while his ex-wife tried frantically to find him.

Nick had finally turned him up in a flea-bitten motel outside a small New Mexico town. He'd persuaded the desperate father to turn himself in, for the child's sake. That hadn't been an easy task, but he'd accomplished it.

All the time, he'd thought about Tabby and wished that he hadn't been so bullheaded when she'd tried to explain why she and Daniel had been making love on her carpet. Now he was worried about her. She was deeply religious and he'd seduced her. She might even be pregnant. What if she did something desperate because he wouldn't listen? When he got back to Houston, the first thing he did was ask his sister if she'd heard from her best friend.

"No," she said quizzically. "Should I have?"

"I thought she might have phoned to tell you how things were going, now that she's been cleared," he replied tersely.

Helen pursed her lips. She knew her brother. He looked haggard and guilty, and she'd already guessed that something devastating had happened to him in D.C. It had to involve Tabby, but she couldn't guess what it was.

"Why don't you call her, if you're so curious?" she asked.

He turned away. "I've got another case to start on," he replied. "I haven't time."

"I've got cases of my own," she reminded him, "but it doesn't take five minutes to pick up a telephone and make a call, does it?"

"Never mind," he said irritably.

She watched him storm out of the office with new interest. He was worried about Tabby for some reason, but he wasn't willing to phone her. Why? Wouldn't she talk to him, was that it?

That night Helen telephoned Tabby. Nick was out of town again on a new case, and there was probably no doubt that he hadn't been burning up telephone lines.

"How are you?" Helen asked without preamble. "Nick wouldn't say why, but he seemed to be worried about you."

Tabby felt her heart leap involuntarily. "I'm fine,"

she said noncommittally. "If he asks, you can tell him there isn't anything he needs to be concerned about. He needn't waste any of his valuable time being worried about me!"

That sounded vicious. Helen grinned. "How's Daniel?"

"He and I are still working on our book. Unfortunately he's discovered that I have a temper. He doesn't want to marry me anymore. Just as well," she said, "because I think I hate men now!"

"You broke the engagement?"

"Yes. Daniel is a fine man, but he deserves more than I have to give him."

"You sound different," Helen said with some concern.

"I suppose I am different," Tabby told her. "I've had a hard couple of weeks, through no fault of my own. I've learned some lessons that hurt."

That sounded vaguely ominous. "Anything to do with Nick?"

"I'm finally convinced that he'll never be desperately in love with me, if that's what you mean." Tabby laughed bitterly. "He gave me the cure. I tried to talk to him and he left D.C. without a word or a note or even a goodbye."

"I'm sorry," Helen said sincerely. "He's been different since he's been back. I'd hoped it might be because of you."

"Not a chance. He can't see me for dust. It's probably just as well. Now that I think about it, I'm sure I wouldn't be happy with a man who can't live without a different woman in his bed every night and a gun under his pillow!"

"He doesn't date anybody these days," Helen remarked. "Not since New Year's, in fact. Isn't that odd?"

Tabby refused to let herself hope. She'd had enough misery on Nick's account.

"He hasn't even been talking anymore about being restless and changing jobs," Helen added.

"That's probably why he's thinking of going with the DEA or the customs people," Tabby muttered. "He said he was."

"Funny, he didn't mention it around here."

"He'll get around to it. I have to go. I've got a lot of papers to grade."

"Sure. Well, keep in touch, will you? I worry about you."

Tabby smiled. "I know. I worry about you, too, believe it or not. You're the only family I have left, even if you aren't a blood relation."

"That goes double for me. I'm sorry my brother is such a blind idiot."

"He's that, all right! Blind, deaf, dumb and stupid as a...!" She forced herself to calm down when she heard Helen's faint giggle. "It wouldn't have worked, anyway. I hardly fit the image of the glamorous party girl with a laid-back attitude toward love."

"Yes, I see what you mean," Helen said ruefully.

"Just tell your stupid brother that he doesn't have anything to worry about. *If* he bothers to ask," she added venomously.

"I'll do that little thing. You take care of yourself."

"You, too."

Helen hung up, her mind going like a watch. Tabby sounded different. Something was going on. She had to make Nick tell her what it was, since Tabby wouldn't.

But she didn't get a chance the next day. Nick didn't

come back. However, a complication did upset the routine of the office.

Harold proposed immediate marriage. Helen, astonished, agreed on the spot, only to be told that Harold was going to have to move to South America for a year to work on his father's construction gang as a prerequisite to inheriting his trust fund.

"What am I going to do?" Helen wailed to Tess Lassiter later that day. "I hate to put you on the spot like this, but I love Harold. I want to go with him. We have to get married now and leave the country in a week."

"You're irreplaceable," Tess agreed. "But I can see that you have to go with Harold. Don't worry," she said gently. "Something will work out."

Something did, hours later. A weeping Kit Morris, Tess's best friend, came storming into the office with red eyes and audible sobs.

"He fired me!" she choked, going into Tess's outstretched arms.

"He? You mean Logan Deverell, your boss?" Tess asked, aghast. "But you've worked for him for three years…!"

"Slaved for him," Kit amended, wiping her big blue eyes. Her oval face in its frame of dark hair was as white as tissue except for her red nose. "But he's got a new lady love. She was terrible to me. We had an argument. She threw hot coffee all over me, and he took her side and he told me to get out and that he didn't want to have to see me ever again!"

Tess was astonished. Kit had worked for Logan Deverell for longer than Tess had worked with Dane before she married him. The two were inseparable during working hours and sometimes even at evening soirees where Kit was obliged to take notes for her boss. Now Logan had apparently fired her over some woman. It was almost too much to believe.

"What am I going to do?" Kit wailed. "I've got rent due, and a car payment, and he didn't say one word about severance pay. I've got no place to go, and not even a job…!" She started crying again.

Tess thought about her problem, and about the agency's problem of losing Helen so quickly. She smiled as she began to arrive at a solution to both their problems.

"Kit," she asked her best friend, "have you ever thought about doing detective work?"

Nick was finally on his way back home again. He'd pursued a bail jumper all the way to San Francisco, only to lose him to a streetcar. The man had underestimated its speed and fallen under its metal mass, dying instantly. Nick had watched. The man had been young, much younger than himself. The experience had shaken and sobered him—much the same as when he'd lost Lucy—making him realize just how short life was. He saw the world through new, more cynical eyes, and he began to see things that he hadn't before. He was going to die someday himself. If he did, would anyone really care except his sister? He was practically alone. No wife, no family, no one of his own to love. No one— except Tabby. She'd wanted to love him so badly, but he wouldn't let her. Now he'd faced mortality; he'd seen death. Everything had changed, all at once.

There was, he decided, no point in continuing to hide his head in the sand. Tabby was a part of his life that he wasn't going to be happy without. He didn't want roots, but it looked as if he had them just the same. He hadn't looked at another woman since he'd had Tabby. He didn't want anyone else.

The thing was, he'd behaved like an idiot. How did Tabby feel after the way he'd treated her? He groaned out loud at the memory of the things he'd said to her, and how she'd reacted to them. Chances were very good that she'd go off the deep end and marry prissy Daniel just to show him. He'd fouled up everything with his callous attitude.

He got off the plane in Houston and took a cab to the office. He reported to Dane and heard Helen's news without really comprehending it.

"Didn't you understand?" his sister asked irritably. "I'm marrying Harold and going off to South America, to the jungle, where pygmies live!"

"That's Africa," he murmured absently.

"Headhunters, then!"

"Wear a scarf and keep it tied," he advised.

She threw up her hands. "What's the matter with you!"

He looked at her, his hands deep in his pockets, glad that they were temporarily undisturbed in his office. "Did you talk to Tabby?"

She shifted her stance. "Yes. Why?" she added, cocking her head.

"How is she?" he asked.

"She sounded strange," she began.

His face began to pale. He caught her by the shoulders. "Suicidally depressed?" he persisted.

"No!" She frowned at him. "In fact, she sounded more mature and independent than ever."

His lips parted on a held breath. "Helen, is she pregnant?" he asked in a choked tone, his eyes wild as they searched hers.

Light bulbs went on in her head. So that was it! Her eyes widened and she smiled. "Well, well," she mused.

He actually flushed. He dropped his hands and moved away, staring out the window with the first embarrassment he could ever remember feeling. "She'd have told you, surely, if she was?"

"She's not," she said, sorry to put him out of his misery so quickly. She'd enjoyed seeing her big, strong brother just momentarily weak.

"You witch!" he burst out, turning, his dark eyes blazing at her. "You might have spared me!"

"Why?" she asked reasonably. "Tabby wouldn't tell me anything. I wanted to know why she was so sarcastic about you. Almost as if she hated you. She told me to tell you that you had absolutely nothing to be concerned about. I wondered what it meant." She grinned. "Now I know."

The flush got worse. "Don't push."

"Sorry. Going to marry her?" she persisted, and her eyes narrowed. "You don't go around seducing nice girls like Tabby," she added. "It's ungentlemanly."

"I know that, too," he replied heavily. "Believe me, it wasn't anything I planned. I loused it all up," he added, throwing up his hands. "Just like I did before, at New Year's. She'll never believe another thing I say. She'll never trust me."

"You could go back and try to talk to her," Helen suggested.

He glared at her furiously. "You conned me into going home before. That's what got me into this mess."

"Tabby loves you. Love doesn't die because of a few harsh words."

"I wouldn't be too sure of that. It might have been nothing more than a long-standing infatuation."

"And it might not. You could—"

"Where the *hell* have you put my secretary?" came a deep roar from the direction of the open office door.

Nick and Helen turned together to find a huge, dark-haired, dark-eyed man glowering at them. He was dressed in a green overcoat and his thick hair was wet. His deeply tanned face was livid with anger. One huge hand was holding the door open, and the other was holding a cigar.

"If you mean Kit," Helen said, "she's out with Tess and Dane."

"Doing what?" he demanded.

"Eating lunch, I guess." Helen shrugged. "Did you need to see her about something?"

"Something." He nodded. "She hid my appointment book before she left and messed up the computer. Every time I hit a button, it throws up an error message at me! I'm going to wring her neck!"

Helen exchanged glances with Nick. "Tell you what, Mr. Deverell," she offered, "I'll come back with you and fix the computer. I think I know what's wrong with it. As for Kit, she'll be back about two, I suppose."

"Back here? Why?" he demanded.

"They gave her a job," Helen said and winced when he proceeded to turn the air blue.

Long minutes later, Helen managed to persuade Logan Deverell back into his own office. It wouldn't do for poor Kit to have to confront him in this violent temper.

What was wrong with the computer, she soon discovered, was Logan Deverell. He didn't know how to use it. Within minutes, she extracted all the information he needed and managed to get an agency to send over a sacrificial victim to do his office work. Then she got out, quickly.

Nick had gone back to his apartment in the meantime, smoking one cigarette after another until he had a vicious cough.

He threw the package on the floor and stepped on it finally and then jerked up the telephone and dialed Washington, D.C.

Tabby had only been home from work for about fifteen minutes. She was still recuperating from her long day with a cup of coffee when the phone rang.

Daniel, probably, she thought wryly as she picked it up, wanting her to do some more research for his book. She wouldn't mind. It gave her a way to fill in the emptiness of her life without Nick.

"Hello?" she asked with twinkling amusement.

The sound of her voice made Nick's heart catch. He felt as if he'd come home. He leaned back in his easy chair and kicked his shoes off. "Hello, Tabby," he said quietly.

She almost put the receiver down.

"Don't hang up," he asked softly. "I haven't called to hassle you. I just want to know."

"About what?" she said curtly, making it hard for him.

"If you're carrying my child," he replied gently.

There was a long pause. "No, I'm not," she said stiffly. "I told Helen to tell you..."

"Yes. She did."

"Then why are you calling me?"

"To make sure there were no misunderstandings," he said simply. "How are you?"

"I'm very well, thanks," she bit off.

"Want to know how I am?" he asked with bitter sarcasm.

"Only if you've had your head blown off or you've got termites in your wooden heart," she said icily.

"Funny girl."

"I've told you how I am."

"So you have. How about flying out here?"

"What for?" she asked coldly.

He stared around at the apartment, and saw for the first time how empty and dull it was. There was no color, no life, in it. "I thought you might like to spruce up my apartment. Make it livable."

"I'd dig a hole and fill it with crocodiles…"

"Venomous," he sighed. "I don't suppose I blame you. I've been a twenty-four karat heel. For what it's worth, I was feeling betrayed, although God knows why I should when I gave you every reason to want to put a knife in my pride. I ran, but you were everywhere I went."

"You don't have to feel threatened because of me," she told him, aching inside. Why did he have to call now and destroy her hard-won peace of mind?

"I close my eyes and see you, Tabby," he said softly. "Feel you. Taste you."

"Me and the rest of the women in the country…"

"I haven't had anyone since I had you," he said quietly. "I won't. Not ever again."

She hesitated. It was a line. Just a line. She had to force herself to accept that. She closed her eyes. "It won't work. I don't want you, Nick. I'm…" She searched for a lie. "I'm going to marry Daniel."

"That wasn't what you told Helen," he said smugly.

She let out a rough sigh. "I'll never tell her anything else as long as I live, you can bet on that!"

"Buy a plane ticket. Come out here," he coaxed. His voice dropped. "Live with me, Tabby."

She had to clench her teeth to bite back an answer. It was tempting. Oh, yes, it was tempting. But living with a man didn't figure in her scheme of things. She wanted a wedding ring and a settled marriage. She wanted children. Nick was only offering an affair.

"No," she whispered hoarsely. "I can't do that, Nick."

"Why?" he asked, his voice more tender than she'd ever heard it.

"It wouldn't work. I'm not...not suited to fervent affairs. I can't come, Nick."

"Affairs...?"

"There's someone at the door," she lied unsteadily. "I have to go." She hung up and then took the phone off the hook.

Tears rolled down her cheeks in torrents. She threw herself down on the couch and bawled. Why had he called, to torment her with temptations she had to resist? As much as she loved him, she could have strangled him for that!

Nick was staring at the receiver with a scowl. What had brought on that comment about having an affair with him, he wondered. He'd asked her to come and live with him....

He slapped his forehead roughly. Of all the stupid things, he'd let her think he wanted her to come and live with him without offering her marriage. Having seduced her twice without mentioning any kind of commitment, how could he blame her for not trusting him? His Tabby would never consent to such living arrangements. She was too conventional for unconventional relationships.

Well, it would be easy enough to clarify that. He dialed the number again. Busy. He kept trying, but she'd obviously taken it off the hook. Just the way he'd done to her before he left D.C. Oddly enough, he didn't get angry. She was entitled to a little revenge.

He gave up at midnight and called the airlines. There was only one way to handle it now. He was going to have to go up and see her. In person, he had a much better chance of making her change her mind.

He caught a plane out early the next morning. Kit and Helen watched him leave the office after speaking to Dane.

"Good luck!" Helen called after him.

"Thanks," he murmured dryly. "I'll need it!"

"So will you," Helen murmured to Kit as a taller, bigger male form replaced Nick's in the doorway and marched in.

Kit paled, but she lifted her chin stubbornly. "I'm not coming back," she told Logan Deverell. "As far as I'm concerned, you can make your own coffee and type your own letters for the rest of your life!"

"You don't think you can be replaced?" he mused coldly. "At this very moment, I have a very capable new secretary sorting out the *mess* you made of my filing system!"

She stiffened. "Your filing system came out of a book! It's the very latest thing…"

"No damned kidding?" he asked sarcastically. "Amazing that I can't find a single file using it!"

"People who can spell," she said pointedly, "find it very simple."

His dark eyes glittered. He jammed his hands into

his slacks pockets, stretching them across the powerful muscles of his thighs. His broad face showed no emotion at all as he looked at her.

"I came by," he said, "to tell you that you left your vegetation in my office in your haste to depart. I'd appreciate having it removed."

"Gladly," she told him. "I'd hate for it to die of poison from those corn shucks you smoke."

"Imported cigars," he corrected.

"They always smelled like corn shucks to me," she said cheerfully. "The masks are in my top drawer, if your new secretary can't take the fumes."

He stared at her without blinking, his very posture intimidating. Kit was tall, but he was taller. Her blue eyes met his dark ones without flinching, but they fell before the arrogant contempt in his.

"You owe me two weeks' notice," he told her.

"Which you'd have gotten if you hadn't thrown a book at me!"

"I didn't throw it. It fell."

"Six feet, horizontally?"

He drew in a rough breath. "What are you going to do in here?" he asked suddenly, glancing around. "Type letters or answer the phone?"

"Neither," she informed him smugly. "I'm going to be a detective."

The laughter that burst from his lips made her flush wildly. "You stop that!" she raged. "It isn't funny!"

He lit a cigar and shook his head as he started back out the door. "Miss Private Eye. Now I've heard everything. You can't even find your car keys when you get ready to leave the office. How are you going to find a missing person?"

"I'll be good at it! At least I won't have to put up with you anymore, Mount Vesuvius!"

His powerful shoulders shrugged. "Poor Dane." He went out and closed the door.

"I had to go and help him work the computer after you left yesterday," Helen confided amusedly. "He couldn't spell the commands. The computer shut down on him."

"Good!"

"Why did he fire you?" Helen asked, frowning. "My goodness, you've worked for him forever."

"I told him his newest conquest had taken her former lover for everything he had. He was a neighbor of mine. He…almost killed himself," she said, grimacing. "I was trying to warn Mr. Deverell. Some fat chance. He makes up his mind, and it's like an edict from Mount Olympus!" she yelled at the closed door. "HE IMME-DIATELY GOES DEAF WHEN HE MAKES UP HIS MIND!"

"Experience is the best teacher," Helen reminded her gently.

"What a nice saying. I'll have it engraved and give it to him for Christmas. It may be the only thing of value he'll have left by then," she added with a cold smile.

Helen didn't say another word. But she had a feeling that this feud was far from over. Meanwhile, she hoped her brother was going to be lucky enough to get Tabby back. It would be a real pity if he finally admitted his feelings and it was too late. Nick had always been a free agent, but he'd been noticeably different since he'd come back from D.C. And if anyone could make him settle down, it was Tabby.

Chapter Ten

Nick rented a car at the airport in D.C. and drove quickly back to his father's old house. It was Saturday now and Tabby would be home. He was counting on the chance that she'd be home alone, and that Daniel wouldn't be anywhere around. He needed to talk to her in private, without any prying eyes. He hoped that would be possible, remembering what an interesting spectacle they'd presented to her amused neighbors the last time he was here.

It wasn't going to be easy. He knew that already. He'd put his freedom and independence above Tabby's pride. He'd treated her shamefully and if she couldn't forgive him, he really didn't know what he was going to do.

He parked the car in the driveway and sat in it for a long moment, gathering up the courage to face her. Finally he got out and started for her front door. But on an impulse, he turned and went around the house.

She was lying on a chaise longue on her small patio,

wearing a one-piece bathing suit that highlighted her lovely figure. He stared at her hungrily, remembering how it had felt to make love to her. His body went taut all at once and he smiled ruefully at his own impatience.

Perhaps, he thought, the element of surprise would give him an edge. He was going to need one.

He moved around the chair and suddenly straddled it just as Tabby's eyes opened and dilated.

"Guess who?" he mused, and lowered his body completely onto hers.

She gasped. "Nick...!"

He smiled as she tried to push him off. He wouldn't let her. His long legs entangled with hers, slowly caressing their bare length as his mouth went down over hers. He began to kiss her slowly, warmly, with aching tenderness. He didn't touch her at all.

"It's broad daylight," she squeaked when he paused to get a breath of air, overwhelmed by his ardor and her helpless need of him. It had been so long. She'd missed him beyond bearing. Her eyes stared up into his with aching adoration.

He didn't miss the warmth in her look. "So it is. Have I ever told you how utterly lovely you are?" he asked softly. He smiled and bent to her mouth again. "Remind me to do that when I stop aching. Put your hands on my hips and hold me against you, Tabby. I hurt like hell."

"The neighbors..." she protested under his mouth.

"They're all watching television," he whispered, levering down between her legs. "Yes," he said unsteadily. "Yes, that feels good, doesn't it?" He pushed, and she gasped and blushed.

The intimacy was shattering. He lifted his head and looked into her eyes, searching them tenderly while he shifted lazily from one side to the other and watched her try to breathe.

"Nick, stop," she protested, and then gave up, her eyes hungry on his face even as she fought to keep her pride intact. "Oh, why did you have to come back!" she raged miserably. "I was just beginning to get over you!"

"No, you weren't," he said knowingly. "No more than I was beginning to get over you. We're stuck with each other, baby. I think I knew that for certain at that New Year's Eve party. That's why I've been the devil to get along with ever since."

"You only want me to live with you…!"

He kissed her mouth shut, very gently. "Yes. For the rest of my life. The rest of yours. I want to marry you, Tabby," he breathed into her parted lips as he slowly increased the pressure of his kiss.

She went under. All her dreams were coming true. She clung to him, oblivious to the whole world. "You went away. You wouldn't answer your phone," she whispered.

"Neither would you, last night. I had to come all this way just to make you listen. Are you listening?" he teased gently. "I want you for keeps. I was afraid of that kind of bond between us, but I'm not afraid anymore," he added grimly. "Seeing you on the floor with darling Daniel convinced me of that in ten seconds flat!"

"It wasn't what you thought," she told him. "Really it wasn't. He was kissing me, not vice versa."

"Who could blame him, really," Nick sighed, looking at her lovely body with possessive eyes. "I know how it feels to hold you like that. The difference was," he added firmly, "that you belong to me. I was your first man, your only man. I mean to be your last man, too."

"You reformed rakes," she managed, laughing.

"We make good husbands and fathers," he informed her. "Marry me, and I'll show you." He pursed his lips and studied her flat belly with intense interest. "I don't know that I mind the thought of deliberately making a baby with you. In fact," he added, touching her stomach with one big, lean hand as he held her eyes, "it excites me. Want to see?"

She cleared her throat and sat up as the man next door began to start his lawnmower. The thing was, he wasn't looking at his lawnmower, he was looking at Tabby. "Better not," she said, glancing past him.

He lifted his head and gave the man a hard glare. Immediately the neighbor began to mow through his wife's flower bed.

"Shame on you!" she exclaimed.

"I don't like him staring at you," he said possessively.

"You jealous man, you."

"I can't help it. You're mine. I tried to keep my distance, after New Year's Eve. You really got to me, and I was afraid of going in headfirst. But when I came back here, I just lost it altogether. What happened in the park that day was inevitable." He winced at her expression. "That, I regret most of all. But I don't regret what came after it," he added fervently. "That night we had together was the most beautiful night of my life."

She felt those words all the way into her heart. "You left," she reminded him.

"I had to. I was so jealous of Daniel that all I could think about was how his head would look in a bowl. I knew by then that it was more than physical with me. But I thought you'd decided that I wasn't worth the risk of your heart. Maybe I was afraid to try to convince you," he added honestly. "I had mixed feelings about being faithful for the rest of my life. Not anymore," he added quietly. "I have no doubts left."

"You know I'm not pregnant," she blurted out. "I told Helen…"

"Yes." He smiled faintly. "I'll have hell living that down, believe me. But just for the record, I do want children. I'm glad that there won't be a baby just yet, though," he said seriously. "Children shouldn't be accidents."

"No," she agreed softly, smiling at him. "They should be wanted, by both people."

He touched her hair gently. "And not born out of wedlock, either."

"No."

"So, that being the case," he breathed against her mouth, "I think I'd better marry you before we try to make one."

He held her gently and kissed her until she was breathless. "I care deeply for you," he said huskily. "You know that, don't you?"

Caring wasn't loving, but it was a start. He wanted her enough to give up his freedom for her. It would be a chance, but she'd already faced life without him. It was less than pleasant.

"You might regret marrying me one day," she began worriedly.

"That works both ways. Marriage is what you make of it."

"I suppose so."

"How will you feel about giving up your job here to live in Houston?"

She started. "I hadn't considered that." It disturbed her. She had put in a lot of time and one day she might head her department. It would mean giving up a lot.

He chuckled softly. "Never mind. I can see that the idea doesn't appeal. To tell you the truth, I'm a little tired of Houston. I'd like to come home to D.C. There's always enough business for a private detective in this neck of the woods. And it's handy to FBI headquarters."

She looked horrified.

He smoothed out her frown. "I'm not going back there," he assured her. "Or to DEA or the customs service, if you're brooding about that. I like detective work enough. I don't want you worrying all the time."

Her heart lifted. "I would never have asked you to give it up," she said.

"I know that. But it would have kept you upset."

"I love you," she said huskily, averting her eyes.

His body tingled all over. He looked at her in wonder. "Still?" he asked. "Even after the way I've hurt you?"

"Love doesn't wear out, Nick. It survives almost everything you do to it."

"It must. I've been a real pain, haven't I?"

She smoothed her hands over his broad chest with the first stirrings of possession. "So have I, I guess."

She looked up. "Marriage isn't something I can take lightly, though, Nick. I can't marry you on speculation. You know, one of those 'we'll get a divorce if it doesn't work out things.'"

He drew her gently into his arms and held her. "I don't want a fly-by-night marriage, either. I'll settle, baby. You'll have to take me on trust, but I won't sell you out or have women on the side. Does that reassure you?"

"I'm not blond and sophisticated," she reminded him. "I may not fit in very well. We college professor types are pretty much loners by trade, and we feel uncomfortable without our trappings."

"You keep forgetting that I studied law, don't you?" he teased, brushing his mouth over her forehead. "Lawyers are very often staid types, too. In fact, I have to confess that I've spent a lot of the past few years being called a bore. Most women who go out with me expect a dashing hero like the ones they see on television. I'm afraid I don't quite fit the image. I'm not flamboyant and I like to talk about famous criminal cases."

"I love to read old Earl Stanley Gardner novels," she confessed. "He was a lawyer himself."

"I knew that. I'm a Perry Mason addict, too." He drew back, searching her eyes warmly. "See? Something else we have in common. I like kids, too."

She smiled wistfully. "It will work, won't it?" she asked nervously. "I mean, you don't feel as if you're being forced into something you don't want to do?"

"I want to spend every night for the rest of my life in your arms," he replied frankly. "Holding you. Loving you. Showing you how much you matter to me. Does that sound like force to you?''

"Not if you really mean it."

"I mean it, all right," he said fervently, his eyes burning into hers. "God knows, I've never meant anything more."

"It isn't just that you want me?" she persisted.

He eased her away from him and helped her into her robe before he led her back into the house. He held her hand warmly in his big one, his eyes on the door, not on Tabby.

He opened the door and let her inside. "Make some coffee, could you? I came straight here from the airport."

"Certainly." She went into the kitchen and started a pot of coffee brewing. She was all thumbs. It showed. "I never got a bill," she said shakily. "I asked you to send me one."

"A bill?" He shook his head. "Tabby! Are you crazy?"

She smiled at him. "I must be. You seem to be an addiction I can't quite cure."

He put his hands into his pockets to avoid temptation. Then he leaned back against the counter to watch her get down cups and saucers from the cabinet. "You look right at home in the kitchen. Take your hair down."

The request was so sudden that she turned and stared at him.

"I love your hair down your back," he mused. "I used to think you tortured it into that bun because you knew I preferred it loose."

She smiled shyly. "I suppose I might have."

She took it down and shook her head to let it fall in natural waves around her shoulders.

He nodded. "That's better." He glared at her. "You had it down that night you were kissing Daniel."

"Not on purpose," she said, soothing him.

He sighed. "Okay. I've missed you. I thought I hated domesticity." He shrugged with a rueful smile. "I hated being alone more."

"So did I." She fiddled with a spoon.

He arched away from the counter and caught her by the waist, pulling her lazily to him. "It's going to be difficult for me at first," he said seriously. "For you, too, I imagine. Learning to live with another person, at our ages, when we're set in our ways is never easy. But I'll try if you will."

"Nick, I'm not sure…"

He tilted her chin up to his dark eyes. "You love me. That makes you sure." He bent and brushed his mouth lightly over hers. "And just for the record, there won't be any heated lovemaking before we say our vows. I started off badly with you. This time, we'll do the thing right."

Her heart lifted. He looked as if he really meant it. "You sound so conventional," she laughed.

"All that upbringing raising its ugly head," he chided.

"Rules hold civilizations together," she reminded him. "When religion breaks down, so does society. I can quote you examples, not the least of which is the reign of Amenhotep IV who became Akenaton, giving his people one god in a desperate attempt to bring religion back to them. It didn't work. Egypt fell into moral decay not too long after he died and eventually fell prey to other cultures. So," she added, "did most great civilizations. It isn't *if* they end. It's when."

"You pessimist!" he accused.

"When you see how many civilizations have risen and fallen over the centuries, cynicism is inevitable." She searched his eyes. "But I'm glad that ours is still around. And that you're part of it. And that you want to marry me."

He smiled. "Kiss me. Then feed me some coffee and let's make a few plans."

They did. He had to go back to Houston several days later to fill in while Adams was down with a cold, and Tabby ached at letting him leave. But the wedding was planned for only three days after that. She was to fly out to Houston, so that Helen could be her maid of honor, and they were going to be married in a Presbyterian church that Nick attended infrequently.

"I'll die of loneliness," Tabby moaned when she put him on the plane. It had been a magical time, one of discovery and delight, as they learned about each other all over again. There had been, as he'd promised, no physical interludes. But it had been difficult, because she wanted him as badly as he wanted her. Only by limiting themselves to brief kisses and no time alone had they been able to keep that resolution.

"You'll be on your way to Houston before you know it. But I've got cases to solve, and a pupil to teach. If Kit's going to take over when Helen and I leave, she'll need all the help she can get."

"Is she pretty?" Tabby asked suspiciously, her dark eyes brooding.

"I never noticed," he said honestly. "She's been crazy about Logan Deverell for years. Now she's breaking the ties, and having a bad time of it. Watching Kit gave me some idea of how it must have been for you, breaking your heart over me," he said solemnly. "You won't ever need to do that again."

"Won't I?" she asked quietly. "You aren't marrying me out of pity, are you, Nick?"

He glanced toward the loading ramp. The first-class passengers were almost through boarding. His group was next. "I have to go. No, I don't pity you." He took a deep breath and went for broke, his eyes staring straight into hers. "I love you, damn it," he said through his teeth. "All right? You finally made me say it. Satisfied?"

Her face began to glow. She could have danced on top of the airplane. "Nick," she whispered, and went into his arms. The kiss she gave him almost made his knees buckle.

"Stop that," he choked, pushing her away. He actually flushed and kept his back to the other passengers while he fought for control.

"Well, well." She beamed knowingly.

He glared at her. "Just don't gloat," he muttered. "I hate women who gloat."

"I can't help it. I feel dangerous." She made a growling sound in her throat. "Let's make love on the floor."

He actually moaned. "I'm going back to Houston. I'm leaving right now!" He picked up his bag, carrying it strategically. "I'll expect you day after tomorrow."

"Oh, I'll be there," she said, peeking up at him demurely. "I bought this black lace nightgown. It's see-through…"

He kissed her quickly and ran for it.

''Coward!'' she called after him.

He grinned over his shoulder as he sprinted down the loading ramp. Then he was out of sight and Tabby was hugging his revelation to her like a teddy bear. Her feet barely touched the ground all the way back to the car.

Chapter Eleven

What seemed like a hundred years later—but actually only three days after Nick flew back to Houston—Nick and Tabby became man and wife in a small, intimate ceremony at the local Presbyterian church in Houston.

Tess and Dane, Helen and Harold, and the rest of the staff were there for the occasion. Kit Morris came with Tess. She still looked drawn and pale, but Nick was very pleased with the way she'd taken to detective work. Her boss's loss was the agency's gain, because she had a sweet personality and a way of talking to people that made them anxious to give her any information she asked for. She had a natural compassion, as well, and a steely inner toughness. He felt sorry for Logan Deverell. The man had set loose a treasure.

After the reception, Kit came up to congratulate her mentor. "I hope you're both going to be so happy," she told Tabby, her blue eyes soft and warm. "Nick's a nice man."

"Thank you," Tabby said, smiling. She looked lovely in her oyster-white wedding dress with its Juliet sleeves and V neckline trimmed with lace. She'd worn a long white veil of illusion lace that Nick had lifted with trembling hands just before he kissed her. It was pushed back over the dainty seed-pearled crown of flowers that held it in place.

She looked lovely. Nick had said so twenty times. Now he said it again.

"Let's go," he said softly. "I'm starving to death."

"There's some cake left," she murmured dryly.

His eyes darkened as they searched hers. "It will take something much sweeter than cake to satisfy this particular hunger. Think you can?"

Her lips parted on a breath of pure excitement. "I don't know," she whispered. "But I'm going to love trying."

His face flushed a little. "Let's go, darling. I want you to myself now."

She clasped his big hand in hers and they said their goodbyes. They were flying down to the Cayman Islands for a honeymoon, but tonight they booked a suite in a local luxury hotel. Nick drove them there and swept her up to their rooms without extricating the luggage.

"My things," she protested when he closed the door.

"Later," he breathed as he drew her to him. His eyes burned into her face. "Much, much later. Right now, you won't need clothes, I promise you."

He eased her out of the beautiful wedding gown, whispering how lovely she looked, how much he loved her, needed her. She let him guide her shy hands to his body and teach her new ways to touch him, to make him even hungrier than he already was.

Minutes later, they twisted feverishly against each

other on the coverlet of the bed, both nude, both in anguish from their sobbing need.

She was crying when he moved slowly above her and held her eyes while his hips very tenderly eased down. He possessed her completely in one smooth, delicate motion, and she gasped at the feel of it.

"It isn't...like it was...before," she managed, trembling.

"I love you," he said unsteadily. "Love you to the height of the world, the depth of the oceans. I didn't know how much until these last terrible weeks without you. This," he breathed, moving gently so that she gasped at the power of his need, "is how much I need you—!"

His voice broke. His mouth covered hers and he groaned as her hands slid hungrily down his back to the base of his spine. He moved, and she moved with him, in a rhythm that was terrible in its slow, sweet intensity. She sobbed, clung, as they drifted into realms they'd never touched before. It was so slow that she began to cry out as she tried to get closer to him and knew that she could never get as close as she wanted, needed, to get...!

She cried out, her voice throbbing in time with his as the deep, tearing spasms caught them both. He stilled, but his body didn't, couldn't. He shuddered and his voice broke on her name as he gave in to the red waves that scalded him.

Tabby cried for a long time afterward. She wouldn't let him go, cradling him to her, savoring the heat and dampness and even the weight of his powerful body in the aftermath.

"I thought I might die," she whispered unsteadily, staring over his shoulder at the ceiling.

"Now you know why the French call it the little death," he said quietly. He lifted his head, searching her wide eyes. He kissed her eyelids, rubbing the tip of his tongue against the spiky wetness of her thick dark lashes. "This is profound," he whispered. "I never realized that it could be like this with someone."

She opened her eyes. "You were experienced," she began, surprised.

"I never loved anyone until now," he said simply. "With you, it's…more spiritual than physical. I loved you. You loved me. It was a physical expression of something intangible." He touched her face in wonder. "I remember thinking I was going to die trying to get closer to you. Even…that close…wasn't enough."

"Yes," she said, her face mirroring her own awe. "I know."

He drew in a breath and laughed unsteadily. "And this is only the beginning," he said, shivering.

He was afraid! She read that in his face. She touched him gently. "It's all right," she said softly. "I'll never leave you. I'll love you until I die."

He stiffened and his face went taut. And then she knew.

She reached up and kissed him, kissed his eyelids, his cheeks, his nose, his chin. She kissed his mouth with soft reassurance. "I'm not going to do anything foolhardy and get myself shot, you know," she whispered.

He made a sound that barely registered, and his arms became bruising, painful as he held her with something bordering on desperation. "If I lose you, I'll die," he choked.

"Oh, my darling, you're not going to lose me!" she cried, her body trembling as she realized just how deeply he did care for her. "Never, never...Nick, love me...!"

She kissed him, moving her hips under him, arousing him to a sudden, violent frenzy. He lost control and took her with such raging need that she found her satisfaction almost at once, and then again and again until his powerful body shuddered into completion.

He cursed viciously as he convulsed, his neck corded, his body lifted above hers so that she could watch him. He felt her eyes and then he went actually unconscious for a space of seconds in a blackness of tearing, unbearable pleasure.

She was bending over him, concerned. "Nick?" she whispered worriedly, touching his face with hands that trembled. "Oh, Nick, darling, are you all right?"

His eyes opened. His face was very pale, his body trembling with the strain it had been under. "I tried not to feel like this," he whispered.

"Yes. I know." She bent and smiled as she kissed his eyelids, his mouth. "I love you so much," she choked, her voice full of tears. "I was dying because you didn't want me...!"

He groaned and pulled her down to him, kissing her with feverish emotion. "I love you. I always did. But I was so afraid. You see how it is now, don't you?" he asked bitterly, laughing at his own helplessness. "I let you watch me, because I wanted you to have it all. I'd do anything for you. God, you own me now!"

He seemed shattered by the knowledge that he was helpless when he was with her, as if it made him feel less than a man. She couldn't have that.

She laid her cheek on his chest. "When you're rested," she whispered, "we'll do that again. And this time, you can watch me. Maybe if you see that I'm as totally at your mercy as you just were at mine, you'll realize that what we feel for each other is mutual. There's nothing shameful about it, nothing demeaning.'' She smiled. ''Nick, love is like that. It overpowers, owns. But I can't gloat. I'm only happy that you care so much. I'll never, never make you sorry that you do. I promise.''

He began to breathe normally, his moment of weakness slowly passing. He stroked her long hair softly and his body began to relax. ''Is it like that for you?'' he asked softly. ''Do you come close to unconsciousness when I satisfy you?''

''Of course!'' She lifted her head and looked down at him curiously. ''Didn't you realize?''

''I haven't been able to watch you,'' he said quietly. ''I was too far gone.''

She smiled. ''Next time, then,'' she whispered.

His eyes softened. ''If I can control myself that long,'' he said with black humor.

''We've got all our lives,'' she told him. ''All the rest of our lives to feel and share and love and be together. Risk everything, Nick,'' she whispered. ''That's the only way to really love.''

''Yes,'' he replied, and his eyes kindled. ''I suppose it is.'' He searched her face. His lean hands caught her bare waist and lifted her to lie on him. ''I've been running. If I let myself care, I knew it would be like it just was. I'd be helpless in my need, in my love, and if I lost you…'' He took a deep breath. ''Maybe Lucy's death affected me in ways I didn't realize. But I think I'm getting it all back in perspective. There are no guarantees. Only love. And we have that. My God, we have it!'' he said fervently.

"Forever and ever," she sighed, and bent to kiss him again.

He pulled the coverlet over them partially and closed his eyes. He was committed now. It didn't feel so bad. In fact, he thought, looking down at Tabby's sleeping face, it felt like heaven. He closed his own eyes and let himself drift. Funny, he thought as he drifted off, that captivity and freedom suddenly felt the same. When he woke up, he'd have to puzzle that out. Right now, he was living a dream and he didn't want it to end a minute too soon. His arms contracted gently around his wife, and he smiled in his sleep.

* * * * *

THE CASE OF THE
MISSING SECRETARY

Chapter One

Kit Morris was just barely lucid as she stormed into the Lassiter Detective Agency, her short black hair falling in wet strings around her face, her blue eyes huge and red-rimmed. Her tall, slender figure was clad in a gray suit that had been immaculate just that morning, paired with a soft white blouse and an extravagant silk blue-patterned scarf. Now, the whole outfit was a dripping mess—like Kit's nerves.

It was Tess Lassiter's day substituting for her husband Dane's receptionist, so she was the first person Kit saw when she dragged into the office. Kit and Tess had been best friends for years, long before Tess married Dane Lassiter, who'd been Tess's boss at the time. Kit and Tess had a lot in common. Not that Kit had a single bald chance of ever marrying *her* boss. Her *ex-*boss, that was. At the moment, Kit would much rather stand him up against a mesquite tree and put a fountain pen through his black heart than walk down the aisle with him.

"What happened to you?" Tess exclaimed. "My goodness, Kit, you look terrible!"

"Of course I look terrible! He put me out of the car on Travis Street!"

"That's five blocks from here," Tess mumbled. "He who?"

"Can't you guess?" Kit wailed. "It was *him!* My boss! My ex-boss," she corrected furiously, shaking her head to get the hair out of her eyes. "He...he hijacked me from the public safety department where I was getting my driver's license renewed!" she exclaimed.

"He *hijacked* you?" Tess had to smother a laugh.

"Yes! I didn't want to go with him, but he picked me up and carried me out to the car. And in front of all those people," she groaned. "I didn't even get my license fee paid! I'll have to go back again and stand in line for another hour!"

"Oh, Kit," Tess began sympathetically.

"I resigned two weeks ago, after all! I don't work for him anymore! He can't talk to me like that!"

"Like what?" Tess asked soothingly, trying to calm her best friend.

Kit's eyes blazed like blue flames. "All these years I've slaved for him." She choked. "Taking his dictation, following him around the world, withstanding his disgusting temper...and he has the gall...the *gall* to say that I'm not worth the salary he used to pay me! As if it was a king's ransom or something. Can you imagine?"

"Mr. Deverell said that?"

"Logan Deverell is a tyrant and a beast." Kit fumed. "The lowest of the low. A worm! No." She caught herself. "Pond scum! That's what he is, only much, much lower...."

"Did you do something?" Tess probed gently.

"Not since I told him about his new conquest, right before I quit," she muttered, trying to hide her feeling of heartbreak. Logan Deverell's new woman was why Kit had quit her job in the first place. "He's serious about her, you know."

"But why did he nab you?"

Kit threw up her graceful hands. "Who knows? Anyway, he tried to coax me into coming back and I told him I wouldn't. He practically jumped down my throat with both feet. He's never used language like that to me, and he said that I was worthless as a secretary and he didn't know why he was willing to hire me again."

Tess wanted to get up and put her arms around the taller woman and coax her to cry. But Kit was stubborn, even in grief. She held her chin high, struggling to maintain her dignity. Tess couldn't undermine her strength.

She could only imagine how her friend was hurting. Kit had been in love with Logan Deverell for years. The silly man never noticed her, except as a piece of office furniture.

"Why was he offering you your old job back?" Tess asked.

"I don't know. We started arguing before he got around to telling me. He was raging like a madman. I didn't even think, I just got out of the car and left."

"He put you out in the rain?" Tess groaned. "How could he!"

"He didn't put me out as much as I jumped out," Kit confessed. "The stupid blind man! I love him so!" Kit choked. Her heart felt as if it were something brittle that had just been smacked with a bat. She was coming unglued. "If only I were blond and stacked!"

"Who is this woman he's seeing?" Tess asked.

"Betsy Corley," she said huskily.

"I don't know her."

"I do. At least, I know *of* her. At one time I was good friends with the man in my apartment building that she took for everything he had." Kit took a steadying breath. "Logan is determined to marry her," she said and laughed hoarsely.

"Oh, Kit," Tess groaned sympathetically.

"At least I have a job, thanks to you and Dane," she said miserably. "I've burned all my bridges...."

"Well, in that case, it's a good thing we're making a detective out of you," Dane Lassiter murmured dryly. He joined the two women, slipping an arm around his wife. He smiled at her before his dark eyes went back to Kit. "We're glad to have you now that Helen's gone to South America where Harold's next job is. He's in the construction business with his father, you remember. And Helen's brother, Nick, is moving back to Washington so that his new wife can keep her tenure at Thorn College. He's starting up his own agency. I'll be two operatives short. That means I've still got to hire another agent. I'm glad you haven't been tempted to go back to your old boss."

"I'd be more tempted to step into a lion's mouth than I would to work for Logan Deverell again," Kit murmured dryly, hiding her pain. "I hope you know how much I appreciate your giving me a chance here." She pushed back her hair again and brushed at the moisture on her suit. It wasn't as wet as she'd first thought, and seemed to be drying slowly.

"We both do," Dane told her, smiling. "But you've

been quite a surprise, you know. If there are such things as natural born detectives, then I think you're one of them. You've taken to the job like a duck takes to swimming.''

She brightened. ''You really think so?''

''I do.''

Kit managed a smile. ''Actually I always used to think I'd make a good detective, because I love poking my nose into things that don't concern me.'' She sighed. ''You really did save my life by hiring me,'' she persisted. ''I didn't have my rent payment. After I stormed out of the office the day I quit, I can't expect Mr. Deverell to send my severance pay after me. I didn't even work a week's notice.''

''I hardly think Logan Deverell will do you out of your severance pay, regardless,'' Dane murmured dryly. ''He's not a vindictive man.''

''If you'd seen him ten minutes ago...'' Kit muttered.

Dane cocked an eyebrow as he peered past her. ''On second thought,'' he mused, ''perhaps he is—''

Before he got the words out, the door flew open and a tall, big dark man in a gray raincoat stormed in.

''I've searched the whole damned city for you,'' he grumbled, his deep voice like muted thunder in the office as he glared at Kit. ''You little fool, you could have been killed, jumping out of a car in the middle of traffic like that! Where in hell have you been?''

''Don't you shout at me!'' Kit raged back. ''You told me to get my nose out of your business, and I did,'' she said with painful satisfaction at the grimace on his broad face. ''You can find someone else to yell at in your office. Dane says I'm a very good detective!''

Logan Deverell lifted a bushy eyebrow and glanced at Dane. "Did you say that?"

"I'm afraid so," Dane replied. "Under the circumstances, it might be to your advantage not to argue with Kit anymore."

Logan glanced at Kit's face and his lips thinned. He was inclined to agree. She looked shaken. That, and totally out of control emotionally. In all the years she'd worked for him, this was the first time he'd seen her in such a state. She was usually calm and efficient. Except for the day she'd quit, of course, when she'd set new records for abusive verbosity. When he'd followed her into her office, where she was cleaning out her desk, she'd actually thrown a book at him and accused him of mixing her up emotionally with her computer.

It had been the cutting remarks about Betsy being mercenary that had cost Logan his temper today. He still regretted some of the things he'd said. Good secretaries weren't a dime a dozen. He hadn't been able to replace Kit. He missed her madly, though it would be unwise to tell her that, of course. He'd hoped to talk her into coming back, and then she'd mentioned some gossip about Betsy. No way was he going to let *any* woman tell him what to do in his personal life!

"I won't take back what I said," Logan told her. "You had no business meddling in my private life. But I'll apologize for letting you walk back in the rain."

"There's no need to apologize," Kit returned. "It was my fault for ever getting into a car with you in the first place!"

He looked surprised. "I was only going to ask you to come back to work."

"I don't want to come back to work for you, Mr.

Deverell,'' she said icily. ''Here, at least, I'm not part of the office furniture. I'm a real live, breathing person with talent and ability, and if I died, Dane and Tess would miss me.''

''We've worked together for three years,'' he reminded her.

''Three years too long,'' she said, regaining her lost dignity slowly. ''I'm sure you'll have no trouble replacing me.''

''None of the temporaries can spell,'' he said angrily. ''They can't file, or project a pleasant personality over the phone. Only one of them has any sense at all, and my mother hired her before I knew it. My brother hates the latest addition to the office. She actually told him to get his own coffee!''

''Your brother should have been getting his own coffee for years,'' she reminded him.

''And my mother's lost again,'' he added irritably, glancing at Dane. ''You'll have to track her down. She told my brother something about a trip to Venice.''

''No problem,'' Dane said. ''Just give me her last known location.'' He studied Kit. ''I might let Kit have this assignment. She knows Tansy.''

''My mother missed you, too,'' Logan told Kit with an angry frown. ''That's probably why she vanished.''

''Go ahead, blame it on me,'' Kit invited with a sweep of her hand. ''I cause your car not to start on cold mornings, I make your coffeepot stop working, I put dust on the windows and make the chairs in the office creak. I probably cause pond scum, too!''

''Will you stop it,'' Logan muttered. He jammed his big hands into his pockets. Looking at her disturbed him. That was new, and it made him irritable. ''Never mind, if you don't want to come back. I can manage without you. Eventually the temporary agency will find me one secretary who can spell, type and answer the telephone.''

''Surely they already have?'' she asked sarcastically.

''Of course. I just said so, didn't I? The agency found me two more to go with the one that my mother hired. At least she can type. Of the two new ones, only one can spell. The tallest of the three can answer the telephone but it takes her until the fifth ring to find it.''

Kit's eyebrows went up. ''Why?''

''The desk is buried in unanswered letters and misplaced files,'' he said simply. ''Don't let that concern you, Miss Morris. I did actually manage before you were first hired. And you might recall,'' he added icily, ''that it was not I who hired you to begin with.''

''How very true,'' she agreed. ''It was your mother, who has excellent taste in employees!''

''We can agree to disagree on that point,'' he said stiffly.

''Should you be getting back to the office, before any more files become…misplaced?'' she hinted.

His broad face hardened even more. ''Cute,'' he said. ''Very cute. Go ahead and be a detective. That should be right up your alley, the way you mind everyone's business but your own!''

''Somebody needs to mind yours!'' she raged. ''That dizzy blonde is just out for what she can get from you—''

''She gets plenty,'' he interrupted hotly. ''*In* bed and out,'' he added deliberately, his eyes piercing as if he knew how she felt and wanted to sink the knife in as far as possible.

He succeeded. It went straight to the heart. But Kit had years of practice at hiding her deeper feelings from him. She just stared at him without reacting at all, except for the sudden whiteness of her face.

The stare got to him. He felt like a fool. It wasn't a feeling he particularly enjoyed, especially with Dane and Tess standing there trying not to laugh.

"I'll get back to my office, then," he said. "Let me have the bill when you find my mother, Dane," he added as he turned. He didn't look at Kit, either.

Kit stuck her full lower lip out as she glared after his broad back. He was as big as a house, she thought irritably. All muscle and temper. If only he'd trip on his way through the door!

"If looks could kill," Tess murmured dryly.

"You couldn't kill him with a look," Kit said wearily. "It would take a bomb. And even that wouldn't hurt him if it *hit him in the head!*" she shouted after him.

He didn't react at all, which only made her madder. The door closed behind him with a thump.

"In all the years you and Tess have been friends, I've never seen you lose your temper until Logan fired you," Dane remarked. "I thought you worshiped your boss."

"His feet melted," she grumbled. "What do you want me to do this afternoon, boss?" she asked brightly, changing the subject.

"You heard what I told Logan. Find Tansy."

She groaned. "But Mrs. Deverell disappears without a trace at least two times a month," she protested. "She always turns up."

"Usually in the hospital or in jail," he reminded her, chuckling. "Logan's mother is a dyed-in-the-wool troublemaker with a fatal philosophy of life."

"Yes. 'If it feels good, do it,'" Tess quoted. "The agency stays solvent because of Tansy's wanderlust."

"Last time she was missing, she started a riot in Newport News, Virginia, claiming to have been kidnapped by a flying saucer," Dane recalled. "We bailed her out of a sanitarium." He laughed. "Tansy just likes to start trouble. She's no lunatic."

"Most seventy-year-old women have the good sense to stay home. Tansy is a renegade. And she may not be a lunatic, but she does act like one," Tess said. "Didn't she go sailboarding in Miami year before last and pick up some middle-eastern potentate who wanted her to join his harem?"

"Yes. And we had to practically kidnap her to get her away from him, to Tansy's dismay. But as they sometimes say, all the wrong people are locked up. Tansy is a breath of fresh air. A totally uninhibited free soul."

"Her son isn't," Kit said.

"Logan's straitlaced. But Christopher Deverell isn't," Dane said. "Chris is as nutty as his mother, and both of them love to get Logan behind the eight ball."

"In other words," Tess said, reading her husband's mind, "this could be a deliberate disappearance. If Tansy knew he'd fired you, this might be her way of getting even. She did like you."

"Always," Kit agreed, smiling as she recalled how well they got along. She suspected Tansy knew how she felt about Logan, too. But remembering it wasn't going to help things, it only made her sad for what her life was like without her temperamental boss.

She missed the silliest things. She missed the way he spilled coffee on his important papers and raised the roof, yelling for her as if she was salvation itself when she came running with a roll of paper towels. She missed evenings when she accompanied him to dinners. It was usually to take notes, and strictly business, but it felt good to wear her prettiest clothes and be in the company of a man who had a mind like a steel-trap and still looked devastating in a dinner jacket.

"Kit?"

Tess's query brought her mind back to the present. "Sorry. I was thinking about where to start looking for Tansy."

"Call Chris first," Dane suggested. "Meanwhile, I'm taking Mrs. Lassiter to lunch."

"Actually we're taking lunch to the baby." Tess chuckled. "I'm still breast-feeding. Don't mind if we're a little late. I hate having to leave him at all during the day, even if he is five months old."

"I think I'd feel the same way," Kit said.

They left and she watched them, faintly envious of the way they seemed to belong together. She'd wanted that with Logan Deverell, but he wanted his scheming lady friend. He was going to get taken to the cleaners, did he but know it, and Kit wasn't going to be around to mop him up anymore. If he spilled coffee, or even tears, somebody else would have that chore. She wasn't sorry, she told herself, she wasn't sorry at all.

She went to work at once. Her first call was, as Dane had suggested, to Christopher Deverell.

"Mother's gone again," he said pleasantly. He was only twenty-seven, just two years older than Kit—but eight years younger than Logan. He and Kit and Tansy were like a different generation. Nobody ever told Logan that, of course.

"Yes, I know, that's why I'm calling you," Kit said with a smile in her tone. "I have to find her."

"Logan's office is a mess," he said. "Logan screamed bloody murder for two solid days and refused to hire anybody else."

"I know," she said. "I was due for a change. I was stagnating in that office with the same routine day in and day out—"

"Bull," Chris said. "You were eaten up with jealousy over the delectable Miss Corley. Everybody knows how you feel about Logan, Kit. Everybody except Logan."

She didn't bother to deny it. Chris knew her too well. "He's going to marry her."

"So he says. He'll find her out in time, though. Logan's no fool. Well, most of the time he's no fool."

"She's very pretty."

"So are you."

"I'm just a walking piece of office furniture that he programmed to do his filing and typing," Kit said solemnly. "He doesn't miss me. He's already found a replacement. Three of them, in fact."

"Mother found him the best one. She's a cousin of ours who used to live in San Antonio, and she can type. The other two...well," he said noncommittally. "Let's just say that they aren't quite what he had in mind. Melody, that's our cousin, is the best of them all, but she can't spell and she's very nervous trying to answer the telephone."

"I would be, too, with a glowering boss peering down his nose at me," Kit muttered. "Don't you have other relatives in San Antonio?" she asked, remembering some veiled references to people Logan didn't ever go and visit there.

"Just Emmett. Don't *ever* mention Emmett to Logan,'' he added. ''He has nightmares about his last visit there.''

''I won't see Logan to mention anybody to him, thank God,'' she said curtly.

''You hope. Logan isn't coping well without you,'' he said gently. ''He won't admit it, but life without you is like going around in a blindfold.''

''I hope he trips over a potted plant and goes out the window.''

''Naughty, naughty,'' he chided. ''Don't you feel guilty, leaving him at the mercy of an office you're not in?''

''No. It's time he knew what the real world is like,'' Kit said.

''From the tidbits I get from Melody, he may try to toss the new receptionist out a window one day soon.''

''Then I hope you know a good lawyer to defend him. I'll be a character witness for the woman. Just call me.''

''Shame on you!'' He laughed.

''I hate your brother. I gave him three of the best years of my life and he never even noticed I was around until I told him his new girlfriend was a miner who'd be digging for gold in his hip pocket.''

''You should have told Tansy instead. She'd have handled that.''

''No, she wouldn't,'' Kit argued. ''Tansy doesn't believe in interfering. She thinks people should make their own mistakes. She's right, too,'' she muttered. ''When he loses his home, his car and his business to his heartthrob, I'm going to phone him twice a day just to say I told you so!''

''Before or after you offer to take dictation for free to help him get back on his feet?''

She sighed. Chris knew her too well. "Where do you think Tansy's gone?"

"To Venice," he said. "She was seen boarding a plane bound for there in Miami."

"Okay. Which airline?"

He told her, along with the flight number and time of departure. She thanked him, cutting off the conversation before he could say anything else. She turned her attention to the task at hand. She had no time to wallow in self-pity.

Minutes later, she knew that Tansy Deverell had bought a ticket to Venice. But the woman who boarded the plane wasn't Tansy. Whoever Logan's cunning mother had gotten to take her place had forgotten to limp as she walked down the concourse. Tansy limped just temporarily because of an accident while she was hang gliding.

Kit laughed. She had to be a natural, just as Dane had said. She was getting the hang of this in a big way. She went back to talk to the skip tracers. They were masters at the game of invention to get information, and most of them could find a needle in a haystack within five minutes.

Unfortunately Tansy was harder to find than a needle. They drew a blank.

"I'm sorry," Doris said, shaking her head. "But she's harder to find than a white bear in a snowstorm. If she paid someone to take her place on that flight, she did it with cash. You'll have to find a flight attendant to ask for a description, and even then, it won't be easy. Those flights to Venice are usually full. Individual faces are hard to remember."

Kit could have ground her teeth. "What do I do?" she moaned. "Dane will fire me!"

"Oh, not yet," Doris said, smiling. "He never fires anyone before Friday."

"Thanks a lot."

"I did get you the name of a cabdriver at the airport who remembers an elderly lady with a limp." Doris chuckled, handing her a slip of paper.

"You angel!"

"No kissing," Doris said, warding her off. "You'll give Adams ideas," she added with a covert glance at the burly Adams, who was playing with a penknife two desks in front of her.

"There's not a thing wrong with Adams," Kit said, smiling. "He's a doll."

Adams overheard her and perked up. He got up, straightening his tie, and smiled in Kit's direction.

"He has homing instincts. You'll be sorry," Doris said under her breath.

"How about lunch, Kit?" Adams drawled with a hopeful smile.

"I'd love it, Adams," she replied, "but I have to go track down a cabdriver. Rain check?"

He brightened. He blushed. No woman in the office had *ever* offered him a rain check. He lost ten years and his morose expression. Doris studied him with renewed interest.

"Rain check," he agreed.

Doris toyed with her pen. "I'm not doing anything for lunch," she said to herself.

Adams thought he might have a heart attack. *Two* women found him interesting in less than two minutes. Maybe his luck was finally changing. Kit was pretty, and petite Doris was adorable, even with salt-and-pepper hair and glasses. "How about a chicken burger, Doris?" he asked quickly. "I'll buy!"

Doris beamed at him. "I'd love that!"

Kit eased out the door with relief and delight. Doris and Adams were both middle-aged loners with no family to speak of. Why hadn't anyone ever thought of tossing them together?

That made her think of salads, and she remembered that she hadn't had any lunch. Thanks to Logan Deverell, she'd probably starve. If she didn't die of pneumonia from standing around in wet clothes. First, she was going home to change and eat a sandwich. Then she'd find that cabbie.

Chapter Two

Kit found the cabdriver without great difficulty. Yes, he did remember an elderly woman with a limp. He'd taken her to the bus station.

With fervent thanks, Kit rushed over to the bus station. One of the ticket agents remembered a silver-haired woman with a limp. She'd taken a bus to San Antonio.

Kit groaned. She shouldn't have taken time to change clothes and eat lunch. By the time she could get to San Antonio, Tansy would be long gone.

She went back to the office, downcast and gloomy, to tell Dane what she'd found out.

"Chris mentioned a relative in San Antonio named Emmett, but I don't know if he's got the same last name as Logan and Chris."

But Dane only grinned. "No problem," he said. "I've got a contact in San Antonio who owes me a favor. This will be a great time to collect."

"Will I need to go out there?" she asked hesitantly.

"Of course not. Logan only wants to know where

she is. We won't be obliged to follow her. Not yet, anyway," he added with a knowing smile.

Kit was given a new assignment, one which wasn't quite as interesting as trying to find an elderly needle in a haystack. A man wanted his wife followed to see if she was two-timing him. This was relatively easy for Kit to do, especially since the woman seemed bent on a shopping spree.

Staying a little behind the woman, Kit was just congratulating herself on her stealth when Logan Deverell loomed up in her path and brought her to a standstill.

"Where is the Dawson file?" he demanded. "Some private detective you are, you can't even put things in their proper place!"

Kit could have hit him. The woman she'd been shadowing couldn't possibly have missed hearing her loud ex-boss denouncing her. Sure enough, the woman gave her a startled glance and dived toward the nearest cab.

"There, look what you've done," Kit cried, exasperated. "I'm on a case! I was shadowing a client, for heaven's sake...!"

"I want the Dawson file," he said. "None of those would-be secretaries have any idea how to find it. You've got to come back with me. I'm going to lose my most influential client if you don't."

"I should *care?*" she burst out.

He glowered down at her. His dark eyes narrowed with irritation. "You're costing me time," he muttered, slamming back the immaculate white cuff of his shirt so that he could see the gold watch imbedded in the thick, curling black hair on his muscular wrist.

"I was on a case," she pointed out. "*You* hijacked me. Speaking of hijacking—"

He was pulling her along as she spoke. "Can't you

be quiet for two minutes running?'' he asked conversationally. ''All you need to do is find a file. What's so difficult about that?''

While she was trying to formulate it in words of one syllable that he might be able to understand, he helped her into his gray Lincoln.

I'm crazy, that's what I am, Kit thought as he got in under the wheel. *He's blown an assignment for me, fired me, humiliated me and here I am letting him lead me to his office to work for him on my own time!* Well, actually, she admitted it was on Dane's time.

''Have you found my mother yet?'' he asked as he pulled away from the curb.

''We're working on it,'' she said.

He cocked a busy eyebrow. ''I thought you were in charge of the case?''

''I am. But I lost her at the bus station.''

He chuckled. ''My mother wouldn't be caught dead on a bus.''

''She would and did, to escape surveillance. Doesn't she have a relative named Emmett in San Antonio?'' she persisted, remembering only then that Chris had warned her never to mention him.

''Oh, yes,'' he said with a vicious glare. ''Emmett lives in San Antonio, as near as not. But I guarantee she wouldn't go there. Nobody in the family will go near the place. You'd have to be out of your everloving mind to want to go and see Emmett, even if you were hiding out from the police!''

The man must be a holy terror, she thought. He was Logan's cousin, of course. Probably it ran in the family.

''Where does he live?'' she asked, and whipped out a pad and pen.

''I told you, she wouldn't go there!''

"Humor me."

He shrugged. "His name is E. G. Deverell." He gave her the address. She jotted it down and stuck the pad back into her purse. Now she had something concrete to go on. She felt like a real detective.

"You can't really like following people around for a living," he said. He glanced at her and back at the road. "I've bought a new computer for the office. It's got a sixty megabyte hard drive and all sorts of software, including a user-friendly word processing program. I bought a laser printer, too," he added. "And the system does forms."

She'd been begging for that sort of system for over a year. He'd argued that it wasn't necessary and he had better ways to spend his money.

"How nice," she said. "For your *new* secretary. Secretaries, that is," she added with a spiteful smile. "Three, isn't it?"

He made a rough sound under his breath. "I don't see what your problem is!" he raged. "I've lost my temper with you before. You never walked out on me!"

"You never allowed one of your women to treat me like an indentured servant before," she countered.

He shifted uncomfortably. "She asked for a cup of coffee."

"Excuse me," she said. "She *demanded* a cup of coffee, and then threw it at me because it was too strong. When I suggested that she might like to go to the restaurant on the first floor and get a cup there, she flew into a rage and called me several names that I won't repeat. Then, the minute she saw you coming, she dissolved into helpless tears."

"She said you threw the coffee at her," he returned,

narrowing one eye. "And you aren't the most even-tempered of women."

"Oh, but I am, as long as I'm not within half a mile of you," she replied venomously.

He had to stifle a smile at the way she was looking at him. How he'd missed these bouts with Kit. The three women he'd had to hire to replace her were frightened of him. Poor Melody was hopelessly intimidated by spelling, and her distant cousin Logan. She could type very quickly, though, and she was efficient.

Harriet, the tallest of the three, could file and do payroll accounts, but she hated everyone in the office and smoked like a chimney.

Then there was Margo, who spelled like a dictionary and wanted nothing more than to seduce him.

Logan, though, had eyes for no one except Betsy, who made his blood run hot and wild through his veins. He didn't want to get married, but it was the only way he was ever going to possess the delectable Betsy. So he'd given in, against his better judgment, and nothing had gone right in his life since he'd proposed. He was no nearer to coaxing Betsy into his bed and he'd lost Kit. Amazing, he thought, how empty the world was without Kit in it. He had no one to talk to anymore. Betsy hardly listened to him, and certainly paid more attention to where they went and who they saw than what they did.

"Betsy was no threat to your job," he told her. "I don't combine my personal relationships with my business ones. I thought you knew that."

She knew that he was going to marry Betsy, and she couldn't bear it. Not only was she losing the only man she'd ever loved, but she was losing him to a woman who'd cut his heart out and roast it over a pile of blazing hundred-dollar bills. Betsy would take him for every cent he had. She glanced over at him curiously. How, she wondered, could a man with a brain such as his be so terminally stupid when it came to women?

"You aren't going to be happy working in a detective agency," he persisted.

"But I am," she corrected. She smiled smugly. "I'm treated like a person there. When I do something right, I get praised for it. When I do something wrong," she added with a meaningful look, "nobody rages at me in disgusting language and threatens to feed me my handbag."

"How boring."

She smothered a laugh and looked away.

"You miss me, damn you," he murmured, smiling at her averted face. "Our daily battles kept you going when nothing else did. You loved trying to get one up on me. Remember the day the Brazilian businessmen came to the office and you spent thirty minutes trying to speak Spanish to them?"

"*You* told me they spoke it."

"*You* should have known that the national language of Brazil is Portuguese. Anyway, you got even."

"Indeed I did," she recalled with a grin. "I borrowed one of the girls from the secretarial pool who spoke no English and sent her in to take dictation from you while I took a two-hour lunch break."

"I almost broke your neck," he said shortly. "She sat there and nodded and smiled at me for thirty minutes before I realized that she didn't understand a word I said."

"The girls in the next office did." She chuckled. "They said you were very eloquent. In fact, one of them wanted to have you arrested."

"The good old days," he said wistfully. He glared at her. "Now I have two helpers who get down on their knees and thank God when I leave the office, and a third who spends her life trying to bend me back over my own desk."

"Oh, my," she said.

"You might pretend to be sympathetic. It's uncomfortable to work in that kind of environment."

"Now you know how women feel," she replied.

He glared at her. "I don't recall ever chasing you around the office or trying to bend you over a desk!"

More's the pity, she wanted to say. But she only replied, "No, sir, you never did."

"Do you know, I've actually thought about reporting her for harassment?"

"If she makes you that uncomfortable, why not just fire her?"

"Because she can spell, Morris." He exploded. "She can spell! That's something neither of the others can do!"

"You could ask the agency to send you someone with good spelling skills."

"I did," he replied tersely. "They sent me Margo of the peekaboo bosom."

She put her face in her hands, but she couldn't stem the laughter.

"Come back," he invited roughly. "I'll give you a raise. You can have a new desk. I'll fix the damned window that sticks."

"I'm very tempted," she said, and meant it. But she'd never be able to stomach Betsy at close range. "But I like my new job too much to quit now."

"I hope Dane isn't assigning you anything dangerous."

"Now, see here," she began defensively.

"Here we are!" He stopped the car, helped her out and escorted her into the building and up the elevator to his office.

"Now," he said, opening the door for her. "Find that file!"

She blinked twice before she walked into the luxurious carpeted office. The spot where Betsy had thrown coffee at her three weeks before was still there. No one had come to clean it up. The coffeemaker was standing empty and very dirty. Three desks were piled high with file folders and stacks of correspondence. Diskettes for the computer were lying around, out of their jackets. One of the women had gray hair and was very tall. She was smoking and her ashes were everywhere. Another was talking on the telephone, apparently to someone male. She smiled at Logan and deliberately leaned forward to show her cleavage.

"Hello, Margo," Kit said sweetly.

"Hi! How did you know my name?" the girl replied, and suddenly went back to the voice on the other end of the line.

"Cute," Logan muttered.

Kit walked toward the third desk, the only neat one, where a third woman, plain and harassed-looking, was flipping through files.

"Not yet, I'm afraid," she told Logan in an apprehensive tone. She looked about twenty, a country-looking girl with a patent vulnerability in her face, and Kit felt a surge of sympathy for her.

"Here, let me help," Kit said kindly. Laying aside her purse, she bent over the stack and in seconds, extricated the one Logan had demanded. "Here."

He took it and glared at the young woman.

"How could I know that it would be filed under Portfolios?" she asked plaintively. "I'm new…!"

"I'm Kit Morris." Kit introduced herself.

"I'm Melody Cartman," came the reply. She glanced toward Logan, who was making a telephone call. "You used to work here, didn't you? No wonder you left! See Harriet over there? She'd stopped smoking for ten years when she came to work here. Now she's gone back. She's smoking three packs a day, and she's got a bottle of Scotch in her desk!"

"I can understand why," Kit mused. Logan, buried in his file, hadn't noticed them discussing him.

"Margo isn't afraid of him. She likes men. Especially rich ones. He has a girlfriend and she's terrible. She expects us to stop everything and wait on her. Not to his face, of course," she muttered. "She's sweetness and light the minute he walks in the door."

"Now you know why I don't work here anymore."

"He's my third cousin," Melody groaned, glancing at him. "He's just like one other terrible member of the family. If I'd had any idea he was like this, I'd never have let Tansy talk me into this job. But the company I worked for went bust and I just couldn't bear to go back to San Antonio." She hesitated. "I'm stuck here!"

"Listen," Kit said, raising her voice, "we're short one detective at the agency where I work…"

"Shut up, Morris," Logan said menacingly as he slammed the telephone receiver back onto the cradle. "You aren't stealing any of my people."

He moved away and Melody groaned. "See? We're slaves. He owns us! I'll never see my apartment again…!"

"There, there, it will be all right. I'll take a few

minutes and explain my filing system to you. Then you won't have this problem again.''

Melody dabbed at her brown eyes and pushed back her thick, blond-streaked light brown hair. It was very long, and she had a sweetly rounded face and freckles. Kit liked her at once. ''I think Harriet carries one of those electrical weapons in her purse,'' Melody told Kit. ''Wouldn't you like to borrow it? You could do him in before you leave. I swear to God, none of us would ever tell on you!''

Kit chuckled. ''I believe you, but he's really not worth the sacrifice. Let's get to work.''

It only took thirty minutes to teach Melody the basics of the filing system, and then Kit gave Melody her telephone number for future emergencies.

''He doesn't like you to know it,'' Kit added, ''but there's a smokeless ashtray in the closet. Two of them, in fact. He used to smoke cigars.''

''He doesn't smoke cigars any more.''

''I know.''

''He smokes cigarettes now. Thin brown ones.''

''Marijuana?'' Kit exclaimed.

Melody laughed. ''Oh, no. Those little cigars, what do they call them? Cigarillos, I think!''

''Not in here, I hope?''

''Yes. Between him and Harriet, I'm a stretcher case with my sinuses.''

''Use those ashtrays.''

Melody brightened. ''If I suggest it, maybe he'll fire me!''

''You needn't look so optimistic. Now that you know my filing system, you're worth your weight in rubies.''

"Drat!"

"If you can become an ace speller, he'll get rid of Margo," she whispered.

Melody's eyes twinkled. "I'll hire a tutor!"

"Good luck!"

Kit walked into Logan's office as she had for the past three years, without knocking. But she realized at once that she'd made a mistake.

Somehow, Betsy must have gotten into the office while she was occupied with Melody. Betsy was there now, blond and fragile, in Logan's arms.

The sight of them that way made something delicate inside Kit go brittle and shatter. Logan's dark head bent over that bright one, his enormous body sheltering hers, his arms compelling her against the powerful length of him, his mouth devouring and insistent on the woman's lips.

He lifted his head abruptly and looked at Kit with the desire and physical enslavement still glittering in his dark eyes.

"Well?" he asked huskily.

Kit didn't say a word. She turned and closed the door behind her, trying not to remember the snide look on Betsy's exultant face as she went. That had been a setup. Betsy knew how she felt about Logan. Everyone knew, except Logan himself.

She gathered her purse and said a quick goodbye to Melody, pausing only to wave at Margo and Harriet before she walked to the elevator.

The stupid conveyance *would* be on the bottom floor, she muttered to herself. She jabbed viciously at the Down button and was almost resigned to going down the staircase when Logan and Betsy came along to stand beside her.

"We'll drop you off," Logan said carelessly. "We have a luncheon appointment."

Kit looked from Betsy, immaculate in a gray silk suit and an ermine coat, to Logan in his blue pin-striped suit and handmade silk tie. Yes, they complimented each other. She'd been living in a fool's paradise to imagine a man such as Logan would ever give her a second look. She was a teacher's daughter with no special beauty or talents. He was related to royalty somewhere in his ancestry and had gobs of money. She held Betsy in contempt for coveting his status and wealth, but he'd probably think that Kit was eager for it as well if she'd ever tempted him deliberately as Margo and Betsy had.

Just as well, she thought, that she'd been allowed to get out when she did. Soon, she'd never have to see Logan again. Betsy would make sure of that.

"I do hope you haven't been trying to tell Logan any of that silly gossip about me," Betsy drawled with a cool smile. "I don't chase men for money. I don't have to. I have money of my own."

Certainly she did. Bill Kingsley's money. Kit's blood ran hot every time she thought about the poor, kind old man. He must have been easy pickings indeed for this blond toad. And here was Logan, waiting in line to be next.

"Some women do chase men for money, though," Kit said quietly. She studied the other woman with cold curiosity. "One of my neighbors was chased after he won a lottery. His name was Bill Kingsley."

Betsy's face whitened. She averted it. "I'm afraid I don't know anyone by that name."

"Well, you wouldn't," Kit said easily. "He used to

live in my apartment building, about the time he won the small lottery.''

"You said he did live in your building? I suppose he left when he won the money?" Betsy asked with assumed politeness, but an underlying nervousness that was visible.

"He left, all right. The lottery wasn't too much, but it was more than he'd ever had. When he found out, he celebrated by buying drinks for everyone at the bar around the corner. That was where he met a young woman who started being nice to him and let him take her around. She was young and pretty and he was a lonely old man with no family. He fell in love with her. She repaid him for his kindness by taking him for every penny he had. She even managed to cost him his savings. After she left, he couldn't believe he'd been such a fool. He simply couldn't live with it. He committed suicide." Kit shook her head, her eyes never leaving Betsy's paper-white face. "If I were that woman, I'd choke on my own greed. And I'd deserve to."

"None of that has anything to do with Betsy!" Logan said angrily.

"No, of course not," Kit replied, smiling at him. "Did I say that it had?"

"It's all right, Logan," Betsy said, having regained her composure if not her color. "You and I have so much, and poor Kit has nothing. Not even a man's love."

Touché, Kit thought. Betsy gave her a smile that would have curled leather.

"Where can we drop you, dear?" Betsy purred.

"I wouldn't want to take you out of your way. I'll just pop onto a bus downstairs. Do have a lovely lunch. Ta, ta." Kit smiled and waltzed to the staircase.

"Morris, come back here…!"

She ignored the demand and kept going. She was shaking inside with rage at Betsy's blatant playacting. The woman was as guilty as sin and felt no remorse at all. She was going to cut Logan up just the way she'd cut up Kingsley. And how was Kit going to stop her? In Logan's eyes, Betsy could do no wrong. But there had to be a way to stop Betsy and save him in time!

She worried the question all the way back to the office, where she had to explain to Dane what had happened.

"I'm sorry," Dane apologized when he could finally stop laughing. "But that's such a dandy little tale…"

"It's the truth!" Kit threw up her hands. "He's my nemesis, I tell you! And one of his very own employees—his third cousin, in fact!—offered me an electrical device and said she'd swear I was innocent if I'd just bump him off for them!"

"Kit, are you sure you've done the right thing to leave an office like that?" he asked her. "Logan is never going to be the same again."

"Good. I hope Margo gets him pregnant."

"Stop that!" He leaned forward and picked up a notepad, whipping off a sheet. "Well I can solve your problems for a day or so. Take this."

"What is it?" she murmured, reading a street address.

"Emmett's address. Get on the next flight to San Antonio and follow these directions. They should lead you right to Tansy Deverell."

"Hallelujah! I'll kidnap her and send Logan a ransom note.…"

"Not while you're on my payroll, please."

"It was just a thought." She folded the note. "I'm sorry about losing the lady I was trailing for you."

"That was hardly your fault. It's okay."

She shrugged, fingering the note. "I seem to get in deeper all the time. I had a neighbor who Betsy Corley took for everything he had." She looked up. "She'll do that to Logan, you know. He's so besotted he won't believe a bad thing about her. She'll lead him right to the slaughter and make him think he's heaven-bound. Just like she did poor old Bill."

"You don't give Logan credit for having much sense, do you?" he asked gently.

She shrugged. "How can I? After all, he sacrificed three years of loyal, slavish devotion and adoration over a cup of spilled coffee, didn't he?"

"He was an idiot there," Dane had to agree. "I'm sorry you've had such a rough deal. Maybe this job will open new doors for you."

She smiled. "Maybe it will. Do you know any more about this address besides its location?"

"Just that Tansy's nephew is something of a hell-raiser. He and Tansy should get along just fine."

"Another Chris," she said, shaking her head.

"Well…not exactly," he replied slowly. "Never mind, just go out there and find out. And, if you get in trouble or have any problems, any at all, just phone here and I'll demand that you come right home to work on another case. Okay?"

That sounded very much as if he were keeping something from her. She wondered what. Her eyebrows lifted. "Now I'm intrigued."

"You will be. That's a promise." He chuckled. "From what we ferreted out, intrigued is an understatement for what most people think when they meet Emmett.''

She put a hand on her hip. "Emmett?"

"Well, most people don't call him that if they want to stay out of emergency rooms. Better make it Mr. Deverell until you know him."

"Should I invest in one of those electrical devices…?"

"Doris will have your ticket."

"Yes, sir." She saluted and walked out. Sure enough, Doris was waving it at her when she approached. Adams was nearby, grinning.

"Don't get involved with the natives," Doris told her. "Those San Antonio men are tornadoes when you get them wound up."

"I'll try to remember that. See you when I can. Goodbye, Adams," she added, waving at him and smiling.

Adams seemed to gain height and masculine beauty as he grinned back.

"Hands off," Doris whispered. "He's all mine."

She said it just loud enough that Adams could hear it, which made his smile even broader. "Good luck," she whispered back to Doris. And with a wave of her hand, she went to get the necessary things out of her desk before she left for her trip.

San Antonio was big. It boasted a million in population and some of the most interesting things to see and do in the country, including the Alamo and the Paseo Del Rio.

Before she went searching for the address and directions in her purse, she checked into the nearest hotel and took time to get a bite of lunch and rest.

Then she got into her rental car and set out for the address Dane had given her.

It was on the southeastern side of town, and not in a subdivision. In fact, the address was something of a ranch, complete with oil wells pumping in the pastures and white fences all around. Red-coated cattle grazed in thickets of mesquite, past flatland that had patches of prickly pear cactus to hallmark it.

She looked at the address a second time to be sure, but there it was. No one had ever said that the Deverells had a cattle-raising relative out here in Texas.

As she drove across the cattle grate and down the long, winding dirt driveway to the elegant two-story Victorian house in the distance, she was suddenly assailed by three war-painted buckskin-clad midgets with bows and arrows and chicken-feather warbonnets.

"Hold it right there, palefacette," one of them drawled "You're our captive."

She shouldn't have stopped, she supposed, but they'd looked so cute! Now they looked menacing and ferocious—if you could call grammar school kids dangerous.

They all looked like boys, but one of them turned out to be a girl. They piled into the back seat and commanded Kit to drive.

"We're the Deverell gang," the spokesperson said. "I'm Guy. That's Polk. She's Amy."

"Yes, we're the reason our daddy can't get married." Polk piped up. "We're savages, like our lus… illl…us…"

"Illustrious," Amy said for him.

"Thanks! Illustrious ancestors, that is," Polk continued.

"They were Comanches!" Amy whispered.

"One of them, Amy, only one," Polk muttered, "and she was our three-times great-grandmother. For heaven's sake…!"

"You said we were Indians," Amy persisted. "That's why we're wearing these silly costumes!"

"It's Thanksgiving in two days," came the reply from the spokesman, Guy. "And we're in a school play tomorrow, which is Monday, so we're rehearsing."

"We're going to kidnap the principal, Mr. Deere, and hold him for ransom!"

I like these kids, Kit thought. *They're my kind of people. I wonder if they know anything about kidnapping financial experts?*

"Stop here," Guy said. "And don't try anything funny, pilgrim."

Amy leaned toward him. "Pilgrimette," she corrected.

As John Wayne impersonations went, it left a lot to be desired, but it wasn't too bad, considering. Smothering a laugh, Kit got out of the car and raised her hands as three ferocious Native Americans with bows raised herded her toward the porch and the front door.

"Knock!" Guy said.

She did. There was the muffled, quick and heavy sound of footsteps approaching and a deep voice asking some kind of question. The door opened, and Kit looked up, way up, to a muscular jean-clad body into the palest green eyes in the most unwelcoming darkly tanned face she'd ever seen in her life.

"Well, I'll be damned," he murmured thoughtfully, glancing at his brood. "Another captive! Bring her in, boys, and we'll build a nice warm fire."

The last thing Kit saw before she hit the floor was the surprise that momentarily softened those fierce features.

Chapter Three

Kit opened her eyes and there was that lean, dark face again. White teeth gleamed in it. Green eyes glittered humorously in it.

"Welcome back," a deep voice said.

"You can't burn me at the stake," Kit said in a rush.

"Beg pardon?"

"Move, Emmett," an elderly voice said stridently. "Don't be absurd, Kit," Tansy Deverell chuckled, "of course he isn't going to burn you at the stake. I tell you, Emmett, these children are even worse than you were at their ages! You've got to do something about them!"

"You want us to go away, don't you?" Guy asked belligerently. "Well, we won't! This is our house, and we can stay here if we want. Tell her, Dad."

"I can't argue with the boy. Look, he's armed," Emmett said reasonably, gesturing toward the bow Guy was holding.

"You're his father!" Tansy raged.

Emmett frowned and looked at Guy and then at Polk

and finally at Amy. "That's what their mother said." He sighed. "I guess they do look like me. Lady, are you all right?" he asked, remembering Kit, who was sitting up dizzily.

"Yes, I'm just getting over the shock. It isn't every day you get captured by a band of Indians and threatened with the stake."

"Aw, gee, lady, we wouldn't have burned you," Polk said. "It's a lot of work to cut that much wood."

Kit stared at him blankly.

"Why did you faint?" Tansy asked curtly, her blue eyes somber in a lovely complexion that hadn't aged, with a frame of beautifully groomed silver hair. "Has my son gotten you in trouble?" she added angrily.

"I'm not pregnant," Kit muttered. "And if I was, it would make biological history. Your son is much too busy getting himself married to one of the world's prime gold diggers."

"Yes, I know," Tansy said wistfully. "He wouldn't listen to me, either. I'm sorry he fired you, Kit. He'll be sorry, too."

"No, he won't. He replaced me." She grinned at Tansy. "It only took him three women to do it. One can do payroll and filing, but she carries an electric weapon and smokes like a furnace. One can spell, but she's trying to seduce him. And the third one could do all three if she wasn't scared to death of him. She's nice."

"That would be Melody," Tansy said, and bit her tongue at the quick, almost violent look Emmett gave her.

"Melody?" he asked slowly. "Melody Cartman?"

"Yes, that's her name," Kit said, too shaken to notice the undercurrents. "If the smoke doesn't kill her, she might work out to be his right hand someday."

"I hate cigarettes," Tansy said with a pointed look at Emmett.

"Cigarettes are a curse," he agreed. Then he shrugged off his bad mood, grinned, pulled one out of his pocket and lit it, daring the onlookers to say a word.

"Okay, Dad. You asked for it," Guy muttered. He whipped around to his back, pulled a water pistol, and quickly extinguished the glowing tip.

Emmett stared at it with a forlorn sigh and dropped it. "Damn. That was my last one."

"And don't try that again, partner," Guy said firmly, twirling the water pistol back into his pocket while his siblings applauded loudly. He grinned at Kit. "Hey, lady, want to come hunting rabbits with us?"

"No, thanks, I feel a bit endangered right now."

"We wouldn't have a post to tie you to out in the brush," Polk argued.

"But there's the brush itself," Amy mused. "It's very dry, and I got one of Emmett's old lighters..."

"Will you stop calling me Emmett?" he muttered at his child. "I'm your father. Show a little respect."

"Yes, Emmett," Amy said politely, pulling the lighter out of her pocket.

She flashed it and Emmett grabbed it. "Not anymore, you don't," he said. "Scat, you varmints! And don't bring back any rattlers this time!"

They scampered out, giggling and murmuring among themselves while Kit caught her breath.

"Nobody in the family ever comes here," Tansy said as she and Emmett helped Kit up. "Can you *guess* why?" she added with a pointed glare at Emmett.

"I could probably make a stab at it," Kit mused.

"He's spoiled them rotten. They don't do anything they don't want to. The only exception he made was school. He insisted that they get educated."

"So I won't have to support them for the rest of my life," Emmett explained. He looked down at Kit and measured her with his glittering green eyes. "How do you feel about brief engagements? We could get married right after lunch."

Kit stared at him. "What?"

"I guess you're one of those girls who believe in long engagements, aren't you? Okay. We can wait until tomorrow to get married, then."

"He does this all the time," Tansy said sadly, shaking her head. "Pay him no attention."

"That's the trouble, nobody does!" Emmett said in exasperation, throwing up his hands. "I've been turned down five times in one month." He narrowed one eye, and glanced at Kit. "Maybe my luck's changing, though. You're not bad on the eyes and you can type. You could handle those kids and help me out in the office, too. We could be a ranching family. Think of it," he said with a gleam in his eyes, "we could found a dynasty here. Several more kids and a few good bulls…"

"Wait a minute, please," Kit said, putting out a hand. "I have just avoided becoming a human sacrifice once today. You really will have to seek a soul mate elsewhere. I have it in mind to become the female Charlie Chan."

"Another private eye." He shook his head. "What is it with you women and trench coats? We had a female private eye down here just a couple of months ago, looking for a missing woman." He glanced toward the door. "Those kids again. They nabbed her at a rest stop and tied her to a tree. Good thing the fire attracted attention from the highway.''

Kit didn't dare ask any more. She simply stood and stared at him as if she doubted his sanity and her own. ''Do you often send your children out to hijack prospective brides, Mr. Deverell?''

''They won't go at all if I don't pay them, the mercenary little devils,'' he told her outrageously. ''They say I'm too cheap to get a really good woman. I don't know, though, you're pretty easy on the eyes. How about it? I've got all my own teeth.'' He grinned to show them.

''Thank you, but I don't want to marry you.''

''Of course not. You don't know me yet. I'll court you over barbecued ribs.'' He frowned. ''You do like barbecue? I simply couldn't marry a woman who didn't.''

She chuckled at the sheer absurdity of it. ''Yes, I like barbecue.''

''You can't marry her,'' Tansy said firmly. ''I've got her all staked out for my son.''

''I don't like Chris that much,'' Kit said demurely.

''You know I wasn't talking about Chris,'' Tansy murmured.

''*He* likes the beauteous Betsy,'' came the terse reply.

''Excuse me, but the two of you are talking about Cousin Logan, aren't you?'' Emmett asked. ''What's he gotten himself into this time?''

Tansy told him while Kit listened.

Emmett shook his head. ''It runs in the family. All us Deverells are fools when it comes to women. Look at me. My ex-wife couldn't wait to marry me so we could have kids. But when we started having them, she got tired of it, so she ran off with a damned mechanic.'' His eyes narrowed with feeling. ''Go figure.''

''Didn't your wife ever want to come back?'' Kit asked.

He shrugged. ''She called a while back, but I lost the telephone number. It's just as well,'' he added, for an instant, there was something not at all easygoing in the glint of his green eyes. ''She got *tired* of the kids…God!''

''There are women in the world who just aren't cut out for motherhood, Emmett,'' Tansy said. ''There are others who would love your brood. Or at least there would be, if your horrible reputation didn't precede you. Nobody will come near the place because of those kids, and you've encouraged them in a most unfatherly way to be hooligans.''

''Straitlaced kids never have any fun, Tansy.'' He chuckled. ''I know. I was raised in a military academy. It took me years to shake off rules and tradition and start having fun.'' His eyes grew wistful. ''Do you know, I've treed more bars locally than the town drunk?''

''Your sins will come back to haunt you,'' Tansy predicted.

''Not before I get a mother for those kids,'' he said. ''They're going to seed.''

''You planted them.''

''I have to work, don't I?''

''I wouldn't call riding in every rodeo from Texas to Montana necessity. You're breaking every bone in your body one at a time.''

''It takes money to keep this place going. The plumbing's half shot. I'll have to bone up on my calf-roping.''

"They'd let you manage old man Ted Regan's place if you'd ask."

"Ted is only five years older than I am. He isn't even middle-aged."

"Everybody calls him old man Regan," Tansy said. "I don't know why, except that he's got prematurely silver hair. Anyway, he'd let you manage his place, but you just won't."

"I don't want to move to Houston."

"Jacobsville," Tansy corrected.

"Not much difference. And old Ted's ranch is so close to Houston that it could be called a suburb. I like San Antonio."

"It would be the best thing in the world for the kids," Tansy coaxed. "Plenty of fresh air, piney woods and green meadows, nice people."

"Girls?" he asked, lifting both eyebrows.

"Nobody is going to marry you until you civilize those children," Tansy warned.

"That's why I've got to get married. A man can't do that kind of job alone," he said plaintively. "I'm only one person, for God's sake! They outnumber me three to one!"

Kit had been listening quietly. This man was a cross between Chris and Logan. She liked him, but there seemed to be a lot more to him under the surface than was visible above it.

"You could hire a companion," she began.

He swept off his white Stetson and held it against his heart, eyes wide and stark. "Lady!" he exclaimed. "I can't bring that kind of woman into my home!"

She burst out laughing. "You're as incorrigible as Chris!"

"He taught me everything I know," he agreed. He

perched the Stetson back on his head. "Yes, I suppose I could get a nursemaid for the kids, but they'd torture her to death the first night. She'd find a snake in her bed or a spider in her bath, or something even worse. I can't do that to some poor unsuspecting woman. I do have a housekeeper, though, who is away on sick leave."

"There are women who have had survival training," she said.

"I don't want a drill sergeant."

"Are you sure? Think of all the fun you'd have, watching her bring them into line," Tansy suggested.

He considered that for a minute. "No," he said finally, shaking his head. "It would break their little hearts."

"The way they're heading, they aren't going to have hearts for much longer. You've got to do something, Emmett!" Tansy said.

"Not right now. Tell us why you're here," Emmett said, turning to Kit.

"I've come to find Tansy."

Tansy's eyes widened. "Logan again!"

"He worries."

"He's a damned busybody," Tansy muttered. "My God, I can't go on a little bitty plane ride without him having me followed and reports filled out on my companions. He's terrified that I'll rewrite my will and leave all my money to someone's terrier."

"That's not true." Kit chuckled. "He's afraid you'll end up married to some twenty-year-old gigolo and kill him with sheer exhaustion."

"How flattering," the older woman said delightedly. "Emmett, do you know any twenty-year-old gigolos we could try?"

"Shame on you," he said shortly. "A nice, decent woman like you ought to be ashamed to say a thing like that to me."

"I don't know why not. Last year, you were running around with that rodeo groupie and she was spending you out of bed and board."

"She was pretty," he argued. "But the kids hated her. First time I brought her out here, she was going to go walking with them. I begged her not to, God knows I did." He shook his head. "Last time I saw her, she was fishtailing her car all over the road trying to get back to the highway, and those damned kids were rolling in the dirt laughing."

"What did they do to her?" Kit asked curiously.

"Damned if I know," he said. "They never would tell me."

"You're staying the night, aren't you, Kit?" Tansy asked.

Kit's eyes widened. "Well, no!" she stammered. "I've got a return ticket late this afternoon for Houston."

"No problem," Emmett said easily. "Hand it over and I'll get you a flight tomorrow afternoon. I'll make barbecue and serenade you with my guitar under a romantic Texas moon."

"Oh, no, not that. Anything but that!" Tansy wailed.

"Shut up," he muttered at her. "I took lessons."

"Don't sing. Trust me," Tansy said, batting her eyelashes at him.

He let out an exaggerated sigh. "Another singing career ruined by critics. Well, I'll play for you, Kit. Kit? What's it stand for?"

"I don't know," Kit said quietly. She'd never talked about her parents. The subject was much too painful, and the last person she could tell was this wild-eyed Texan. "I didn't bring a bag…"

"I'll loan you one of my pajama jackets," Emmett offered.

"You can have one of my gowns, Kit," Tansy said, elbowing a grinning Emmett out of the way. "Will you stop? Honestly, anyone would think you'd never seen a woman before!"

"Well, I haven't," he argued. "Not like this one. Chris is always ranting about how nice she is, and if you like her, that's a character reference in itself. She'd make a perfect mother for those kids."

"She's going to marry Logan one day. He just doesn't know it yet."

"I'd tell him fast if I were you, by the sounds of things."

"I wouldn't have Logan on toast!"

Emmett pursed his lips and made a whistling sound. "That sounds suspiciously like cannibalism. Speaking of cannibalism, did you know that there's fossilized evidence that *Homo erectus* was a cannibal and ate his own kind? There are smashed bones and burned bones in late Pleistocene camps…"

"Go away!" Tansy wailed. "Emmett, don't start on this poor child. She's not a prehistoric culture addict like you."

"I did a course in anthropology and I did my minor in paleontology," Emmett confessed. "Dinosaur bones, that sort of thing. Did you know that there's a fossilized link between birds and lizards? A fellow called archae-opteryx—"

"Later, later, Emmett. Now what's this about Betsy?" Tansy persisted.

Emmett watched them walk toward the living room.

He could sure do worse than that sweet young thing. She was only about ten years his junior and the kids had already taken to her. For an instant, he remembered what Tansy had said about Logan's new secretary, and his blood began to burn. But he forced the thought of Melody away. He wouldn't have to see her, thank God. He never went near Logan's office. On the other hand, Kit was right here and he liked her a lot. He started whistling as he went out to feed the horses in the barn....

"Well, I won't come meekly home with you and that's that," Tansy said at supper.

"A Christian should be meek," Amy piped up. She and the boys were cleaned up, but they still looked pretty much alike. With her very short haircut, Amy could have passed for a boy.

"That's right," Kit said, smiling at the child.

Amy smiled back, and without mischief. "You're nice. Are you going to marry Emmett? We voted, and it's okay with us. You'll have to learn the rules, of course."

"Right," Guy agreed. "Bedtime is at eleven sharp. No card playing on Sunday. When Dad's got a girl in the living room, no peeking over the back of the sofa, no matter what sort of noises you hear..."

"Guy!" Emmett exploded.

"And most of all, if he's been drinking, don't get in front of him on account of he might fall on you," Amy finished.

Emmett put his hands over his face.

"You should be ashamed!" Tansy muttered, glancing at him. "Reprobate! You really are the black sheep of the family."

"He isn't black, Aunt Tansy," Polk said. "He's dirty. He always looks like that when he's been in the barn with the horses."

Kit had to wipe her mouth suddenly, but over it her eyes twinkled with unholy glee.

Emmett looked up, and the sight of those very blue eyes in merriment made him feel suddenly younger. He blinked and began to smile.

Uh-oh, Kit thought. She wiped the smile off. Here was one complication she could do without.

"You're fighting it, Kit." Emmett sighed.

"I told you, you can't have her," Tansy reminded him.

"There are plenty of women in Houston," he began.

"I've been working on this one for three years. Eat your barbecue, which is rather good, by the way. Did I ever tell you about the Russian count I met at Maxim's in Paris the last time I was there?" she added, waxing reminiscent. "He was one of the last of the Romanoffs, and he actually remembered the siege of the Winter Palace."

Emmett looked at the barbecue on his fork and began to pale.

Tansy shot a covert glance at him and continued. "There were fires everywhere. Some of the soldiers were thrown into them…"

Emmett put a hand over his mouth, dropped his food, and ran from the room.

"No guts," Guy said disgustedly, looking after him.

"Disgraceful." Polk nodded.

"Whatever are we going to do about him?" Amy sighed.

"You did it last time," Tansy reminded them while

Kit sat, dumbfounded. "Bringing that...that 'not alive' thing in here on a dustpan to show him."

"Yeah," Guy chuckled. "He didn't even *make* it to the bathroom that time!"

"You ought to see him at the rodeo if there's any blood," Amy piped in. "He goes green and white, all mixed up, and his stomach churns."

"Except if it's him that's bleeding," Guy pondered. "Weird, ain't it? Never bothers him if it's his own blood. And if it's ours, and an emergency, he's never sick. But sometimes you can turn him green real easy if you talk about something yucky."

"What a terrible way to treat your poor father," Tansy chided them. But her eyes were twinkling.

When Emmett came back, his eyes were glittering with imminent retribution.

"Great barbecue, Dad. We're going in to watch that new survival show on the educational channel, okay?" Guy blabbered.

He and the others murmured excuses and ran for it.

"Little monsters!" he called after them. "I'll get you for this!"

"Why do you let them do it to you?" Tansy asked. "You know it's terminal to show weakness to children."

"Well, look who started it off," he said, narrowing his eyes at Tansy.

"Couldn't resist it," she sputtered. "You are a case, Emmett."

He picked up his fork and forced himself to eat a bite of barbecue. Amazingly it stayed down.

Kit listened to the conversation without taking part

in it. This man was one of the more interesting people she'd ever met. She wondered what was going to become of him.

Logan Deverell was sitting on the doorstep of the Lassiter Detective Agency the minute it opened the next morning.

"I want to see Kit," he told Dane.

Dane lifted both eyebrows. "You can't. She's out of town running your mother to the ground."

"Where out of town?"

"San Antonio."

"Oh, no! Why in God's name did you let her go *there?*"

Dane didn't move. "It's only your cousin, Logan."

"No, he isn't only my cousin, he's got these three pint-sized assassins and they hate women! They'll burn her at the stake. And if they don't, Emmett will have her in front of a minister...I've got to get out there and save her!"

He was gone before the last word hit the air, with a shell-shocked Dane looking after him. Tess came to stand beside him, staring toward the closed door.

"Logan?" she asked.

He nodded.

"Where'd he go?"

"To San Antonio to save Kit from Emmett."

She turned and looked up at him. "I beg your pardon?"

"It seems that Emmett is in a perpetual state of readiness to marry the first available woman, but he can't get her past his three kids. Logan's gone to the rescue."

"I thought he wanted to find Tansy?"

"We did. She's staying with Emmett."

"And so is Kit, because she phoned last night with

some story about being hijacked by white Indians and narrowly escaping being burned at the stake.''

He smiled down at her. After a minute, he bent and kissed her with slow, lingering warmth. "I need a very strong cup of black coffee, and then you can tell me that again. Join me?''

She looped her arm through his. "I'd be delighted."

The thunderous knocking at the front door woke Kit, who'd overslept from sheer exhaustion. She and Tansy and Emmett had been up very late. Emmett had serenaded her. His voice grated like a nail file, but he did play the guitar quite well and she enjoyed listening to him. Then they talked about rodeo—which was the passion of his life—and about his plans for the future. They didn't talk a lot about the kids, who were carefully concealed behind curtains and under chairs listening. They'd been told three times to go to bed, but they never paid any attention to their father. Anyway, they were bent on finding out everyone's opinion of them.

The knocking stopped, but it was followed by a familiar bellow.

"Where is she?'' Logan demanded.

"What a hell of a nerve, practically breaking into my house at this ungodly hour!'' Emmett muttered. "Quiet down or I'll turn those kids loose on you!''

"Oh, God, not that, anything but that!'' Logan groaned.

There were muffled giggles down the hall.

"Anyway, Tansy's asleep. Or she was, until you tried to knock the house down around our ears.''

"I'm not looking for Tansy. Where's Kit?''

Kit's heart leaped in her chest. She couldn't believe that he'd come all this way for her! Had he seen Tess

Lassiter and become concerned when he knew she was out here with the volatile San Antonio Deverells? Had he missed her?

She sat up in bed, just in time for Logan to throw open the door and confront her. She was dressed in the concealing flannel gown Tansy had loaned her.

"So there you are!" he growled.

"My, what a pretty picture." Emmett sighed as he saw her. "Darlin', you would look lovely propped up in my bed like that…"

"Out!" Logan shoved his cousin unceremoniously out the door and slammed it. "You lecher! She's only a child!"

"I'm going to marry her…" came through the door.

"Over my dead and decaying corpse!"

There was a muttering sound, like gagging, and quickly retreating footsteps.

"So much for him," Logan said with satisfaction. He stared at Kit for a long moment. "You can't marry him. It isn't love. He just likes women. There are so few who can get past those kids, he'll gladly latch on to anyone they like."

"I'm not blind," she said primly, folding her slender hands in her lap. "Why are you here? I thought you wanted me to find Tansy. I did."

"I know that. But you had no business moving in with the Family from Hell."

"What a way to talk about your own cousins!"

"Everybody knows about them. Nobody will even come near the place for fear of disappearing in the brush! Emmett lets those kids do anything they want to since his wife left. He doesn't care enough to make the barest attempt at control. He's too busy riding in rodeos to prove he's still a man, and getting his body broken to bits in the process! He can't get over the fact that his ex-wife left him.''

Kit began to see the carefree Emmett in a new light, and he didn't seem quite so carefree anymore.

''Poor man,'' she said quietly.

''Poor man, the devil. He isn't your problem. Go home!''

Her eyebrows arched defiantly. ''I don't work for you anymore. You can't tell me to walk to the corner!''

''No? Let me show you what I can get you to do, Miss Morris,'' he said, and started toward her.

Chapter Four

Kit froze. She'd never been alone in this kind of intimate setting with Logan, not even when she'd had to accompany him out of the country and they'd stayed in hotel suites together. Then, it had been all business and he'd never noticed her, no matter how she dressed or looked.

But now, the gown she was wearing might have been transparent as his dark eyes slid over the bodice and seemed to see right underneath it. He had a sophistication that was vaguely alarming. A woman's body was no mystery to him. She'd seen enough women come and go in his life in the past three years to know that he was experienced.

Her fingers grasped the cover and drew it up sharply to cover her breasts. She flushed as he paused by the bed and looked down at her.

Something changed in his face. He lifted one bushy eyebrow and deliberately let his eyes fall on her softly parted mouth.

He'd never wondered what it would feel like to taste

Miss Morris's pert little mouth. But suddenly, he wanted the knowledge with a longing that corded his powerful body. Betsy was pushed to the back of his mind quite suddenly while he grappled with unbelievable desire for his ex-secretary.

"Will you please get out of here?" she squeaked.

He made an odd, hesitant movement and sat down on the bed beside her. His big hand, half the size of a dinner plate, folded around both of hers and detached them from their death grip on the coverlet.

"What are you afraid of?" he asked.

It was a tone he'd never used with her, a deep, husky pitch that was like warm velvet. She looked into his eyes closer than she'd ever seen them and became lost in their dark brown depths.

She wasn't breathing quite naturally. Neither was he, if the rise and fall of his broad chest under its charcoal-gray suit and white shirt was any indication. He smelled of some exotic cologne that appealed to her senses, and he was clean-shaven. The elegant Mr. Deverell was never disheveled or less than immaculate. Kit couldn't imagine him wearing jeans and chambray shirts as Emmett did.

"Answer me, Kit."

That was new, too—her name on his lips. It was always Morris this, Morris that. She searched his eyes helplessly. "I'm not afraid of you," she said absently.

Her vulnerability had a devastating effect on him. Their fights had become legend in the office building where he worked. Kit had a fiery temper and a stubborn nature, and he enjoyed the explosions that resulted from his prodding of both.

But she wasn't fighting now. She was sitting in his grasp like some exotic kitten, her big blue eyes wide and afraid and yet…almost welcoming. She had a beautiful complexion, he thought, and a mouth that looked as if it would feel like warm silk.

His body tautened with longing. He wasn't even thinking of consequences or other commitments as he captured her face in his big, warm hands and slowly bent to her upturned mouth.

She gasped as she felt his breath, coffee and mint scented, and the tentative brush of his mouth on her parted lips.

He felt her body jerk instinctively. His nose drew against her own. All he could see, think, breathe was the shape of her mouth under his. "I won't hurt you," he whispered, moving closer. "I can be gentle, even if I've never given you cause to believe it."

She felt his mouth touching hers, and it was like electricity. So many dreams, and here was the incredible, pulsing reality of his mouth against her own, his body so near that she could feel its heat and strength. She was floating, drowning.

She heard his breath catch, a tiny burst of sound that she knew was going to be a prelude to something volcanic and utterly destructive. And even as she yearned hopelessly for his touch, she knew that she couldn't give in to this madness. She didn't dare let him…!

She froze. "What about Betsy?" she said quickly.

His hands tightened on her head and his head lifted. His dazed eyes stared into hers. "What?"

"Don't forget Betsy!" she managed unsteadily, fighting his pull on her starved senses. "Remember Betsy, Mr. Deverell."

Mr. Deverell. He was Kit's boss and Betsy's would-be lover. He wondered how he could have forgotten that. His heavy brows met as his head lifted and Kit's

pale face suddenly came into stark focus and he regained his lost wits.

Abruptly he let her go and stood up, turning his back
while he struggled with unfamiliar feelings. He could
feel his heart beating against his ribs, feel the tautness
of his body with what he recognized dimly was desire.
What was wrong with him? He didn't want Kit! He'd
fired her. Betsy was warm and soft and loving, and her
body promised heaven if he could ever maneuver her
into bed. Kit was young and untried, very probably
she'd never slept with anyone. God! he thought, and
his body reacted sharply to the thought.

Kit pulled the covers back over her and averted her
face. "I'd like to get dressed, if you don't mind," she
said hesitantly.

"What? Oh. Certainly." He went out the door without a protest, and Kit thanked God for small miracles.

She couldn't quite believe what had almost happened. She had to be very careful from now on. Logan
had made his opinion of Betsy quite clear, along with
his commitment to the woman. Why he'd tried to kiss
her, she couldn't comprehend. All she knew was that
she mustn't, for her own sake, ever let him get close
enough to try again.

Unrequited love was something she'd lived with for
three long years. She knew Betsy and she didn't want
Logan to fall victim to the woman, but there had to be
another way to stop it. She really couldn't allow herself
to become embroiled in a hopeless affair with him,
even to save him from financial ruin. She'd certainly
lose him that way. And when he'd had his fill of Kit's
inexperience, probably Betsy's sophistication would
snare him for sure. The thought was depressing, but it
had to be faced. She couldn't let herself dream about

him anymore. She had to get used to being without him in her life, in any capacity.

She got dressed in jeans and a sweatshirt, and went to the dining room where the rest of the family, Logan included, was sitting down to an enormous breakfast.

"Can he cook, or can't he?" Tansy enthused over the biscuits. "Emmett, you've missed your real vocation. God meant you to be a chef."

"I'd get dishpan hands." He chuckled. He glared at Logan. "That was a low blow, what you did in the hall."

Logan didn't look up from his scrambled eggs. "Yes, it was. I'll kill myself if you like."

Emmett didn't believe he'd heard that from his staid cousin, so he ignored it.

Kit didn't. Logan didn't sound like himself. She stared at him until he lifted his head, and what she saw in his eyes then made her blush furiously and look away.

Logan felt his fingers tremble on his fork. Damn it, what was *happening* to him? Only this morning, he'd been in complete control of his life. Or had he? He hadn't phoned Betsy to say he was leaving for San Antonio, or offered to bring her with him. He hadn't even phoned the office to tell them where he was. Chris would be dragged in to sub for him, which would make his brother furious. And why had he come dashing out here in the first place? To save Kit from Emmett.

That threat, at least, certainly seemed real enough. Emmett stared at her dreamily and kept making veiled references to how well he could provide for a new wife. The kids wanted to take her hunting with them, he added, which was a real honor.

"No, thanks." She chuckled. "I'd look sad with arrows sticking out all over me."

"Oh, none of that," Emmett protested. "They hunt with those electronic spotting guns. Toys, you know. I wouldn't dream of turning them loose with real bullets!"

"Did you know that if you get close enough with a radio signal you can ignite a dynamite cap?" Polk asked conversationally, which caused his father to choke on his biscuit.

"Out!" Tansy told the three, who had finished eating, while she hit Emmett on the back to dislodge the biscuit.

"I didn't say we'd ever done it," Polk muttered defensively. "Anyway, we couldn't get the man to sell us any dynamite."

"Oh, my *God!*" Emmett wailed.

"Wouldn't you like to enlist them in the Marine Corps?" Logan suggested. "You could lie about their ages."

"You won't feel like that when you have kids of your own," came the droll reply. "Flesh of your flesh, blood of your blood..."

"Speaking of blood, they're after the cat again," Tansy remarked.

Emmett muttered something violent and went to yell out the window. When he came back, he looked even older.

"I can't stand it. Please, for God's sake, marry me!" he pleaded with Kit, dropping to his knees by her chair and draping one long, muscular arm over her lap. "I'll reform. I'll stay home and cook barbecued ribs and breakfast and manage old man Regan's ranch. *Anything.* Just save me from those kids!"

Kit doubled over laughing. She just shook her head. "Thank you for the offer, but I really can't. I have to find missing people."

He looked up at her thoughtfully, his lips pursed, one eye narrowed. "Find people, do you? Okay. How are you at the reverse? Couldn't you hide me where those *kids* can't find me?"

"Why, you craven coward," Tansy chided. "Get off your knees and act like a proper father."

"I did try, Tansy," he said good-naturedly as he got gracefully to his feet. "But just as I broke the switch, one yelled to distract me, the second one positioned himself behind my knees and the third one knocked me over the second one into the river. I haven't really tried to hit one of them since."

"You don't have to hit them," Tansy continued, unabashed. "You could discipline them in other ways. Take away their television privileges."

He stared at her. "We don't have a television. Those kids threw a bowling ball through it. Thank God we have a good volunteer fire department here."

"Emmett, you're not the man I remember," Logan said, shaking his head.

"I'm not sure I ever was. Things have gone from bad to worse since she left me," he said, obviously referring to his ex-wife. "Since I got custody, no sane woman will have me. Maybe I could lock the kids up until I got one to the altar. Too late for you, of course," he said with a wistful smile in Kit's direction. "It's got to be a woman who doesn't know they exist until we're legally married!"

"Buffaloed by three children," Logan scoffed. "Imagine that."

"You try dealing with them," Emmett dared.

"Not me. I'm on the first plane to Houston this afternoon."

Emmett put down his coffee cup. "Why not stay until tomorrow?"

"Yes, why not?" Tansy seconded. "You and I get no time together these days, Logan. You're either too busy making money or traveling around the world or escorting that taffy-brained woman friend of yours around town."

He glared at her. "Let's leave Betsy out of this, shall we?"

"Suit yourself," Tansy replied. "You could fly back tomorrow with me. I can't stay around much longer. I'm only filling in for the housekeeper."

"My housekeeper," Emmett said. "The only woman west of the Pecos who isn't terrified of those kids."

"She had to have some minor surgery, but she'll be back tomorrow. Come on, son," Tansy coaxed. "You could use a day off. Besides, it's too late to go home and try to get anything done."

He didn't want to admit how much he wanted to stay. The way he felt about Kit was changing by the minute. He didn't want to leave her.

"You stay, too, Kit," Tansy commanded. "It's too late for you to go now, anyway."

"But I have my ticket…"

"You can use it tomorrow," Emmett coaxed, smiling at her. "I'll take you to a concert. Our local symphony has several this time of year. How do you fancy Aaron Copland?"

"Fanfare for the Common Man!" Kit said enthusiastically. "Oh, I'd love to go and hear some of his music!"

Logan was mildly surprised. The topic of music in

any personal way hadn't come up since Kit had started working for him three years ago. He had no idea she liked Copland. So did he.

"How about Stravinsky?" he asked. "His work is largely of an experimental nature. A lot of people don't care for it."

"I like it," Kit said.

"So do I," Emmett seconded. "I think *The Firebird* is a tribute to his ability as a composer." He hesitated. "Let me make a couple of telephone calls. There's a special charity concert being given by a visiting orchestra, and I think they might include Stravinsky in their program. Let me find out."

He came back shaking his head. "Wrong night, I'm afraid," he said ruefully. "But there's a Mexican folk group in the city. Want to go see a Mexican ballet?"

"What about the children?" Kit asked.

"They like concerts and music of any sort," Emmett said. "They'll sit like mice. You wouldn't recognize them properly dressed and behaved."

"*I* certainly wouldn't." Tansy sniffed.

"That's because they used my flexible ropes to tie her to the bed the first night she got here," Emmett explained. "She taught them some new adjectives."

"You, too," Tansy chuckled. Her eyes twinkled. "It's so alive here, Kit. You really ought to marry Emmett. You'd never be bored."

"Not until the kids got grown, at least," he added. "Be a sport. Two little words—I do."

"I'm not that much of a sport, thanks just the same." She laughed. "I don't want to get married for years yet."

"It's a shame to wait for something that may never happen," Tansy said gently.

Kit's eyes were eloquent as she begged Tansy not to give away to Logan how she felt.

"All right," the elderly woman said, laughing softly. "I'll quit playing matchmaker. I would like to point out, though, that I have a perfectly marriageable son who thinks you're wonderful…"

"I have never said…!" Logan began fiercely, color burning along his high cheekbones.

"Chris, my dear, *Chris,* not you," Tansy scoffed. "You've already announced to all and sundry that you can't wait to talk the beauteous Betsy into letting you support her for life in the manner to which she'd like to become accustomed."

"Betsy has money of her own," Logan said shortly.

"Indeed she does," Kit said, burning inside at the injustice of it.

"If you have something to say, Morris, spit it out," Logan challenged.

"Very well, I will." She threw down her napkin and got to her feet. "Your beautiful blond spider caused my nice old neighbor to kill himself over a stupid lottery ticket. He killed himself because she played him for a fool and got him to sign over every penny he had to her! That's why she's got money, Mr. Deverell. That's how she'll get yours, too," she added huskily. "She'll wind you around her little finger and promise you that lovely body. But you won't get it until she's got your name on a legal document of some sort. And then you still won't get it. But she'll have you. Drawn and quartered and bled to death, she'll have you."

She turned and left the room. The closed expression on Logan's broad, dark face had told her that he wasn't buying a word of it.

You simply couldn't talk to a stone wall.

* * *

Emmett caught up with her outside a few minutes later. He was smoking a cigarette and looking all around.

"It looks safe enough right here," he said, shoving his free hand into his jeans pocket. Under the wide brim of his hat, he was smiling as he joined her in the middle of the path that led into the distant pastures. The cool, dull brown horizon stretched out forever, a reminder that winter was almost here. "I have to pick times and places to smoke," he added ruefully. "Those kids have radar and smoke detectors and water guns in every shape and size. I guess they're right. I really should quit."

"It doesn't do your lungs much good, I suppose," she said.

"Mine or anyone else's. I don't smoke in closed rooms. It's too dangerous for bystanders." He flicked off an ash. "Funny, you know, the Indians used tobacco for hundreds of years, but they used it mostly for ceremonial purposes. Same thing with peyote. Mostly those substances weren't abused because they considered it sacrilege. Our culture abuses damned near everything."

"Especially natural resources." She turned and looked up at him. He seemed different when he wasn't pretending to be something he really wasn't. He looked somber and quiet and very, very masculine. If it hadn't been for the way she felt about Logan, she could have found herself falling all over this man.

"Did I put my nose on upside down again?" he asked with a cynically cocked eyebrow.

She laughed. "No. I was just thinking that you're many-faceted. I don't think I've seen the real you yet."

He shrugged. "Most people are pretty complex." He

studied her face for a long moment. "You're without guile, aren't you? You have an honest, open face. I'll bet you return quarters you find on restaurant floors and obey parking signs and never tell lies."

"I try not to," she corrected. "I was raised not to cheat."

Her face closed up as she got the words out, and he saw her reaction.

"You tense when you get close to the subject of your parents."

"Do I? How big is this ranch?"

He hesitated, but only for a minute. He smiled and proceeded to describe the size and operation of the ranch for her, until a perplexed and irritated Logan came out to join them. He'd made all the necessary telephone calls, and he was still seething at Betsy's spitting fury because he hadn't phoned her sooner. He didn't like aggressive, snarling women. He respected intelligence, but Betsy had displayed cold, icy self-interest. Even through his physical infatuation for the woman, he recognized that.

"Do you know where the children are?" Kit asked suddenly. "Should I go look for them?"

"You'll find them in the barn with the new kittens," Emmett said. "That's where they usually are these days. Pretty little things, all different colors and all with long fur and blue eyes. Old Walt wanted to get rid of them, but we've got mice in the barn, so I figured they might as well stay."

He had a warmth about him that probably drew women like flies, Kit thought. She'd never had warmth from Logan, not even the two or three times she'd had flu or a virus since she'd worked for him. It was never "poor Kit." Rather, it was "when the hell are you coming back?"

"I'll go with you to look for them," Logan said, smoothly interposing himself between Kit and Emmett. "Sorry you're too busy to come with us," he said with a smile at his cousin. "But I know how it is."

"Not yet, you don't," Emmett said enigmatically, with a gleam in his eyes. "But you'll find out. How about that ballet?" he asked.

Kit hesitated. "I really don't feel quite up to it, but thanks anyway. Maybe Tansy and Logan...?"

"Not me," Logan replied.

"Oh, well, maybe next trip," Emmett said. He winked at Kit. "If you married me, we could go to all sorts of cultural events."

"Right now, we're going to look at kittens and kids, thanks," Logan told him, taking Kit's arm. "Come along."

"Okay, I get the picture," Emmett said. He tipped his hat at Kit and strode away, whistling.

"I don't want to go anywhere with you," Kit snarled at Logan.

He let go of her arm and linked his big hands behind him to study her. He was wearing a long-sleeved white shirt and tie with his dark gray suit slacks. The shirt-sleeves were rolled up to the elbow and he was wearing boots instead of street shoes. His dark, thick black hair was windblown and it gave his broad face an untamed appearance. Against the sky, he looked as if he were part of the history of the place.

"Who were your ancestors?" she asked unexpectedly.

"One of them was a lieutenant under Santa Ana," he mused, smiling at her shock. "You did know that the enemy troops sometimes raped and pillaged in the local communities? One of my ancestors was unfortunate enough to be in a house alone when they marched through. Along with the Mexican blood, I've got some very upper crust French and British.''

It was a reminder that his background was much more monied than her own. She averted her eyes as they walked. ''You're very dark.''

''Most of that is from the sun. I spend a lot of time in the Mediterranean.''

''Yes, I know.''

He followed her toward the barn. It was warm for a November day. She pulled off her sweater and left her arms bare in the long-sleeved white shirt she was wearing with off-white jeans and boots.

''You look pretty western today,'' he remarked. ''Didn't you live on a ranch once?''

She winced. ''A long time ago. Look, there are the children…!''

He caught her arm and swung her back to face him.

''Your parents divorced, didn't they?'' he said quietly.

He knew. She'd never been quite sure where he found out, or who had told him. She did know that her job required a thorough background check, and that he'd had one done before Dane's detective agency even opened for business.

Whoever had searched around in her record had certainly hit pay dirt. She didn't even bother to deny it. His eyes told her there was no point.

''It was a very messy divorce,'' she said averting her eyes. ''They were arguing all the time. I don't like to remember those days. They both remarried after the divorce, but they only had a few years with their new spouses. Both my parents are dead now.''

He pulled her into his big arms. She was warm and soft and vulnerable, and he loved the feeling it gave him to comfort her. That should have warned him that his emotions were teetering on the edge, but it didn't.

"Here, now," he muttered. He drew out a handkerchief and dabbed at her red, wet eyes with it. "Blow."

She did, hiccuping at the same time. "I never cry."

"I know. Not even when I yell."

He wiped the rest of her face and pressed the handkerchief into her hand. "Keep it. I've got dozens. Tansy has them hidden in every other drawer in my house. She thinks a man should have an endless supply."

"Why do you always call her Tansy instead of Mother?" she asked curiously.

"She doesn't seem old enough to be my mother at times," he replied with a wistful smile. "She's unique. Not that she doesn't worry me out of my damned mind just by being unique."

"Not every woman her age would try sailboarding."

"This is true." He pushed back the disheveled hair from her eyebrows. "You have skin like milk, Kit," he said, sketching her cheekbones. "It's almost transparent."

She flushed. "My mother…my mother had skin like that."

"Did she? Your people were ranchers, weren't they?"

"Yes. From over around El Paso," she said wearily. "Poor farmers. I come from a long line of poor people."

"Wealth or the lack of it never made character, Kit," he replied.

"It opens and closes doors, though."

He didn't argue. "I know the memories won't ever fade completely," he said. "But surely you're doing yourself no favors by burying them so deeply."

"It seemed best."

"I suppose so. Feel better now?"

"Yes. Thank you, Mr. Deverell."

He sighed. "Kit, after three years, don't you think you could manage to call me Logan?"

She searched his dark eyes in a long silence.

"Surely we know each other well enough," he persisted. He touched her lower lip, startled by its softness, its warmth and fullness. He couldn't seem to drag his eyes away from it. As he watched, her lips parted and his breath lingered in the very back of his throat.

His blood began to pound in his veins. His hands settled on her waist and drew her to him. There was nothing in his eyes except her mouth and even as he bent toward it, he knew he was going to regret this for the rest of his life.

"There's Betsy," she croaked defensively, pressing her hands flat against his broad, hard chest.

"Damn Betsy," he bit off against her soft mouth.

Chapter Five

Kit froze, but only for an instant. The reality of Logan's hard, expert mouth on her lips was all of heaven. She closed her eyes and felt as if her body was on fire from head to toe. He knew what to do with a woman's mouth, she thought dizzily, pressing closer. He knew *exactly* what to do!

Years of anguished longing, and it was happening. It was actually happening! These were Logan's arms enveloping her, this was Logan's mouth grinding so hungrily against her own.

She knew she'd live on this memory for the rest of her life. Her body lifted closer to his, and she moaned. The pressure of his mouth lessened and he began to tease and softly probe her lips, breaking through any defenses she might have had left, demanding surrender.

She gave it willingly. Her mouth opened to his penetration. She leaned into his big, powerful body and let him bring her so close that she could feel the corded muscles of his thighs, the flatness of his belly, the warmth of his broad chest against her soft breasts as his arms tightened.

He groaned and she answered him, her body so perfectly attuned to his that she matched every single movement he made.

Slowly her arms inched around his waist and she moved helplessly against the muscles of his body. He was against her, around her, sheltering and comforting her. Nothing could ever harm her again.

His tongue teased lightly into her mouth and then began quite suddenly to stab at it, producing the most intensely private sensations in the lower part of her body.

She tensed and tried to pull away, but his arms refused to release her. The movements became quicker, rhythmic, deep. She made a sound that she'd never made before and tried to twist upward in his arms, seeking blindly for a contact that would ease the powerful need he was building in her untried body.

As if he knew what she needed, his hands suddenly dropped to her hips and lifted her into the cradle of his own, bringing her into a contact that shocked even as it aroused.

She protested under his mouth. He lifted his head and watched her eyes with sensual mastery as his hands contracted, pressing her belly into a most blatant evidence of capability.

Her eyes shared everything with him: her fear, her vulnerability, her shock, her delight in his masculinity. Everything.

"Yes," he whispered gruffly. He nodded and his mouth settled slowly back on her own. She was no longer protesting anything, and his hands were moving her in a lazy rhythm, which produced choked little cries of pleasure.

When the building tension was more than she could bear, he wrapped his arms around her and all but crushed her, groaning into her mouth as he felt her shiver.

He was breathing raggedly and his legs were unsteady, as was her whole, soft body. He wanted her. There was a barn nearby, but it was full of kids. There was a house behind them, but it was full of adults. The ground was hard and cold, and very public. He cursed under his breath in anguish and his big body shuddered in response to her need.

He drew back, his face hard with passion and frustration.

Kit looked up at him, blazing with needs she hadn't even known existed. Her legs almost went out from under her, her body throbbed so with unsatisfied desire. "I hate you!" she said, choking. She hit his chest, hard, once, twice, shaking with what she supposed was rage at his presumption and his teasing.

"Here, it's all right," he whispered. His arms enveloped her, leaving a little space between their bodies as he comforted her, stroked her hair and whispered words of soft reassurance.

Tears ran down her cheeks as she struggled for composure. He felt a tremor in his own body. It had been a near thing. Imagine, he thought, with Kit, of all people!

His eyes opened and he saw the barn. The doors were closed, thank God, although there was one kid in the loft getting an eyeful. Polk. The quiet one. He darted back when he saw Logan's head lift.

"Spying on us, the devils," he murmured against Kit's temple.

"What?" Her soft voice was shaken, beautiful.

He lifted his head and smiled down at her. "The kids. They're up in the loft watching us."

She blushed. "Oh, my!"

His eyes kindled as he studied her. She was vulnerable. Now he knew it, but he didn't know what to do about it. His whole body ached from the heat of hers.

"You dress like someone who was raised in a convent," he said quietly. "But you kiss like a wild woman."

"Now you know what kind of night school courses I took year before last!" she said sarcastically, pushing at his chest.

He let her go, watching her try to get herself together. It amazed him that he could knock the logical, very prim Miss Morris off her pins. It delighted him. Betsy was a woman of the world, but this unique little sparrow wasn't used to men at all. The contrast was surprising. He found that he much preferred teaching Kit to having Betsy tutor him in what pleased her.

"Innocence in these confused times is a rare jewel indeed," he murmured, watching her.

She glared at him. "My jewel is none of your business," she muttered. "And how do you *know*, anyway?"

"I don't," he agreed. He grinned slowly. "But I could find out in ten minutes flat with a little cooperation," he added. "How about it?"

She latched on to what he was suggesting at once. "Mr. Deverell!"

She didn't know whether to gasp or laugh or kick

him very hard. She walked on toward the barn without saying anything at all.

The barn door opened and all three kids smiled at them with very knowing faces.

"Where are the kittens?" Kit asked.

"Right over here," Amy volunteered, leading them. "Uh, Polk and Guy and I have to go get cleaned up. We'll see you later!"

There was a scurrying sound and the barn door closed, but Kit would have bet her socks that the kids were still inside.

She exchanged a glance with Logan, who actually grinned.

"Aren't they cute?" she asked, reaching down to pick up a kitten and stroke and caress it.

"Yes, they're cute," he mused, paying much more attention to Kit's rapt face than the small felines. He knelt beside her and gave the cats equal attention.

Nothing else was said for several long minutes.

"Damn!" came a long-suffering exclamation from Guy, who stood up along with his siblings, cast a disgusted look at the adults and stalked out of the barn. The other two went with him, trying to look both sheepish and angry at the same time.

Logan chuckled. "I suppose they were expecting a floor show."

"Those kids know too much already," she said, refusing to be baited. "But they're sweet children."

"They are not! Why do you think the family avoids this place like the plague? My cousin Belinda came down here to spend the night last year and the little monsters put an armadillo in the bed with her."

She whistled. "I'm glad they like me!"

"You'd better be. They defanged a rattler and

shoved it in my room the first time I was fool enough to spend a night here.''

"What did you do?"

"I went out the window, of course," he said. "Stark naked, because that's how I sleep, and I think I took at least two-hundred dollars worth of pane glass with me."

She could almost picture it. "Weren't you hurt?"

"Only my pride. The glass did very little damage. Fortunately for them. I haven't been back since, until now." He cocked an eyebrow at her. "But they'll be nice to me this time. They think I'm going to kiss you, and they can catch us at it and we'll be embarrassed."

"That's not a nice thing to say!"

"Why do you think they were hiding in here?" he asked patiently and smiled at her confusion. "Well, hide your head in the sand. But they're getting old enough to be curious, you know, and I'll bet Emmett hasn't told them zilch."

"He has so!" Amy interjected until two small hands, one on each side, clapped over her mouth.

"You varmints!" Logan raged at them. They'd eased back in and were crouched just inside the door behind a wall. "You'll swing for this, you sidewinders!"

"You'll have to catch us first, and you're old!" Guy called. The three of them escaped at a dead run.

"They're right," Kit said thoughtfully, eyeing him. "You *are* old. Thirty-five just this year."

He glared at her. "How would you like to be flattened out on the hay here for a few minutes?" he asked, glancing around. "The kids could sell tickets."

She cleared her throat. "I take it all back. You're young. You're in your prime, in fact."

"I was in my prime at eighteen, actually," he remarked. He smiled wickedly. "But I can still go all night."

She leaped up in the wake of outraged embarrassment, brushed off her jeans and stalked out the door just in time to connect with three small, warm bodies.

They all went sprawling, Kit included.

"I told you they were both too old," Guy muttered as he helped his siblings to their feet. "You have to watch teenagers to find out that sort of thing, not old people. Come on. We'll go down to the river and spy on Josh Landers and Cindy Gail when they get through fishing!"

Flushed with glee they rushed off again, leaving Kit muddled and out of sorts.

"I told you," Logan said from behind.

Emmett passed the kids, whirling around as they went by him like cyclones. He didn't ask where they were going. He wandered on down to join Kit and Logan.

"Why are you sitting on the ground?" Emmett asked Kit conversationally. "Is there a sudden chair shortage?"

"I'm just where your offspring left me, flat in the dirt," Kit told him. "They were down here spying on us—" She broke off when she realized what she was saying.

Emmett lifted an eyebrow and looked at Logan, who had a disgustingly smug and triumphant look on his face. "Oh," Emmett said. He smiled a little sadly, managing with one word to convey total understanding of the situation and regret on his own account.

"They're just curious," Emmett added after a minute, rocking back on his heels. "I told them the basics, and how to stay out of bad trouble with it all. They cleared their throats and pretended not to listen.'' He chuckled.

''Well, they were on their way down to the river. Something about a couple of teenagers fishing there...'' Kit told him.

''Ohmigod!''

Emmett did an about-face and rushed off in the general direction the kids had taken.

''No wonder he's so slender and fit,'' Kit remarked, watching his figure slowly grow smaller in the distance. ''I don't think I've seen him sit for five straight minutes since I've been here.''

''The kids keep him on his toes. When he's here.''

''Rodeo is very dangerous, isn't it?''

He nodded. ''And for him more than most. His father died in a bull riding competition, right in the ring.''

''How terrible for him!''

''That's not all of it. His mother killed herself soon after the funeral. That was when Emmett got married.'' He said it pointedly.

''He was lonely and grieving, wasn't he?'' she asked.

''And determined to have a family so that he could fill up the house and banish the bad memories as quickly as possible. But the woman he married didn't take to motherhood, and she was really too young to settle down. She fell head over heels in love with a pretty ordinary man who'd worshiped her since high school. Emmett was never at home back then. He was paying off the mortgage on his father's land and just getting started good on the rodeo circuit. She should have stayed around. One of our more well-to-do relatives died last year and left Emmett fixed for life. I think Emmett's ex-wife married too young and wasn't really in love with Emmett.''

''Then he doesn't have to do rodeo,'' she said.

''Not financially,'' he told her.

''Oh. I see.'' And she did. Emmett was harboring a wealth of hurt. Perhaps the pain and danger of rodeo made it go away for a while, or brought him close to memories of happier times when his father was alive. ''But it can't be good for his kids.''

''Maybe he does it to escape them,'' he murmured dryly.

''But they adore him. You can tell that they do, and it's mutual. But...''

''But he's afraid to get too close.'' Logan looked down at her with sudden comprehension. ''He's afraid to love, because he's afraid of being left alone again. One way or another, he's lost every single person he ever loved.''

Kit didn't reply. She kept walking and so did Logan, but the thought lodged in his mind and wouldn't be coaxed out. Was he that way, afraid to love? Betsy was temporary. Even as he'd admitted his physical need for her, there was never a time when he'd pictured her as a permanent part of his life. She hated cooking and housework and she and he never thought alike on the important issues. They argued often on politics and religion and just about everything else. The only real common ground they had was when Logan took her in his arms. But even that was superficial, shallow. There were times when he was almost certain that her enjoyment was nothing more than a facade.

Kit had said as much. She had to care about him, to be so protective. They'd been together a long time, he supposed, so maybe she felt a proprietary interest in his happiness. Still, she'd been upset enough to quit. Was she jealous?

He stuck his hands into his pockets as they walked, the big, husky man and the slender, graceful woman. It felt good to spend time with her. She didn't chatter or talk fashion and gossip at the expense of more serious subjects. Kit only spoke when she had something to say.

"Betsy was upset because I didn't bring her with me," he remarked.

She didn't look up. "You could ask her to fly out and meet you."

Logan gave Kit a calculated glance that she didn't see. "She'd want to sleep with me," he lied. "Emmett would go through the roof. He doesn't believe in that sort of thing."

She hated the very idea of Betsy in Logan's bed. Her hand clenched at her side, but she didn't make any remarks.

She didn't need to. The small movement didn't escape Logan's dark eyes. He smiled.

"Tansy's being very agreeable, don't you think?" she said, changing the subject.

"Yes. Suspicious, isn't it?" he added. "She probably didn't expect you to be this good at tracking her down." He stopped, and the look in his eyes was thoughtful. "In fact, it really was good detective work."

"I'm not just a typist, you know," she murmured. "I do have a brain and a few skills."

"If I never realized that, why would I go off and leave you in charge of the office for days at a time?" he asked. "I always recognized your talents, Kit."

Her heart jumped in her chest. "You never said you did."

"Why would I do a stupid thing like that?" he asked, amazed. "If I'd mentioned that you were being wasted in my office, you'd have quit and gone to work for a detective agency or something." He glowered at her. "As it happened, you did it anyway."

"After your beloved threw scalding coffee all over me and you took her side against me!"

"Of course I did, damn it!" He bit off the words. "I wasn't trying to get *you* into bed, was I?"

She went scarlet. Her palm itched to land against that massive jaw, but she restrained it—barely.

"You hopeless little prude," he said shortly, dark eyes blazing. "To you, like Emmett, sex is something that only happens between married people, I suppose?"

"Yes, it is. Or it should be," she said forcefully. "I suppose you think it's right that carelessness produces thousands of unwanted babies? Or that it's all right to sleep around indiscriminately and spread terrible diseases?"

He didn't reply immediately. "No," he said finally. "I don't think it's right. I believe in prevention and safety, and I practice them."

She didn't have a comeback for that. She started walking again.

"How's your secretarial staff?" she asked. "Are they coping with your absence?"

"Chris is having something of a problem with one of them."

"Which one?"

"Margo."

"The one with the cleavage who can spell."

He chuckled. "That's right. She likes rich men."

She bit her tongue to hold back a remark about another woman close to him who did, too.

"Don't hold back," he told her, smiling as if he knew what she was doing and thinking. He stretched lazily. "The chain-smoker has bronchitis, but she's still dragging in to work. The other one seems to be managing, too, now that you'd shown her where you hid all my most important files."

"I didn't hide them." She gritted her teeth. "I filed them."

"Only an idiot would file an oil account under *T* for Texas."

She glared at him. "It isn't *T* for Texas, it's *T* for Texas Premium Oil Company!"

"Well, I had the girls refile things so that I could find them. Oil accounts under Oil, tax accounts under Taxes and clients under the last names."

"Not under the company names?"

"It's none of your business anymore," he said smugly. "You quit."

"I did not! You fired me!"

He shrugged his broad shoulders. "We had those potted things moved out into the hall, too."

She gasped. "They'll die! They were by the window so that they could get sunlight! They can't live in the shade."

He frowned. "So that's why they're wilting."

"My poor plants!"

"There's probably still time to save them," he remarked casually. He glanced at her. "You could come back. I'd give you a raise."

"And stand by while darling Betsy practices her Napoleon impression."

"She is not tyrannical!"

"Ask Melody or Margo or Harriet," she shot back. "I dare you! She may be sweetness and light to you, but she's poison to everyone else—especially to her own sex! What she did to poor old Bill Kingsley she's going to do to you, and I'll be the last one crying when you're sleeping in a downtown mission!"

His chest rose and fell roughly with anger. Damn, she was a bossy woman! He had no intention of letting her lead him around, tell him whom to date, what to think!

"Betsy is *my* business," he said harshly. "You're only jealous, because she's beautiful and you aren't!"

He'd never said that before, even if he'd always thought it. Kit was used to people looking through her. She knew she wasn't pretty. But that was hardly why she disliked Betsy.

She didn't fight back. It would have been admitting that he was right. She walked on, alone, her eyes sad and quiet.

Behind her, Logan slapped his fist angrily against his thigh. Damn his tongue! He'd been furious, but those hurtful words had really slipped out unconsciously.

It was pure cussedness, he knew, but he couldn't think of any way to take it back—and still save face. Kit went very quiet when she was hurt. It was the only time she didn't spit and claw. He remembered how she'd responded to him earlier, and how protective she was. She was probably in love with him, and he had more power to hurt her than anyone else on earth.

He watched her with a gnawing hunger. Love wasn't an easy thing to throw away. All the same, he was getting married and Kit was off-limits. He shouldn't have kissed her like that. She'd said that it was unfair to Betsy, and it was.

The problem was that Kit aroused him even more than Betsy did. He couldn't let that situation develop. He had principles, even if he was only just discovering them. He might as well let Kit think he had a low opinion of her looks. Perhaps it would spare her any more hurt at his hands if he could turn her infatuation to dislike. He was going to marry Betsy. All he had to do was keep that in mind, then perhaps he could stop having these inconvenient urges to seduce Kit.

But she didn't hate him. That was all too apparent when he stared at her across the supper table and her eyes fell in blushing confusion to her plate. His heart began to race in his chest as he realized how easily he could disconcert her. His eyes fell to her mouth. He remembered much too vividly how it felt to kiss her, to hold her. He'd tried for the rest of the day to put that sweet interlude out of his mind, but he couldn't. The more he thought about it, the more he wanted it again.

With an angry movement of his hand, he reached for his coffee cup and accidentally hit it, sloshing hot coffee right across the table onto Kit's white blouse.

She gasped, grabbing a napkin to dab at it. While Logan tried to apologize, she glared at him. "Been taking lessons from Betsy, have we?" she asked with cool sarcasm. "No need to worry, it will wash out. Excuse me, please."

She was grateful for the incident in a way, because it gave her the opportunity to escape. Everyone was looking at her. The kids were probably recalling every lurid minute they'd witnessed from the barn, and Emmett was speculative and a little sad. Tansy was hiding amusement. Logan—well, Logan was a puzzle altogether. But Kit had felt like a lab specimen. By the time she changed and went back downstairs, supper would be over and she could escape.

After she stripped off the blouse, she soaked it in the bathroom sink. Her flimsy bra was wet, too, from the coffee. That, she thought resignedly, would have to be washed as well. As she unfastened it, her elbow caught a bottle of shampoo and knocked it across into the bathtub with a heavy thump. The noise concealed a brief knock at the door, and her own movements, as she retrieved and replaced the shampoo, masked the sound of footsteps.

She slid her bra into the sink and was swirling it through the water when a soft sound beside her made her turn her head.

Logan was holding the door open, and he was making no pretense of not looking. His eyes, dark with surprise and fascination, slid over her breasts as if they belonged to him, savoring their firm, tip-tilted contours, enjoying their dusky hard tips and creamy texture.

He hadn't expected this when he'd come after her, albeit reluctantly, to apologize. Seeing her half nude had knocked every sane thought right out of his mind. He was enthralled by the utter beauty of her. He leaned against the door frame and gave his eyes free rein. "I don't think there's any work of art in the world that could compare favorably to a woman's bare breasts," he said quietly, and without offensive intent. "Yours are beautiful, Kit. Absolutely breathtaking."

They must have been, because she actually saw his breathing change. Her eyes fell and she saw something else change, too, before she quickly lifted her eyes again and quickly folded her arms over her breasts.

"I won't embarrass you any more than I have," he

said softly. "It's all right. I only came after you to apologize. Spilling the coffee really was an accident."

"I knew that," she said. Her voice was husky and she felt her body ache with new sensations, new hungers. Her breasts began to swell and tingle and throb. His hands were like plates, she thought as she stared at him. They would cover her breasts completely. They would be warm and a little rough, and her body would tremble because it would feel so sweet to have them on her bare skin.

The feelings frightened her. She shivered, her eyes wide and a little apprehensive as she looked at him.

Logan saw her hunger and reacted to it. He wanted her. God, he wanted her! And if her vulnerability was any indication, she wanted him just as much.

"You've never known a man's eyes or hands before, have you, Kit?" he asked very gently.

She couldn't get a word past her tight throat. She shook her head.

His eyes traced her body with quiet, aching appreciation. He had to touch her. He couldn't help himself; he had to! "There is, as they say, a first time for everything, little one," he said.

He sounded almost solemn. And as she watched, he pushed away from the doorframe, walked slowly inside and closed and locked the door behind him.

Chapter Six

Kit couldn't find the right words to express what she felt. It would have been muddled if she had. She wanted him to look at her; she ached for him to touch her. But it was wrong, because he was only interested in the physical intimacy, and because he was going to marry Betsy. She should scream her head off and order him out of the room, and her brain wanted to, but her body trembled helplessly as he walked toward her. Her eyes told him that he could have anything he wanted.

His own eyes were stormy, not easily read at all. His broad face was without humor or teasing. It was as solemn as if he were in church.

Without a word, he reached and disengaged her hands from her breasts. He moved them away from her body and brought them to her sides. Then he looked at her, with awe and quiet delight while she struggled to breathe normally and failed.

When one big hand came up and gently touched just the tip of her breast, a weak cry escaped her throat.

''This is where you're most sensitive,'' he said, tracing the hard, erect tip. He watched her eyes while he touched it, savoring its heat and hardness with his fingers and then with his palm. "It frightens you to be vulnerable, doesn't it?"

"Yes," she whispered.

"Don't you think I am?" he asked surprisingly. His fingers went to the Western-cut shirt he was wearing and flicked open the pearly snaps.

Her eyes lit up with pure delight as she gazed at the thick dark hair on his broad, bronzed chest.

"Here. Touch me where I'm touching you."

He drew her fingers to his chest, and let her feel the hard tip over his heart.

She traced it and he caught his breath, laughing softly at her surprise.

"When men and women make love, there's no real master," he said, moving so that his big hand could completely cover her soft breast. "Both become vulnerable. Fragile…"

He bent and kissed her parted lips with a tenderness that was indescribable. His hands were gentle on her body, tracing, learning, exploring, until he knew every centimeter of skin above her waist.

Kit, too, was learning. Her hands buried themselves in that thick pelt and tugged at it with a pleasurable rhythm. But all too soon, it was no longer enough, and without conscious intent, she stepped even closer to him and relaxed completely against his aroused body.

"No," he whispered. His big hand dropped to her hip and gently moved her back. His mouth teased hers again. "This isn't the time or the place."

She looked up into his dark, patient eyes. "It makes me ache," she whispered, trying to put her feelings into words.

"Yes. Me, too." He drew his face against hers. Both hands slid over her breasts and gently caressed them. "You're like silk all over, aren't you?" he whispered. His mouth slid down her throat, over her shoulders and her collarbone. It eased down, down, until it suddenly opened on her soft breast. He touched it with his tongue, producing new and volatile hungers that arched Kit's body like a bow.

"Hold on, baby," he whispered roughly.

While she was trying dizzily to comprehend what he meant, his head lifted. For an instant, the coolness of the room was uncomfortable on the moist place he'd left on her skin. Then he burrowed against her, found the hard nipple, took it completely into his mouth and began to suckle it.

For a few seconds, Kit froze. Then she tautened until her muscles felt in danger of shattering. Her body arched and drew in and she pushed up against his mouth as if it were the source of life itself.

Her hands were in his thick, dark hair. They clung, trembling, as the fever he kindled burned high and bright. She shivered, and shivered again, and began to moan. He made a fierce sound and the suction grew harder, more insistent.

Something snapped in Kit's body. She shuddered as a wave of pleasure hit her right in the core of her body and convulsed her into utter satisfaction.

She couldn't stop trembling. Her legs were too weak to hold her up. Logan had lifted his head and was looking at her, but she was too busy trying to get her breath back and stop her heart from shaking her to bits to notice. Gently he pressed her bare breasts against his equally bare chest, starting up new sensations as she felt the sexy abrasiveness of his body hair against her warm skin.

He held her cheek there, and under his muscular chest she could hear the irregular beat of his heart as he smoothed her hair back, and brushed soft kisses against her temple.

She thought that she could never look him in the face again. Her abandon had embarrassed and sickened her.

She tried to pull away, finally, but he wouldn't let her. He tilted her shamed face up to his eyes and searched it quietly. It was somehow more profound because he didn't speak. His fingers touched her face, cherished it, while he examined every facet of her from the chin up as if he'd never looked at her before.

"I'm plain," she said in a brittle tone. "You said so."

"You infuriate me at times. I say a lot of things I don't mean and you know it." His voice deepened. "You know me better than anyone else in the world does, except in one way. In the ultimate way."

Her cheeks burned with heat.

"I satisfied you, didn't I?" he asked, his voice soft and intimate. Her eyes fell and she couldn't speak. "Yes, I thought so. You're incredibly naive, Kit. You have no real comprehension of what sex is all about. Perhaps now you understand a little better how powerful a force attraction can be." He put a fist under her chin and tilted up her rebellious face. "I could have you right here, standing up," he said harshly. "And after the first five seconds, you'd be tearing the clothes away from our bodies for me. That's how much you want me."

"That's cruel," she choked.

"That's the truth." His hands framed her face. He

bent and kissed her forcefully, roughly, and jerked his mouth away. "You'd walk to hell for me if I asked you to."

She stiffened in his embrace and her face turned deathly pale.

"This is why you left in the first place," he said huskily. "You had to get out because it was killing you to see me with Betsy! You love me!"

The truth of it was in her wide, wounded eyes, blue pools in the white oasis of her face. She looked at him as if he'd put a knife through her.

Until he'd said the words, he hadn't really known. But now he did, and suddenly the past three years fell into place. So much of his life was involved with Kit's. He'd fired her, but he hadn't really wanted her to leave. He'd missed her, ached for her company. Now he ached in another way, in a damned inconvenient way, and he'd just crossed the barrier between friendship and sex. And he'd compounded the error by doing it with a woman who was madly in love with him.

"I never used to be cruel," he said almost to himself. He winced as he searched her face. "Everything I say makes it worse, doesn't it?"

"Would you hand me a towel, please?" she asked dully.

"Of course." He turned away and removed one from the rack to give her. She wrapped it around her like a blanket and stood there, defeated, humiliated, drained.

"If you could make some excuse for me," she said, her voice so low that he had to strain to hear it. "A headache?"

"I can do that."

Her eyes closed, shutting him out. She wished she

could go through the floor. What must he think of her now?

He drew her forehead to his chest and held it there, his expression troubled. "I'm sorry. I had no right to touch you like that."

She bit back tears. She didn't say a word, or yield an inch.

His teeth ground together as silvery waves of pleasure teased his body. Even the smell of her was enough to trigger it. "My God, I want to make love to you, Kit!" He choked.

She wanted it, too, but it was impossible. "You're engaged," she reminded him. "What happened... wasn't right."

He sighed heavily. "Yes, you're obsessed with doing the right thing, aren't you? I used to be, too, until Betsy came along and my glands all exploded. I'd been so busy making money and speculating on ways to make more that I'd all but given up women in the past six months, until Betsy walked in the door." He brushed his lips over her hair. "There you sat, waiting for me to wake up. But I turned the wrong way, didn't I?"

"You can't help loving someone."

She should know. But she was assuming he loved Betsy, and he didn't. He wanted her and the only way he could get her was to get married. Now, he wasn't sure that it actually was what he wanted anymore. He scowled as confused thoughts began to gnaw at him.

"Let me go, Logan," she said, tugging at his hands. "You'd better leave now."

He stared at her with undisguised longing. "If we were anywhere else, I'd ask you to come to bed with me. I could protect you, Kit. There'd be no risk at all."

She stared back, wavering. But there was Betsy, and

sleeping with a man she wasn't married to was wrong. No. She couldn't do that. Her eyes fell.

"Even if that kind of thing is right for the whole rest of the world, it isn't right for me. I...I'm not made for one-night stands."

He watched her while he snapped his shirt buttons back up, his face taut and somber. "I don't think one night would be enough," he said. "You're starved for me, Kit. Not just hungry. Starved."

"I am not!" she said miserably, lifting wild blue eyes to his.

"If you're not," he replied quietly, "then explain to me how I managed to fulfill you just by putting my mouth to your breast. Or do you think it's a common occurrence for women?"

She felt her face go even whiter at the charge. "If you're implying that I'm wanton...!"

"Oh, yes, you're wanton," he said huskily. "Sexy as hell and heaven to kiss. I'd give my right arm to go all the way with you."

In that moment he looked as if he actually meant it. His posture was as intense as the way he was looking at her.

"You're engaged," she said sadly.

"Yes."

She felt cold. "I'm sure that...that Betsy attracts you just as much. And probably any experienced man could have made me feel the same as you just did."

"I wouldn't bet on it."

"Maybe I should ask Emmett..."

"I'll break your neck if I catch you so much as looking at Emmett!" he burst out, but returned to normal in a flash, his usual domineering, impatient, outrageous self.

"How interesting," she said calmly.

"You little fool, he's out of your league," he persisted, hating the very thought of her with his cousin.

"He wants to marry me. He said so."

Logan's lips compressed. He glared at her. "He can't have you."

She felt intimidated by the look he was giving her. He was bristling with bad temper, she thought, and felt an involuntary surge of compassion for him. He wasn't a bad man. He loved Betsy, that was all. Probably he was missing her, and Kit had been a stand-in. She felt sad, knowing that.

"Logan, you have your own life," she said gently. "Your own priorities. However I feel, and you don't really know," she emphasized, "Betsy should be your main concern right now."

His eyes narrowed in anger. "I can manage my own private life, thank you."

"Good. Why don't you go and do it?"

"I might as well," he said irritably. He gave her one long, lingering look, and found that he had to force his legs to move. She'd been so sweet in his arms. But she was right. He had Betsy to think about. Touching Kit had been in no way honorable, even if it had been heaven.

He finally started toward the door. He didn't say another word. He unlocked the door and didn't even bother to close it on his way out.

Much later, when Kit was in bed, Tansy came to check on her.

"Logan's outside howling at the moon," Tansy said. "He's utterly demolished half a glass of good Scotch whiskey. Your doing, I presume?"

"I, uh, we had a slight misunderstanding. He seems to feel that he can be engaged to Betsy and still make a grab for me if he feels like it," she said through her teeth, without elaborating on her own part in her downfall.

Tansy took one of Kit's hands gently in hers. "Let me tell you something you may not realize. In three years, you've been all Logan ever talked about when he came to see me. It was always Kit said this, Kit did that. You've been his world all that time."

"Then why is he going to marry Betsy?"

Tansy let go of her hand and shrugged. "Who can fathom the mind of a man?" she asked. "I think perhaps he hasn't realized yet how much a part of him you are. Sometimes it takes a drastic change to make a man look a different way at something. I don't believe he's ever really seen you, Kit. How's that for irony?"

He'd seen her in ways she couldn't tell his mother, too. She didn't dare bare her soul that far. "If he marries that woman, he'll never recover," Kit said sadly. "But he won't listen. He just won't listen!"

"He's not going to admit that he made that kind of mistake, I'm afraid," Tansy said. "Logan never would admit to being in the wrong. Too, perhaps he resents having you try to nurture him. He likes to think that he's doing the nurturing. But Betsy is a bad woman, Kit," she added quietly. "A bad egg. I know the danger Logan is in. I just don't know what to do about it, short of having the kids kidnap Betsy." She frowned thoughtfully. "I wonder if I could get Emmett to bribe them...."

Kit laughed reluctantly at the thought of Betsy tied to a stake. "It's an idea."

"Kit, please don't give up on him," Tansy pleaded.

"Chris and I are the love 'em and leave 'em type. But Logan is different. He's deep and when he loves, it's with everything he has, everything he is. A man like that who loves the wrong woman paves the way to his own destruction."

"Yes, I know," she said. "But if he loves her..."

"If he loved her, he wouldn't have been shut up in a bathroom with you for several minutes," Tansy said with a wicked grin.

"How...?"

"Those kids, how else?" Tansy sighed. "They were up here trying to take the doorknob off with a screwdriver when Emmett caught them. Don't worry." She chuckled at Kit's horror. "The walls are two inches thick, nothing gets past them. But if they'd managed to get the doorknob off, things would have gotten a bit interesting..."

Kit buried her face in her hands. "Oh, dear," she whispered, thinking how embarrassing it would have been, even though nothing terribly indiscreet had happened.

"Don't be like this, sweetheart," Tansy said gently. "My goodness, you do take life so seriously. How do you expect to live if you can't bend the rules occasionally? It isn't as if you're a promiscuous person who thrives on flaunting herself. You're a nice, decent woman, and I do wish it was you instead of Betsy that I was going to have for a daughter-in-law."

"Nothing really terrible went on in there," she began.

"So what if it had? Since when have you been perfect?" Tansy smiled. "My dear, you have a very rigid and rather unflattering view of God if you think He's as narrow-minded and petty as most human beings are.

Give Him credit for knowing all about you, not just what shows.''

"I thought you didn't go to church," Kit said, amazed.

"I don't. There are too many denominations fighting each other, when they should be trying to please God. Fellowship is nice, but I don't think just going to church alone will get a mean person into heaven."

"Maybe not," Kit said. "But without some kind of rules, what would we have?"

"What we've got," Tansy told her. "The most confused generation of kids who ever lived on the planet. There are no rules, no values, no heroes. Have you ever studied ancient civilizations, Kit?"

"Not really."

"The first sign of a declining civilization is a decline in the arts. And I think we have a very definite decline in culture and art. It's been replaced by video games and plastic toys and television and VCRs."

"I'm glad the kids don't have a video camera," Kit said with faint humor as she began to relax a little.

Tansy chuckled. "Remind me to give them one for Christmas."

"Poor Emmett! He'll never get a bride then!"

"Are you feeling better?" Tansy asked. "A little less tormented?"

"Yes. You're nice medicine."

"I've never been called that. Well, off to bed. We go back to Houston in the morning." Her eyes twinkled at Kit. "After that, who knows?"

"Tansy, you won't vanish again!"

"Dear girl, if I stay in one place very long, I'll die there. At my age, one must keep moving or freeze up. If old age catches me, it'll have to outrun me." She got up and went to the door. "I'd lock this," she said. "The kids don't have a VCR, but they do have a Polaroid camera…"

Kit leaped out of bed without an argument. She could imagine the kind of photographs she might appear in if she left that door unlocked, even though she didn't sleep naked.

At breakfast the next morning, the kids were gathered around and snickering faintly as they looked from a hung over, very quiet Logan to a shy Kit.

"I hid the screwdrivers, Kit, don't worry," Emmett said with a wicked glance toward her and then Logan. "You're safe this morning. All the same, I wouldn't lock myself in any more bathrooms with Logan around here, if I were you. They've got this Polaroid camera and a saw…"

"What screwdriver?" Logan asked with restrained shock.

"The one they were using to take the doorknob off Kit's bathroom door," Emmett said smoothly.

Logan put down his fork. "My God!" he exclaimed, staring at the children.

"He never tells us nothing!" Guy muttered, and when he scowled at Emmett, it was like looking at a miniature of the man.

"Emmett, have you ever considered giving up rodeo for a season and raising your kids?" Logan asked curtly.

Emmett glared at him. "They're my kids and it's my life. I don't come up to Houston and try to tell you how to live, do I?"

"Somebody ought to," Tansy remarked pleasantly, "before he ruins it."

"Thank you very much," Logan growled at his mother.

She smiled vacantly. "Why, you're welcome, dear. Emmett, wouldn't you like to bring the kids and come and visit Logan? I'd *love* for you to meet his new fiancée...!"

"I don't have spare bedrooms," Logan said abruptly.

"You do so," Tansy argued. "Three of them."

"They're being remodeled."

"They are not," she argued.

"They will be by tomorrow," he said under his breath. "Besides, Emmett's riding in a rodeo out in Montana."

"In the snow?" Tansy exclaimed.

"Arizona," Emmett corrected lazily. He glared at Logan. "Some cousin you are. I offer you the hospitality of my home and loving family, and you don't even want us to stay a night with you."

"Loving family?" Logan's eyes widened. He looked at the kids. "Them?"

"We're loving," Amy said, glaring at him.

"All of us," Guy seconded, scowling.

"You better not say we ain't loving, mister," Polk added.

"That's my kids," Emmett said smugly. "Listen up, you kids, how would you like Kit there for a mother?"

"She ain't pretty," Guy said.

"She's nice, though," Amy interrupted. "And she doesn't have to fix her face every two minutes and paint her fingernails like that lady in the glittery dress that you brought home that night you thought we were asleep," she reminded Emmett.

Polk frowned as Emmett's dark face flushed. "He

sure took her away in a hurry when he saw us, didn't he?''

"Will you stop?" Emmett asked him.

Kit chuckled to herself. She did like Emmett. But not enough to marry him.

"You could marry that glittery lady," Polk suggested. "She said she sure did like your money. She didn't like us much, though. What was it she called us, Guy?''

"Guy, shut up!" Emmett raged.

"You were so married to our mama, weren't you, Emmett?" Amy asked. She called her father by his given name, a habit he'd reluctantly gotten used to because he couldn't seem to break it.

"Yes, I was, Amy," he said.

"So that means we're not—''

"*Amy,* I'm warning you!" Emmett threatened.

"Oh, very well, Emmett," she said primly, dabbing at her mouth. "May we be excused?''

"Why? Are you in a rush to hijack a truck or something?''

They glared at him. "We're helping Mrs. Gibbs bake a cake. She's the foreman's wife," Amy explained to everyone. "She said we could.''

"God help Mrs. Gibbs.''

"Some father you are," Logan muttered as the kids escaped out the backdoor, heading for the foreman's house.

"Mrs. Gibbs has nerves of steel and they listen to her," he argued.

"They ought to be listening to you," Logan persisted.

"Talk about soreheads!" Emmett said, making a clicking sound. "Frustration sure doesn't sit well with you, does it? And you ought to be ashamed of yourself, making advances to Kit when you're engaged to that Betsy woman. Something I would *never* do if you got engaged to me, Kit, my dear,'' he added silkily.

"Oh, for God's sake!'' Logan roared. He threw down his napkin and walked out of the room.

His back was growing very familiar to Kit, who saw more of it lately than she ever had.

"I really can't marry you, Emmett. I'm sorry,'' Kit said.

"I'm persistent,'' he remarked with a lazy smile. "Don't say I didn't warn you.''

She smiled, but it wasn't an encouraging smile.

Two hours later, they said their goodbyes and Logan drove Kit and Tansy to the airport. Their seats were widely separated, and for that small mercy Kit was glad. It was good to go home and get away from the enforced intimacy with Logan. He barely spoke to her now, and she was equally glad to avoid him. After the explosive interlude they'd shared, she didn't know how to behave with him. All she knew was that she didn't want to end up in his bed because he was frustrated and she was weak. Going back to Houston and keeping out of his way seemed the only sensible thing to do.

Logan was thinking the same thing. He'd just begun to realize what a horrible mistake he'd be making if he married Betsy. But admitting it was next to impossible. It would kill his pride.

On the other hand, Kit's well-meant interference had only made him dig his heels in deeper. All the way back home he did his best to convince himself that Kit was wrong and he was right about Betsy. But the doubts were beginning to outweigh the certainties in the relationship. He was at a crossroads and he honestly didn't know which way to turn.

Chapter Seven

Dane was fascinated by the report Kit gave him when she got back to the office.

"You're kidding," he remarked when she finished. "Nobody has children like that in real life. Are you sure you haven't been reading fiction?"

"Why don't you go out there and see for yourself?" she suggested dryly.

"No, thanks!" He shook his head. "What a family. Tansy went home with Logan, did she?"

"Yes, but nobody knows how long she'll stay. When Betsy walks through the door, I expect Tansy will vanish again," she said dejectedly.

"That means more business for us." Dane chuckled.

"I suppose."

Dane gave Kit a new case to work on, tracking down a bail jumper this time. But the man wasn't a dangerous criminal; he was a forger who'd made "bush bond."

With a little help from the skip-tracing department, specifically from Doris, Kit latched on to an address downtown in the red-light district. There was only one way to get close to that address, and she didn't find it at all amusing.

The sacrifices I make for this job, she thought as she adjusted her skin-tight, green sequined miniskirt and black halter with matching black silk hose. She over-applied her makeup and saturated herself in sweet perfume. Then she drove to the address and started to walk, rather self-consciously, along the crowded sidewalk between two adult bookstores.

"Hey, who are you? This is my spot! What do you think you're doing, girl?"

The questioner was the real thing, with bleached blond hair and good skin, of which most was on blatant display.

Kit glanced around nervously and moved closer to the blonde. "I'm a detective," she whispered. "I'm trying to find a bail jumper. Please don't give me away."

The woman looked impressed. She pursed her lips and nodded. "A detective? For real?"

"I'm afraid so." She eyed the other woman curiously. "I saw *Pretty Woman.* You aren't…?"

Delighted laughter met her query. "No. But I wouldn't mind meeting somebody with an expensive car who brought me flowers. Now in this job, that's *real* fantasy!" She and Kit both laughed.

"Who's this dude you're looking for?" the woman asked, glancing around. "Maybe I know him."

"This is a copy of his driver's license photo," Kit said, producing it. She didn't mention how she'd managed to obtain it, and the hooker didn't ask.

"I've seen him!" the woman said. "He doesn't have much time for us, but he passes here every night on his way to that adults only video place at the corner. Matter of fact, he'll be along about nine, if he follows his usual routine.''

Kit glanced at her watch. ''Mind if I stick with you?'' she asked, nervous now that she was attracting attention from men and pimps alike.

The hooker chuckled. ''This isn't your scene at all, is it, honey?''

''Well, no.''

The other woman smiled at Kit—really smiled at her. ''You haven't looked down your nose at me once.''

''I don't think any of us are so good that we can look down on anybody else,'' Kit replied with a shrug, then shivered a little in the cold. ''How do you keep warm?''

''The street people have fires in barrels down the alley. We usually take a break and go stand down there. They don't mind us. Society's cast-offs stick together.''

Kit felt a surge of sympathy for the woman, who looked to be in her thirties. But she had a worn-out look in her eyes. ''Don't you worry about, well, about diseases?''

''All the time,'' she was told. ''I had a friend who died of AIDS last month.'' She shook her head. ''We're all careful now. *Real* careful.''

''Why do you do this?''

''It's all I know how to do. Even this was better than home, when I was thirteen,'' she said with a haunted look in her eyes. She shivered a little, and suddenly looked so fragile and pathetic that Kit could have cried for her. ''Well, would you look at that hunk?'' she said suddenly, nodding toward an approaching crowd. ''He sure isn't down here for a pickup, I'll bet.''

Kit followed her gaze and caught her breath. No, she thought. No, I can't be seeing this.

But she was. It was Logan, breathing fire in a figurative sense. And not only did he see Kit, but he obviously knew she was here.

"Doris told me," he said without preamble. "Dane must be out of his mind to let you come down here alone at night! What's the matter with you, are you daft? Don't you know what kind of people these are?"

Kit was offended. She glared at him. "Yes, I know," she said. "But do you? Don't insult my friend!"

The hooker looked as shocked as Logan did.

"You could be out here if circumstances hadn't made you rich," Kit said. "Anyone could. Look around you! These people didn't wake up one morning and decide to wander around the back streets of the city!"

Logan hesitated. He glanced at the blonde, who was gaping at Kit.

"You know her, I guess?" the hooker asked.

"She works for me. At least, she did before I fired her."

"If you fired her, you're pretty stupid for a handsome, rich man," the hooker said, but she smiled. So did Logan.

"Hey, look, there he is!" the hooker said urgently, pointing to a small, dark man in a camouflage jacket.

"Glory be!"

Kit was running before the other two could say a word. When the man realized that he was being chased, he took off. Kit followed him. The high heels were hampering her. She stopped just long enough to strip them off and kept running, panting for breath as the small man dodged cars to cross the street, with Kit in hot pursuit.

"Stop!" she yelled after him.

He looked over his shoulder when she yelled and lost his footing. He went down with muttered curses, tripping other people on the way.

Kit ran to him, dragging out the handcuffs she'd brought from the office. She flipped him over, linked a cuff over one wrist, crossed it over the other and cuffed that one, too.

She laughed, her senses heightened with success, still panting for breath as she dragged the small man upright and held on to him. Her feet were freezing.

"You're a damned cop, I guess?" the man grumbled.

"No. I'm a private detective," she told him.

He made a sound and glared at her.

Logan and the hooker caught up, both laughing when they saw Kit with her prize in cuffs.

"Hey, a cop couldn't have done any better!" she said enthusiastically. "That looks like fun!"

"It is." Kit grinned. She held out her hand and the hooker shook it. "Thanks."

The hooker left and Logan propelled Kit to his car, one big hand wrapped completely around her arm while she held on to her bail jumper.

"Who's got who in custody here?" the little man asked.

"I've got you and he's got me, I guess." Kit sighed. "Just my luck. I can't even go on a stakeout on main street without ex-bosses popping out like measles."

"You mean you used to work for him?" the little man asked. "What a lucky escape you had!"

Logan scowled over his shoulder at the bail jumper. "Watch your mouth."

"Oh, aren't we in a nasty temper tonight," the prisoner mumbled.

"There's a policeman," Logan remarked, having spotted one.

"I can't…!" Kit protested, but it was already too late. Logan dragged her, and thereby the bail jumper, off to confront the officer.

"This man is a bail jumper," Logan said, propelling Kit and the man forward. "Can you tell me where to take him?"

"You aren't taking him anywhere…he belongs to me!" Kit raged.

"I do not," the bail jumper said indignantly. "You attacked me! Officer, this hooker attacked me and put me in handcuffs! I demand that you arrest her for assault!"

"I am not a hooker, I'm a private detective! Look, I have my ID right here…uh-oh."

She didn't. It was on her dresser at home, where she'd left it. She looked at the policeman, whose eyes were narrowing as he considered action. She looked at the bail jumper, who had a smug I'll-get-you-now look on his face. She glanced at Logan, who was obviously not concerned with trying to save her.

"Nice night," she remarked. "Well, toodle-ooh!"

She turned and took off, bare feet and all. There was a whistle and several shouts, but she kept running.

"Quick, in here!"

She followed the voice, and the hooker that she'd met earlier jerked her into the shadows of the alley.

"Now I'm in real trouble," Kit wailed. "I'm on the lam!"

"No. You're hiding from the heat."

"Oh. Sorry."

"Listen, go around the block and down the next alley, but go careful, you hear? I'll scout out the hunk and tell him where to find you."

"Thanks!" Kit said fervently.

"No problem. Run!"

She waved and darted through the alley.

Ten minutes later, Logan picked her up at the corner, the policeman having long since given up and taken the handcuffed man to headquarters to have his story checked. That wouldn't work to the agency's advantage, because Kit couldn't now claim that she'd collared him. But the client would have his money back just the same, and maybe Dane wouldn't fire her.

"Of all the harebrained, stupid stunts!" Logan shouted the minute he had her in the car. He turned the heater on full blast and pulled out into traffic. "You'll probably have pneumonia!"

"Go ahead, rub it in!" she muttered.

"I intend to, good and hard," he returned. "Do you have any idea how much trouble you could have found out there?"

"Of course I do, but it goes with the job," she replied. "Besides, I'm tough." She spoiled the pose with a loud sneeze, and wrapped her arms close around her shivering body.

"Tough, my elbow," he said heavily. "You're turning my hair gray."

"I'm not your problem," she reminded him, exasperated. "For heaven's sake, I don't even work for you!"

"My mother considers that you do. So does my brother."

"They don't count."

"They all blame me because you left."

"And you don't think they should!" she exclaimed.

He made an uncomfortable sound. "I must have been out of my mind to fire you," he said under his breath. "Nothing's been the same since. I can't find files, I can't get letters out the same day I dictate them, half my clients have quit because they think I'm running a brothel…"

"A what?"

"The one who can spell tried to seduce the last three men who came into the office," he said icily. "I fired her!"

"Good for you. Who's doing the spelling now?"

"Cousin Melody. The smoker with acute bronchitis is now in the hospital. She says she won't come back."

"I don't blame her."

He glared in her direction. "You can keep quiet. One way or another, you've cost me plenty since you left."

"Since *you* fired me," she corrected.

He dragged a big hand through his thick hair. "Damn it, Kit, you know I never meant you to take it seriously! You never did before! My God, I fired you every other week, but you never actually left!"

"That was before Betsy came along and made vanilla pudding out of your brain," she replied stiffly.

"She didn't do anything except make me ache."

"While trying to pick your pockets," she said through her teeth.

"She isn't like that!" he raged, despite the fact that he was seeing Betsy with new eyes since he'd come back from San Antonio. In fact, he was discovering for himself that Kit was right and Betsy was exactly "like that." He wasn't admitting it, though. No, sir!

"The devil she isn't like that!" Kit shot back, turning in the seat. Her dark hair was damp and her mascara had run. Her hose had runs in them. She looked like a third-rate clown.

Logan couldn't help himself. He chuckled.

"That's right, laugh at me," she blustered. "You always found something about me to make fun of. If it wasn't my cat, it was a man I dated or something I wore…!"

"What ever became of the cat?"

She shrugged. "He moved to Detroit with a little girl down the street."

"Well, I'll be."

"He wasn't much of a cat, anyway. He ate half my potted plants before he left."

He shook his head, still laughing. "You have the most unorthodox life-style of anyone I know."

"You don't know me, Mr. Deverell," she told him flatly. "You never did. I was just a dictating machine with legs."

He glanced at her with a raised eyebrow. "Very nice legs, at that. You never bothered to display them at the office."

"God forbid that I should be accused of coming on to you," she taunted.

"That would have been the joke of the century." He turned the corner and eased the car into the underground garage at his apartment building. "I always did wonder why you were so nervous of being alone with me."

"You were forever yelling at me," she mumbled. "I wanted to have the door open so I could get a head start running if I had to. And why are we here? I'm not going up to your apartment with you!''

"You are," he replied grimly. "I'm not taking you home looking like *that!*"

"I left home looking like *this!*"

"I hope nobody saw you," he said curtly. "Or you may not have a home to go to."

"I went out the back," she said involuntarily. "I don't have anything else to wear...."

"I'll loan you a shirt and some jeans."

"Yours?" Her eyes imitated pie pans. "Great! Have you got some string so we can tie up the legs...?"

"Chris's would probably fit you. You're about the same build," he said with exaggerated patience. "I keep a change of clothing for him at the apartment in case he needs it."

"Why do you have an apartment and a house?" she asked, and then went scarlet at the look he gave her.

"Don't ask embarrassing questions if you don't want embarrassing answers."

"You can count on me, sir."

He helped her out of the car and into the elevator, careful to keep her out of sight beside his formidable bulk. Fortunately the hall was empty when they got to his floor. He whisked her into the apartment with an audible sigh of relief.

"Now just stay there while I—"

"Logan, are you finally home?" Betsy called half angrily from the bedroom. "I've been waiting for hours! Why didn't you call— Oh!"

Betsy was suddenly standing in the doorway of the bedroom, in a pink negligee. At the sight of Kit, her eyes bulged.

"You!"

"Hello, again, Betsy dear," Kit said prettily. "Logan brought me home for companionship, but since you're here…"

"Logan, how could you?" Betsy wailed, bursting into mock tears. "How could you?"

Logan cursed roundly under his breath. He threw off his overcoat. "Get into the shower while I fetch those clothes for you!" he told Kit. "In there, the guest room!"

He shoved her through the door and closed it with a loud thud. Afterward, there were loud voices and louder voices and thuds and silence and then a vicious slam. Kit got under the shower and used the fragrant soap to clean off her horrid perfume and makeup.

When she was scrubbed clean, she lifted a thick white robe from the back of the door and slipped into it. It must be Logan's, she thought. It smelled of the same sexy cologne he favored. She drew it closer while she wondered if she dared open the door. Betsy was probably still out there, waiting to cause an even worse scene.

Logan would want to get rid of Kit as soon as possible, she was sure, with Betsy waiting for him in all her glory. Kit could have screamed and wept, but it wouldn't help the situation. Betsy was in possession, and they all knew it. Logan might rescue Kit for old time's sake, but he wasn't emotionally involved. She wasn't stupid enough to mistake concern for love.

She opened the door and peeked around it. Logan was sitting sprawled in an easy chair, his jacket and tie off, his shirt open at the neck. He was sipping a glass of something amber colored. He looked broody and out of sorts. He was alone.

He spotted her and scowled. "Well, come on out of

there," he said icily. "You've sure blown my evening to hell."

"You could go after her," Kit said miserably, her big blue eyes accusing. "I'm sure she'll get over it when you explain what happened."

"Explain?" he asked with a careless smile. The expression in his eyes wasn't careless; they were blazing. "Like hell I will! If she wants to take this at face value, let her. I don't give a damn."

"But, you must!" she protested. "You're engaged!"

He opened his palm and held out a huge diamond engagement ring. "Not anymore. Not since five minutes ago, thanks to you," he added with barely contained fury. He tossed the ring onto the coffee table.

She tugged the robe closer with a long sigh. "It's not my fault," she said miserably. "I never asked you to come storming into my stakeout."

He glared at her. "You think I could have left you there with a clear conscience?" he asked, exasperated.

"Yes, you could!" she muttered. She dug her hands deep into the pockets, aware of her bare feet and even barer body under the robe, her hair damp and tousled from the bath. "You don't have to wander the city at night looking for me. I'm not your responsibility."

He swirled the amber liquid in the glass, his big, dark eyes on her face. "So you keep telling me."

He looked older. There were deep lines in his broad face, and as she watched him sip whatever he was drinking, it occurred to her that she'd never seen him this way. Even when she'd traveled with him, there had always been a very formal atmosphere. He'd never taken off his jacket and tie in her presence, or done anything more than roll up his shirtsleeves. She'd learned more about him physically in San Antonio than she'd learned in three years.

In the intimacy of his apartment, she was more aware of him than ever. If only he loved her, wanted her, needed her, she thought miserably. If only there wasn't Betsy. As he'd said in San Antonio, she'd waited for years for him to notice her, and when he did, he'd turned the wrong way—toward Betsy, who was searching for a means of support, not a man.

"You look as worn as I feel right now, Kit," he said quietly, watching her as closely as she'd been watching him. "I don't suppose your evening was any bed of roses, either, even before I came along."

"I didn't realize what it would be like on the streets," she confessed, moving to sit on the sofa, poised on the very edge with her bare toes curling into the carpet. Her senses were all aroused, but still she felt at home with him, as if she belonged here. That was silly, and she pinched herself mentally. "Life is pretty terrible for some people, isn't it, Logan?"

"I suppose it is. You shouldn't have gone that far looking for your bail jumper."

"I know that, now," she admitted with a rueful smile. "I was gung ho on doing my job. Dane will probably fire me when he finds out what I did."

"Not Dane. He'll promote you for going above and beyond the line of duty." Logan laughed mirthlessly, his eyes slow and quiet on her face. "You've always given more than anyone asked of you. You used to stay late at the office night after night when I needed you, and I never heard you complain. I wasn't very kind to you, was I, Kit?"

"Why ruin your image on my account?" she mused dryly.

He chuckled. "I suppose it would have. I enjoyed our disagreements. I miss them."

"Hire someone who talks back."

"I tried. They run into the ladies' rest room when I start yelling." His big shoulders lifted and fell. "I suppose I'll have to learn to be polite."

"What a comedown."

"You don't know the half of it, honey."

He wasn't a man who used endearments, but that one sounded as if he meant it. In his deep, smooth voice it was seductive.

"I could go and talk to Betsy for you," she offered after a minute, because she did feel guilty.

His eyebrow jerked. "What would you tell her?" he asked curiously.

"The truth," she replied. "It seems to work best."

"After that blatant statement that you came back here to entertain me?"

"Well, I'm sorry about that," she said slowly. "It shocked me to find her standing practically naked in your bedroom."

"You might not believe it, but it shocked me, too. Since I came back from San Antonio, Betsy has been pushing me toward a quick ceremony, but I was resisting." He sipped his drink. "I think tonight was a dead-end play. She was going to make sure of me."

Kit flushed and looked away.

"Wouldn't you, if you were engaged to someone?" he persisted. "The risk of pregnancy would certainly be an incentive to an honorable man."

"You said you never took that kind of risk."

"Not normally. But any man can be pushed off balance by a seductive woman and driven crazy. Too crazy to give a damn about precautions."

She picked at the robe and didn't look up. "You don't seem the type to lose your head, Logan."

He smiled secretively and his dark eyes wandered all over her as though they were caressing hands. "Don't I, Kit? Well, why don't you take off that robe and I'll prove to you that I am."

Chapter Eight

Kit stared at him in disbelief. Perhaps she'd heard him wrong.

He didn't look as if he was kidding, though. His eyes were steady and very dark. Deliberately he put his glass on the table beside his elbow. He leaned back and slowly one big hand went to the buttons of his shirt and flicked them open. Under the shirt, his broad chest was darkly tanned and thick with curling black hair. He pulled the shirt out of his slacks and unfastened his belt. He tossed it aside, too, and then kicked off his shoes.

Still watching Kit, he stretched out full-length on the sofa with a cushion under his head.

"Come here," he said quietly.

There were, of course, fifty perfectly good reasons to ignore him and lock herself in the bedroom. She went crazy trying to focus on any one of them. But with him lying there, sensuous and warm and welcoming, nothing in her brain seemed to work.

"Logan, I can't," she said hesitantly.

He didn't speak. He simply held out an arm.

She loved him. In the final analysis, there was nothing else that mattered, she told herself. Not the fact that he was on the rebound from Betsy, or that he didn't love her.

She got up and went to him. But when she sat down, he caught her arm and wouldn't let her any closer.

"The robe," he said, his voice deep and quiet and deadly somber. "Take it off, Kit."

"But, I can't...!"

"If you love me, you damned well can," he replied.

Her nerve gave out. He wanted more than she could give. What had she expected, anyway?

She started to get up, but his hands caught her wrists and held her there, gently but firmly.

"You only want consolation," she said. "I can't be an interlude or a diversion. I'm sorry. I...I want much more than that from a man before I can give myself," she added softly. "I'm not like Betsy."

His hands slid into hers, locking with them. He searched her eyes slowly. "I never had Betsy," he told her, his voice deep and still in the silent room.

She felt her cheeks going hot. "You were engaged to her."

"All the same, until tonight, she was intent on a legal ceremony beforehand."

"I see."

"I don't think you do. I know I didn't, until she perched there in her negligee and I realized for the first time that she was bargaining, not being moral." His eyes narrowed. "You wouldn't bargain with me, would you, Kit? You'd never use sex as a medium of exchange."

"I wouldn't know how," she said honestly.

"Little Miss Muffet," he murmured, studying her

pixie face. He smiled. "All right, I won't seduce you. Is that what you want?"

She didn't. Her eyes fell to his chest and she wanted to feel her breasts burying themselves in that thicket of hair. Unfortunately he knew enough to realize that.

His big hand went to the knot at her waist and lingered there. He searched her eyes slowly, intently. "Despite all your hang-ups and principles, you want me. I could slide my hand inside this robe and touch your breasts, and you'd lie with me without a protest. I know that, and so do you. But I won't do it. If you sleep with me, you have to have both eyes open and no coercion about it."

"I suppose you know that I want to," she said miserably.

He nodded. "It's pretty hard to miss. What are you afraid of?"

"Everything," she said unhappily. "That you'll think I'm cheap, that I won't be able to live with it, that I'll get pregnant, that everyone will know..."

"I'll use something," he said curtly. "There will be no risk of your getting pregnant. No one will ever know except you and me. And for God's sake, how can I think you're cheap when you're a virgin?"

She lifted her eyes to his and smiled mirthlessly. "Don't men always say these things to make women give in?"

"Of course," he admitted. "Except that it's usually a casual arrangement with no strings attached. That isn't the case with you and me. You're in love with me. I know it. Do you think, under those circumstances, that I could ask you for a casual hour or two in bed to satisfy a passing urge? Do you think my conscience would let me?"

She hadn't expected the question and she couldn't quite answer it. She studied him without speaking while her mind whirled.

"Then...then what do you want?" she asked.

"I want you to love me," he said huskily. "I want to lie in your arms and be loved by you until I'm too exhausted to do anything except sleep."

"Betsy...Betsy loves you."

He shook his head. "No. And you know it. I've never been loved. Not like you'd love me."

"But it would only be one night..."

"Will you marry me, Kit?" he asked.

Her body clenched. The thought was so ecstatic that her face burned with color. "You don't want to marry me!" She laughed nervously. "Not for just one night!"

"It won't be for just one night. I'm thirty-five. You're twenty-five. We know each other much too well, in the important ways, not to get along."

"An hour ago you were engaged to Betsy," she said through her teeth.

"Because you were so damned determined to save me from her that you pushed me right into her web!" he muttered. "My God, don't you know anything about men?"

"I know that they're selfish and manipulative and domineering!" she shot back.

"Who's domineering?"

"What do you mean, who's domi— Oh!"

He jerked her down against him and flipped her onto her back, taking her mouth with one slow, smooth motion. He groaned as he felt her lips part, felt the anger quickly transmuted into passion, and then into pleasure.

Her arms were under his, sliding around him, her hands caressing the hard, warm muscles of his back.

She felt his heartbeat growing quick and erratic against the robe and then, without warning, against her bare breasts. The thick hair that covered him also covered her now, a soft abrasion that made her moan as he drew himself against her.

"Tell me to stop if you like, but do it now," he said over her mouth. "Hurry!"

His hands were on her, and she arched into them. "I can't," she whispered, shaken. "I don't want to! Logan... Please don't make me pregnant...!"

"I won't," he promised unsteadily. "I promise. Kiss me...!"

He drew her completely against him, so that she could feel the swollen contours of his body in passion. His hands threw off her robe and drew her hips into the curve of his body.

"Wait..." His mouth fastened hungrily onto her stomach and while he had her in thrall, he got his own clothing out of the way. When he slid back down against her, there was nothing between them, not even the air.

She wept, because the pleasure was so sweet and slow and terrible that she thought she wouldn't be able to bear it. His mouth on her body was heaven. His hands, touching her, exploring her, were ecstasy.

"The sofa...it isn't big enough for what we're going to do," he said against her mouth.

He moved and moved her, but he shuddered at the silken brush of her body and groaned. "I'll never make it to the bed," he whispered hoarsely.

She felt her back against the carpet and Logan's formidable weight above her. His mouth ground into hers as he slid over her, against her, his warm, hair-roughened thighs parting hers in a sensual movement that was as arousing as his tongue in her mouth.

"Here," he said roughly, pressing something into her hand. "Help me."

He taught her how, the touching intimate and exploratory as he whispered at her ear.

Then his kiss grew suddenly deep and demanding and his hips moved down. She felt him slowly invading her and she stiffened instinctively.

"Does it hurt?" he whispered.

"Not...not really," she whispered back, embarrassed by the question.

"Look at me." He forced her flushed face up and looked down into it as he moved with deliberate sureness. She gasped and clutched at him. The expression on her face aroused him beyond bearing. Submission was there, and need, and sudden understanding of what had been a mystery before.

"I'm going to take you," he said huskily. He moved, stilling her body with a firm hand. "I'm going to take you, Kit. Right now."

As he spoke, he arched down, and she gasped as she felt him completely possessing her.

She couldn't move, or breathe very well. He was heavy, but it was other sensations that she noticed. It was the heat of his skin, the beat of his heart, the pleasure that the rhythm began to build in her body. It was a trembling tension that slowly blocked out every single thought except the need to make it stop, any way she could.

She clutched his broad shoulders and her head thrashed. "Logan..." she whispered. "I can't...bear it, I can't...bear it!" she whimpered feverishly.

He laughed deep in his throat and moved harder.

"Love me," he said, one big hand catching in the hair at her nape as he forced her to look at him. "Love me!"

"I...do!" Her eyes held his, bright with passion and love and spiraling pleasure. "Logan...I love you... more than my life!"

He blurred suddenly in her eyes as the harsh movements created a blinding red oblivion. She heard him speak, but her mind was totally intent on achieving satisfaction. She moved helplessly, her body demanding more than he was giving her, her voice pleading with him, sobbing as she climbed up and up and up.

The roughness of the carpet, the quick breathing, all blurred into a crescendo of movement and sudden throbbing stillness.

She sobbed helplessly as the waves swept over her, her voice mingling with Logan's harsh groans. Shuddering, they clung until the last trembling thread snapped and they spun away together.

He wouldn't let go. That registered as sanity came floating back. Kit opened her eyes and saw the ceiling over Logan's broad, damp shoulder. It wasn't quite steady. His heartbeat was rough against her breasts. His skin was wet and cold where it touched her.

"You made me whole," he said, shaken to his soul. His lips traveled softly over her face, her closed eyelids, her nose, her mouth, her cheeks, her chin. "Oh, God, Kit, you gave me ecstasy!"

"Yes." She smoothed back his damp, unruly hair, her eyes soft and serious as they met the black fever in his. "I love you," she whispered.

"I know. My God, how I know!" He kissed her with warm, slow passion, his body moving sensually above and within her. "It would be sacrilege to do that with another woman now!" he said under his breath.

"Would it, really?"

He lifted his head and smoothed back her soft hair tenderly. "You were with me every step of the way," he said huskily. "Every step! Do you have any idea how rare that is between lovers?"

She flushed and turned her shy face into his throat.

He laughed gently and held her there. "You're my lover," he whispered into her ear. "And I'm yours. After all these long years, we made love, Kit."

"You aren't sorry?" she asked worriedly.

"No. Are you?" he asked, lifting his head to study her.

She probably should have been, but she wasn't. She said so. Her fingers touched his hard mouth and she watched in wonder as he moved and she felt him, still a part of her.

"I know," he whispered at the expression on her face. "It awes me, too." He kissed her again, delighted in the feel of her body, the softness of her hair, the perfume that lay subtle and intoxicating on her throat. He groaned softly as the fever began to burn in him, but even as he felt the need, he denied it.

"No," he whispered on a shaken sigh. "No, we can't."

"Why?" she asked.

He told her, watching her blush. "And besides that," he murmured dryly, "I think you're probably going to be a bit uncomfortable for the next day or so. This takes getting used to."

"Oh."

He lifted away from her, poising there long enough

to make her blush before he chuckled and rolled over onto his back. "Now you know," he murmured.

She sat up, wincing a little at the unfamiliar discomfort. He watched her and smiled with pure masculine triumph.

"I'll strut for a week," he murmured as she pulled the robe from the couch and wrapped up in it. "I could never have imagined the very prim and proper Miss Morris clawing my back raw and begging for satisfaction."

"You can stop that," she said, hitting his chest. "Conceit doesn't become you."

"Yes, it does." He sat up and pulled her across his chest to kiss her roughly. "I've got you and I'm keeping you," he said, his dark eyes possessive and unblinking. "You'll never get away. First thing tomorrow, we're getting a license. As soon after that as possible, you're marrying me."

Her eyes mirrored her shock. "But...!"

"But nothing. Marriage is an honorable institution. I do have my reputation, and yours, to consider. Satisfying a passing urge is one thing, but what you and I just did, Miss Morris, has no relation whatsoever to fleeting lust. That, by God, was lovemaking. The real thing."

"I won't get pregnant." She faltered. "You took care of that."

"Kit, that isn't why I want to marry you."

"Oh. It's because you...deflowered me?"

"*Deflowered?*" he teased.

She glared at him. "What would you call it?"

"Delicious," he murmured against her mouth. "Sweet heaven. A taste of immortality. I could go on, but it would take weeks until I ran out of adjectives."

"Logan," she protested weakly.

"Are you hungry?" he asked softly. "I can cook bacon and eggs."

"I can cook, too," she replied.

He smiled at her, his eyes so warm and affectionate that she hardly recognized them. "We'll manage together. Then we'll sleep, in my bed, in each other's arms."

Her body tingled at the thought. Heaven seemed very close.

He got up and pulled on his slacks, holding out a hand to help her up. "Can you make cinnamon toast?" he asked, bending to kiss her gently.

"Yes."

He smiled. "Good. Come on. We'll share the work."

Breakfast at almost midnight wasn't at all bad, Kit thought. They washed up together, and that was nice, too. But the best part was lying with her head pillowed on Logan's broad chest in the dark bedroom, with the sounds of traffic outside. She curled into his body with absolute trust, so much in love, so happy, that she wanted to die if tomorrow meant giving it up.

He meant it about marriage. She didn't even question his motives. She loved him too much to say no. He wanted her, and there was something...something... in his expression when he looked at her. If it was only physical infatuation, it would wear off. She'd face that eventuality if she had to. But the look in his eyes gave her hope that it might be something more than an affair. She had that thought to cling to as she closed her eyes and went to sleep with the sound of Logan's breathing under her ear.

The next morning, she was aware of movement and

sound as her eyes opened. She frowned, disoriented as she looked around. This wasn't her apartment, and it certainly wasn't her robe that she was sleeping in.

She sat up and looked around the room, and the night before came back to her in a flash of vivid impressions that made her face go rosy. She'd made love with Logan and slept in his arms all night. Now it was morning and time to pay the piper.

She got up and dressed in Chris's things that Logan had thoughtfully left on the chair, along with her flimsy, and by now quite dry, underthings.

"Are you ever going to get out of the bed and have breakfast?" came a disgruntled voice from beyond the door. "The eggs are congealing, for God's sake!"

"You're so impatient!" she muttered, throwing open the door.

He leaned against the jamb, tall and muscular and devastating in just slacks and a T-shirt with Atlanta Braves plastered across the front. "I wasn't last night," he reminded her wickedly.

She couldn't argue with that. She laughed up at him.

"You look very nice in Chris's jeans," he remarked, studying her trim figure. "Perhaps we could raid his closet while he's on vacation and see how you fill out the rest of his clothes."

"He probably looks much better in them than I do," she said.

"Not from where I'm standing. Come here." He lifted her by the waist onto a level with his big, dark eyes. "Kiss me, sweetheart," he whispered.

Tingling from the endearment, she leaned forward and put her soft mouth against his wide, hard one. "Good morning," she whispered back.

"Good morning yourself." He savored her lips,

aglow with the wonder of having her this way, with the silky soft memory of the night before making him weak all over. He hadn't slept a long time. He'd woken long before first light and lay looking at Kit with wonder. So many years they'd been together, and he'd never seen how lovely she was. He really had been blind.

He kissed her slowly, barely brushing her mouth with his lips. "Come on and I'll feed you," he said. He put her back on her feet with flattering reluctance. "That isn't what I really wanted to do, of course. I want to throw you on the floor and ravish you, but it's much too early for that sort of thing. Besides, I'm too much a gentleman to seduce you on the floor of my apartment."

Remembering the carpet burns on her back she was hesitant to agree with him. He chuckled at her expression.

"Next time we'll use the bed," he murmured ruefully. "I couldn't hold out long enough to get into the bedroom."

"You said you weren't impatient?"

"I seem to have a low threshold with you, don't I?" He brushed back her short hair. "Are you sore, Kit?" he asked matter-of-factly.

"A little," she said nervously.

"There's nothing to be embarrassed about," he said gently. "I shouldn't have been quite so rough. I wanted you very badly."

"I wanted you, too."

"What a scarlet blush," he remarked. He smiled. "We'll eat and then we'll go apply for a license."

"It's Sunday."

"Is it? Well, we'll go apply for a license tomorrow,

then.'' He seated her. "You can't make love again comfortably today, can you?''

She could hardly breathe. "I don't know…''

"There are ways, and ways,'' he whispered, bending to kiss her with soft tenderness. "I'll teach them to you.''

He sat down beside her and poured the coffee. As they ate, Kit watched him and tried to imagine that he was the same man who'd been yelling at her for years over mistakes in dictation and fouled-up appointments and misfiled files—most of which were his own fault.

"Something bothering you?'' he asked.

"It's really you, isn't it?'' she replied vaguely. "I'm just having a little trouble believing it, that's all. We've worked together for a long time.''

"And I've never looked at you until a few days ago,'' he agreed. His face went somber, almost grim. "I might have married Betsy. Why didn't you do something?''

"I did!'' she shot back. "I tried to tell you, and you fired me!''

"I didn't know you were in love with me then,'' he said quietly.

"It wouldn't have stopped you if you had,'' she returned.

He didn't speak. His eyes were on his plate. "I haven't been very good to you over the years. I've been selfish and overbearing. Do you think you care enough to put up with me, Kit?'' he asked, raising a curiously still face to hers. "Suppose you were only physically infatuated? After all, you knew nothing of men before last night.''

Did he mean that? Or was he looking for a way out? She panicked and it showed in her eyes.

"Now what's wrong?" he asked gently.

"You're sorry about what happened, aren't you?" she blurted out.

"In a way," he had to admit. "I let you go to my head. I had no right to put you in that position. Despite the fact that I didn't let you get pregnant, you gave me something that you were saving for marriage."

"In which case, you would have had it anyway," she told him.

"Yes." He studied his fork. "But in the proper sequence. I find that I'm more conservative than I realized. I cheated you of a proper wedding night. I'm sorry."

"It wouldn't have been any different, really." She faltered. "I'd have been more nervous, I suppose..."

"You're still nervous." He caught her cold hand in his and warmed it. "Why?"

She couldn't quite explain it. "I'm shy, that's all. I've never slept with a man before."

He chuckled. "Are you sure it's that?"

She glared at him. "You don't have to make fun of me."

"Was I?" He sobered at once. "You're right. I shouldn't tease you about something that profound." His eyes slid down to the shirt she was wearing and lingered there until her breathing quickened. "I used to watch you sometimes and wonder what you looked like under your clothes. I was careful not to let you know, of course."

She smiled faintly. "I used to watch you and wonder what you looked like under your shirt."

"Now you know."

"Oh, yes."

Her eyes were faintly acquisitive. They made his

body begin to throb all over again. He got up and stood over her. With a smooth motion, he pulled the T-shirt over his head and tossed it over a chair.

Kit's lips parted. "Oh, Logan," she whispered, her eyes as hungry as the hands she lifted to caress him with. "Logan, I love to touch you…!"

He groaned, lifting her into his arms. His mouth took hers roughly, claiming it. "I want you," he said harshly.

She clung, not protesting, as he carried her into the bedroom and came down beside her on the bed. She didn't say a word as he unfastened the shirt and removed it and her bra and leaned above her, studying her bare breasts with hot, hungry eyes.

"Make love to me," she whispered. "I want you, too."

"And hurt you?" he asked, forcing his eyes up to hers. "Because it would."

"I don't care," she told him. Her eyes smoothed over the broad, hair-roughened muscles of his chest. "I love you. It will be all right."

"You have a lot to learn about bodies and intimacy, little one," he said quietly. He held her eyes and unsnapped the jeans. The sound of the zipper was loud in the room. He slid his hand under them. "Let me show you what I mean."

He touched her, intimately, and watched her flinch. He wasn't rough. It was only that her body was new to passion, and very sensitized.

"You see, Kit?" he asked gently. "Remember how we were together last night, and try to imagine how it would feel when I went into you."

She went scarlet and gasped at the imagery.

"I know. It's blunt talk. But this kind of thing gets unmanageable. I can't start and then stop."

"No…"

He looked at her with aching need, his breath lodged in his chest as he withdrew his hand and smoothed it up her belly to her breasts and softly caressed them. "You are every dream I've had in my life," he whispered roughly.

With trembling hands she felt for a fastening and found it, moved it. His eyes widened and he gasped. His hand caught her wrist.

"No!" he said roughly.

"You want to," she breathed. She lifted her mouth to his and kissed him, feeling his hold begin to slacken. "You know you want to, Logan. You want to…!"

He groaned and gave in to her. There were times, he thought blindly, when surrender was positively a virtue.

Chapter Nine

Logan drove Kit home late that afternoon, reluctant to let her go. But she'd insisted that she had chores to do, to get ready for work the next day.

"At lunch, we'll take out that marriage license," he told her firmly as he left her at her door. "You'll never get away again."

She smiled lovingly. "As if I'd ever want to," she said. "Am I dreaming?" she added somberly, searching his dark eyes. "I must be. I couldn't be this happy otherwise. I'll wake up…"

He was thinking the same thing as his eyes caressed her radiant face. "No, you won't," he said tenderly. He bent and brushed his mouth gently over hers. "I'll see you tomorrow."

"You aren't sorry?" she asked worriedly.

He stared at her for a long moment, seeing her with eyes that knew all about her. Everything. "Not if I died in my sleep."

"You're sure that you want to marry me?"

"Kit, do you think we've had enough of each other

yet?'' he mused. ''I could go to you on my deathbed, don't you know? I'm in over my head, and so are you. Marriage is the only way for us.''

''Your mother and brother...''

''Will be delighted. Especially my mother.'' He frowned. ''Which reminds me. Kit, you have to find my mother.''

''First thing tomorrow, I promise.''

''My future wife, Jane Bond.''

''How about Shirley Holmes?''

He chuckled. ''Our kids will be born wearing trench coats and following the doctor around the delivery room.''

She flushed. The thought of having a child was delightful—in wedlock. ''I like children.''

''I used to, before I got to know Emmett's,'' he said dryly. ''I imagine we won't be so intimidated by our own.'' He frowned. ''You were afraid last night that I might accidentally make you pregnant.''

''Yes,'' she agreed. ''I don't want to bring a child into the world without a stable relationship. I don't think you do, either.''

''I don't suppose I do, Kit.'' He held her gently by the shoulders. ''I'm no less conservative than you are, and I agree that children shouldn't be accidents. That's irresponsible.''

She studied his face with eyes that adored it. ''It's hard not to give in when you love someone,'' she said quietly. ''I don't think I ever really understood losing control until last night. I couldn't say no. I couldn't stop.''

''For what it's worth, neither could I. I'll take care of you, Kit.''

''I'll take care of you, too,'' she promised.

He started to speak, but she put a soft hand over his mouth.

"It's not shameful to let a woman care about you and try to protect you," she told him.

He kissed her fingers. "Isn't it? All right." He sighed. "I'll work on it."

She smiled and reached up to kiss his square chin. "Good night, Logan."

"Good night."

The next morning, she started right out on her quest to find Tansy. But complications erupted before she'd even begun. Tess couldn't come in, so the office was shorthanded. And when she tried to find Tansy, the trail led to a medical center on the outskirts of Houston. To top off the confusion, Emmett and his three children came careening into the office just before Logan was due to pick up Kit.

"Emmett said we must come and see you, Kit." Amy grinned. Polk and Guy grouped around her as well, while a smug Emmett stood beside the desk with his white Stetson in hand, looking rather elegant in a gray business suit. The children were less presentable, though. Amy was wearing a stained and wrinkled dress. The boys had on jeans with holes at the knees and their hair needed washing.

"What are you doing here?" Kit asked, aghast.

"We came to see Tansy. She said we were welcome anytime," he added, his pale green eyes twinkling in his lean face, "and I'm in town for a rodeo. We thought the kids could stay with her while I work." He frowned. "But she's not at home."

"I'm looking for her," Kit said, without mentioning the medical center. She was reasonably certain that Logan didn't know about it, either, and until she found out what the problem was, she couldn't tell him. She didn't want him worried until there was something definite to worry about. Tansy might, after all, just be getting a checkup.

"She's done another flit, has she?" Emmett mused, pursing his firm lips.

"Looks like it. Oh, there's Logan!"

Logan came in the door, saw Emmett and the kids and began scowling.

"Hi, Cuz," Emmett said pleasantly. He rammed his hands into his pockets. "We came to stay with Tansy, but she isn't home."

"Don't expect to stay with me," Logan said with no hint of welcome. "I don't have room for you."

"Logan!" Kit exclaimed.

"Don't mind him," Emmett said imperturbably, smiling at Kit. "He's only jealous because he hasn't got any kids. Thought any more about marrying me, sweet thing?"

"She's marrying me," Logan said with a violent glare. He moved to Kit's side and caught her close. His sheer size was intimidating even without the black scowl he gave Emmett. "So get any thoughts in that direction right out of your mind."

"I was afraid it might come down to this." Emmett grimaced. "Ever since those kids overheard you two in the bathroom, I've expected to hear wedding bells."

Kit blushed and Logan glared at the grinning, innocent-looking children.

"Well, I've got to get signed up. What am I going to do with the kids?" Emmett groaned. "I was counting on being able to leave them with Tansy for the afternoon."

"Can't you take them with you?" Kit asked.

Emmett looked hunted, the kids snickered. "I did that last time I rode in a rodeo here. I'm afraid too many people remember them."

"I can't imagine why," Logan muttered darkly. "After all, having longhorn cattle standing in the middle of main street must be a common occurrence. Not to mention the two calves that invaded the local French boutique and tried on one of the designer dresses…"

Kit hid a smile. Emmett shrugged.

"Kids will be kids," he said, smiling fondly at his brood.

"Those aren't kids," Logan replied. "They're a commando group!"

"Thanks Cousin Logan!" Guy said with a grin.

"I have to leave them somewhere," Emmett repeated.

"Don't look at me," Logan said tautly. "I'm taking Kit to get a marriage license."

Emmett shrugged and looked so lost that Logan gave in. "All right. I know where we can leave them," he said, without mentioning that he was going to volunteer poor Melody. It was probably a terrible mistake, but there really wasn't anyone else available. Besides, Emmett had to face her sooner or later, and she had to face him. Today was a good time. "Come on."

"Logan…!" Kit protested squeakily.

"Keep quiet," he said under his breath, "or we'll get landed with them!"

Kit knew when to give up. She followed him out the door with the rest of them, waving discreetly to Doris as she left.

Melody was the only one left in Logan's office, with Harriet in the hospital and Margo gone permanently.

She was bent over the computer, her long honey-streaked hair hanging down around her flushed face, wearing a trim beige suit that was stained with coffee and newsprint from the *Wall Street Journal*.

"May I help you...?" she began, lifting soft brown eyes with a smile. She saw Emmett and the world tilted on its axis. Her expression was a study in quiet shock.

Emmett's normally pleasant, easygoing personality went into eclipse. He glared at her. He turned and stared furiously at Logan. "What the hell do you mean, bringing me here when she's in residence?" he demanded.

Melody swallowed, averting her eyes. "I work here," she said stiffly.

"You never said she was going to be permanent," Emmett told Logan, and there was frightening impact in those glittery green eyes when he turned to the other man. "What a hell of a relation you turned out to be, you damned turncoat!"

Logan glowered at him. "This is my office," Logan reminded him. "She's bright and capable, and I appreciate her talent."

"Her talent for what?" Emmett asked sarcastically.

"That isn't fair," Melody cried, glaring at him out of a white face. "It isn't fair at all! I had nothing to do with your divorce!"

"Your *brother* eloped with my wife!" he said through his teeth. "Do you think I can stand the sight of you?"

So that was it. No one had told her why Emmett clammed up when Melody's name was mentioned, but now she knew. Kit felt a surge of sympathy for Melody, who looked as if Emmett had struck her.

"It's hardly Melody's fault," Logan pointed out.

"Did our mother leave because of you, lady?" Amy asked.

"No!" Melody protested, coloring.

"But it was your brother who took her away!" Guy muttered.

"All of you, shut up," Kit said, intervening. She glared at Emmett, a little intimidated by that hard, unyielding countenance but determined to protect Melody. "No human being is responsible for the acts of another. It's terribly unfair of you to blame Melody for something her brother did."

Emmett didn't say another word. He glared at Melody. "I won't leave my babies with that woman."

"Who asked you to?" Melody asked through numb lips.

"Let's go, kids. You can come with me."

"I don't want to go to the arena," Polk muttered. "I hate cattle."

"You're the son of a rancher," Emmett began.

"I like computers, not cows." Polk went to the desk and stood beside Melody, refusing to budge. "I want to stay here."

"There's a television," Amy enthused, walking to the corner of the waiting room. She switched channels, "Look, *Sesame Street!*" She turned it up and sat down.

Guy glared at his brother and sister. "Turncoats. I'll go with you, Dad," he said, standing beside his father.

"That's my boy," Emmett said. He gave Melody a furious scowl. "Amy, Polk, let's go!"

Melody wanted to protest, but she could see that it wouldn't do any good. Emmett had despised her ever since he'd discovered her with his wife Adell and her brother Randy. She'd helped them pack and was standing with them while they caught a plane. There had been a terrible scene. Adell had cursed Emmett, and Emmett had cursed Randy and Adell and Melody roundly, for everyone to hear. It had been terribly embarrassing, especially for eighteen-year-old Melody.

She'd never forgotten her humiliation or her fear of Emmett, whose temper was legendary locally. He'd beaten Randy to a pulp before he'd stormed off, leaving Adell and Melody to patch up the cuts.

Melody hadn't seen him since, and that was deliberate. She'd moved to Houston to get clear out of his orbit. She'd taken the job with Logan because she knew Logan and Emmett never got along and didn't ever see each other. What a shocking development this was, to find Emmett here.

Amy and Polk rejoined their father. They looked dangerously vindictive.

"You'll be sorry, Emmett," Amy said sweetly. "I like Big Bird."

"You can learn to like cattle. Both of you. Let's go."

Emmett didn't put his foot down often. When he did, all three kids snapped to attention and did what was expected of them.

Emmett glared at Melody. "How long are you going to work here?" he demanded.

"For as long as she likes," Logan told him, getting between them. "It's no concern of yours. You live in San Antonio. Remember?"

"You hired her because of me," Emmett accused.

"I hired her because Tansy asked me to," Logan replied. "She's kin to us, you might remember, in a remote way. She was alone in Houston and needed work. I hired her." He looked at Melody and smiled reassuringly. "As it happens, I'm glad I did. She's an asset. Not up to Kit's record yet, but she's good."

"Words of praise from you?" Kit gasped. "I'll faint."

"Not yet," Logan chuckled. "I want your signature on a marriage license first."

Melody was frozen at her desk. The telephone rang and she answered it, capably if a little unsteadily.

"It's for you, Mr. Deverell," she told Logan. "Mr. James."

"Damn," Logan muttered. "I'll have to take it, Kit."

"That's all right."

He caught her hand. "Come on. I won't say anything you can't hear." He led her into the office and closed the door. A minute later, Melody heard him pick up and transferred the call.

Emmett was still glaring at her. She ignored him and went back to work, forcing her mind to the job at hand.

But her hands were trembling. Amy, who never liked other people, saw that and shyly approached Melody. "She's trembling," she said softly. She studied Melody's averted face and caught her breath. She glared at her father. "You made her cry, Emmett!"

"I'm not crying," Melody muttered, wiping her wet cheeks.

"But you are!" Amy protested. "Oh, you mustn't. Emmett didn't mean it. Did you, Emmett?"

"She helped your mother run away," Emmett said icily.

"That's right," Guy replied. "Come back here, Amy."

"But—"

Emmett's temper overflowed. "Damn it, I said let's go!" he shouted, his green eyes flashing at Amy.

Amy had never seen her parent so enraged. She

obeyed him at once, a little afraid of the fierceness in his lean face.

Melody didn't look up as the door opened and then closed. She rested her hands on the computer keyboard and drew in deep breaths as she fought for control. She felt sick all over. The confrontation had been totally unexpected and shattering.

Logan and Kit came back out minutes later. By then, Melody was pale but composed.

"Mr. Deverell left," she told Logan.

"You know how bitter he is about Adell," Logan said gently. "Don't let him upset you. He'll be back on his way to San Antonio in a few days and you won't have to see him again. At any rate, it's unlikely that he'll come to the office anymore."

"Good," Melody said stiffly.

"He's a bitter man," Logan said. "I'm sorry he took it out on you. But it won't happen again."

"It's all right," Melody said. "Honestly."

"You're doing a good job," Logan told her. "I hope you'll stay."

"So do I," Kit agreed. "Even when we get married, I won't be coming back here to work. You're stuck."

Melody managed a laugh. "Then I'm glad. I enjoy the job. It's very interesting." She glanced at the door and gnawed her lower lip. "If you're sure that *he* won't be back."

"I'll guarantee it," Logan promised. "I'll be back about two. Can you cope?"

"Yes, sir," Melody promised him.

He smiled, and escorted Kit out the door.

"Emmett is a…" she began hotly.

"Yes," he said, leading her to the elevator. "I've never seen him be so savage with anyone like that," he added. "Least of all someone as young as Melody. My God, what a temper!"

"He takes after the rest of the Deverells," she said dryly.

He glared at her. "I don't pick on young women."

Her eyebrows raised over stark open eyes. "What do you think I was when I came to work for you, you slave-driving tyrant?"

"I am not a tyrant," he said, pushing the Down button hard. "I was terrific to work for."

"When?"

He narrowed his eyes as he studied her. "Do you want to marry me or not?"

"Of course I do."

"Then be nice to me."

She moved close, glancing down the deserted hall. "How nice do I have to be?" she whispered, and suddenly plastered herself against his big body.

He chuckled and pushed her away. "Not that nice," he told her. "Not until it's legal, anyway. From now on, we're doing it by the book."

"Party pooper."

"All right, if you really want to make love on the floor of the elevator…!"

"No!"

He laughed delightedly as she backed away from him. "Well, what did you expect? I'm pretty vulnerable with you."

"So I noticed." She fanned herself with her hand. "And you a respectable stockbroker, too."

"I'm an engaged man. Damn this sluggish elevator…!"

The door opened finally, and a broody, muttering

Emmett and three red-faced children stared out of it at Kit and Logan.

"Now what?" Logan asked curtly.

"Big Bird," Emmett said through his teeth.

"What?"

"She incited them." He gestured toward the other two. "They're in it all together. They stood in the middle of the sidewalk and told God and the rest of the world that I was stunting their natural development by denying them educational programming. Then," he added viciously, "they overturned a fajita stand and dumped salsa on a fat lady."

Kit leaned against the wall, laughing so hard that she could barely stand.

"Well, you needn't look at me," Logan told his furious cousin. "I'm not keeping them for you. And if I were you, I wouldn't go near Melody. She'll probably throw a keyboard at you if you so much as stick your head in the door!"

"I'm not stupid," Emmett replied. "Go on," he told the kids. "I hope she stuffs you into a drawer!"

"I don't want to go!" Guy muttered. "She stole our mother!"

"This isn't the time or the place," Logan said. "Go on, Guy. Try not to upset Melody anymore, if you please. Your father's done a great job on her nerves already."

"All right," Guy muttered. He glanced back at his father. "But I'm on your side, Dad."

"I know that," Emmett replied quietly. "Go on. Don't…give her any trouble." He shrugged. "I guess I was pretty obnoxious."

"That's an understatement," Logan said as he got into the elevator with Kit and a subdued Emmett.

"She's terrified of you, couldn't you tell? Two years have passed since you beat her brother to his knees and verbally assaulted her, and she still starts shaking the minute she sees you. Quite a feat, cousin," he added venomously, watching Emmett shift his eyes. "You didn't use to stoop to terrorizing children."

"She isn't a child," Emmett said stiffly.

"But she is. She's barely twenty," Kit said quietly. "And she isn't worldly at all."

Emmett scowled. "Twenty?"

"You didn't know?" Kit asked, staring up at him curiously.

His broad shoulders rose and fell. "I never thought about it." He went broody, avoiding Logan's sudden stare.

They left him on the sidewalk and went to get into Logan's sleek Lincoln.

"Is Emmett really like that?" Kit asked. "He seemed so easygoing and kind..."

"He's a hell-raiser," Logan told her as he put her into the car and got in beside her. "He always was wild, even as a boy. He married Adell just days after his mother died and he insisted that they start a family right away. She seemed to care about him, and we thought he'd settled down. But he took off rodeoing and left her there alone with babies and cattle, and she was never suited to either. She met Randy, fell in love for real and just took off. Emmett blamed her, blamed Melody, blamed the kids, blamed everybody except the real guilty party—himself. He hated marriage and responsibility. He was trying to find a way out when Adell presented him with one. His pride was bruised, but he never loved her."

"He got married because of what happened to his mother?"

"Yes, I think he did. He was lonely and Adell thought she loved him. It was only infatuation, though." He stopped at a traffic light and looked at Kit worriedly. "Do you love me?" he asked suddenly. "Do you love me enough, Kit?"

Her lips parted as she studied his broad, leonine face. "I'd do anything in this world for you," she said quietly. "Anything, Logan."

That didn't sound like infatuation, and combined with the look in her eyes he was convinced. He took her hand in his as the light changed and wrapped it in his fingers. "That's all I wanted to know."

Which told Kit very little about his own feelings. It was impossible not to know how much he wanted her. As he'd said, they did get along well together. But what if he discovered one day that what he felt for Kit was only a physical infatuation? What if he fell in love with someone else and took off?

"Stop brooding," he said, smiling at her. "We've got plenty going for us. We'll make it, Kit. I promise you, we will."

Her long fingers curled into his. "Okay. I won't worry."

But she did worry. They took out the license and she went back to the office to continue her search for Tansy. It was much more imperative now to find her, with the impending marriage. She wanted Tansy there. More, she wanted to make sure that her future mother-in-law was all right. The fact that Tansy had checked into a medical center was very worrying indeed. Usually when the elderly woman sought medical assistance, it was after some wild stunt that bruised her. But there hadn't been any wild stunts. Tansy had gone in deliberately, on both feet. And that in itself, Kit thought uneasily, was cause for concern.

Chapter Ten

Kit found the hospital without a problem. Then she sat in the car, worrying about how to proceed. There was a good chance that Tansy would be very angry if Kit just walked into her room and started asking questions. On the other hand, there was little else she could do.

Leaving her car in the parking lot, she proceeded into the hospital and found which room Tansy was in. She hesitated outside the private room, but only for a minute. With a deep breath, she knocked gently at the door and opened it.

Tansy Deverell stared at her without speaking, her eyes very wide in a thin, pale face which held pain and worry.

"And here you come again," Tansy murmured, with a hint of a twinkle in her eyes.

"Yep," Kit said, smiling.

"You're too good a detective, Kit," Tansy said. "This time I didn't want to be found."

"I had that figured out for myself." She moved to

the bed, and sat down beside it, her blue eyes quiet and steady on the worn face in its frame of untidy silver hair. "Why are you here?"

"I won't tell you that."

"Are you ill?"

"I won't know that until I get the results of the tests."

Kit held her breath. "Tests for what?"

Tansy couldn't conceal her worry and fear. "I don't know, Kit," she said in a choked tone. "I've been getting tired a lot, and I can't seem to stop losing weight. I don't know, but it could be cancer."

"Oh, Tansy," Kit wailed.

"And if it is," she continued, "I don't want my boys to have to suffer through the uncertainty with me. When I find out for sure, then I'll tell them."

Kit felt terrible. She knew she should tell Logan and Chris, but Tansy looked crushed enough already.

"It isn't fair to keep it from them," Kit began gently.

"Yes, it is, dear," came the soft reply. "You're all heart, aren't you, Kit?" she asked. "Nothing like that curvy cash register he thinks he's in love with."

"The delectable Betsy?" Kit replied with a quiet smile.

"Chris's description." Tansy nodded and she smiled. "He'll come to his senses one day."

"I'm delighted to tell you that he already has," Kit told her. "We just got a marriage license. I'm going to be your daughter-in-law."

Tansy held out her arms and hugged the younger woman with pure delight. "You couldn't have brought me happier news if you'd looked for years. Kit, how wonderful!"

"He doesn't love me yet," Kit told her. "But maybe I love him enough for both of us."

"Give him time. Commitment is new to him. He's my son. He can't be completely stupid."

Kit laughed. "Of course he can't."

Tansy could sympathize with Kit. It was hard to love so deeply and not have it returned. If only her eldest son wasn't so blind!

She rubbed her cold hands. "Go away, Kit. I love seeing you, but this is something I have to do alone. And don't tell my sons. Not a word," she said sternly.

"But…"

"Not one word," Tansy repeated, her eyes piercing. "This is my business. Mine alone."

Kit knew when she was beaten. "All right. But I'll be back to see about you," she said firmly.

"I knew that already," Tansy said, and smiled. "You're a sweet child."

"No. I just have good taste in people," Kit murmured.

Tansy laughed, although her eyes didn't.

"When will you know, one way or the other?" Kit asked.

"Tomorrow."

"Then I'll see you tomorrow. Can I bring you anything?"

"Not really, Kit. But thank you for asking."

She studied the older woman, noticing that her hands were shaking. "Tansy…"

"I'm freezing," Tansy said. "And starving to death. You know, no matter how much I eat or drink, I can't seem to get full. All that hunger and thirst, and look at me." She laughed. "Skin and bones." She lay back and closed her eyes. "Life is so complicated sometimes."

"Don't we all know it," Kit mused.

"How is Melody working out?"

"I don't know if he'll still have her by sundown," Kit replied. "She's baby-sitting Emmett's kids, and he hates her. I mean hates her!"

Tansy's eyes opened and she looked less frail. "Oh, my goodness. Poor child!"

"She's a trooper. Amy and Polk like her. Guy is his father all over again. I imagine he's giving her the devil."

"She's too young to bear the brunt of Emmett's hatred of her brother. I shouldn't have recommended her for the job, but she'd just lost a job she'd had for two years and she was too afraid of Emmett to even live in the same city he did. I saw a chance to help Logan and Melody. But if Emmett is going to make a habit of coming back here, I may have done more harm than good. Poor child!" she repeated.

"Emmett didn't even look like himself," Kit said, recalling with a mental shiver. "I thought he was easygoing and funny."

"Did you? Emmett wears a mask. Most people see through it a lot sooner than you did. He has plenty of enemies."

"If he's like he was today when he rides in a rodeo, it wouldn't surprise me to learn that he wins every event," she said. "He's ruthless."

"He always was. It's his way or no way." Tansy shook her head. "I'll have to apologize to Melody. But Emmett won't be in town for long, I'm sure. Logan will protect her."

Kit wasn't certain about that, but she didn't say so.

She stayed and talked for a little longer, before she looked at her watch and realized that she was already past due back at the office.

"I have to go," she said, bending to kiss the thin cheek. "You know where to find me if I can do anything for you. And I won't tell Logan or Chris where you are. I promise."

Tansy studied her face for a long moment, reading accurately the acquiescence in it. "That's a deal. Come back tomorrow. Maybe it will be good news."

She didn't sound as if she expected it to be. Kit was an incurable optimist, though, and she knew what a strength of will Tansy had.

"I'd bet on you, no matter what," she told Tansy. "You're too special to lose." She smiled and left the room before Tansy had time to reply.

It didn't help that later in the day Dane Lassiter wanted to know about her progress.

She considered lying to him. That didn't seem particularly bright. Dane was a detective himself, and much more experienced. If he wanted to find Tansy, it would take him no time at all. And it would be dishonest to lie.

So she asked to speak to him privately and told him everything.

"So you see," she said miserably, "I don't know what to do. I told Tansy I wouldn't tell Logan a thing. Professionally I'm bound to." Her eyes searched his stern face. "Where do you draw the line?"

"In this agency, we stand behind our detectives," he said, smiling gently. "It's your decision."

"Thanks for not firing me." She got up from the chair she'd been sitting in.

"Don't be absurd," he murmured. "I trust your

judgment.'' He sighed. "God, I hope it's not cancer. Logan pretends that his mother is a trial to him, but he loves her.''

"So does Chris,'' she added.

"Of course he does. But Logan will take it harder.''

She nodded. He was right about that. The icy Mr. Deverell had a surprisingly soft side, and he did adore his mother. Even if he raised the roof over some of her antics from time to time.

"Kit,'' Dane said as she started to leave, and he looked solemn, "think very carefully about the position you're putting yourself in. You and Logan are engaged. Keeping this sort of secret between you could irreparably damage your relationship. I won't blame you if you do give in and tell him. No one would, least of all Tansy.''

"I don't know about that.'' She clung to the door. "If I tell Logan, I'll be betraying Tansy's trust.''

"It's a hard decision, I know,'' Dane said. "Just remember, you have to live with the consequences of your actions. I don't. Neither does Tansy.''

"Yes. I know,'' she said quietly.

Kit had hoped that she wouldn't have to lie to Logan. The following day, after all, she'd know for certain about Tansy. But she had no such luck.

Logan telephoned less than ten minutes before she was due to leave the office that afternoon. In the background, boisterous yells and shouts interrupted him.

"I'll pick you up about six and we'll eat out,'' he said. "Can you kids shut up?'' he yelled. "My God, they're driving us nuts! Emmett promised to be back by five, and he isn't here! I don't know what to do!''

"Bring them with you," Kit suggested, buying time. "We can look after them."

"Kit, are you out of your mind?" he asked.

"I guess so. But we can't ask Melody to have them, not the way Emmett treated her."

"I know." He paused. "Have you found my mother?" he asked abruptly.

The question shook her. She took a slow breath and steadied her nerves, preparing to hedge the question. She was flirting with finishing their relationship before it began, and she knew it, but Tansy trusted her. She had to consider that before she considered her personal feelings.

"I've got a good lead that I'm following up," she replied carefully, mentally crossing her fingers at the lie. "I should know something by lunch tomorrow," she added, praying that she would, and that it would be good news.

"I thought you were an ace detective, Miss Morris."

"Detective work can be slow, Mr. Deverell," she countered. "And you might remember that I am very efficient."

"So you were." He chuckled. "Come on over here and go home with me. We can pick up your car in the morning."

"Okay. I'll be there in fifteen minutes," she promised.

She and Emmett arrived together. He was unusually quiet as he rode up in the elevator with her, totally uncommunicative.

"Did you get signed up for the rodeo?" she asked.

"Yep."

And that was all he said, all the way to Logan's

office. He walked in, saw the kids sitting all in a row on the sofa with their hands angelically folded and did a double take.

A harassed, black-eyed Melody glared at him. "You can take them with you, now, if you don't mind," she said stiffly. "I hired on here to be a secretary, not a baby-sitter."

"We ain't babies," Guy muttered with a hard glare in her direction. "And we ain't scared of that electronic gadget in your desk, neither!"

"What electronic gadget?" Emmett said with deadly menace.

Melody looked straight at him, opened her desk, picked up a black box and pointed it at him. She pressed a colorful button. Death ray sounds out of a Grade-B science fiction movie filled the room.

"Tomorrow morning when you wake up, you'll have green skin and antennae," she promised him. "And warts."

Emmett's eyebrows lifted.

"She tried to turn us into Martians with that thing, but we weren't scared of it, Emmett," Amy said proudly. Her haughty expression wavered just a little when she glanced at the black box. "But, we'll go now, won't we? Before she points it at us again, I mean."

"Witch," Emmett accused. "Scaring little children."

Melody put the black box back in the drawer. "Those aren't little children," she said icily. "They're a homebound terrorist unit, complete with hardware. Look at this, for heaven's sake!"

She started pulling things out of the desk. When she finished, there were screwdrivers, Swiss Army knives, fingernail files and other assorted tools in a heap before her. "Just look! They could break open a safe with this!"

"No, we could not," Polk said indignantly.

"We only tried one," Guy reminded his brother. "And it was old. If we worked on a new one..."

"That's right!" Amy agreed.

Exasperated, Melody stared at Emmett. "Congratulations," she said. "You can visit them all in federal prison next year after you're through riding in rodeo competitions."

Emmett stared at his children. Comprehension was dawning. He'd spent two years hating his ex-wife and blaming her for all his problems. He'd spent an equally long time running away from the kids.

Now, here they were, and he was just beginning to see what his neglect had accomplished. Instead of normal, wholesome children, he was raising a family of potential second-story men.

"Where did you kids get that stuff?" Emmett asked, nodding toward the desk.

"We'll never tell," Amy said, making a motion across her lips like a zipper closing.

"That's right," Polk agreed.

"We'll see about that," Emmett said grimly. "Let's go. I've booked us into a hotel for the night."

"Great!" Guy said. "At least we can escape the wicked witch of the stock market before she makes Martians out of us."

Emmett herded them to the door. He paused, glancing at Melody, who was composed and not very communicative. "Kind of you to watch them," he said reluctantly.

"I'll quit before I do it again, even if it means starving," she said quietly.

His lean face hardened. "No stomach for children, Miss Cartman?"

"I like most children," she replied.

"There's not a damned thing wrong with those kids," he said furiously.

She didn't reply.

"Emmett, that's enough," Logan said with quiet menace. "Go away."

"You hired her to get back at me, didn't you?" Emmett accused his cousin.

"You think everyone is out to get you, don't you?" Logan asked quietly. "Your biggest problem is your own lack of trust."

"I trusted Adell. Until *her* damned Romeo brother," he pointed at Melody, "waltzed in and carted her off!"

Melody colored. Her hands were shaking. She clasped them together tightly. "Adell said she got tired of dirty diapers and living alone with three toddlers," she said with pure bravado and a shaking voice, "while you strutted around with pretty young girls at rodeos."

Emmett didn't say another word. His face hardened to stone. He turned and went out, slamming the door so hard that the windows shook.

"Well, he did," Melody muttered, shaken.

"I know," Logan replied. "You don't have to tell me about Emmett. I'm sorry, Melody. I won't let him in here again."

"Thanks," she said quietly. "I seem to set him off."

"Everything does. Get your things and I'll lock up. I'm taking Kit out to eat. Want to come along?"

Melody smiled. "Thanks, but I've got a nice pot full of soup waiting."

"That sounds good on a cold night," Kit remarked.

"Well, good night, Melody," Logan said.

* * *

Logan took Kit to an elegant restaurant and they drank expensive wine and ate perfectly cooked steak, paying much more attention to each other than to the food.

"Two more days," he groaned when he kissed her good-night at her door. "I'll never make it!"

"Yes, you will," she said, smiling with delight at his hunger for her. "Good night, Logan."

He kissed her one last time and reluctantly let her go. "Good night. If you find out anything about Tansy, call me, all right?" he added.

She cleared her throat and averted her eyes. "Certainly I will!"

Logan saw that suspicious, guilty look and scowled. "You aren't holding anything back, are you?"

"Logan!" she exclaimed. "Of course not."

He stuck his hands into his pockets and stared down at her, frowning. "I love my mother, despite her shenanigans," he reminded her. "If you know something, and you don't tell me, I won't forget it."

Her conscience was killing her. She wanted to tell him. She should tell him. But she couldn't force the words out. She groaned. "There's nothing to tell yet," she said.

"When?"

"Soon. Really."

He nodded, but his eyes were watchful. And there was a blatant withdrawal in his manner when he turned and walked away from her.

She closed the door behind him, locked it and leaned back against it. Her heart was beating her to death with its mad rhythm. Blast her own tongue! She wasn't good at lying. Now Logan was suspicious, and Tansy would never forgive her if he found out anything too soon. But, then, how could he?

By the time she went to bed, she'd convinced herself that he had no way of knowing that she wasn't telling the truth. And Dane wouldn't blow her cover. No, she had nothing to worry about.

Late in the morning, after she'd gone through her files and done some legwork on an unrelated case, she drove to the hospital and went to find Tansy.

She knew by the expression on the older woman's face that it wasn't cancer.

"You're all right, aren't you?" she asked Tansy, smiling. "It wasn't cancer after all, was it?"

"No," Tansy sighed, smiling. "Thank God, it wasn't."

The door opened suddenly and Logan Deverell came in, his face like a thundercloud. "So here you are," he told Tansy. "Hiding out in a hospital…what's wrong with you?"

Tansy stared at Kit and grimaced. "You told him! You told him, after I begged you not to!"

"No," Kit began.

"Why are you here?" Logan demanded from his mother.

Tansy glared up at him. "I thought I had cancer."

He went stark white. "And…?"

"It's not," she said shortly.

His dark eyes, relieved, went to Kit's white face and kindled again. "You lied to me, damn you," he said softly. "You told me you didn't know where she was! She's been in here with the threat of cancer hanging over her and I wouldn't have known!"

Kit didn't reply. She couldn't. She felt as bad as he must.

"Oh, Kit, I'm sorry," Tansy began.

"Dane's going to get an earful about this, and I damned well hope he fires you!" he said, bristling with rage at her betrayal. He'd trusted her, planned to marry her. But she didn't trust him. She'd covered up his mother's situation and her hospitalization. She'd deliberately lied to him about it! He was so furious that he could barely speak.

"Get out of my mother's room!" he said viciously. "Get out of my life, while you're about it! You can take that damned marriage license and rip it up, because I wouldn't go five feet toward the altar with a two-faced, cold-blooded little liar like you!"

Kit felt the tears welling in her very soul. They both blurred in her blue eyes as she turned and went out of the room with the tatters of her dignity around her.

"But it's not her fault," Tansy was saying loudly.

She didn't hear what Logan said. She kept walking.

Eventually she found her car, through a mist of hot tears. Her eyes were red and swollen long before she got back to the office and went to tell Dane Lassiter what had happened.

Tess was with him. They both gaped at the sight of her.

She blurted out the whole story and then dried her eyes and blew her nose. "He wants you to fire me," she told Dane. "I guess I deserve it. I was only trying to do what Tansy wanted me to, but she wasn't paying us, Logan was. He said he had the right to know."

Tess hugged her warmly. "Now, now," she said soothingly. "It's all right."

"I'm not going to fire you," Dane said. "If Logan wants to refuse to pay, that's his affair. The agency won't lose that much. But he will," he added curtly.

"The next time Tansy takes a powder, he can damned well track her down himself."

"Not on my account," Kit pleaded. "I don't want any of you in trouble because of me."

"You're our employee," Dane said curtly. "That makes you family. Nobody, but nobody, threatens family around here."

Kit forced a smile. "You're very kind."

"It's easy to be kind to nice people. You go back to work and get your mind on another case. Consider this one closed."

"Okay. Thanks," she added.

"We're going shopping tonight," Tess reminded her. "It will cheer you up."

"I could really use that now," Kit replied.

She went back to her desk. Adams paused beside it, frowning. "You okay?" he asked. "I heard Deverell took a bite out of you. Don't let it get you down. We all catch hell sometimes, you know." He grinned sheepishly. "Want me to go bash his nose in for you?"

She laughed, her blue eyes twinkling. "Would you do that for me?"

He blushed. "Sure. If you want me to."

She reached out and took his big, hammy hand in hers. "Adams, you're the nicest man in the world."

He only smiled, looking even more sheepish.

"How about supper?" he began. "Doris and I know this place that makes great Irish stew," he added, glancing at Doris, who smiled and nodded. "You could have supper with us…"

The sound of the front door opening caught their attention. The person entering had full view of Adams holding Kit's hand and smiling at her.

Logan Deverell stared at them from a face that would have done justice at a murder trial.

Kit's eyes sparkled with anger. Her injured dignity sat up and growled. "Yes, Mr. Deverell, can we help you?" she asked. "If you'd like to speak to Mr. Lassiter, I'm sure he'll be happy to oblige you. I've already told him that you're dissatisfied with my handling of your case. Sadly for you, he doesn't feel it warrants firing me."

"This the guy you were telling me about?" Adams asked Kit, looking big and pugnacious, an expression he'd cultivated back in his homicide days on the police force.

Logan glared at Adams. "I hope your medical insurance is paid up," he said levelly, "because I'm a Tae Kwon Do blue belt."

"I don't need a bodyguard, thanks just the same, Adams," she added, gently disengaging her hand.

"Well, if you do," Adams said, glancing toward Logan, "just whistle."

He ambled away and Logan shoved his hands into his pockets as he moved to stand just in front of Kit's desk. His broad shoulders rose and fell. "Mother told me all of it." He looked uncomfortable. "I shouldn't have jumped to conclusions."

"If that's an apology, it isn't necessary," Kit began.

"Isn't it?" His dark eyes slid over her face. "You've been crying."

"Tansy was angry with me," she hedged.

He scowled. "Was that the only reason?"

She lowered her gaze to her locked fingers, lying cold on her desk top. "How is she?"

"Diabetic, apparently," he said. "They've had to put her on insulin. That explains her weight loss and the gnawing hunger and thirst and weakness. They're sure she'll be back in top form in no time.''

"Did it come on suddenly?"

"Apparently not. But she didn't recognize the symptoms. She was thin for years, and then she started to gain weight. They said she was a textbook Type II diabetic who could be controlled with diet. Her penchant for sweets put her over the line.'' He shifted. ''It may have saved her life. She very nearly went into a coma.''

"Poor Tansy."

"In more ways than one. She felt guilty about you. I caught hell for what I said to you,'' he mused, smiling faintly.

She refused to rise to the bait. She was tired of being cut to pieces by him. She lifted a composed face. ''Did you want to see Mr. Lassiter? Our receptionist is still out of the office, but I can buzz him for you.''

"No, I don't need to see Dane," he replied. "He can bill me for services rendered, no argument. You found her. It's her fault I wasn't told, not yours.'' He searched her weary face. ''You're very loyal, Kit.''

She didn't react. "If that's all," she said without expression, ''I have another case I need to be working on.''

"A case, or Adams?" he asked with a speaking glance in the general direction of the office where Adams had disappeared.

"Adams is…"

"As Nick used to say, a tick," he said, lowering his voice. ''If he attaches himself to you, you'll never get rid of him.''

"That's my business, Mr. Deverell," she reminded him. ''You have no right to interfere in my personal life.''

He recognized the quote, and she'd meant him to. He pursed his lips. "Throwing my own words back at me?" he asked. "I suppose I don't deserve any less."

She didn't reply.

He searched her blue eyes for a long moment, and delicious sensations shot through his powerful body as he let the look linger. Kit blushed and averted her face, and his heart jumped in his chest.

Three years, he thought. He'd never really looked at her. He'd never let himself look at her. Now she was out of his office, out of his life, and he couldn't seem to stop looking at her. Betsy had been a remedy for boredom, but Kit was…everything. He looked down at her and loved her, suddenly, unbearably. He'd given her hell for something that wasn't her fault, broken their engagement. And after all that, to discover that he was in love with her…

He shrugged. His eyes slid over her body. "Tansy wants to see you."

She nodded. "I know where she is."

"I really am sorry," he said unexpectedly. "I was thinking that you'd betrayed me, that you hadn't trusted me enough to be honest with me. I…lost my temper."

"I noticed."

"Damn it, Kit, you have to marry me!" he burst out.

"Why?" she asked haughtily, aware that everyone in the office was staring at them.

He looked around at the audience and sighed furiously. "Don't you all have anything better to do?" he demanded.

"Not me," Adams said. "How about you guys?"

The other detectives and skip tracers shook their heads.

"Oh, hell," Logan muttered. He rammed his hands

into his pockets and looked down at Kit with pure repressed fury.

"What does it matter to you that you broke the engagement?" Kit asked. "You never wanted to marry me in the first place. I was just a substitute for Betsy!"

Logan searched her flushed face and couldn't drag his eyes away. She was so lovely. He remembered her laughing, and crying, and he knew that nothing would fill the gap in his life if she left him.

"Actually, Kit, it was the other way around," he said finally. "Betsy was a substitute—and a very poor one, at that—for you."

Chapter Eleven

"That isn't true," Kit said quietly.

"Isn't it?" He moved to the desk and stood over her. "Did you tear up the marriage license?"

"I meant to," she returned.

"Where is it?"

She hesitated. She reached into her desk drawer and pulled it out. They'd had the blood test the same day they'd taken out the license. They could be married legally today.

"Come on," he said gently. "Let's get married."

"But, Logan," she protested.

He drew her out of her chair. "City hall, eleven o'clock," he told the office. "You're all invited!"

There were so many congratulations and well-wishes that Kit couldn't get anyone to listen when she said it was a mistake, and she wasn't marrying Logan.

It did no good to try. He put her into her coat, took her out the door and drove her down to city hall.

"But what about Tansy?" she groaned.

"We'll go and see her afterward," he replied. "She was delighted when I phoned her."

"You didn't know that I'd have anything to do with you after this morning," she said icily.

"I knew that you loved me," he said simply. "If I've learned nothing else in life, it's that love doesn't wear out."

"Mine might have. You starved it."

"Yes. And now I'm going to feed it until it becomes overweight," he promised. "Ten minutes after you say I do I'm going to take you to our apartment and make love to you until you're too weak to walk!"

She flushed. "Hush!" she exclaimed, glancing around.

"We can make love on the carpet, like we did the first time," he said imperturbably. "Except that this time, it's going to be very, very different."

"Because you've resigned yourself to marriage?" she asked dully.

He turned her face to his and held her eyes. "Because I finally woke up and realized what was happening to me. I love you, Kit," he said with quiet wonder, searching her shocked face. "I suppose I did all along. But I didn't know it until I broke the engagement and sent you running out of Tansy's hospital room. I worried that you might have taken me at face value, that I wouldn't be able to get you back."

"You love me?" she asked, staring at him blankly.

"Oh, yes," he said huskily, putting more feeling into the words than she'd dreamed anyone could. "Can't you see it? Feel it?"

She could. Her heart ran wild. "I thought it was because you wanted me."

"I do, desperately," he said.

"You were so angry with me, Logan," she began.

"I know. I'm sorry." He drew her hand to his mouth. "I love Tansy, too, you see."

"I knew that. I was trying to protect you," she said miserably. "I thought if I waited, as Tansy wanted me to, until we knew the truth, it would be easier for you."

"You can't protect me from life," he said quietly. "I'm a grown man. I have the right to know what I'm up against. I've never run from anything."

"Except me," she murmured with an attempt at humor.

"You caught me, didn't you?" he mused.

"Well…"

"Tansy will be all right," he said. "She's sorry for what she thought, and I'm sorry for what I said. We'll both make it up to you somehow."

"There's no need for that."

"Yes, there is. Want me to tell you how I'm going to make it up to you?" he teased softly.

"No," she said, dropping her eyes to his chest. "You can wait…and show me."

He did. It took hours and hours, while he caressed her in the silence of their apartment, sprawled in loving abandon with her on the big king-size bed with all the lights blazing away.

He laughed at her shock, delighted in her hungry response, loved her from one side of the bed to the other and, finally, onto the floor with his inexhaustible ardor. It was dark before he was sated enough to rest.

They slept. When they awoke, he carried her into the bath and they lay together in the Jacuzzi, gently kissing, while they bathed. Afterward, they fixed steaks and salad in the kitchen and ate.

"Tansy was glad to see us," she said when she was curled up in his lap on the sofa, when they'd put the dishes into the dishwasher.

"And happy for us," he agreed. He bent and kissed her with soft possession. "I love you, Kit," he said huskily. It was evident in the eyes that swept over her, in the very softness of his voice. "I'll love you all my life."

"That goes double for me, Mr. Deverell," she murmured contentedly.

He leaned back with a long, happy sigh. "At least, we're free of Emmett," he said with a smile. "Tansy said he called and after the rodeo tonight, he'll be on his way to San Antonio with the kids."

"Who's keeping the kids?" Kit asked.

"A baby-sitter at the hotel." He chuckled. "I expect the poor woman will retire after tonight."

"No doubt." She linked her arms around his neck and lay her head on his broad chest. "I'm tired."

"So am I. And we both have a job to go to in the morning," he murmured. "I'm sorry I'm not a man of leisure. I'd like to stay in bed for several days."

"Me, too." She sighed. "But I guess life goes on."

"Thank God, it does." He tilted her face up to his and searched it hungrily. "I'm glad you didn't give up on me, Kit."

She smiled and drew his face down to hers. "How could I, when my life began the day I met you? Bad temper and all," she whispered against his hard mouth.

"I do *not* have a bad temper," he muttered.

"You do so!"

"I have never— What the hell are you doing?"

She pushed him down on the sofa and sat on him, laughing at his expression. "Showing you who's boss," she whispered. She laughed with aching delight as she eased down to his mouth and kissed him while her hands smoothed under his shirt. "Do you mind?"

"I don't know. That depends on whether you can make me like it," he whispered with ardent pleasure as her mouth settled on his. He chuckled as his hands went up to help her with his shirt. "So get busy. Show me!"

And several delightfully feverish minutes later, it was pretty evident that she'd done just that.

* * * * *

A
mysterious
Woman

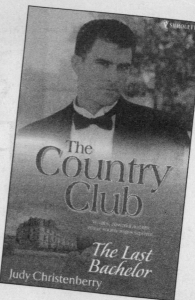

The Country Club

No.1 *New York Times* bestselling author

NORA ROBERTS

One spectacular summer transforms two women's lives...

Summer Pleasures

Two heartwarming stories
Second Nature *One Summer*

Available from 16th July 2004

*Available at most branches of WHSmith,
Tesco, Martins, Borders, Eason, Sainsbury's
and most good paperback bookshops.*

0804/121/SH78 V2

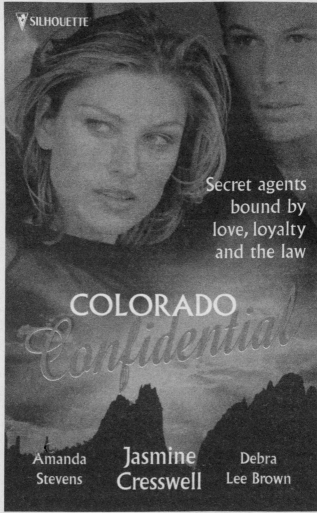

▼ SILHOUETTE®
DESIRE™

are proud to introduce

DYNASTIES: THE BARONES

Meet the wealthy Barones—caught in a web of danger, deceit and...desire!

Twelve exciting stories in six 2-in-1 volumes: